Angels jagged out before Barrin. Their magna swords sliced
Phyrexians. Blades bit into s   t clean through
to hunched legs. They cleft   s
ran black and golden wit   l
become a bloody thing, pa

Barrin lashed out with   ll
turned Phyrexians on each   n-
dreds more with carbuncles of rust. Catching   rin
unleashed a simple but effective fireball, melting metal and bone
and flesh. As he gathered another enchantment, Barrin's steed
smashed hooves atop Phyrexian heads.

Still, there were so many shock troops—too many. Phyrexians
rose from every hollow and every deadfall. Plague-infected claws
sank into angel throats. Pincers ripped wings from their sockets.
Stingers pumped venom into pure hearts. Serrans dropped like
moths.

Experience the Magic

MAGIC The Gathering®

INVASION

INVASION CYCLE • BOOK I

J. Robert King

Front cover art by Eric Peterson
Back cover art by Michael Sutfin
Internal art by: Brian "Chippy" Dugan, Dana Knutson, Todd Lockwood, Anson Maddocks, r.k. post, Mark Tedin, and Anthony Waters
First Printing: October 2000
Library of Congress Catalog Card Number: 00-101635

9 8 7 6 5 4 3 2 1

ISBN: 0-7869-1438-6
620-T21438

U.S., CANADA,	EUROPEAN HEADQUARTERS
ASIA, PACIFIC, & LATIN AMERICA	Wizards of the Coast, Belgium
Wizards of the Coast, Inc.	P.B. 2031
P.O. Box 707	2600 Berchem
Renton, WA 98057-0707	Belgium
+1-800-324-6496	+32-70-23-32-77

Visit our web site at **www.wizards.com**

Dedication

To Jess Lebow,
for good friendship, expert direction, and exemplary cigars.

Acknowledgments

It is a great pleasure not only to work with a talented group of professionals on a project like this but also genuinely to call them friends.

Thanks go first to my terrific editor, Jess, who's stuck with me through thick and thin on four books and is stuck with me for two more.

Thanks go also to Scott McGough, the Magic continuity editor. He is both a fierce defender of Dominaria and a welcoming host who makes the world truly shared.

Thanks go as well to Mary Kirchoff, Peter Archer, Daneen McDermott, Tyler Bielman, Kyle Murray, Bill Rose, Mark Tedin, and all the others who contributed to the Invasion summit. What a great meeting of the minds!

Finally, thanks go to all the thousands of designers, editors, artists, authors, marketers, and administrators who have made Magic what it is, and to the millions of fans who make it what it will always be.

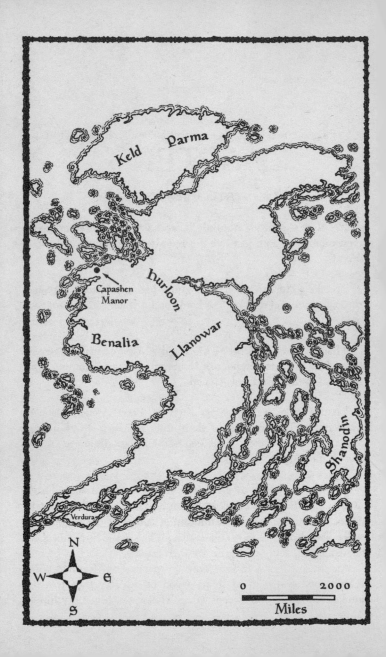

CHAPTER 1
To Fight Phyrexians

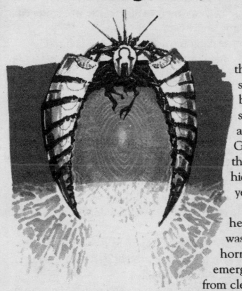

White clouds fled through blue skies. The sea chanted fearfully below. Waves crowded shoulder to shoulder and shoved each other. Gray land crouched at the edge of Dominaria, hiding itself in veils of yellow steam.

Evil hung in the heavens. Something was coming, something horrible, and it would emerge without warning from clear air.

It came. The thing carved a sudden line in the sky. The trough it cut deepened. It tore water from the air and hurled it outward in white flames. This was no meteor, no dumb stone from heedless heavens. This thing clove the sky with intent.

Air streamed away from a lancing prow and saw-toothed keel. It drummed gunwales of living wood on its way into roaring intakes and across wide-swept wings. This was a ship, a skyship—

1

the sort that had ruled Thrannish skies. Loose tongues told of new fleets built by Urza and secreted away to fight Phyrexians, but who believed in Urza? Who believed in Urza's bogey men? Who had ever seen even a single skyship?

Until now.

It was a sleek and glorious, horrible thing, this *Weatherlight*. Nature cringed away from it. Still, it was not the dreamed-of evil. Something else was coming, something far more horrible than *Weatherlight*.

Tiny figures stood on her wind-ravaged deck—human figures.

Behind a gleaming ray cannon on the forecastle was strapped a man with black hair and angry eyes.

He shouted into a speaking tube, "Coordinates, Hanna!"

A powerstone embedded in the mouth of the tube snatched up his voice and hurled it a hundred feet aft to the glass-enclosed bridge.

The words raked out over a slim, hunched woman. Rules and styluses were clutched in one of her hands. The other jotted slide-rule calculations in a hasty column.

Blowing an errant strand of blonde back from her face, Hanna did her own shouting into the tube, "Working on it, Commander Gerrard!" Across her navigation console, compasses and gyros reeled. Hanna's eyes spun as she watched them settle. "Good luck finding another navigator who can pinpoint longitude without stars."

"I don't want another navigator," Gerrard answered from the forecastle. He threw a grin back toward the bridge. "I just want my favorite navigator to get us to Benalia."

Hanna summed three columns of figures and assigned functions to them. "We're still twelve hundred miles out, this time north by northwest."

"Damn! That's the farthest of the three," Gerrard said. "Where's the problem?"

"Not here," Hanna replied, confirming the calibration of her altimeter.

"Not here, either," reported another woman, standing at the

helm. Her corded shoulders and ebony skin seemed part of the ship's wheel she clutched. "Rudder, keel, airfoils—everything's performing perfectly, including me."

"I know, Sisay—" Gerrard answered, quickly adding—"*Captain*. But something's throwing us off course. Karn, is it an engine problem?"

The call echoed down tubes into steamy darkness—the engine room. A vast drive-core dominated the space. Mana conduits added their green light to the tepid glow of bolted lanterns. Two crewmembers worked a giant torque wrench, closing a valve. They did not pause to answer the commander. A third crewmember, who seemed simply another engine subreactor, spoke. Karn was a massive man made of silver, and his voice was like a waterfall.

"No engine problem yet, but soon."

His silver back was bent toward the machine, his hands embedded in twin operations ports. Micro-fibers extended from the controls into his fingers, linking him to every corner of the ship. All the rest of *Weatherlight* had endured the planeshifting stresses well, but the engine was beginning to overheat.

"We're having to douse the manifolds to keep them from melting down. Push it too far, Gerrard, and you'll have a puddle where your engine used to be."

Gerrard's laughter answered through the tube. "You know me, Karn. I push everything too far. Sick bay, how are the wounded holding up?"

"We're all fine down here," replied the ship's healer as she tightened a strap over one of her patients. Sweat beaded her forehead, and she raked her turban off. Out spilled dark hair braided with coins. "The second planeshift knocked my patients unconscious. There's been less complaining since then."

"How're you holding up, Orim?" Gerrard asked.

"All this flashing into and out of existence makes meditation sort of redundant," Orim said wryly.

Another laugh came from Gerrard. "That's my crew. Stout-hearted comrades and complainers, all. Sisay, let's have another go."

"Aye, Commander," said the woman at the helm.

"Hanna, pinpoint Benalia City, the Capashen Manor." Gerrard reflexively glanced down at the Capashen symbol tattooed on his left forearm. He would not likely be welcomed in his old home.

"You got a street address? A house description?" Hanna teased as she slid longitude and latitude indexes until they aligned. "Locked in, Commander. Heading three, seventeen, twenty."

"Aye," Sisay acknowledged. She turned the wheel, bringing the prow up toward a roiling mass of cloud. "Karn, initiate jump sequence."

The silver man's voice was drowned out by the engine's eager surge.

"Hold on, everybody," Sisay called out.

Behind his ray cannon, Gerrard hunkered down. He tightly clutched the handles of the fuselage. The cannon harness was sufficient to hold him in place on a rolling deck in the middle of a dogfight, but even those straps were stressed by a planeshift. Gerrard shot a glance over his shoulder to the starboard-side cannon. There, a minotaur gunner clung with equal fury. Tahngarth's teeth were gritted in determination, the closest he came to smiling.

Gerrard did smile. This was his ship. This was his crew. They were the best damned fliers and fighters in Dominaria and Mercadia, in Rath and Phyrexia. For years he'd heard how he and his friends and this ship were supposed to save the world. For the first time, he felt like they could.

That wasn't the only reason he smiled. There was no better place to watch a planeshift than strapped to a forecastle ray cannon.

Beyond the rail, Dominaria vaulted suddenly forward. The sky stretched out. Clouds frayed away to ropy lines of mist. The heavens began to fold in on themselves. Where before there was only beaming blue and white, now black verges appeared in the separating seams of reality. The sky held together only a moment more. It came to pieces. Scraps of blue and white tumbled in a black wind.

Were Gerrard beyond the rail, that wind would have torn him to pieces. It was chaos, pure and simple, the ocean of potentiality in which all actual worlds floated. Anything material that touched the chaos wind was dissolved away into sparking energies and nothing.

Weatherlight and her crew were wrapped in an envelope of saving air. It died to stillness around them. The roar fell silent. Beyond the energy envelope, storms of power raged. Within it, only *Weatherlight's* engines sounded.

"Command crew to the bridge," Gerrard barked. He undid the straps of his gunner's harness and strode across the forecastle toward the stairs leading amidships.

Tahngarth followed. The minotaur leaped the stairs and landed amidships with a thump. Gerrard joined him at the bottom, and they marched across the trembling deck. From the central hatch ahead, Orim emerged. Her feet trod softly between hoof and boot. The three approached the bridge. A fourth crewmember scuttled up to join them.

Gerrard arched an eyebrow. "Since when are you part of the command crew, Squee?"

The goblin winced downward, as though accustomed to being cuffed. He smiled all the same. "Karn can't make it. He say Squee go talk for him."

"That'll be the day," Tahngarth rumbled.

The four comrades climbed the stairs from amidships to the bridge. They opened the hatch and one by one clambered through. Mana conduits glowed around them.

"Here it is!" Hanna declared from the navigator's console. "Look, here—three loci of topographic disturbance."

Gerrard stalked toward her and stared down at a map of Benalia. Hanna was marking **X**s in an equilateral triangle above the nation.

"Three loci of—?"

"I've calculated it all out," Hanna said. Her blue eyes flicked impatiently as she rapped the back of her hand on a pile of figures. "There are disturbances here, here, and here. Geometric disturbances."

"Geometric—"

"Distortions in the fabric of space. Stretched-out geometry. They shunt us off our target like a drop of rain off an umbrella. That's why we can't get to Benalia."

Gerrard's eyes were grim beneath stormy brows. "Good work, Hanna. Any idea what might be causing these distortions?"

She breathed deeply, pausing for the first time in hours. "We ourselves make a geometrical disturbance every time we planeshift. It's a simple fold of space with a localized effect—two hundred yards or so. These things are warping space for a thousand miles each."

"That's a heck of a big ship," Squee offered.

Hanna shook her head, hands in sudden motion again as she dragged a folio of Phyrexian ship designs from beneath her desk. They were plans she had gleaned from the wrecked armada base in Mercadia. She spread them out. The ships depicted there were massive and grotesque. They bristled with hornlike protrusions. Their hulls seemed bone or carapace.

"No, even the largest ships we saw in Mercadia could not make that kind of disturbance."

"Brace for reentry," Sisay warned.

The crew each grasped handholds and watched as reality swam up around the ship. Scraps of sky and sea schooled densely beyond the dissipating energy envelope. The blackness of chaos was shut out behind bright, sinuous order. Fleeing cloud, clashing wave, cowering land—it might have been the exact same spot they left.

"Coordinates," Gerrard asked gently.

"Working on it, Commander," Hanna answered, ship plans cascading from her desktop as she noted new magnetic readings.

Squee scrambled to gather the plans.

"They aren't ships," Sisay broke in from the helm. She guided *Weatherlight* smoothly through racks of cloud. "Ships would make only a momentary disturbance. Unless they were continuously planeshifting in and out of the same spot, it wouldn't be ships."

"Unless they were portal ships," Gerrard said in sudden realization. He took the ship schematics from Squee, unrolled one, and spread it on the console. It showed a massive ship that seemed a crab claw opened wide. "When these pincer portions here and here pivot downward, they create a portal between them." He dragged the schematic away and pointed at the three spots on the map. "Those are huge aerial portals opening above Benalia. We're not talking about three Phyrexian ships. We're talking about hundreds pouring out of three separate portals."

Despite the flurry of paper on her work space, Hanna finished her calculations. "We're twelve hundred miles southwest of Benalia City."

Sisay hissed, "Even at top speed, it would take us nearly two hours to get there."

Tahngarth pounded his palm with his fist. "The Phyrexian ships are already coming across."

"Pinpoint the center of one of the disturbances," Sisay ordered. "If we strike the umbrella in the exact center, maybe we won't be shunted aside. Maybe we can break through."

Eyebrows furrowing, Gerrard said, "You think *Weatherlight*'s got it in her?"

"I know she does," Sisay replied.

Gerrard shrugged. "She's your ship."

Leaning to the speaking tube, Sisay said, "Karn, what do you think? One more planeshift, down the center of one of those things?"

The response seemed to come from the ship herself. "One more. We can do one more."

"Coordinates locked, Captain," Hanna reported as she tightened the bolts on the longitude and latitude levers.

The engines barked once and then droned with fierce life.

"Brace for planeshift!" Sisay called.

The planks bucked. Beyond the bridge, air wavered as if from heat stress. An envelope of calm rose around *Weatherlight*. It pushed back the shimmering sky and sea. Once again, reality stretched beyond its breaking point. Black seams snaked across the sky. The heavens unraveled. Scraps of the world fled away. Then there was only the vast blackness.

This planeshift was different, though. Instead of gliding through emptiness, the ship seemed to be plunging forward through muck. The power envelope rattled. The engines whined. Everything felt sluggish and hot. A wall of energy appeared ahead. Supercharged chaos slowed to take on momentary form. In seconds, *Weatherlight* struck that endless barrier.

Despite their handholds, the crew pitched forward. Sisay and Tahngarth kept their feet. Gerrard staggered to one knee. Squee scampered up beneath the navigational consoles and clutched Hanna's legs.

Then they were through. Reality coalesced again out of chaos.

Below, the plains and woodlands of Benalia spread to the horizons. Above, the sky was cluttered with clouds. In their steamy midst hung a vast black hole, a hole in the heavens.

"There's your Phyrexian portal," Sisay noted quietly. "But where's the portal ship?"

Through gritted teeth, Gerrard growled, "On the other side—in Rath, or Phyrexia, or wherever. Makes it impossible to destroy from here."

"That hole is big enough to admit three ships abreast," Tahngarth whispered.

Gerrard nodded. "And there they are, coming through."

Light failed beyond the lip of the portal; though within it, in murky crimson, huge and horrible figures appeared. They were ships—dragon ships the size of *Weatherlight*, cruisers thrice her displacement, and some larger still, massive things covered with holes.

Here was the long-dreamed evil.

"Plague ships," Orim growled.

"They've seen us," Sisay said, pointing. "Look."

Two of the cruisers nosed through the gap. The sunlight of Dominaria broke upon them. Spiky rams led their prows, and behind them were rank on rank of scabrous ribs. Black shadows became black realities. The central hulls of the ships seemed cancerous carbuncles piled atop each other. Next came flaring spines, razor wings, and clouds of oil soot. They were huge ships, the size of floating cities.

Swarming antlike across them were Phyrexians.

"Evasive action?" Sisay asked.

"Take us to them, Sisay. Battle stations," Gerrard responded. He repeated the order into the tube. "Battle stations!"

Tahngarth yanked back the forward hatch and descended amidships on his way to the forecastle guns. Sisay meanwhile hauled hard on the wheel. *Weatherlight* banked and climbed. Behind her, Hanna nearly bit a stylus in two as she worked out new calibrations. She spared a moment to swat Squee out from under her desk. The goblin retreated toward the poop deck door and huddled there.

"Get to the aft gun. You're not as craven as all that," Gerrard said.

"Who? Squee?" whimpered the little green man.

"Yes, Squee. You're the one who shot Volrath out of the sky, right?"

A glad light came to the goblin's eyes, and he hurried out the aft door.

"What, if I might ask, is your plan, Commander Gerrard?" Sisay shot over one shoulder.

He smiled winningly. "To fight Phyrexians."

Then he too swung down through the hatch. It was his last chance for bravado. The ships were closing fast. Gerrard sprinted across the amidships planks, vaulted up the forecastle stairs, and rushed to his gunner's rig. Even as he fastened straps about him, he pumped the foot pedal that charged the gun. A moan began in the metal. It shivered and grew warm. The powerstone arrays in the center of the gun's housing glowed to life.

Across the forecastle, Tahngarth swung the massive barrel of his ray cannon about. He spat on the shaft, watching the white glob hiss away on impact.

"Fore starboard gun ready!" he shouted.

Gerrard likewise spun his weapon to fore and spat on it. "Fore port gun ready!"

From amidships, Dabis and Fewsteem reported in from their gun encasements.

"Squee, too," came a squeal through the speaking tube. "Squee, too."

The belly gunner and top gunners reported in.

Gerrard shouted to them all. "They look awful, sure, but they've never been in battle. They've never tested their ships in combat. Shoot for the power conduits. Shoot for intakes and stabilizers, anything that'll make one shot count for two."

Weatherlight mounted up the sky. Her engines screamed in the ascent. The cruisers didn't seem to get any nearer, only bigger.

"They've got to have fifty guns per ship," Dabis gasped. "How do we stand against fifty guns?"

"We'll stand, and they'll fall," Gerrard said. "Sisay, take us between the ships."

Her voice was shrill in the tube. "*Between* them?"

"You heard me. Thread the needle."

"You mean run the gauntlet," Sisay growled. "Threading the needle, Commander."

After the stress of shifting, this kind of tooth-and-nail ascent was like poetry. Never before had *Weatherlight* been so powerful. Skyshaper, Juju Bubble, Bones of Ramos, Power Matrix—the engine had almost doubled in size since leaving Dominaria for Rath. It showed. *Weatherlight* rose with a vengeance.

Ahead the two Phyrexian cruisers formed the cliff walls of an aerial canyon.

Weatherlight was still accelerating as she drove between them.

"Fire at will!" Gerrard roared.

He squeezed the cannon handles. A great bolt of radiance roared out of the flaming end. It struck clear air, melting it to red plasma. A hissing comet, the flare arced across the racing sky. It smashed fistlike into the starboard intakes of one cruiser. Sparks and great shreds of metal danced in the engine. A black plume belched out the rear of the ship. Tahngarth scored a similar strike on the cruiser on his side. Dabis and Fewsteem squeezed off a few shots.

Then black bolts answered. They shot out like sooty spider webs from ports along the ships' baselines. These were no webs. They were mana beams, their touch bringing death. They reached out toward *Weatherlight*.

"Cut those lines!" Gerrard shouted. His cannon unloaded three rounds in quick succession. The bolts grabbed Phyrexian flack from the air and obliterated it.

Tahngarth's cannon shouted. It ate away a pair of webs just before they lashed *Weatherlight*'s hull. He shot a third time. This beam sliced through the air to punch into a set of mana conduits on the starboard cruiser's flank.

Already, the air was black with fire from the cruisers.

"What have you done?" Tahngarth roared even as he loosed a new volley. "We'll never survive the crossfire!"

"*They'll* never survive the crossfire," Gerrard shouted back.

Black bolts filled the air between the cruisers. Most of the shots went wide of *Weatherlight*. They continued on, slamming into the opposite vessel. The Phyrexian cruisers were slaying each other.

A black blast struck *Weatherlight*'s hull just below Fewsteem's gun.

"Forget the ships!" Gerrard shouted. "They're already done for. Defensive fire!"

Over the tube came Sisay's voice. "Shall I take us out of here, Commander?"

"Sure, Sisay. Straight forward. Take us up, through the portal!"

CHAPTER 2
Day Trip to Rath

"Take us where?" Sisay's voice echoed in the speaking tube.

Gerrard had expected her to resist. He squeezed off two more blasts, watching gaseous plasma smack against the lateral thrusters of one of the cruisers. The mechanism melted, and the Phyrexian warship listed farther.

Through a grim smile, he called back to Sisay, "We've got to destroy the portal ship. We can't shoot it from this side."

"On the other side, there's an armada," Sisay protested, "and Phyrexians."

Gerrard spat dismissively. "Their ships are crap." As if in proof, he fired twice more. The shots soared out like twin stars and smashed through the main bridge of the cruiser. It lit lantern bright. "And their crews are no match for ours."

"I agree with you there," Sisay replied.

Weatherlight surged with new speed toward the portal. The engines roared their resolve. Karn, below, was reworking the intake-exhaust ratios to maximize thrust. *Weatherlight* shot from the gulf between the cruisers. A whoop went up from the crew, followed by a second one, even louder.

The port-side ship foundered and plunged from the sky. It rolled massively over, its guns still firing. Webby mana trails tangled about the shuddering vessel. Explosions rocked it. The stern cracked away, propelled on red flame. The cruiser's main body shown in cross section. It tipped on end, smashed to ground, and shattered like a rotten egg.

A third cheer erupted, cut short by a sudden explosion.

Weatherlight was still a thousand yards from the portal when a black-mana bolt struck the starboard amidships. It ate the rail and part of the gunwale and swept toward the starboard ray cannon. Fewsteem, strapped there, shouted as his gun blazed. Red energy punched through the center of the black mass. It was not enough. Inky death spattered the cannon and fell on Fewsteem. Metal hissed. Flesh turned to rot and white ash. The gun belched green smoke and went dark. Fewsteem was gone—nothing more than a pair of legs beneath a puff of soot.

Without its counterpart, the remaining Phyrexian cruiser was unloading its arsenal.

"Tahngarth, blast that cruiser!" Gerrard shouted. He struggled to wrench his gun about, but its angle of fire couldn't reach starboard aft.

"It's behind the wing!" Tahngarth shouted back.

Sisay initiated a series of swooping lunges. Ropy charges of black-mana spent themselves in empty air beside and behind the ship.

Crimson charges rushed out from the stern ray cannon. Squee stood in its traces, blasting away. The pulses danced erratically through the air. Many shots missed their mark. Others batted down the cruiser's fire. Two rounds won through the barrage and sank into the exhaust port of the main engine.

The enormous craft hiccuped. It shuddered once. Its attacks faltered.

In a sun-bright blaze, it exploded. Hunks of ship hurtled outward, trailing fire. They raced toward *Weatherlight* at twice her speed. Had she been in clear air, the shrapnel would have hailed across *Weatherlight* and dismantled her. Fortunately, it was just then she punched through the portal.

Fortunately? The blue skies of Dominaria gave way to twisted clouds in red and black. The wide plains and deep forests gave way to volcanic rills and tortured lava tubes. Worst of all, though, in place of two Phyrexian ships, there were thousands.

Airships were stacked to the sky. As devilish as they had seemed in the sunlight, in shadow these vessels were demons in hell. Wings of skin. Dripping claws. Jetting fires. A dozen of the ships were as big as mountains. A hundred were the size of the cruisers already destroyed. A thousand were the size of *Weatherlight*.

"Forget the armada!" Gerrard roared. "Target the portal ship!"

Fire answered from the six remaining guns. A sunburst of scarlet energy raced out from *Weatherlight*. The charges soared up toward the vast metallic claw that hung in the skies of Rath. The ship seemed to glare down at them, robotic arms twitching impotently in the portal. One by one, the shots impacted the claw. Flowstone panels slumped. Fires hissed forth. The flames seemed impossibly small on that massive machine. Already *Weatherlight* was out of range for more attacks.

"They're getting through!" Squee shouted through the aft speaking tube.

Two more cruisers nosed beneath the portal ship, toward undefended Benalia.

Gerrard shouted. "Turn the ship! We've got to stop them!"

"Turn the ship—?" Sisay shouted. Her objection was cut short.

The portal ship spewed black smoke. Its gleaming vision of Dominaria flickered. Explosions bloomed in the joints of one pincer. It cracked free, toppled, and dropped toward the twisted ground of Rath. Like a soap bubble, the portal popped. Sunlight died. Benalish skies were gone.

Gone too were the front halves of the two cruisers. The closing portal had guillotined the ships. The shriek and groan of failing metal was punctuated by explosions from severed engines. In tandem, the cruisers' afts sputtered sparks and soot. They tipped, crashing down atop waiting craft below. In a storm of fire and smoke, five ships impacted the flowstone ground. The first power core went critical. It sent a column of black force a thousand feet into the sky and fifty feet into the ground. Hunks of flowstone pelted a second craft. Its power core cracked, and then a third. More ships went down there before the closed portal.

"Nice work for the first ten minutes of the invasion!" Gerrard shouted to his crew. "A ruined portal and a dozen ships down!"

"And ten thousand ships trapped on this side with us," Sisay warned. "We've got company."

Though cruisers and plague ships were too slow to pursue *Weatherlight*, the dragon engines were not. To the untrained eye, they seemed merely dragons. The sinuous constructs were as agile, as sleek, as intelligent as their natural kin. Beneath scales of enameled titanium were meshes so fine as to form skin and muscles. The beasts wheeled about and swarmed after *Weatherlight*. They opened jaws lined with true scimitars and breathed breath as powerful as any ray cannon blast.

"Punch it, Karn! Full speed!" Gerrard called.

"This *is* full speed," came the rumbled response.

"Evasive action," Gerrard shouted.

"This *is* evasive action," Sisay responded.

"Laying in planeshift!" Hanna called.

"Belay that," Gerrard responded. "Stay here on Rath. Lay in a course to the closest active portal ship."

"Aye, Commander."

"One armada isn't enough for you to take on?" Sisay asked through the tube.

"We'll shut down that one just like we've shut down this one."

Weatherlight jagged, her keel smashing a dragon engine that had flown up beneath it. The metallic wyrm plunged from the air to tumble brokenly across the tortured ground.

"Nice flying, Captain!" Gerrard said.

"How about you *shoot* some of them?" she replied.

"Yeah, how about it?"

Gerrard's cannon blazed. Blood-red energy dragged plasma from the air. It roared down the open gullet of a dragon that swooped up to port. The eyes of the beast glowed for a brilliant moment before going black. The dragon engine's wings folded, and it plummeted away.

Two more engines soared up to take the place of the first. They spat their own fire. It mantled the fore hull and made wood instantly blaze.

Had *Weatherlight* been a ship of dead timbers, she would have gone up like a jack straw. But *Weatherlight* lived. Her hull was living wood, her Thran metal fittings grew, even her engine was a vital organ, capable of agony and joy. The silver golem attached to that engine served as a kind of brain for the machine. Together the components of *Weatherlight* made a powerful being, more than capable of her own defense. Sap oozed from the living hull, extinguishing the fire and salving the charred grains. The port-side landing spine jutted suddenly, and the ship rolled. The sharp metal spine lanced through the dragon engines, slicing their chests. They veered off, falling through the swarm of their comrades.

"Course locked in," reported Hanna. "A hundred miles to the next portal ship."

"They're targeting the wings!" Sisay shouted in warning.

The ship swooped to avoid a killing blast of breath. Shots from Squee's cannon destroyed the offender. Another dragon engine followed, unshakable.

Gerrard growled, "Karn, can we fly without wings?"

"Like a rocket, fast and fatal. It'll be almost impossible to steer."

"Not for Sisay. Fold the wings. Rocket us to the next portal." Gerrard expected a chorus of dissent. The others were either inured to his requests or dumbstruck.

The wings folded, ratcheting inward on chains. For a moment, *Weatherlight* lost lift. Then her intakes opened wide, and her exhausts narrowed to blazing jets.

"Hold on!" Gerrard shouted.

It was futile. He could not be heard above the sudden roar. Besides, anyone who was not strapped down or inside the ship would have been blown from the deck.

Weatherlight rocketed away from the pursuing cloud of dragon engines. Her exhaust vents painted the folded masts vermilion. The afterburn lit the eyes of the metallic serpents. They fell back, their jaws snapping on nothing.

As the yawing hull settled into its roaring course, Gerrard let out a whoop. "Would you believe it? All the time I spent running from my Legacy—if I'd known it was so damned much fun—"

"There has been a casualty," Tahngarth reminded through the speaking tube.

"Yeah," Gerrard acknowledged. He drew a long breath and pivoted to stare at the starboard amidships gun. The black rot that had once mantled its barrel had spent itself, hissing away to nothing. The goo had taken Gunner Fewsteem's body with it, had burned away even the harness that had held him. Gerrard muttered, "Fewsteem. He was a brave man. There have been so many lost. . . . Yes, that's why I ran for so long—"

"I'm picking up an even larger armada at the next portal ship," Hanna reported, her voice tense in the speaking tube. "We're going to need every gun."

"Any chance of repairing Fewsteem's cannon?" Gerrard asked.

Karn answered from the engine room. His connection to the ship allowed him to sense its every fiber as part of his body. "There is a single ruptured conduit in the plasma supply field. Replace it, and the gun will work again."

"I'm on it," Hanna said, moving away from the speaking tube before Gerrard could countermand her. Moments later, she descended from the helm to amidships, the needed part in one hand and a big wrench in the other.

He had to grin. It was classic Hanna. Her blonde hair whipped in the wind. She leaned steeply to make her way forward. She seemed so slender there, against the racing landscape of Rath, the coiling red clouds. Gerrard was glad she had a wrench to weigh her down. She reached the gun, removed a split panel, and worked at loosening the ruptured conduit.

"That's my girl," Gerrard said, shaking his head in admiration.

"Gerrard, you see what we are flying over?" Sisay asked at the helm.

He had not. Eyes that had seen only Hanna against the red turmoil of Rath now shifted their focus. His face darkened.

On the unruly hills below waited a huge army of Phyrexians. Their forces stretched to the horizons. There were no tents or bedrolls, for these creatures needed neither shelter nor rest. There were only patient ranks of troops and penned beasts to feed them. No campfires, either—Phyrexians did not need heat and preferred their meals raw, indeed live. There was not a stick of furniture and no provision for comfort—unless gladiatorial circles could be called comfort. There was only order and slavish obedience and savagery.

"Waiting to board troop ships, you think, Sisay?" Gerrard conjectured.

"Waiting for something but not troop ships. There're too many soldiers."

"Gun's fixed," Hanna announced triumphantly. She repositioned the split panel and staggered to her feet.

Sisay let out a hiss. "Incoming!"

A plague bomb dropped from a sentry craft overhead. It fell straight toward *Weatherlight*. The ship jagged out from beneath it, but the bomb burst in midair. Shrapnel hailed across *Weatherlight*'s amidships. Shards bounded briefly against the planks before being ripped away on the winds.

"Everybody all right?" Gerrard shouted.

"Just a little scratch," Hanna answered. She gripped her stomach and smiled bravely. "Makes me want to fire this gun."

"The job's yours. See Orim about that scratch as soon as we're out of here."

"Look sharp," Sisay shouted. "There's the next armada."

Beyond the dipping prow of *Weatherlight*, a vast black cloud appeared. It swelled quickly outward until it filled the whole horizon. Instead of mist, though, this cloud was made of ships—Phyrexian warships.

There were dragon engines, cruisers, and plague ships but also hundreds of others. Many had been specified on the plans Hanna had stolen from the Mercadian hangar. Solid-hulled ram ships hovered like barracudas. Fat barges provided floating laboratories for Phyrexian vat priests. Bombers bore payloads of plague on bat-like wings. Helioslicers held themselves aloft with whirling blades that could mince whole armies. Icthus ships seemed winged spiders, with eight articulated lances for spearing merfolk. There were ship types for slaying every creature in land and water and air. They lined up to soar through the pincers of the portal ship.

"Let's not give them time to fire," Gerrard commanded. "Karn, keep the wings folded and the engines roaring."

"Aye."

"Sisay, we need perfect flying. No collisions and straight through the portal."

"I'll fling us through. You clear the way and shut the door behind us."

"Right. Tahngarth, Dabis, Hanna—we'll have just one chance at this."

"Don't worry. I'm pissed," Hanna said. She clung to the starboard amidships cannon, pivoting it fore.

"Just hold on. You're not strapped."

"Can't get rid of me that easily," she said, flashing him a grin.

He returned the look. "Here we go!"

Weatherlight blazed across Rath like a shooting star. Her engines lit the sagittal crests of the troops that crowded the land behind. Her ray cannons flung blazing light at the stacks of hovering ships ahead. Red plasma spattered arsenals, punched its way through engine walls, ripped open carapace hulls, slew the slayers on the threshold of the world.

Gerrard's cannon barked. Scarlet energy shot in a long column outward. It struck the rear stabilizers of a ram-ship dead ahead. The heavy craft pitched forward, driven over by the cannon fire. The ram head cracked into a troop ship below. The two halves of the troop ship split. Phyrexians spilled out like pepper from a mill. *Weatherlight* rocketed through the vacated space.

Tahngarth meanwhile lined up a shot, his bullish nostrils snorting. He fired. Red-hot energy pounded the aft of a command cruiser. The blast ripped free the flying bridge of the craft. It toppled aside, taking its controls and staff with it. The rest of the ship began to yaw slowly like a falling maple seed.

"Bull's-eye!" Gerrard shouted to him.

The minotaur squinted and rumbled, "Don't get cute."

Weatherlight cleared the spinning wreck. The portal ship appeared beyond, just visible through the waiting armada. The first two cruisers were making their leisurely way through.

"Save your shots!" Gerrard called. "Time this right."

In moments, they were in range.

"Aim. . . . Fire!"

Six of the seven ray cannons could bear on the portal ship, and they all discharged. The racing blasts seemed red spokes on a vast wagon wheel. Each one soared unerringly to strike the pincers of the ship. They sparked and flared. Fires erupted from the ship. There was no time to see more.

Weatherlight shot through the portal. Blue skies replaced red. Benalia replaced Rath.

"Did it close? Did it close?" Gerrard shouted.

"Negative," called Sisay. "The cruisers are coming through—"

Four quick blasts came from the aft gun. Squee pumped the hissing weapon. Tracers stretched back to sock the bow of the half-emerged cruiser. Explosions popped along its hull.

"Great shot, Squee!"

The cruiser foundered, halfway through that hole in the sky. It listed to port. Its masts raked along the side of the portal, ripping at the superstructure. With a sudden boom like thunder, the gateway slammed closed. The prows of the two Phyrexian cruisers were severed from the rest of the ships. They fell away. The wrecks tumbled, sparking.

Benalia received its invaders with the wide-open arms of a brick wall. Each hulk shattered on impact.

"Hanna, find that third portal."

"We've got to land," Karn interrupted ominously from below. *Weatherlight*'s wings raked out, and her engine slowed. "We're overheating."

"Fine—land—but get us to Benalia City. Get us to the Capashen Manor."

CHAPTER 3
When Gods Do Battle

On a lofty ridge in eastern Benalia stood two men. They might as easily have been two armies. Power armor encased their bodies. Metallic, hypertrophic, veiny—the suits were set with powerstone arrays. Thick capes draped their shoulders. Bladed battle staves leaned in their grips. Flight dynamos jutted from arms and legs. Black crystals gave gauntlets the touch of death. Whole armies had been defeated by these two men.

They were not men, not truly.

One was a millennium-old mage, with short gray hair, mutton chops, and a pair of wide-spaced mustaches bracketing his mouth. He wielded the power of skies and seas, of volcanoes and verdant fields. The armor he wore was a concession to his friend. Even without it, the mage could bring the heavens down to kiss the dust.

The other man was a near-god. His body was nothing but a convenience of his concentration. Nothing but will held him in one place. He stepped among and between worlds as easily as other

21

men stepped stone to stone. For him, the power armor was a vanity. He could have simply imagined the suit into being, but he loved to build machines.

Urza Planeswalker drew a deep breath of the cool air. Wind dragged at his long, ash-blond hair and goatee. It snapped his cape behind him.

"Do you sense it, Barrin? Do you sense what *Weatherlight* has just done?"

Mage Master Barrin nodded. Time had wrinkled his flesh and clouded his eyes. Still, he seemed a young protégé to Urza. Indeed, he was. Though Barrin had lived a millennium, Urza had lived four.

"Yes, my friend. I sense what they have done—your savior and my daughter and their ship." The words sounded sharper than he had intended. It mattered little. Urza was oblivious to social slights. "They've closed two of the portals."

"Splendid." Urza rarely smiled, but he did now. "Gerrard at last is testing well." He glanced at his friend. Caprice shone in the planeswalker's gemstone eyes. "You said it was a mistake to create him. You said no man could live up to the destiny I assigned to Gerrard."

"I said no man could *endure* Gerrard's destiny." Shrugging his eyebrows, Barrin added, "We have yet to see. I only wish my daughter had chosen another man to love. It is dangerous business to love a savior."

"Hanna chose as her mother chose," Urza said offhandedly.

Barrin scowled, regret boiling in his eyes. "There is still this third portal." As if to banish memories, Barrin stared out over the wide plain. Wild wheat filled the fields, nodding white heads in the wind. "We should summon the aerial contingents. At top speed, they could arrive even as the portal opens."

"No," Urza said flatly. "I will summon them, but they will come slowly. They would be weakened after a more speedy flight." He activated gems imbedded in his staff.

"Better to field many troops early than to perish before stronger troops arrive," quipped Barrin.

"Haste makes waste. Better to bide our time," replied the planeswalker.

"If it were up to you, Urza, we would bide forever."

"If it were up to you, Barrin, we would do the same."

"But it is not up to us. It is up to the Phyrexians," Barrin said.

Urza's temples reddened. He had no need to blush. The capillaries that suffused his flesh were mere figments of his mind but, as figments, were all the more receptive to Urza's mood.

"If we succeed in this war, nothing ever again will be up to the Phyrexians," replied Urza.

Barrin grasped Urza's armored shoulder and pointed toward the wide heavens. "Here they come."

The sky opened. Blackness ripped a hole in blue. A portal yawned wide. From its lightless depths stared a malign presence.

Urza's hand tightened on his battle staff. "My old foe. He is gazing at me."

"And you are gazing at him."

"Were it not for him, I could simply walk to that portal and shut it down, but he knows me. He shoves at me, even here."

Ships—small, fleet ships—shot from the yawning portal. They buzzed outward and swarmed there, watching for attack. Some were dragon ships, their necks and tails coiling. Others were smaller still, single-pilot jump-ships configured like fleas. A few were puppet craft, unmanned and controlled distally. All flew in intercept patterns as the first big cruisers made their way through the portal.

"They've learned from *Weatherlight*'s tactics," Urza observed grimly. "We'll not be shutting this one down in Gerrard-fashion."

"He's shoving at you, Urza," Barrin said. "Shove back."

Nodding in satisfaction, Urza raised his battle staff. "First— some old friends. Do you think they will remember my falcon engines?" He pressed a certain stone.

From among waving heads of wheat, metal things surged suddenly skyward. There were ten thousand of the birds—little more than wings of steel, gemstone eyes, and nostrils that craved glistening-oil. In their brave breasts the falcons bore Thran-metal shredders. When they struck Phyrexian flesh, the shredders emerged to dig through.

Falcons rocketed skyward. Their pinions shrieked in the ascent. In moments, they had reached the foe. Falcons converged on the vanguard of Phyrexian vessels. Many cracked through jump-ship windscreens and punched into the chests of Phyrexian pilots. Most hurled themselves onward to the cruisers that lumbered above. Plasma batteries answered from the huge ships. The falcons easily evaded. They reached the cruisers, delved into whatever hollows presented themselves, and coursed down corridors into chambers where Phyrexians stood their posts. There, they shredded.

Once again, there came that impossible grin on Urza's face.

"You're enjoying this," Barrin observed grimly.

"It's a sort of chess match," Urza replied. "Two foes, ancient and powerful, battling over little squares of turf."

Barrin's face was bleak. "Two not dissimilar foes—"

"He has led with his knights and bishops. I have led with my pawns. They are swarming and destroying his pieces."

"*Weatherlight* is not a pawn. That ship, and Gerrard, and my daughter—it's your king. You're leading with your king."

Urza gestured as jump-ships fell in a regular rain from the skies. "It is beautiful. How can you not smile?"

"In this chess match, Master Urza, you have sixteen pieces and he sixteen thousand."

"I have sixteen billion," Urza said. "I have every fluttering heart on this planet." He brought his staff down.

From the rocky peaks all around came the whine of cables snapping suddenly taut. Enormous trebuchet arms arced up from machines hidden in cut branches. Their uplifted baskets flung Metathran troop transports high into the air. The small ships spun skyward. They were simple in design—mere wheels hurled on the air. Within those wheels sat Metathran shock troops—blue-skinned warriors bioengineered for this very war. They were held against the walls by simple centripetal force. The transports had no engines of their own. On the perimeter of each disk, five powerstones in the five colors of magic were imbedded equidistant. In dynamic opposition, they made the wheel into a mana magnet. It was drawn inexorably to the most powerful mana source nearby, where it would clamp tight.

Reaching the height of their arc, the transports sensed the cruisers emerging above. One after another, they whirled upward. Dragon engines flew down to intercept them. A few disks struck the dragons, knocking them aside and continuing on their steady flight upward. The pull of gravity was nothing next to the pull of magic. Like sucker fish around a shark, the disks schooled up around the nearest Phyrexian cruiser and latched on. Immediately, Metathran warriors climbed from their wheels, boarding the enemy vessel.

"They will not survive the battle," Barrin noted.

"They are bred not to care whether they do," Urza said.

"So are Phyrexians," Barrin replied.

"Then they should be a fair match," Urza mused. His eyes glinted. Whenever he stared intently, the faceted gemstones in his skull showed through the masking glamour they wore. "I only wish I had batteries of ray cannons. That was my one great oversight."

"One . . . great . . . oversight," Barrin echoed sardonically.

Urza raised an eyebrow. "Phyrexians inherited Thran powerstone technology undiluted. They had six thousand years and a world laboratory to improve on it. I've had to dig Thran hulks from deserts and volcanoes and guess at glyphs and work in impoverished isolation." He gave another rap of his war staff. A hundred more troop transports launched overhead. "Of course they have ray cannons."

"*Weatherlight* has Phyrexian ray cannons. You could study them there. Your titan engines could use such weapons."

"I would not interfere with the development of the crew."

"They wouldn't even know you were there," Barrin interrupted testily. "You are Urza Planeswalker, after all."

The new batch of troop transports swarmed a third cruiser, just then emerging from the portal. The first two ships, sharks drifting side by side, no sooner cleared the gap than black-mana bombards hurled destruction from one to the other. Ropy lines of energy spattered the sides of one cruiser, eating it away.

Urza nodded. "I see the teams have reached the fire controls."

The attacking ship banked inward. Its huge hulk ran up alongside the neighbor ship. Lateral spikes sank like fangs into the wounded vessel's flank. Sparks ringed the gouges, and oil bled forth.

"They've reached the ship's bridge too," Barrin added.

The cruiser ground a deep cleft in the side of its cohort, severing vital conduits. The second cruiser began to list.

"You don't need ray cannons when you have strategy," Urza thought aloud.

The sky leviathans seemed to fuse. They scissored together, shearing away metal as they went. One lost lift. Spewing flames, the two massive machines pitched toward the plains.

"And now, they've shut down the batteries," Urza said as commentary. "They should be returning to their transports. Once the mana batteries are dead, the transports will rise." His gemstone eyes followed the battleships as they plunged. Not a single transport had disengaged from the hull. "Any moment now, and they will whirl away to attach to the next ship."

The ships formed a huge **V** as they struck ground. Their prows dug deep. Soil mounded ahead of them and splashed outward like water. The ships compacted. What air once resided in those oily chambers shot forth in angry hisses. Panels blasted loose. Explosions followed. They began in shattered power cores and spread on plumes of oil and ignited even the white heads of wheat. Then the raving flames were extinguished by a black implosion that sucked air into its empty belly.

Grass was pulled from its roots. Trees were leveled in converging rings. Barrin himself would have been sucked into the vortex had it not been for Urza's stony hand grasping his shoulder. The whole world seemed to gasp in that moment. It was a deafening drone. Slowly the roar died to a sound like horses screaming, then sudden silence.

Releasing his comrade, Urza said hoarsely, "Not as I had planned it."

"Nothing will be as you had planned it," rasped Barrin. To

soften the comment, he said, "Thank you for anchoring me."

"I was only returning the favor." Urza hitched his goatee skyward. "Enough observation. We had best wade in ourselves."

"Yes," Barrin replied.

The two rose into battle. Azure crystals embedded in their power armor lifted them with the silent alacrity of bubbles through water. This was not so much flight as levitation, keyed directly to the minds of the suits' wearers. Soon the wind set up complaint at their passage. It tore at shoulders and wrung cloaks. No one was supposed to rise this quickly, not even a mage master and a planeswalker.

They had planned greater affronts to nature.

Barrin swept his battle staff through three arcs. Blue energy formed a sphere of protection around him. It was barely complete when a great tarry fist of black mana struck the shield. Dark energy spattered the sphere and crawled around it.

Pressing his lips together in irritation, Barrin whirled his staff again. It peeled back the shield as though it were an orange rind. He gathered the black-dripping shards of blue energy, mixing the colors. Swinging the staff in a final wide arc, he flung the glittering ball up to impact the belly of the third cruiser.

The ball tore through plates of metal to rip open a barrack. Out tumbled Phyrexians, cockroaches from a rotten log.

Urza meanwhile dodged red blasts from a ray cannon as he approached the cruiser.

The shots grew more precise. The gunners worked with frantic fury. One gunner had once been a human. Now it was a tortured thing of crisscrossed cables and gearwork implants. It caught Urza in its sights and fired. Red fury belched from the smoldering barrel of the cannon.

Urza lifted leathery gauntlets and deflected the hot plasma as if flinging away globs of wax. Heedless, he neared. Another volley spewed from the machine. This time, Urza caught the killing stuff and hurled it back at the gunner.

Gaseous plasma struck its tortured face. Its head collapsed like a balloon. It slumped in the straps of the machine.

Urza was glad to see that the ray cannon itself was unharmed.

The other gunner had never been human. A vat-grown monster, its body configuration was arthropodal. Beneath a red skull piece lurked a round mouth set with in-curved fangs. Its four forward appendages were poison barbed, and they lashed out to strike Urza. The reach of those things told of their unnatural origins.

The first jab caught Urza in the side. He had been too distracted, admiring the weapon. Now he was focused. Stingers the size of bull horns cut through power armor, sank into his side, pierced viscera, and met in the middle of him. Their fangy tips pumped venom.

Any man would have been killed. Perhaps that was why the **O**-shaped mouth wore a leering grin. Urza, however, was no mere man.

He ripped the stinger from his flesh. It was agony but an agony he could survive. He yanked the creature's arm out by its roots. Poison jetted from one end and bug-gore from the other. Urza jabbed the stingers into the Phyrexian's astonished mouth. Poison pumped. The gunner thrashed briefly before slumping beside its partner. Urza flung the dead arm away.

Almost as an afterthought, Urza reshaped his flesh, squeezing the venom out of him. His viscera and muscle regrew. Even the power armor repaired itself, now a mere projection of his mind. As long as the planeswalker could think, he could heal.

With a single almighty yank, Urza broke the ray cannon from its mounting. The huge weapon cracked loose from the walkway. It weighed an easy ton. Clutching the gun, Urza floated away from the cruiser. He slowly turned the cannon about, so he could engage its fire controls.

With a mere touch, Urza understood this machine. His eye glinted in the crosshairs. His hand compressed the trigger.

Red plasma blazed from the barrel, first taking out others guns like it. Next, Urza aimed at engine banks, at power stations, at stabilizers. It was short work with the single cannon to cripple the third cruiser. The massive ship began to sink.

Urza set his feet on it and paused to breathe. He did not need to breathe, but it helped him think. This ray cannon would prove very helpful. He would ride the cruiser to the ground and see what else he could salvage.

A cry came from overhead. Urza looked up. A huge dragon engine hovered there, its scales limned with blue motes of magic. From the back of the engine, a familiar figure called down.

"I requisitioned a ride. Where are you going?" Barrin asked.

"I'm riding this one down to see what else I can salvage," Urza said, happily hoisting the ray cannon. "Then I have pressing business elsewhere."

"Pressing business?" Barrin echoed incredulously. He gestured over his shoulder, where two more ships emerged, spraying flack. "*This* is pressing business."

"Yes," Urza replied. He pointed beyond the cruisers. Small white figures descended out of the sky—Metathran warships and flights of Serran angels. "But you have some new help. This battle is well in hand."

Barrin could only stare incredulously as Urza slid away atop the plunging cruiser. With anger meant for his old friend, Barrin savagely dug his heels into the sides of the dragon engine.

"Get up there, now. We've got a battle to win."

The dragon could not resist the blue thrall of Barrin's magic. Its wings surged, and it climbed into the sky.

Barrin patted the metallic neck. "You and I are the same, dragon. Enthralled. Driven into someone else's battles. One of these days, if we last long enough, we will awaken."

CHAPTER 4
Blind Visions

Weatherlight was a fine ship—and more than a ship. Part machine, part organism, part miracle, she fought with all the nerve and innovation of a great warrior. When the battle was done, also like a great warrior, she staggered to the nearest haven to make a controlled crash.

"There!" Gerrard shouted where he stood in the prow. He jabbed a finger beyond broad grasslands to a walled metropolis. "Benalia City!"

He would always remember the gleaming limestone of that place—thin white towers with conic hats, tall windows with elegant tracery, larger-than-life statues gazing over endless grasslands. Gerrard had trained there, had become a master-at-arms in the Benalish military. Benalia City had taught him the deadliness of blades and politics. He would still be among those sword masters except for Sisay's abduction. He had left his division to help save the ship's captain.

30

"Karn," Gerrard called into the bow speaking tube, "can you get us there?"

There came no response from below decks except a shudder of exertion that jiggled the whole ship. Sisay's voice came through.

"He's already drawing on his inner reserves to keep us aloft. He'll get us there."

"How bad is the damage?" Gerrard asked.

Hanna replied, "She'll heal herself. There's lots of heat stress— worn contacts, overworked parts. Give her an hour or two, and she'll be ready for another fight."

An alarm rose from the grand walls of the city.

"Speaking of a fight," Gerrard hissed under his breath.

In marketplace stalls, citizens looked up and pointed skyward. Soldiers clambered up the walls to reinforce the guards. Crossbow archers cranked bolts into place. Swords glinted in the sun. These were among the best-trained warriors in Dominaria. Ballista crews wheeled their siege engines about, loading them with thirty-foot spears of spruce. The iron-tipped bolts could rip their way through *Weatherlight*'s hull. Just now, ten such machines targeted the ship's bow.

Gerrard raised his arms in the Benalish signal for alliance and parley. The ballistae and crossbows remained trained on the smoldering ship.

"Peace!" Gerrard shouted in a voice that sounded like war.

With massive grace, the ship edged out over the elegant turrets of Benalia City. Pennants snapped above hipped gables. Among colonnades of limestone stood gaping dignitaries, their robes hanging in mute amazement from their arms. The whole city blinked in wonder and a little fear.

Gerrard drew a deep breath and listened for the sound of hull-staving bolts. No such traumas came from beyond, but from within . . . a great blast from the engine room sent a jet of fire out of the manifolds.

Folk in the marketplace below shouted. A single anxious quarrel leaped up. It cracked off the rail beside Gerrard and tumbled away. It was the only shot fired. The other archers held their attacks, and the white-garbed civilians in the marketplace held their breaths.

Weatherlight had found her haven, uneasy though it was. Landing spines jutted from her hull and reached for the cobbled courtyard. She cast a deep shadow over the stones. An apple seller scrambled to wheel her cart out of the way. Apples hopped off the shuddering conveyance like children leaping from a hay wagon.

The courtyard, once thronging with buyers and sellers, was now empty of everyone except a single, wizened madman. Shabby in gray robes, he had been proclaiming death from the skies. The great, smoky airship nicely fulfilled his prophecies. That was not why he remained. Eyes wrapped in a kerchief, the blind man simply did not realize *Weatherlight* was about to settle atop him.

From beneath a broad-brimmed hat, the man continued his lament, ". . . monsters more hideous than creatures in a child's nightmare. Ancient, evil, twisted, bent on destroying all that is fair and beautiful. They think this world is theirs. They think we are the usurpers. They want to kill us, every last one. They think they save us, but they will kill the weakest and enslave the strongest and change us into monsters. They will change you! And you! And you!" The blind man pointed accusingly. His gnarled fingers failed to indicate anyone in the empty courtyard. "Arm yourselves, Benalia! Arm yourselves! Each of us shall have to fight, even the aged, the blind, the mad—and I am all three!" He laughed dryly, the sound ending in a hacking cough.

Only then did the blind man notice the huge ship, hissing as it settled on its landing spines. He didn't seem to hear it but rather to feel the sudden shade it cast on his shoulders. A look of puzzlement puckered his old lips. The hull gently shoved his back. He staggered forward as the ship stopped just short of crushing him.

Turning angrily, the old man pushed at the side of the ship. "Watch your wagon, goodsir! Give me room!"

Grim-faced soldiers marched up in a line behind the man. Boots cracked smartly against the stones. Cocked crossbows set an uneasy whine in the air.

The blind seer turned, lips white with anger. "What is this?

You come to haul me away? My warnings are disbelieved? The truth teller goes to prison?" He held out his arms in melodramatic surrender.

The captain of the guard glared past the madman to the rail of the airship. "Ho, there! Give account! Who are you, and what is this . . . thing? What is your purpose?"

A wry laugh came from above. Gerrard set one booted foot on the rail, leaned on his knee, and smiled. "I am Gerrard Capashen, scion of the first house." He rolled up his left sleeve, displaying the Capashen tattoo—a tower with seven windows. "I learned to fight there, in the lower yard, and I learned to tryst there, in the grotto. This is *Weatherlight*, ancient airship and Benalia's greatest defender. My purpose is to defend you in the coming war."

"Defend us? Against whom?" asked the guard captain.

"The monsters from the skies!" the blind man cried. "I have told you over and over, but you will not believe."

"Shut up, old man," the guard advised.

Gerrard snorted. "He's right, in fact. This blind man *does* see something. Yes, there is an invasion underway—beasts falling on us from the skies. Return to your homes. Arm yourselves. Every house must become a fortification, every person a warrior."

The guard captain spat into the dirt. He glanced at the blind seer. "Is this sky-flying lunatic your son?"

Patting *Weatherlight*'s hull, the wizened man said, "Well, why not?"

"I demand an audience with the chief of the Capashen Clan. I demand to address the chiefs of the seven clans."

"All right, come down here, Gerrard Capashen," the guard captain said, motioning. "And bring your command crew."

Gerrard called into the speaking tube, summoning his crew. Sisay, Hanna, and the others left their posts, heading fore.

"Make it fast," the guard captain barked.

A line snaked down from the rail. Gerrard slid easily down it. Tahngarth, Sisay, Orim, and Hanna followed quickly afterward.

"Don't forget Squee!" came a call from above. The green fellow followed his comrades down.

J. Robert King

"We won't forget you," the guard captain promised as his men seized Gerrard.

Commander Capashen reached for his sword, but already it was raked from its scabbard. He tried to drag loose his thigh daggers, but three men held each of his arms. Next moment, irons clapped in place, and he was driven to his knees.

Sisay, Hanna, and Orim were similarly overwhelmed.

Tahngarth hurled back the men that swarmed him. He drew a curve-bladed striva from his shoulder harness and swung it around him, clearing space.

Beneath the leaping blade darted Squee, who ran headlong into the minotaur's leg and clung there piteously. Tahngarth roared, shaking off the clinging creature. Gathering his courage, Squee turned and held up his hands in a pale imitation of a martial master. He even managed a small roar of his own.

The minotaur kept the ship to his back as he eyed the soldiers. "What is the meaning of this?"

The guard captain rubbed a clean-shaven chin. He seemed to take Tahngarth's measure. "This man here is a deserter from the army of Benalia. I am taking him prisoner. Perhaps deserters are not dishonored among minotaurs."

A hissing growl was Tahngarth's only response.

"Then surely you will not oppose the rightful arrest of this man."

"What of the others?" Tahngarth rumbled.

"Would your . . . people allow a fully manned warship to remain in the center of one of your cities?"

Tahngarth changed the subject. "My commander speaks the truth of the coming invasion. We have fought these beasts. You must listen to him."

"We will determine that. Gerrard Capashen will have his audience with his clan chief, but until then, he and his crew will wait in safety."

The white cast of Tahngarth's knuckles on the striva handles told of his mood.

Gerrard nodded to him. "Tahngarth, please. These are my

34

people. You can't fight them. We'll sort this out, and I'll owe you."

"You bet you will," said the minotaur as he surrendered his striva and submitted his wrists to be shackled.

"Squee surrenders too," announced the goblin, lifting his hands and falling to his knees. Benalish soldiers chained him and then ascended to round up the rest of the crew.

The blind seer growled as his own shackles clicked into place. "At least I'll have some company, for a change."

* * * * *

The Benalish military brig had the same grand reserve as the city above—slim but strong bars, efficiently arranged cells, guards as decorous as statues. It was a familiar place for Gerrard. The city had taught him to fight and tryst and defy authority. It also taught him the consequences.

"It's urgent you deliver my message to Chief Raddeus!" Gerrard demanded.

The guard captain smiled humorlessly. "Oh, he'll be notified." He clanged the doors closed on Gerrard and his crew.

"It's urgent! Thousands of plague ships are descending even now!" Gerrard insisted as he clung to the bars.

"Tell them about the monsters," urged the blind seer. "Tell them about the monsters!"

"Quiet!" Gerrard shouted. It didn't matter. The guard captain was already gone.

Flinging up his hands in resignation, Gerrard turned and set his back against the bars. "Why did I think I needed to warn them?" He sank down to sit on the ground.

"A familiar complaint," the blind seer replied. He felt his way forward. "How did you find out about the monsters?"

Gerrard waved a dismissal. "It's a long story."

The old man sat down. His face was fully shadowed by the broad-brimmed hat he wore. "We have time."

Drawing an angry breath, Gerrard said, "I've known about them forever, even before I knew what to call them. I used to blame the

'Lord of the Wastes' for everything the Phyrexians did to me. Now I know better."

"Everything they did to you?"

"Yes," Gerrard replied. "I know this sounds crazy, but everything I've lost in my life, the Phyrexians have taken from me: my true parents, my foster parents, my brother Vuel, my Legacy, my friends. . . . Now they want to take the rest." He grasped Hanna's hand and drew her toward him, wrapping her in an embrace. "They would take Hanna, here, and my crew—*Weatherlight*, Benalia, Dominaria. I won't let them. I'll fight for every last one. I would rather lose myself to the Phyrexians than lose anything else to them."

"Don't be too eager to lose yourself," the blind seer warned.

Gerrard turned his gaze on the old man. "So, you really see visions?"

The old man's mouth was grim beneath the bandage that wrapped his eyes. "There are two kinds of blindness—not seeing anything and seeing everything. I am blind because I see everything."

"You see everything?" Gerrard snorted. "How come you don't know anything about me?"

"If I focus, I could probably tell you all about yourself."

"Right," Gerrard replied. "How about you focus on whether we're going to win this war?"

The man took a deep breath. "There are some things even I cannot see."

CHAPTER 5
Losing Battles

Like gnats swarming dragonflies, Metathran hoppers buzzed Phyrexian cruisers.

Fast, maneuverable, light—hoppers were spheres of glass and polished metal that shrugged off ray cannon fire and plasma bolts. Small metallic wings jutted from all sides, hinged to fold against the craft except when needed. Hoppers could turn in midair, could fly sideways or top-onward and could fire exploding quarrels from any of twelve ports. A well-placed shot from a hopper could gouge a ten-foot hole in the outer armor of a cruiser. Hopper pilots were strapped to the central node of their craft, allowing them to pivot through two hundred ninety degrees. They used their fingers and toes to access the controls that filled the cockpit. Pilots divided their attention between strafing runs, vector targeting, and chamber reloads. Short, wiry, fearless, and focused, they were bred for this task. Unlike Metathran ground troops, fliers were not towers of muscle. If Urza had had time, he would have given them hollow bones like birds.

37

"Form up!" Barrin shouted, signaling from the back of his dragon engine.

A swarm of hoppers responded eagerly to his signal.

Trailing these frenetic ships were angel platoons. Their long white pinions carved the air with a slow grace that the hoppers lacked. Still, these creatures were anything but slow. With one surge of their wings, the Serran angels overtook the hoppers. Magna swords—halfway between sabers and cleavers—glinted in their hands, and featureless metal masks covered angelic faces. These otherworldly creatures were refugees of a collapsed plane. They owed their very lives to Urza and Barrin and would likely repay that debt today.

Barrin signaled for a strafing run. Clutching the wire mane of the dragon engine, he crouched above the creature's neck and sent it into an arrow-straight dive.

The hoppers and angels flocked afterward.

Below, a dozen Phyrexian ships cruised above the Benalish plain. A dozen more lay in wreckage amid burning grasses. If even one craft landed safely, more than grass would burn. Each vessel carried an army of Phyrexians. The huge ship in the midst of the armada carried something even worse—plague. In gray, putrid clouds, contagion cascaded slowly from the craft. Disease ate every living thing in the wake of the ship.

Barrin's dragon engine tucked its wings. It dived. Air shrieked about the plunging beast. Angels and hoppers bobbed in its slipstream. Wings of feather and metal clung tight to their sides. Angels readied their magna swords, and Metathran pilots whirled in a frenzy of preparation.

The Phyrexian fleet seemed to swell outward, eclipsing the plains. Webs of black energy leaped up from the machines.

Barrin signaled for the hoppers and angels to execute a topside strafing run on the plague ship. He himself would fly below.

As the attack squadron approached, hoppers spread their wings. Angels began a piercing song. Their voices woke white magic from the very air. It enveloped them as they shot outward in a long attack.

A wall of black energy and red plasma rose dead ahead.

Hoppers punched through, the stuff spattering from polished

metal. A few caught the plasma in weak seams or intakes. They disintegrated in midair or gummed up and tumbled from the skies.

The angels were untouched. They sang the music of the spheres, which burned away all that was impure. Joining their gleaming comrades beyond, they swarmed down on the plague ship.

Hoppers sent exploding quarrels into the side of the ship. Crimson fire scooped out sections of hull and engine. Phyrexian limbs and skulls hailed from the blast sites. Angels severed power conduits, bringing geysers of energy spewing from the ship. White smoke belched out all around.

For all their success, though, the hoppers and Serrans were merely bees stinging a mammoth. They could nettle it but not kill it.

Barrin lost sight of the squadron. His dragon engine swooped beneath the plague ship. He prepared a spell. White energies crawled down his arms. Drawing them through the air, he garbed himself in a suit of scintillating lightning—and only just in time. Clouds of plague rolled up around him. The air crawled with contagion. It pressed upon the envelope of energy around Barrin and hissed on the metal skin of the dragon engine.

Barrin stared up through the death cloud. It grew more dense ahead. He was approaching the main plague port beneath the ship. Its shaft would lead directly to the disease banks. It was Barrin's target. If he could send a blast up through the main plague port, he could purge the disease. What blast, though? A fireball or lightning strike would only spread the contagion. Barrin gathered white power from the vast plains below. He had intended these spells for the wounded after the battle, enough for a thousand Metathran warriors. Better to use them to save millions of civilians.

A ball of white power filled his hands. It grew incandescent there in the midst of the plague cloud. Sensing the spewing port above, Barrin hurled the sphere upward. It disappeared. A bright flash pierced the cloud, showing up the lip of the port. Moments later, the healing spell smashed within the plague channels. Another burst of light showed mana energy scouring the knobby mechanisms within.

"I've still got it," Barrin croaked wearily as the dragon engine carried him out from beneath the plague ship. They broke from the cloud.

Healing magic gushed from the plague ship. White energy overtook black disease. The spell that had sterilized the ship now cleansed the air beneath it.

Barrin clung to the dragon engine. That vast conglomerate spell had exhausted him, but it had worked. It had saved millions.

As the metal dragon soared out into clear sky, the plague ship dipped. Smoke poured out of it. The hoppers and Serrans had done their work. Wounds gaped across the horn-studded flanks of the ship. Listing slowly, the vessel slumped. It spiraled, a log in a whirlpool. Phyrexians were flung from its deck. They fell, writhing in air. The ship also fell. It keeled over, the empty plague port yawning one last time. A pair of bony masts struck ground first and dug deep furrows before snapping off. The fuselage followed. Decks cracked away. Engines exploded in long lines. Twin pillars of smoke shot up into mushroom clouds.

Barrin allowed himself a tired laugh. It had been an unconventional salvation but a salvation still.

His silent satisfaction ended too soon. Above the laboring wings of the dragon, he glimpsed another plague ship emerging from the portal. The Phyrexians were evidently shifting their forces from the portals Gerrard had shut down.

"Where's Urza?" Barrin hissed under his breath. "What business could be so pressing elsewhere?"

He knew he should not have been surprised. Urza had often left him to fight overwhelming odds. There was a time on Tolaria when Barrin had led an army of young students and old scholars against hordes of Phyrexians—all without Urza's aid. He had nearly lost that war. It was as though Urza would not fight a losing battle. He left those to the capable hands of the mage master.

Barrin thought of his wife, Rayne—another losing battle. Her death had ripped his heart out. It was almost a relief to fight Phyrexians. It was easier to close a hole in the sky than a hole in the soul.

Barrin stood in the saddle, signaling for the Metathran hoppers and Serran angels to form up behind him. They came with their customary alacrity. He drove his dragon engine up toward the plague ship. Perhaps he could muster another set of healing spells. Perhaps he could clog the contagion channels.

Perhaps it didn't matter. The Battle of Benalia might well be a losing one.

While Barrin fought to close the hole in the heavens, Phyrexian cruisers soared out across the ground, heading for distant Benalia City.

* * * * *

Beyond waving heads of grain rose columns of smoke. They vented from new mountains, hulking on the horizon. Those steaming peaks were not volcanic but Phyrexian—mountains that had fallen from the sky.

More mountains still soared there. Twelve Phyrexian cruisers glided above the grasslands. Stalks of grain trembled in their vast shadows. The underbellies of the ships were flat and plated, almost crocodilian. As quiet as predators, they coursed over the plains, seeking a spot to deploy.

Twenty miles beyond the portal, the cruisers fanned out across a wide field. They hovered until each of the twelve craft had reached its place in the giant arc. Sending forth sudden jets of steam, they eased themselves to ground. Grasses bent and crackled. The final impact of each ship shook Benalia. It was as though twelve gods had set foot on the world. Gigantic doors dropped outward, forming ramps. At the top of them were poised Phyrexian legions, ready to deploy.

They were figures out of nightmares—scaly and grimly powerful. Poison fangs, goring horns, blood-sucking shunts, acid ejectors, exoskeletal proliferation, pincers, barbs, paralyzing stings—every adaptation that nature had given the foes of humankind the Phyrexians had given themselves.

Out marched the first ranks of shield folk, the scuta. They were stooped creatures. Their skulls had been flattened and elongated into wide shields that guarded their scuttling legs. There was little room for brain anymore in that bony bonnet and little need. These fleet-footed beasts were bred on instinct to rush into unknown territories and flush out ambushers. They seemed giant horseshoe crabs, inhuman except for the vestigial faces, stretched and vacant, on their lower skulls. Shoulder to shoulder, they bounded down the ramp and swept outward, sniffing with enhanced olfactory cavities. Scuta were kept hungry, that they would seek their victims not only for sport but also for sustenance.

The next ranks were utterly different. Grown for brute strength, stamina, and savagery, bloodstocks had a second pelvis and a second pair of legs grafted across their stomachs. They leaned forward perpetually as if in a vicious charge. Steel beams pierced their shoulders, widening them by three feet and providing artifact arms above their natural pair. The bloodstocks pounded down the ramp and tore out across the field. They were as fast as wolves and charged like rhinos. If the scuta flushed out more forces than they could slay, the bloodstocks would paint the plains in blood.

After the scuta and the bloodstocks came phalanx after phalanx of Phyrexian troopers. These vat-grown troops were less specialized, with generally human configuration and intelligence. They were tall and lean, their shoulders bristling with horns, their faces taut like leather sacks. The ribs of Phyrexian troopers had thickened into a full-torso breastplate, and implants had developed into subcutaneous armor across their bodies. Mechanical talons replaced hands and feet. It was impossible to tell where flesh stopped and mechanism began. Phyrexian troopers were meant to march and haul and dig as well as fight. They were also meant to follow orders instead of instincts.

Order and instinct had their mutual apotheosis in the final figure to emerge. She did not come down the ramp among the shouldering hordes of Phyrexians. She was not one of the rabble. She was their leader, their god. It had been part of the indoctrination of these troops that when they looked up at Tsabo Tavoc, they saw mother and ruler and slayer, all.

Tsabo Tavoc's eight legs helped the image. They were mechanisms, silvery and knife shaped. Even in a crouch, they lifted her torso ten feet off the ground. Fully extended, they made her stand taller than a house. Between those massive legs rose a great, bulbous abdomen. It was a mechanism, as well. A four-foot-long stinger jutted beneath it, dripping venom. Powerstones within that abdomen linked Tsabo Tavoc to her every minion. She could sense everything they sensed.

Above it all rose a powerful thorax, half human and half machine. Brown robes draped from four massive shoulders and mantled a bald, young, strangely beautiful head. Tsabo Tavoc had once been a fair maiden with ivory skin and supple arms. Her beauty had somehow been only heightened by the torturous modifications she had undergone. Even her eyes, the way they sparkled, might have been alluring were they not so plainly compound.

Tsabo Tavoc stepped down from the prow of her command cruiser. Her legs picked gracefully forward among the waving heads of grain. She watched with all-seeing eyes as her troops lined up on the plains of Benalia.

Tsabo Tavoc loved them. These were her children. What seemed almost a smile formed on her segmented lips. She sent her children the sum of her will.

Welcome, my sweet ones. Welcome to Dominaria. This is our home. Do you feel it in your blood as I do? Do you feel how the hills call to us? They remember when we walked this place. They have longed for our return. We come to them, compleated and glorious, their worthy rulers.

There is another race here, though. They have ruled this world for these six thousand years, ruled wrongly. They are the remnant of us, those who would not ascend. They remained in squalor and have thrived here only because they had no natural predators.

We are their natural predators. We have come to take this world back from the soft-skinned, cowering vermin that have overrun it. We will feed upon them, as is our right, and claim dominion over Dominaria, as is our destiny.

Array yourselves, my children. This is the first great battle of many. Before the sun sets this day, we march upon the center of Benalish power. We march upon Benalia City.

CHAPTER 6
To Sting A Spider

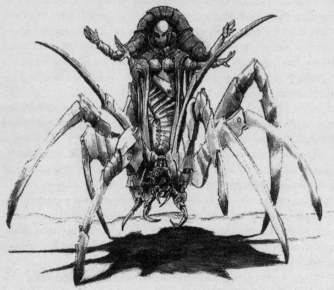

From Benalia City above came muffled booms and sudden shouts. The cell floor shuddered. Iron clanged on iron. Sand sifted from the stony ceiling.

"Do you hear that?" Gerrard called to the brig guardsman. "That's the invasion we spoke of. Those are the monsters out of the sky."

The blind seer stood beside him, clutching the bars.

"They'll be calling you in a moment," Gerrard continued. "They'll need everybody to fight. They'll need us too. Let us loose!"

The guard was young and pallid. He took a step toward the cell, his hands on the keys at his side. A shout came from above. He craned his neck up the passageway and listened to barked orders. Each word jolted him bodily, as if he were a scrap in the mouth of a dog. Suddenly, he charged up the stairs.

"Wait!" Gerrard shouted.

It was too late. A deafening concussion sounded at the head of the stairs. The guard—a mere rag doll now—tumbled down to sprawl at their base.

"Damn it," Gerrard growled, staring at the crumpled young man. He rattled the cell door in frustration. "We've got to get out of here. It won't be long before Phyrexians start flooding down."

Tahngarth rose from the corner where he had sat. Snorting angrily, he stalked across the cell, gripped the bars, and hauled hard on them. Muscles snapped like steel cables. The sinews of his massive shoulders rolled beneath mottled white fur. Beads of sweat broke out over his bovine brow. Still, the bars did not budge. With a roar of anger, he released his grip and dropped to his knees, panting.

Shaking his head, Gerrard said, "How about you, Hanna? Could you jimmy this lock?"

The slim, blonde navigator shrugged as she came forward. "Just because I studied artifice doesn't mean I know anything about locks." She crouched beside the door and peered into the keyhole. "If this were powerstone driven, I'd have a shot. As it is, I don't even have anything I could use as a lockpick."

"How 'bout dis?" interposed Squee, suddenly at her side. He clutched a white, pointed object.

"That might be just the thing," Hanna replied, taking hold of it before she realized it was the tip of Tahngarth's horn. The kneeling minotaur cocked an eyebrow at her, and she let go, smiling in apology.

"Those horns have bashed down plenty of doors, but never lock-picked them," Tahngarth snorted.

Another explosion shook the brig. More rocks fell from the ceiling.

Gerrard patted the minotaur's back. "I hate to ask it of you, but they took anything else we could have used to pick the lock. They even took my belt, as if I'd use it to throttle a guard. They left it with our weapons—with your striva."

"All right! All right!" the minotaur growled. "Use my horn! It'll just make me more deadly when I get out."

Hanna gingerly took the tip of it and directed it toward the keyhole. "Forgive me, Tahngarth. I'm not exactly an expert at this."

"Squee's good! Squee know how to do dat!" the goblin said emphatically. He clambered up Tahngarth's stooped back and leaped to the bars, where he clung like a monkey. He brushed Hanna aside, peered into the keyhole, and said, "Aw, yeah. Easy tumbler. One strike. I do dis easy." He grabbed Tahngarth's horn and shoved it into the keyhole. The minotaur overbalanced, his head ramming against the bars.

Hanna and Gerrard wisely retreated.

Tahngarth steadied himself and was about to protest when a cascade of fist-sized stones fell from the ceiling, pummeling his shoulder blades. He was going to be very deadly when he got out of this.

Squee twisted the minotaur's horn. It shrieked pitiably in the metal encasement. The goblin switched his handhold. His wrist twisted.

"No good. Angle all wrong. Maybe we break off dis horn!"

"Maybe we break off dis goblin!" Tahngarth roared.

Squee was too busy clinging to the bars and rattling the horn in the keyhole to notice he was in mortal peril. Exasperated, he squeezed his way through the bars.

"Squee try this from outside."

He braced his feet on the outside of the cell door and yanked on Tahngarth's horns, ramming the bull-man's head again into the bars.

"Squee! Squee! Stop!" Tahngarth bellowed.

"Squee almost got it!" shouted back the goblin.

"You've got it already, you imbecile! You're outside the cell! Grab the keys!"

"Wuh—?"

"From the dead guard! Grab the keys!"

Releasing the minotaur's horn, Squee dropped his webby feet to the cold stone floor. He brushed off his hands, frowned, and shrugged.

"Well, if you tink it'll be quicker—"

"Get the keys!" the *Weatherlight* crew shouted in unison.

Squee cringed beneath the auditory assault and retreated to the body sprawled beyond. Deft hands won the key ring free of tangled clothes. Squee brought them back to the door. Griping under his breath, he fitted key after key into the slot.

"Dis just cuts it. Squee save your butts in Mercadia ten hundred times, and now he save your butts here, and all you say is 'Get dose keys, Squee! Get dose keys!' "

A loud boom sounded above, and a small landslide swept down the stairway, burying the guard.

Gerrard watched feverishly from the other side of the cell door. Quietly, he advised, "You'd better hurry, Squee."

" 'Hurry up, Squee! Hurry up, Squee!' " the goblin groused.

Down that landslide ambled inhuman creatures. They had claws the size of butcher knives and serpent-slitted eyes. They climbed over the body of the dead guardsman and charged the cell door.

"Hurry up, Squee!" the goblin told himself. "Hurry up, Squee!"

The lock clicked. Squee hauled on the door, yanking it open. He rode the swinging bars back, keeping the door between him and the charging Phyrexians.

Tahngarth followed the door out. He burst from the cell with a full-fledged roar. It echoed through the trembling chamber as though the brig itself screamed.

At that sound, even the Phyrexians faltered. They paused in their charge, glimpsing a great mass of muscle headed their way.

Tahngarth barreled into the front two Phyrexians. Horns that had been twisted in a Rathi torture chamber caught and gored their first monstrous victims. Golden oil-blood rained from the beasts as Tahngarth lifted them to the ceiling. He shook his head. The horns eviscerated the monsters. Guts tumbled out on either side of the minotaur. Like impaled bugs, the Phyrexians writhed on his horns. A brace of their comrades charged Tahngarth. He hurled the dying beasts from his horns, toppling the others.

Gerrard and Sisay rushed from the cell to the minotaur's side. Sisay clenched her teeth in fury.

"What do we use for weapons?"

Gerrard demonstrated with a roundhouse. Knuckles impacted a Phyrexian jaw, just between a pair of venomous horns. The bone beneath cracked. The beast reeled and dropped like a plank. Grinning, Gerrard blew across his knuckles.

"These, I guess."

Nodding philosophically, Sisay ducked the swiping claws of another beast. She kicked out, breaking its leg at the knee. Four Phyrexians were down, but dozens more flooded down the stairwell.

"We're done for, you know?" she said blandly as she stomped the head of the creature she had just felled.

Before he could respond, Gerrard drove the nose of one beast into its brain. He peeled the thing's claws from his own bleeding throat.

"I know."

* * * * *

Tsabo Tavoc trembled in delight as she strode through the shattered outer wall of Benalia City. Dead citizens lay everywhere. Only a few had been fed on yet. Most lay with wide-open eyes and mouths frozen in final screams. Tsabo Tavoc had heard those screams through the ears of her children. She had tasted the blood of this one, and that. It was as though she herself had killed them all. Even now, more murderous moments flowed over her, as bracing as the waters of a cool stream. Tsabo Tavoc trembled. There was such an ecstasy in the harvest.

A herd of bloodstocks bounded eagerly through the breach in

the wall. They passed among her legs. Tsabo Tavoc was delighted at the touch of her children. She watched the bloodstocks converge on Benalish soldiers. The humans set their pikes for the charge, but these were not horses with hollow chests. The bloodstocks ran full speed onto the pikes. Metal heads struck wedge-shaped sternums, cut along broad ribs, and slid ineffectually out the severed pectoral muscles. Such injuries maimed one arm, but bloodstocks had three others. With them they ripped apart the pike men. It was a glorious sight—a red fountain bursting into being in the cobbled square.

Ah, what ecstasy there was in the harvest! Tsabo Tavoc drew a deep breath.

Perhaps the sweetest triumph of the day had been capturing the flying ship *Weatherlight*. Any Phyrexian would have recognized that queer little war machine. It had caused havoc on Rath. It had destroyed the Phyrexian fleet on Mercadia. All Phyrexians recognized the ship if only as the laughably puny creation of Urza Planeswalker. It was merely a wasp—small and ludicrously vicious but capable of delivering a painful sting.

Not today. The ship's crew was gone. It had been guarded only by Benalish soldiers. They were dead now, replaced by Phyrexians. Every chamber of the ship had been searched. Where was the crew?

Something sad touched her: the piquancy of loss. It came from there, from the ruined infirmary. It seemed a place of victory. A ray cannon had ripped the roof off. One brick wall was blown out. Bunks lay overturned. Between them were red fragments of bone where the inhabitants had fed scuta. Even Capashen Chief Raddeus and his wife Leda had been surprised there, visiting the ill. They were gibbeted high enough that the bloodstocks could bite off only a toe or two. Above ground was victory.

Below ground was defeat. A deep brig lurked there. Twenty of her children lay dead, and not a single prisoner was slain. What sort of prisoners were these—?

With a sudden shudder of realization, Tsabo Tavoc knew. She sent out her will. *Hold them, my children. Do not slay them. Neither allow them escape. These are the master's former friends. They are Urza's saviors.*

The reply came back, as always it did, with grateful obedience. The thoughts were borne on a current of death—the deaths of her servants.

I must go see this Gerrard Capashen myself, Tsabo Tavoc thought.

Her legs galloped. In moments, she reached the blasted infirmary and stood at the top of the stairs. Agony broke in exquisite waves over them. Tsabo Tavoc's hearts pounded in her thorax. She tucked her venomous abdomen up beneath her and folded her legs in a cage over her head. Metal scraped on stone as she rolled down the steps. She landed on a rubble pile at the foot of the stairs. There was a still-warm body beneath her feet, but she paid it no heed. Unfolding her legs, she surveyed the scene.

Her children lay, twenty-some, dead before the crew of *Weatherlight*. How had fists and horns bested claws and fangs?

Tsabo Tavoc spoke. It was a grave moment when she spoke aloud. Her voice had the sound of cicadas rasping in chorus.

"Surrender, Gerrard of *Weatherlight*. You will not be harmed by me. My master has want to see you. Surrender, and live."

The black-bearded man she addressed wore a most unusual grin as his bloody knuckles felled another foot soldier.

"You overestimate . . . how fond I am . . . of life."

Rarely did Tsabo Tavoc speak aloud. When she did, she was always obeyed.

There in that tight space, her legs scraped the ceiling as she lunged for Gerrard. A minotaur—foolish bovine—stepped before the man and rammed his horns into Tsabo Tavoc's belly. Her own pain was not as lovely as others'. With one slim hand, she wrenched the twisted thing from her flesh. The horn was slick with her oil-blood. Tsabo Tavoc shoved the minotaur away as though he were a newborn calf.

A dark-skinned woman kicked the belly wound. Her foot sank into the oozy hole.

Tsabo Tavoc constricted her thorax and trapped the foot. Her assailant writhed in agony. Heedless, Tsabo Tavoc dragged the woman toward Gerrard.

He took a swing even as he stumbled away. Tsabo Tavoc caught his fist and hauled him up by it. He tried to break free but was too weak. It was like crushing kittens.

Tsabo Tavoc gazed into the angry face of this young man, this creature bred out of millennia for his task. Her voice buzzed through the brig.

"You cannot defy me, Gerrard, nor my master. I have taken your country. I will take you as well. My master will take your world."

What was this? He spit on her face? Could he possibly defy her still?

"What is your name, that I can brag of killing you," the bearded man asked.

"I am Tsabo Tavoc," she replied placidly, "but it is quite the other way around." Her abdomen curled up beneath Gerrard. A huge stinger dripped venom. Poison sacs pulsed. Tsabo Tavoc clamped onto Gerrard's side.

Oh, this was the greatest pleasure of all!

Sudden light and noise filled the place. The weighty ceiling came to pieces. It dropped all about them. Every chunk of stone was limned in red light. Phyrexians were crushed. A hunk of rock knocked the dark-skinned woman unconscious. Another tore a deep gash in Gerrard's side. Only those in the cell were protected.

Just one rock mattered, though—one deadly boulder. It smashed Tsabo Tavoc to the ground. A twenty-foot slab of stone pinned the legs of her left side. She struggling to claw free.

Worse, Gerrard got away. His hand was in bloody ribbons. He dragged his dark-skinned companion with him. Her foot was badly burned from Tsabo Tavoc's blood, but they got away.

A grotesque goblin clung to the bars and pointed skyward. "Squee love Karn! Squee love Karn!"

Tsabo Tavoc looked up. Drifting above the smoking crater was that damned ship. Someone had remained aboard—someone who could fly the ship and fire the ray cannons by himself.

"Squee love Karn! Squee love Karn!"

Gerrard and his crew clambered out of the cell, over rocks and bodies.

Tsabo Tavoc lashed out with her right legs.

The little monsters were just out of reach. They climbed out of the prison and into the ruined shell of the infirmary. *Weatherlight* edged out above the wreckage. Its anchor clattered down, smashing through the remnant of a wall. The crew crowded onto that swaying piece of metal. It slowly rose.

He would die, this Gerrard. It mattered little what the master wanted. Here was a man who had grinned his defiance, had spat in her face, and had lived to tell the tale.

Already, *Weatherlight* slid away.

Tsabo Tavoc gathered the strength in her trapped legs. There was only one that was inextricable. The rest could pull loose, given the chance. Tsabo Tavoc gave them the chance. She yanked free. The metallic interface of the single doomed leg raked out of the meat and bone of her pelvic girdle. Her own blood painted the stone as she drew her good legs forth. It made her angry. Her own pain was not as sweet as others'.

For this and other indignities, Gerrard would die.

CHAPTER 7
How Forests Fight

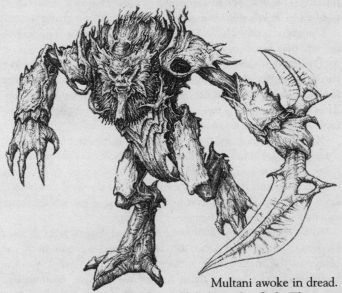

Multani awoke in dread.

He knew he was dying. He could feel it in his flesh. There was sudden cancer—a numbness that ate away feeling and replaced it with living death.

Last night, he had been well. He had sent his consciousness into every bud in the treetops and every hair root below. The great forest Yavimaya was his body. Magnigoth trees were his endless limbs, elves and pixies his darting thoughts, surging sap his pumping blood. Last night, the forest had been well.

This morning, all was different. Yavimaya was suddenly filled with pockets of darkness—cancer.

It had fallen from the skies. The contagion sifted down through clear air. Minute spores tricked their way into every stoma on every leaf. A tingling numbness followed. It flowed down stems into twigs and branches and trunks. It converted all to living rot. Whole boughs were corrupted.

It was worse than that. An intelligence controlled this cancer. Something called to the rotten limbs—something black and hungry. This was not just a killing plague. It was a resurrecting plague too. It killed in order to revivify the dead wood and control it. Gangrene worked a slow possession on Yavimaya. The forest's life was becoming an alien unlife.

The malign power hovered above. Sensing it, Multani rose through a millennial magnigoth. In moments, he had ascended the three-thousand-foot tree. His presence flooded into healthy leaves. They were retinal structures, attuned to light. Through them Multani could see stars no mortal eye ever guessed at.

Now he did not see stars. He saw an achingly blue sky with three immense rents in it. Out of those holes drifted enormous black carbuncles. They were gnarled like diseased wood. One eclipsed the sun. It cast down a shadow that covered a thousand acres. The sun shone in corona around that great scab. Figures moved there, carapaced figures—Phyrexians.

A millennium ago, Multani had joined Urza's fight against Phyrexia. He granted Urza the Weatherseed—drawn from the center of the forest's most ancient tree, the Heart of Yavimaya. From that seed grew the living hull of *Weatherlight*. Multani had aided in breeding perfect defenders for Dominaria. He had even trained Gerrard Capashen in maro-sorcery.

All these preparations seemed punily insufficient now. In the face of this onslaught, what good was an army of Metathran and a living airship and a reluctant hero?

Multani's mind darkened. He seeped down through ancient wood and spread his soul in vines and tangled boughs. He wanted to reside in every tree, every pulsing heart. Only when he encompassed the whole of the forest could he glimpse the divine world. It was painful to be stretched so thin, to feel the trembling terror of the forest. Once he touched on every tendril, though, he sensed his mother watching.

Gaea, you have known of this dread hour since before I even was. You knew of it from Argoth and before, from Halcyon of the Ancients. I am a fool. You see how little I am prepared. Save me, Mother. Save your son. I beg of you. Save me.

There came no response from the world-goddess. Never did she speak.

Her silence was terrible. Multani winced back from it. He withdrew, no longer in every strand of cellulose. In withdrawing, he lost sight of the divine principle and saw instead only the circling vortex of ships above the forest.

Dragon engines, cruisers, troop transports, rams, plague ships—they formed a horrible black whirlpool in the sky. The cyclone widened. Ships descended to attack the shores. Others would overtop the forest in a great killing dome. There would be no escape. There would be no miracle from Gaea. There would be only a long, vicious fight that Multani must lead.

He sent his mind into the elven cities in the canopy. In natural hollows, children played. Across bridges of vine, women worked air nets. In thatched villages, men gossiped. Multani spoke to them all. Fey oracles suddenly saw all he had seen. Fey warriors learned what he knew. Chiefs and kings prepared for all-out war. Multani reached even into the minds of common elves and awoke nightmares.

He gave them a new definition of hate. The angry distrust they felt toward humanity was love compared to this. To kill a Phyrexian was to serve good. To die killing a Phyrexian was to join the eternal forest. Each pixie, each sprite would hate and fight and kill for Yavimaya.

Multani sent his mind into the deep root clusters of the magnigoths. There, in lightless seas, dwelt great serpents and fishes as large as villages. Druids lifted their eyes to the ceilings of their root cells. Multani twisted among their chants and prayers. He whispered terrors into their ears and charged the druids to marshal their might. A fanatic heat entered them. Druids were furious by nature but solitary and sedate in their anger. When one of their gods united their rage, though, woodfolk became warriors.

How could fey and druid stand against Phyrexia? What good were songs and poetry against plague and poison?

Heart despairing, Multani stretched his will once again through the great wood, to every dumb beast. These were not warriors. The fiercest were mere predators. The gentlest were leaf-licking molds. But cornered, wounded, with death inevitable, every creature will attack. Multani infused them with the surety of their doom. They would fight, every last one. Giant ground sloths would rip Phyrexian heads from their shoulders. Green boas would wrap themselves around whole phalanxes and squeeze until glistening-oil jetted from every pore. Apes would emerge from their warrens and pummel the monsters to mush. Sky leeches, great forest hogs, gobbet raptors, fire ants—they all would fight and die in the fighting.

Was this the salvation Gaea offered her mortal folk: to die fighting?

Multani watched in aching dread as the storm of ships deepened over Yavimaya. Plague engines spewed tree-toxins. Phyrexian fliers stretched leathery wings. When the canopy was ripe with rot, they would soar down upon the elven kingdoms. Other troop ships neared the shores. They would off-load Phyrexian armies, who would race unopposed among the ancient boles.

Multani took a shuddering breath through manifold stomas.

Perhaps Multani should have made himself Urza's servant. Perhaps he would have gained ships and monster machines of his own.

Troop ships hovered above the wide-flung shores of Yavimaya. They edged up over root tangles that reached into the sea. One by one, great doors opened, swinging down into ramps. Hundreds of thousands of troops appeared. They stared toward Yavimaya with eyes like sockets scooped in meat. The invaders started down the ramps, their claws scraping.

Soon, every creature in Yavimaya would have lightless eyes.

Except that Gaea had heard his prayer. She was silent, yes, but she had heard.

The tangled roots, reaching far out into the salty sea, moved. They slid across each other with the ease of snakes. Inextricable knots untied themselves. Roots reached out like grasping fingers. All around the island, fibrous hands grasped Phyrexian troop ships. Some roots simply crushed them. Others shot straight through metal, piercing the beasts within. More still struck the craft down like hands slapping flies. Not a single monster reached the safety of the shore. Those who survived the crushing, spindling, shattering attack tumbled into the water. Phyrexians hated water, especially salt water. It destroyed their metal parts. But more than water waited down there for them.

Other Dominarian defenders rose. Fins slapped and froth churned. Sharks fed in plenty, yes, but other creatures too—dolphins and giant squids, stingrays and barracudas. In their midst were merfolk, their tridents spearing Phyrexians. Side by side, the folk of the sea feasted on the flesh thrown to them.

The forces of the sea had never before aided their old foes, the forces of the forest. Why now?

Multani understood. Gaea was not merely a forest goddess. She was the world-goddess. Seas were hers and the creatures therein. As Multani had marshaled the dumb beasts of the forest, she had directed some other mind to gather the beasts of the sea.

This is why he had not allied with Urza. This was the way the forest fought. Exultation replaced dread.

Overhead, aerial troops leaped from their skyships. Wings of skin barked on the wind. Down soared Phyrexians in thick swarms. They swirled down toward the elven kingdoms in the treetops.

Multani gathered himself from the island's perimeter like lightning gathering itself from the sky. He vaulted up the hollow core of an ancient magnigoth tree. In the crown above, the largest of the elven kingdoms spread.

Multani emerged. He took his shape from a shaggy vine, bringing with it blankets of moss, a number of parasitic plants, and a section of loose bark. All these, Multani assembled into a vast, shambling form. He had no body aside from this forest, but in its flesh he had flesh. Multani climbed to the elven kingdom. En route, he dragged a venom-vine into his being. It spread through him, its poisonous thorns positioning themselves as fangs, horns, and claws.

Already, the elf warriors gathered in thorn brakes and atop lookout spires. They trooped like ants across the foot-worn branches. Some crucial bough-bridges had already succumbed to rot. They had taken on a wicked life of their own, lashing out at nearby troops. Crews busily doused rotten sections with pine spirits and set them ablaze. It was a horrible sight—elves torching trees.

Multani dug one foot into a sap channel and sent a signal to the heights of the magnigoth. There, vast seed pods opened prematurely. Soap-down, as white as snow and as slippery as ice, spewed upward. The stuff rose to envelope Phyrexian wing-troops. Oily fibers dragged across batwings and talons. The soap-down filled air holes and blinded eyes. Everything it touched grew slick.

Hissing and spitting, Phyrexians dived out of the choking cloud. They soared down to the leafy crowns and converged on the lookout aeries.

Elf sentries loosed slim shafts.

The arrows ripped wings and thudded into Phyrexian chests and skulls. A few fell from the sky. They cracked against branches in their long descent. Others reached the aeries, shrieking their attack. Wings folded. Talons gripped branches. They slipped, overbalancing. Elven swords were there to catch them. Impaled, Phyrexians writhed like bugs on pins. The wiser elves hurled their fouled swords from the aeries. Those who kept their blades lost their lives. Phyrexian fangs bit through skulls. Phyrexian claws ripped through chests and heads. It was impossible to tell the slayer from the slain.

Below, the main mass of the aerial troops landed in the kingdom's center. Those that came down atop elves got spears and arrows in their bellies. Those that landed on footpaths slipped to spill from the boughs. Elves crowded in tight companies and flung beasts off birch shields.

A massive Phyrexian, a seeming gargoyle, lunged into a group of elves. It bit an elf in half and lifted its head back to swallow the torso. Swords jabbed the Phyrexian's neck, unintentionally pinning the corpse within. The gargoyle gasped, choking.

Elsewhere, another winged monster found itself swarmed with vines. The living wood drew stinging thorns across its hide, cutting to muscle. Moss crowded into the thing's mouth and air holes. Thistles raked wings to bloody rags. Vines constricted, strangling the beast. It fell on the bough and hissed to stillness.

Multani withdrew from the corpse. He pulled his bloodied vines off the shapeless figure and reassembled himself. The twin thistle blossoms that made up his eyes glimpsed a new atrocity.

Elf children fled backward over a sheer drop. They clung to rough bark and vines to escape a Phyrexian mob.

Multani ran for the mass of the creatures. He could kill one at a time, perhaps two at once. Still the monsters would slay the children.

A thought came to him. He dived into the wood. His vine-body sloughed from him into a pile on the surface. Multani sped inward along sap lines. Up through a fat bole and a twisted girdle he went. Spreading through a meaty branch, he possessed it. The thing swung downward, the arm of a colossus.

It struck the Phyrexian mob and hurled them from the tree.

Multani took no time to admire his work. Phyrexians filled the treetops. He lifted the bough again and brought it down to mash them. Leaves became blades. Tendrils became scourges. Branches became staves. Boughs became rams. All dripped with glistening-oil-blood.

This was how the forest fought.

CHAPTER 8
Battles Above Benalia

Engineer Karn had made good use of his time alone aboard the wounded ship. Outwardly, he crouched down, impersonating an inert engine module. The trick fooled Phyrexian crews. Inwardly, Karn activated the ship's healing routines. Once *Weatherlight* was skyworthy again, a jolting takeoff ripped her mooring lines from the ground. Karn rolled the ship to fling Phyrexians from her deck. He ignited her ray cannons and blasted his way into the brig.

Together, he and *Weatherlight* had rescued the crew.

Now, aloft, Karn proved more powerful still. In flight, the ship was his body. In it, he charged across the heavens like a thoroughbred. A pack of Phyrexian ships howled in his wake, but none could even approach him.

Weatherlight ruled the skies beyond Benalia City. In a series of lightning attacks, she strafed troop transport ships and cruisers, pinning them in their deployment arc. None could get off the ground. The cruisers' heavy batteries hurled flack into the sky, too slow to strike the shrieking vessel. Phyrexians scrambled from damaged engines and melted cannonades. They were no match for *Weatherlight's* crew.

Sisay worked her own magic at the helm. She soared down the throat of Phyrexian cannonades, hopping *Weatherlight* away before plasma split the air. The incandescent stuff narrowly missed the ship, instead blanketing pursuers. Flinging off hunks of magma, Phyrexian fighters collapsed and plunged from the sky. They impacted cruisers docked below or troops off-loading from them.

Hanna, meanwhile, pinpointed the Phyrexian vessels' critical sectors—fire controls, fuel tanks, power conduits, flying bridges. . . . She plotted strafing runs that cut straight across numerous engine cores. In a steady stream, she barked out heading directions and blast coordinates.

"Target thirty degrees to port, the red 'midships manifolds. You're warm! You're hot! Bull's-eye!"

As flames engulfed the vast structure, Tahngarth shouted from the starboard prow cannon, "Stop calling them bull's-eyes!"

"Yeah," rejoined Gerrard at port. "That was *my* shot!"

"Get ready for another," Sisay warned. "A cruiser's lifting off."

Hanna growled out hasty instructions. "Three degrees left, vault over this next ship, and bring us in low."

"Low?" Gerrard called back. "It's lifting off."

"She's plotting a course beneath it," Sisay guessed.

Hanna worked out the vectors.

"Beneath it?" Gerrard echoed.

"The engines are exposed on the underside. The hull guns won't be operational yet," Hanna explained. "It's the safest route and the surest kill."

"What if we shoot it so well it falls on us?"

"Have a little faith in Karn," Hanna replied, smiling wryly at Sisay. "Three degrees to port, and dive, Captain."

The ship plunged above the smoldering heap of a grounded cruiser. *Weatherlight* raced over black mountains of mechanism, past splayed Phyrexian corpses, past shattered cannonades and batteries spewing corruption into the air. *Weatherlight's* plunging keel sliced through a cloud of plague spores, which rose in white canyon walls around the ship. The ship rocketed out of the killing tunnel.

Dead ahead, a cruiser labored into the air. It was a mountainous ship. Tangled grass and clods of dirt rained beneath it.

"Take us below," Hanna called.

With a gut-wrenching drop, *Weatherlight* plummeted. Her own keel sliced grasses. She left a wide-boiling wake of stalks behind her. A surge from her engines sent the ship screaming beneath the enormous cruiser.

Dust pelted down from convoluted pipework. It stung the gunners and anyone else on deck. *Weatherlight* arrowed beneath the huge black shelf and above the trammeled ground. Her spars cracked occasionally against the cruiser's belly. Her keel gouged lines in the dirt.

"Where's this exposed engine you promised?" Gerrard shouted through the tube.

"You'll feel it," Hanna said.

They did. Sudden, incredible heat tore across the deck. It radiated from a network of huge black cylinders, each bristling with thermal fins.

"Fire!" Gerrard ordered even as he squeezed off a few blasts.

The rays looked vermilion against the ship's dark underbelly. They tore outward, striking column after column. The huge cylinders cracked open, their hulls seeming as brittle as eggshells. Pure energy oozed from the engine cores. Tahngarth's own blasts mixed red power with black, blood and rot commingled.

"Cease fire," Gerrard called. "All power to the engines!"

Weatherlight leaped. Even her running lanterns dimmed.

The Phyrexian cruiser jolted, descending in a great rush. It fell like a mountain from the sky. The air trapped beneath it fled in roaring waves out of the way. *Weatherlight* was caught up on the currents.

Gerrard and Tahngarth clung for dear life to the hot chassis of their guns. The leather straps strained to hold them in place.

Weatherlight's masts scraped the cruiser's underside. The keel plowed through the ground. With a last shriek, *Weatherlight* vaulted from the collapsing space. She shot into clear air. The ruined cruiser smashed to ground.

The air was clear no longer. Pulverized ground rushed out. After it came shards of shattered metal. The cruiser exploded. Wild energy cratered the plains down a hundred feet. The fireball lashed out, toppling two adjacent ships. It flung them onto another. The blaze was so bright, it cast *Weatherlight*'s streaking shadow before the cruiser.

"That'll keep them out of the sky for a bit!" Gerrard crowed. "Let's give the ground troops some help."

"I think we're a little late," Sisay reported grimly.

Gerrard's breath caught in his throat as he looked out beyond the rail. "Take us in slow, Sisay!"

The city was destroyed. While *Weatherlight* had slain ten thousand Phyrexians in their warships, a hundred thousand had overrun the city. Every house poured black smoke into the air. Every threshold was strewn with bodies. Some had been eaten half-away—the sweetmeats first. Others had been too badly burned to be consumed. They were little more than tarry skin stretched over black bones.

It wasn't just the homes that were destroyed. Ram-ships had felled every tower and turret along the outer wall. Some guards had been chewed to pulp by falling stones. Their comrades decorated the remains of the walls. Soldiers were piked on their own weapons.

Phyrexians loped like wild dogs through the city. The garrisons were decimated, the manor houses, the infirmary . . .

"Slow down. Come in lower," Gerrard said, glimpsing a pair of gibbets beside the infirmary's ruins. Gerrard stood behind his ray cannon, straining against the straps to see.

There, nailed to a pair of tall posts, were Capashen Clan Chief Raddeus and his wife Leda. The spikes driven through them were twelve inches long. Something had climbed the poles, making a feast of the bodies—empty eye sockets, teeth showing past missing lips, a purple cavity beneath the ribs. . . .

Gerrard turned away, closing his eyes. I'd rather die than lose anything more to them.

Sisay's voice was gentle in the speaking tube. "There is nothing more we can do here. There is no one left to defend."

"There are Phyrexians left to kill," Gerrard hissed bitterly. "Turn us about. Take us back over the cruisers."

"There will be other battles, more important battles, elsewhere. Benalia is overrun. A single ship cannot stop it. The Capashens are gone."

"I am a Capashen!" Gerrard growled. "Bring us about!"

"Aye, Commander," Sisay replied.

Weatherlight banked, pulling swiftly away from the devastation. She cut through a column of black smoke. It dragged covetously across the ship. The ravaged city shrank below. The Phyrexian fleet—a range of mountains on the horizon—swelled outward.

Gerrard felt a heavy hand on his shoulder.

"We did all we could," Tahngarth rumbled.

The commander's eyes were bitter as he watched the demonic skyline. "You're the one who always talks of those I have lost. Now I have lost a whole nation."

"You can't save everyone, Gerrard."

"What are you doing away from your gun? We're coming up on a strafing run. With the starboard gun amidships unmanned—"

Tahngarth let out a sudden roar and vaulted down the forecastle ladder. He rushed toward the port gun amidships. There, Gunner Dabis thrashed beneath a gigantic spider.

Tsabo Tavoc! She must have clambered onto one of the airfoils when the ship hovered above the infirmary. Despite a missing leg and the oozy flesh where it had torn loose, the Phyrexian commander was still fast and powerful.

Clutching Gunner Dabis, she jabbed a long metallic stinger into his belly. Her abdomen pumped venom. The gunner convulsed, falling to the deck. Tsabo Tavoc pivoted toward Tahngarth. Her stinger reluctantly withdrew from the black wound in the man's side. He was a dead man now, and Tahngarth could be next.

In midstride, the minotaur reached up over his shoulder for his striva. His hand fastened on empty air. His weapon lay in the rubble of the infirmary.

It was too late to stop the charge. Tahngarth bulled forward, ramming his horns deep into the seven-legged thorax of the spider woman. Ivory sank into spider muscle. Golden oil-blood poured down. Tahngarth thrashed his head, ripping the monster's flesh.

She shouted in fury and drew herself upward.

Tahngarth hung from his horns. He growled, kicking. Hooves struck to either side of the spider's darting abdomen. Her venomous stinger jutted between his knees. The barb was crazed in Dabis's blood. An inch-wide hole in the end gushed poison.

Tahngarth twisted his head. Horns broke free of the monster's thorax. He hurled himself in a back flip, away from that stinger. The world tumbled once magnificently. His hooves struck the deck, slick with poison. He slipped and fell backward.

Tsabo Tavoc was quick. She lunged. Three of her seven legs slid about Tahngarth, clutching him tightly. They constricted. His arms were trapped at his sides. Metallic limbs closed implacably. Tahngarth couldn't move, could little breathe. Tsabo Tavoc squeezed him beneath her thorax. Her wounds seeped over him. Above a massive torso and mantled shoulders, Tsabo Tavoc's queerly beautiful face stared down in cruel satisfaction.

Her look suddenly darkened. In compound eyes, a rushing figure reflected.

Gerrard.

His sword, too, was missing. He had snatched up what he could—a short-handled gaff hook—and leaped to the charge. The hook arced overhead and sank into Tsabo Tavoc's belly.

She reared back, clutching Tahngarth all the harder. Her four remaining legs scratched back to the rail.

Gerrard would not let her go. Hanging onto the hook, he climbed. He braced a foot on Tahngarth's bloody horn and swung his free hand toward her face. The roundhouse cracked her jaw. Knuckles left a gray print beside her segmented mouth.

Hissing, Tsabo Tavoc slid one of the three legs free of Tahngarth and reached up around Gerrard.

He wriggled the hook loose and drove it into soft flesh above the spider woman's collar bone.

Spitting black bile, Tsabo Tavoc yanked Gerrard and the gaff away. The hook snapped through her collar bone. She flung Gerrard brutally to the deck.

He landed in a roll and smashed into the far rail.

The spider woman, with Tahngarth in tow, crept over the rail, preparing to leap.

"Oh, no you don't," Gerrard growled.

He hurled himself across the ship just as Tsabo Tavoc slipped below the side. Gerrard swung the gaff. It pierced flesh. He clutched the rail and braced himself. Only then, through the rail posts, did he see that the gaff had impaled Tahngarth's shoulder. The minotaur's whole weight—as well as that of the spider—hung from that single hook.

"Do you kill him," Tsabo Tavoc purred in a voice like summer cicadas, "or do I?"

Winds tore sweat from Gerrard's brow. He stared down into Tahngarth's eyes. Despite the obvious agony, there was no fear, no resentment in the minotaur.

Segmented mouth parts worked. "Either way, I win. I have killed your land. I will kill your world."

Gerrard felt his own shoulder pulling out of the socket. He clenched his arm. Bone ground against ligaments.

"Even if you win," he panted out, "we won't stop fighting."

Tsabo Tavoc's compound eyes became inky black. "*Fool.*" She lifted her stinging abdomen, curling it up toward Gerrard's clenched fist. The trembling stinger oozed white poison. It drew itself up to strike.

A gash of red light tore through the air. It curled the hairs on Gerrard's arm. The blast struck two of the great spider's legs. They vanished in the crimson gush. More energy raked across her belly. The hook wound was immediately cauterized. She shied back from that blast, letting go of Tahngarth and dropping. Her remaining five legs balled about her. Landing, Tsabo Tavoc rolled amid her troops. Warriors were unmade by her lashing metallic legs. At last, she came to a stop and stood.

Meanwhile, Gerrard hauled Tahngarth up over the rail. Despite the minotaur's mass and the tearing winds, Tahngarth felt suddenly very light. Gerrard caught him in his free arm and laid him on the deck.

"Now, I'm a . . . bull-fish," Tahngarth growled out.

Gerrard smiled grimly. "I thought I'd got that leggy thing, not you."

"But . . . who shot the . . . ray cannon?"

They both looked up to see the blind seer, white knuckles clinging to the fire controls of Gerrard's gun. Gaseous plasma dripped from the muzzle.

Gerrard gabbled at the man, "H-how did y-you know t-to shoot?"

Beneath his dark hat, the man spoke simply, "I know things."

Orim emerged from the hatch and rushed to kneel beside Tahngarth. She set her hands on the gaff hook, sending an enchantment down into it. With a slow, smooth motion, she pulled the hook forth and stanched the flow of blood.

"Another thing I know," said the blind seer, descending the forecastle steps, "is that you're wasting your energies here. There is only vengeance here—and death."

Gerrard stared grimly down at Tahngarth's clenched teeth. "Yes, old man. I think you are right."

"There is a better Battle of Benalia. There is another army—heroes after your own stripe. An easy thousand of them. You must go lead them."

Arching his brow, Gerrard said, "Another army? Who? Where?"

"The Atrivak Mounds—Benalish Penal Colony."

"Military prisoners?"

"An easy thousand. Powerful warriors, but incorrigible."

Gerrard gave a dry laugh and shook his head. "Heroes after my own stripe."

CHAPTER 9
Teferi's Realm

Barrin soared through the skies over coastal Zhalfir. The day was sultry. Clouds stood in steamy stacks all around. Lurking among them were three more portals, newly opened. Soon drifting black racks of Phyrexian armor would appear. Then there would be death in Zhalfir as there was in Benalia.

Barrin's Metathran fleet had been crushed in Benalia. Only a small squad of hoppers had survived. The rest had sacrificed themselves downing cruisers and debilitating plague ships. The Serrans had fared better, though one in two angels had been killed. At last, Barrin and his troops had fought near enough to the portal that he could send his healing magic into the wound in the sky. He sealed it and ended the air battle but was utterly spent in the effort.

He and his last fighters had withdrawn to the next aerial rendezvous. The Serrans soared to their aeries to regroup.

For Barrin, there was an all-too-brief night of study and sleep before the next battle opened above distant Zhalfir—another powerful source of white mana. He teleported to a western point that he knew well. The battle of Zhalfir would unfold just as the battle of Benalia had—too few defenders flinging themselves in suicidal fury against too many attackers. Such had always been the model for Urza's battles. For Urza, survivability was not as important as victory.

One of these days, Urza will orchestrate a battle that even I cannot survive, Barrin thought grimly.

Topping a long slope of saw grass, Barrin glimpsed the battle on the fields beyond. A portal gaped wide in the sky. It was black and ragged among the clouds, as though some jealous god had gripped the heavens and ripped a hole in them. From that black tear emerged cruisers, plague ships, dragon engines, and a new class of sleek-bowed vessels—dagger-boats. Fighters filled the air like wasps, buzzing beside the droning hulls of larger ships.

"Urza and I against an armada," Barrin said, clucking.

He had spoken too soon. Someone had brought defenders to the field—amazing, powerful, glorious defenders. Figures played on the wide plains amid shrubs and fruit trees. In their draping white robes, they seemed children, hands and heads upraised as though guiding kites through the skies. In fact, they were archmages. Above them moved gossamer, streaming sorceries. Mistmoon griffins and giant eagles, angel warriors and armored pegasi—these were summoned creatures, ideals made material. Alabaster dragons and duskrider falcons, winged paladins and flying unicorns—they were guided in their battles from below.

White talons tore dagger-boats to shreds. Angelic swords clove ray cannons from their embrasures. Griffin beaks plucked ballista bolts from the sky and rammed them back into the swarming ships. Even unicorn horns were put to their original use, the merciless goring of the despoiled. Phyrexians died in their thousands. So, too, did these summoned creatures, but they were not true beings.

They were ideas given flesh and blood for a time, granted the will to fight, and ideas never died.

Barrin smiled. This was the battle of a fairer mind than Urza's. White ideals clashed against black realities and steadily won. On a ridge overlooking the savanna stood Urza and that fairer mind—Teferi.

It was a strange tableau. Teferi stood to the fore, gazing out at his sorcerous army. In his manifold blue robes, the black-skinned man seemed taller than Urza— bolder, more powerful. One of Teferi's feet was poised on a stone. He leaned avidly toward the battle and spoke in rapid, exited tones. Urza meanwhile stood behind. He never stood behind. His feet were planted like fence posts. His hands hung empty and idle at his sides.

Barrin allowed himself a laugh at his old friend's expense. Urza was never so miserable as when someone else was in control.

Spreading his war cloak like the wings of a settling hawk, Barrin swooped down to light on the arid hilltop. The rustling robes drew the eyes of the two men upward. Urza's gaze was both nettled and pleading. Teferi's was triumphant.

The tall, ebony-skinned man smiled broadly and extended his hand to shake Barrin's. "Ah—a pleasure to see you again, and so soon—"

"A pleasure!" hissed Urza in exasperation.

"Welcome, Master Barrin, to Zhalfir."

Barrin studied the extended hand with feigned caution before grasping it. "No shocking grasp? It's almost a letdown, Teferi. Still, it's nice to know you haven't reverted to your old tricks."

Teferi shook his head vigorously. "Only new tricks, Master Barrin. Plenty of new ones."

"He won't let us help," Urza blurted in place of a greeting.

"Won't let . . ." Barrin echoed incredulously. He searched Urza's queer eyes, looking for signs of humor. It was a futile search.

Teferi's eyes brimmed with joy. "It's not that I won't let you *both* help—just not Master Urza alone. No offense. If Tolaria taught me anything, it taught me that Urza is a danger to himself and everyone else unless he's working with his lab partner."

"Which would be me," Barrin said through tight lips. The two masters of Tolaria traded rueful looks. Teferi had always been a bright, good-hearted troublemaker—just what Barrin and Urza needed. "Well, I'm here, now. How can we help?"

Teferi took a glad breath, stroking his chin and looking out at his proud forces. "That's a good question. The Mage Corps of Zhalfir seem to have things well in hand."

"Impressive," Barrin said. "I have never seen spells used this way before."

"Phoenix flocks," Teferi said. "An innovation of mine. It keeps the battle in the air, keeps the casualties to Phyrexians. Our warriors are all creatures of fancy—ideas battling monsters. That is very appealing to me."

Barrin watched tracers of white-mana magic rise, slim and graceful, from a mage on the dusty field. The power spread outward, blossoming into a great spectral eagle the size of a mammoth. Its wings swept out. They could cover whole companies. With a shrieking cry that raked the heavens, the enormous raptor crashed into a Phyrexian cruiser. Pinions of pure energy enveloped the ship. The bird's figure disintegrated. Lines of magic limned every hackled spine and barbed strut of the ship. The lines solidified into unbreakable cords of power. They constricted inward. The shimmering white force cut beneath armor plates. It sliced bulwarks and causeways. Sparks showered from the cut marks.

"Why don't they simply land, crushing your forces?" Barrin asked.

"Watch," Teferi replied quietly.

The cruiser that had been overwhelmed by the spectral eagle began to disintegrate. Sections of the ship cut loose and tumbled away. Strangely, though, the pieces did not plummet toward the savanna. Instead, they rose, tumbling into the air. Some of the hunks impacted Phyrexian ships above. Sharp wedges lodged in the bellies of the craft. No, not the bellies. Only then did Barrin realize that all the Phyrexian ships floated upside down in the sky.

"It's a simple but powerful enchantment, reversing the pull of Dominaria," Teferi said. "It's a time-field effect, like those I learned on Tolaria. In backward time, the world repels rather than attracts

71

objects. Meteors leap into the sky, feet are propelled away from the ground, and instead of stumbling, drunkards vault upright. I've extracted that single vector of movement and enacted it in a broad space above the plain. My sorcerers can stand on the ground, but a hundred yards above their heads, gravity reverses itself. Those ships are laboring toward the ground just as they would labor into the air. If any of them actually neared the envelope of the reversion field, they would plunge to their destruction."

Above the massed fleet of Phyrexian ships ascended the wrecks of hundreds of other vessels. They rose into empyrean spaces. Many had been dismantled by Teferi's phoenix flocks. Others had met more mundane ends.

A cruiser halfway out of the portal flipped violently over. It veered, crashing into a nearby plague ship. Beyond them, another cruiser unleashed its battery of black-mana guns on a flock of angels. In the topsy-turvy field, though, the muck spattered a nearby squadron of dagger-ships. They cascaded into the sky. Even plague spores, even the dead, did not fall toward the ground.

"It's interesting what difference a single inversion can make," Teferi noted blandly. He cocked an eye at Urza. "It's a benefit of having a sense of humor—I'm used to thinking of what things look like when they're flipped over. Funny, mostly. In this case, flipping stuff over makes it look really lovely." He gazed at the cyclone of wrecked ships heading skyward.

Barrin sighed. "I think he's right—"

"I have a sense of humor," Urza interrupted testily.

"No, not about that," Barrin soothed. "I think he's right that he doesn't need us—"

"That's not what I said," Teferi broke in. "It's a simple spell, but a draining one. Eventually one of those ships will crash on Zhalfir and contaminate it. I need your help to shut down the portal."

"At last—reason!" fumed Urza Planeswalker.

"What do you suggest?" Barrin asked.

"It's a simple enough principle. We planeswalk into the portal—"

"Won't work," Urza growled. "Rath is warded against us."

"We don't planeswalk to Rath. We planeswalk into the portal

and then back out again. We repeat the process until the spatial-temporal fluxes melt the thing down."

"The backlash will kill us," Urza said. "It'll kill us and everything in a hundred-mile radius."

"I've worked out a spell to draw off the energies. A most impressive spell. I can personally vouch for the safety of my people. Oh, and you'll survive too, Urza."

"I thought you said you needed me for this operation?" Barrin reminded him.

Teferi's smile was the brightest so far. "I need you to shame him into it."

Eyes blazing and face as red as a campfire, Urza barked, "Let's 'walk, pupil."

The two planeswalkers traded looks. Something of Urza's solemnity entered Teferi's features, and something of Teferi's cockiness infused Urza. Abruptly, they were both gone. Only the dry weeds remained. The pair flashed again into being, and simultaneously out. It was as though they were mere boys, racing for the water hole. A capricious light shone in their eyes when next they appeared.

Above, Barrin could see why. The portal seemed to be boiling. The energies in that black space crisscrossed and reversed, warring against each other. Surges of black energy tore into coils of red power. White sparks and blue-green shafts of force battled for predominance. Grinding teeth of magic chewed an emerging cruiser to shreds. It belched smoke downward and rained ruin up.

Faster they flashed, and faster. Their grins only deepened.

Barrin shook his head, smiling also.

A light awoke—a blinding thing. A new sun was born above Dominaria. It flashed, casting the fleet's shadows on the plains below. Whatever ship still labored in air ceased its struggles, plunging upward like ash on the heat of a fire.

Barrin winced back. The whole hillside and all Zhalfir could be consumed by that sudden blaze.

Then, it was done. Neither blinding fire nor black portal shone in the sky. Neither Phyrexian fleet nor phoenix flocks circled there. The sorcerers of the Zhalfir Mage Corps stood on the plain, eyes lifted heavenward and hands applauding. It was as though they had just watched a fireworks show.

"What happened?" Barrin wondered aloud.

"Come," said Teferi simply, appearing out of nowhere to grasp Barrin's arm and drag him away in a spontaneous planeswalk.

The world folded around Barrin, spinning into chaos. As quickly as Zhalfir had flashed away, it returned, though now a mile below. Barrin floated in blue skies beside Urza Planeswalker and Teferi of Zhalfir.

"Very impressive," Barrin rasped. "Very, very impressive."

"Where did you put the energy?" Urza asked suspiciously.

Teferi shrugged. "I put it away for another spell."

Urza cleared his throat—exactly the sound he had made as Teferi's headmaster. "Well, now that we have helped you save Zhalfir, you must help us save the world."

"Save Zhalfir?" the dark-skinned man echoed. "You think closing a single portal makes Zhalfir safe in this worldwide conflagration?"

"Safer than most places," Urza replied evenly, "but safety isn't the issue. Defeat of the Phyrexians is."

Teferi nodded. All the joking had gone from his face. "This is where you and I differ, Master. Safety is the issue. You've never wanted to save your people. You've only wanted to defeat your foes—Mishra, Gix, K'rrik, and now Yawgmoth himself. You would sacrifice us all if you knew it would doom him."

"I am willing to sacrifice myself to defeat Yawgmoth," Urza replied solemnly. "I have neither sympathy nor patience for others who are not."

The old, cocky Teferi had returned. "As I said, Master, this is where we differ."

"You can't save your people, not single-handed," Urza said.

"Oh, I do not do it single-handed. I've had the aid of thousands and the consent of millions. You yourself helped me harness the final measure of power to complete the spell. It is triggering even now below us."

Below, Zhalfir shuddered. Something passed over it—not over it, but *through* it. The same energies that had boiled through the doomed portal now shot through the land. Every rill was lined in scarlet ribbons of energy. Every field was sketched in shimmering white. The shorelines flashed waves of blue fire, and the veins of every woodland leaf glowed green. Then all was subsumed in a great colorless grid, as though the land and the plants, the animals and the people, were being caught in a vast blueprint.

"If spells can make ideas into reality, they can make reality into ideas," Teferi said quietly.

The transformation picked out every mote of Zhalfir. Lines fused. Grids merged. For one dazzling moment, all the colors combined into a blinding radiance. With a flash, Zhalfir was gone. Where it had been, only a red afterimage remained in Barrin's eyes. Then came a boom like a hundred thousand thunderbolts in synchrony.

Barrin blinked, struggling to see. Winds tore past him, but Teferi's magic held him in place. The red glow where Zhalfir had been faded to black—a black wound the size of the great land mass. It was bedrock. Teferi had taken the whole peninsula, a mile of air above it, and a mile of rock beneath.

The ocean stood for a moment in astonished walls all around. Then its green rim turned white. Water cascaded into the deep gash. The belly of the ocean slumped. The first gush smashed to bedrock and churned eagerly out across dry stone. The head of the flood was overtopped by new waves, which crowded the shoulders of the slumping water and poured into the cauldron.

Urza gazed in silent consternation at the churning sea.

Barrin gaped. "What did you do?"

"I saved my people. They dwell now in immutable ideas," explained Teferi.

"Y-you killed them!" Barrin stammered.

"No. They will return when the world is safe again. For them, not a moment will have passed."

"There will be tidal waves," Urza said darkly. "Thousands will die."

"Millions have been saved," Teferi replied. "This is how I save my people. This is how you and I differ."

"Yes," Urza replied. "This is how we differ."

CHAPTER 10
Heroes of the Same Stripe

Gerrard had deep misgivings about this plot. His Benalish commander's uniform fit poorly. He'd not donned the garb since leaving his division half a year ago. The quilted sleeves constricted his biceps. The maroon waistcoat and bandoleers bulged across his pectorals. The linchpin in this contraption of doom was the official orders being forged even then by a blind man.

The blind seer sat at Hanna's navigation desk. He pinned a hunk of parchment beneath one hand. His other clutched a quill. With strong, jagged strokes, he wrote: By this writ, command of the Benalish Military Penal Colony shall be surrendered to Commander Gerrard Capashen.

"This isn't going to work," Gerrard groused, flinging his hands out. He turned to Sisay. "We'd better abort, Captain."

"Too late, Commander," Sisay replied placidly from the helm. "They've already seen us." She gestured beyond the bridge.

Silhouetted against the sunset, the Benalish Penal Colony seemed a dark diadem topping the Atrivak Hills. Tall walls of stone hemmed in the inner wards. Guard towers stood at the many corners. Crossbow nests bristled beneath the descending night. In the center of the yard, a gaunt wooden tower presided over it all, and from there an alarm bell sounded.

"We won't get a second chance at this," Gerrard muttered. He reached down, snatching up the parchment. His eyes widened in amazement. The document looked convincing, well ordered and with an impressively embossed seal. Gerrard read aloud:

To: Captain Benbow, Warden of the Brig at Atrivak

From: Capashen Chief Raddeus

Greetings,

In the sudden peril that has swept across our nation, I require the fighting might of every warrior under my command. I have sent my ward, Commander Gerrard Capashen, recently returned from epic battles against our foes, to gather the prisoners in your charge and lead them into combat. Please provide him every assistance to liberate, arm, and provision the troops previously imprisoned in your facilities.

Blessings,

Chief Raddeus

Gerrard nodded, mollified. "Perhaps we do have a chance." He peered down at the mysterious old man. "There's more to you than meets the eye."

"Yes," the blind seer said smoothly, "since nothing meets my eye."

"Hand me that map tube," Gerrard said, reaching toward the desk.

From the map rack, Hanna snatched the tube. Gerrard pulled its cap and upended it. Out slid a detailed map of Benalia City. Not a single structure, so carefully rendered on the map, remained in reality.

Gritting his teeth grimly, Gerrard rolled the forged document, set a daub of candle wax on it, and printed the wax with his own Capashen ring. He slid the roll into the map tube and lifted his eyes toward the fore window of the bridge.

The sun seemed to blaze within the prison. Guard towers and needlelike palisades reached their clawing shadows up the deck of *Weatherlight*. Soon, the ship was swallowed in darkness. The silhouetted brig hovered spectrally above. Just beneath it lay a natural shelf of stone, covered by the western overlook of the mounds.

"We land there, where *Weatherlight* will be shielded from Phyrexian eyes and bombs. We don't want to be pinned down."

"Aye, Commander," replied Sisay. She eased the ship up toward the shelf.

"So far so good. Let's just hope Benbow falls for the forgery."

* * * * *

"Guards!" Captain Benbow shouted. The warden's voice echoed through the block-walled station house. He glowered at Gerrard and his command crew. Benbow's meaty hands clutched the forged letter, and his red brows bristled. "Guards!"

They flooded in. Guards were common enough in the Benalish Military Brig. In field plate with yellow tabards, the warriors surrounded Gerrard and his crew.

"Wait!" Gerrard objected. "You must believe us. Benalia needs every fighting arm! An invasion is underway!"

"Clap them in irons!" Benbow bellowed. The guards converged.

Gerrard had surrendered to Benalish forces once—and Benalia City was destroyed while he sat in the brig.

"Attack!" he shouted.

Tahngarth snorted his approval. He flung a wooden chair beneath the chin of the nearest guard. The man barked once and fell forward, landing atop the chair that had knocked him out.

Hanna was not as fortunate. A guard grabbed her from behind in a headlock. He breathed angrily in her ear. More a lover than a fighter, Hanna turned her head and intercepted his lips with hers. The warm contact produced a sudden weakness in the man's grip. Hanna pulled forward and lifted her heel in the angle often induced by a kiss. The guard went down, clutching himself.

Sisay hurled her opponent's tabard up about his face and spun him to attack one of his comrades. While he fought, she casually tripped a warrior who was about to grab Squee.

For his part, the goblin detained guard after guard by surrendering to them, allowing them to fit shackles to his too-slim arms, and then sliding out of them.

Gerrard was most pressed of all. He had drawn a sword and dagger from his belt. With the smaller blade, he caught and flung back shackles heading for his wrists. The chain bloodied the guard's nose.

The man reeled, sitting down beneath a canopy of clattering blades.

Gerrard's sword lashed out in a strike meant to intimidate. The blade sliced through the false writ and threatened the shaggy pate of Warden Benbow.

Benbow was a seasoned fighter, and his sword hung on the wall behind him. Dodging Gerrard's lunge, Benbow rolled rapidly out of his seat. He got his feet beneath him and, with a grace that belied his girth, snatched his sword from the wall.

Gerrard leaped up to the desktop. He brought the flat down in a braining blow.

Benbow blocked the strike. Metal clanged. He flung his foe's sword aside and spun. The warden's blade swept the desktop in a stroke that could have cut Gerrard's feet from beneath him. Gerrard jumped amid a flurry of prison records. He hurled his sword in a second flat attack. This one won through but weakly. It whapped Benbow's sunburned head. The warden reeled back, giving Gerrard a second chance to plead.

"You must believe me. They'll be here in hours—in moments."

"Who? Your next of kin?" Benbow growled, swinging his sword higher.

Gerrard hopped again, evading the knee-capping blow. "No, the Phyrexians!"

"Phyrexians?" Benbow shouted back incredulously, "Bogey men? Fairy-tale monsters?" His third swipe was aimed at cutting short a dearer appendage.

Gerrard blocked the attack, meanwhile kicking open the desk drawer.

It soared out on hidden bearings, as fast as a ramrod. The heavy drawer struck the warden. Benbow yelped in pain and doubled over.

Just before the man's bulk obscured the desk drawer, Gerrard spotted a large key ring lying within. His hand darted down.

Benbow guessed his foe's intention. Despite his agony, Benbow lunged forward to slam the drawer with his hips. Hidden bearings bore it inward. Just before wood closed on wood, Gerrard snatched the keys out.

Benbow was not as quick. He bellowed in agony.

Gerrard turned, spotting Tahngarth in the melee, and shouted, "Tahngarth, take these keys. Release the prisoners!" He flung the ring out over darting blades.

Swords jabbed up to intercept the keys. One blade flung them sideways. A second caught them, spinning, for a moment. The third was no blade at all, but a crook-ended cane. The ring of keys jangled down around the gnarled wood to clack in place in the blind seer's hand.

"I'll let them out," the old man vowed.

"Tahngarth, go with him!" Gerrard shouted.

The minotaur nodded. Decisively, he kicked aside a pair of blades and brought his fists down on the heads of the adjacent warriors.

"Me, too," Squee volunteered. He'd managed to get three guards chained together and bolted to the bars on one window. They cursed as he trooped happily to the minotaur and the blind man.

"I'm free," Sisay offered, glancing down at a warrior who lay prone at her feet. His legs were pinned beneath a chopped corner of the desk.

Hanna still battled. She was a fair enough fighter when roused to anger but typically had no stomach for it. Just now she wielded a tall brass coatrack against a single swordsman.

"Looks like I'll stay . . . unless—"

She charged the man suddenly, catching his armored collar in one hook of the rack. With an almighty heave, she set the stand upright. The soldier riled impotently, unable to bring his sword to bear.

Brushing her hands, Hanna retrieved her fallen blade and said, "I'm in."

"Excellent," Gerrard replied. The twenty-some guards had all been felled one way or another, none having suffered a worse setback than a concussion. Warden Benbow still lay on the desk top, struggling to free himself.

"I do hope you recover quickly, Warden. We could use you out there," Gerrard said, leaping down from the desk. He smiled, gesturing to his crew. "Let's go. We have an army to liberate."

Through the door they filed. Tahngarth led, a naked blade before him. He'd not used it in the battle so far and had no intention of killing with it, but a minotaur with a sword does wonders for inspiring the human sense of self-preservation. Next in line was Squee, whose own sense of self-preservation attracted him to such a defender. Hanna was third, guiding the blind seer. Hanna's other hand twitched as though she wished she still had the coatrack. Gerrard brought up the rear. He dragged a chair after him, closed the door to the stationhouse, and propped the chair beneath the doorknob.

"That ought to keep them."

"Gerrard," came Hanna's tremulous voice ahead. "Gerrard!"

He glanced up, seeing her pull a bloody hand away from her side. Gerrard rushed to her.

"One of those bastards get you?"

Turning toward him, she said, "No." She dragged the crimson tunic up from her side. "This is that wound. That one from the shrapnel in Rath."

Gerrard knelt beside her. "You said it was only a scratch!"

Hanna blushed. "It was a little more. Orim cleaned it and dressed it on the way here. Healing magic didn't work. . . ." She glanced beneath the blood-soaked bandage. The wound beneath was necrotic. Blood flowed from its center, but the skin and muscle around it were turning black. Fingers of corruption reached out from the spot.

"It is the Phyrexian plague," said the blind seer bleakly. "There is no cure."

Hanna's eyes darkened. She looked from the old man to Gerrard.

Giving a smile he did not feel, Gerrard said, "You may know a lot, old man, but you don't know Orim. She'll find a cure. In the meantime, let's stanch that blood flow." He knelt, ripping the sleeve from his commander's jacket. "Damned thing was too small anyway."

While he tended Hanna's wound, Tahngarth continued down the corridor to the first cell.

The inmate there had heard his approach and was cursing at what he expected to be another guard. When he caught sight of the massive bull-man and his keen sword, the inmate scrambled back from the bars.

He gabbled, "What in the Nine Spheres are you—?"

"Shut up," Tahngarth advised. The man complied. "If you vow to fight for us, we will release you from your cell."

"Wh-what if I want to stay here?" the man asked.

"You'll probably be killed when the prison is overrun."

"Overrun? By whom?"

"By Phyrexia."

* * * * *

The thing about vows is this: Honest men don't need to swear them, and dishonest men don't hesitate to swear them. Of course, Tahngarth would not have realized this. A dishonest minotaur was an oxymoron—or at least a moronic ox. It understandably surprised Tahngarth when the first five hundred prisoners liberated by Gerrard rebelled against him.

The crew were crossing the main yard when the liberated prisoners mobbed them. Though Gerrard and his command crew had been a match for twenty guards, they were not a match for five hundred warriors. These particular warriors gave a new definition to the term "irregulars." Many were inhuman—hulking things that looked like animate rocks, half-lizard men armored in the bones of victims, minotaurs with shorn horns and peg legs. Human, elf, dwarf . . . prison had molded them all into a single species—killers. In moments, the crew was overwhelmed, their weapons stripped. No one was injured in the brief struggle— Tahngarth was too stunned to fight, and Gerrard was too accustomed to ironic reversal.

With rough chants, the liberated prisoners escorted their liberators to the central guard tower in the yard. They drove them up the stairs that ascended the tall framework of beams. The nearest prisoners used the crewmembers' own weapons against them. Those farther out wielded whatever came to hand—chains, pipes, broken bottles, splintered boards. . . . Disarmed and shackled, Gerrard and his crew climbed the switchback stairway. Defeat replaced victory on their faces.

They staggered, one by one, through the hatchway at the top of the stairs and onto a ten-by-ten-foot covered platform above. No sooner was Gerrard through the hatch than it slammed shut, and a bar slid into place.

Though Gerrard had gotten a bloody lip for his attempts to explain, he staggered to the guard tower window for another try.

"Listen to me! Listen!" he shouted to the chanting prisoners. "*We* have freed you! Why do you fight *us*? We are the same. It doesn't matter what you once did. Even treason! Even murder! Whatever wrong landed you here, it is nothing compared to the wrongs of our true foes. I revoke your sentences! You must revoke ours! I return your freedom! Return ours! Together we will fight the true enemy. Together we will fight Phyrexia!"

As Gerrard spoke, the chanting ceased, and the crowd grew

slowly quiet. By the time his last words rolled out, a fearful hush filled the courtyard.

It was so quiet, the crew could hear a single man among the prisoners when he said, "Let them out of there."

Wide-eyed nods came from the prisoners, gaping upward. One man hurried up the switchback stairs to unbar the hatch.

Gerrard smiled incredulously and turned to his comrades. "I'd never really thought of myself as an orator, but this time I . . . I guess I got their attention."

Sisay shook her head gravely. "You didn't," she said, pointing skyward. "Someone else did."

There, in the black belly of night, the lights of hundreds of Phyrexian ships made ghastly new constellations.

CHAPTER 11
Allies from Old Foes

The Battle of the Mori Tumulus would
decide the fate of Yavimaya. Multani fought beside his people—
displaced elf kings, pods of angry sprites, clans of great apes,
clutches of giant spiders, and a handful of fire-eyed druids. These
last ascended from the volcanic caverns that riddled the rocks
beneath the vast tumulus.

Of course the Phyrexians chose to land their invasion fleet
along the Mori Tumulus. It was the highest point of Yavimaya.

Its trees rose five hundred feet above their neighbors. The extensive boughs provided landing platforms for Phyrexian cruisers. From those crowns, the Phyrexians could command the canopy and seep downward to dominate the land. It was more than that, though. The Phyrexians were drawn to the Mori Tumulus because it was a scar they themselves had left on the world.

The Mori Tumulus was a break in Yavimaya's millennial bones—a wound struck by the Argoth event. The world-shattering blast Urza had unleashed to destroy the Phyrexians four millennia ago had cracked the continental shelf beneath Yavimaya. It thrust the broken halves against each other. They ground together and rose. The Mori Tumulus mounded up. It formed a three-hundred-mile ridge, five hundred feet high. Magnigoths struggled to clutch the rift closed. They straddled it like massive stitches. Still, the rent widened. Once in a while the world poured forth its blood and lymph in lava and steam. Even the green might of Yavimaya could not heal it. Something seethed below.

Of course it drew Phyrexians, as an open sore draws maggots.

That's why Multani feared this battle. Here Gaea was weakest of all.

Already Phyrexians had corrupted the crowns. The wound in the world below was mirrored in the treetops three thousand feet above. Here Phyrexian ships clustered, pouring spores down out of the stormy night. Leaf molds and cellulose macrophages turned once-proud heads of green into black rot. Minute mechanical caterpillars ravaged leaves. Metal bugs sank shiny feet into stalks and extracted magnesium, iron, and zinc to use in growing their razor wings. Flocks of battleflies rose to flay armor and skin and muscle from bone. Other machines—spiked treadmills fronted with bear-trap mouths—devoured whatever flesh they found, storing it away for testing inside the cruisers. Phyrexians had a damnable interest in the physiology of their foes.

Pestilence and machines and monsters drove elves from their kingdoms. They fled downward into murky, wet hollows and shelves. One part refugee camp, one part military staging grounds, the camps bustled day and night. Other sentient defenders came here too—sprites, druids, great apes, and of course giant spiders. These nimble beasts, onetime foes of their elf neighbors, allied with them now. They even offered themselves as mounts to carry elf mages into combat.

It was in a war council of such mages, held in a wide and lofty crotch of a magnigoth, that Multani took form. He assembled his body from a termite colony and the desiccated wood that made it up. His flesh literally crawled with large white bugs. He rose, twelve feet tall and ominous, in the midst of the murky circle.

The folk in the crotch of the tree startled momentarily, but they had been waiting for the forest spirit. They welcomed him, bowing. Foxfire lanterns dangled from the sleeves of the elf sorcerers, sending a green glow inward. The light shone across the swords and arrows of elf warriors and oval wings of swarming sprites. The great apes crouched beyond, blinking intelligently in the darkness. Behind it all lurked giant spiders—their multiple eyes like grapes dangling in an arbor.

"Our forces are gathered, Master Multani. We are ready," said the eldest mage, eyes glinting beneath a mantle of white hair. "What is our objective?"

Multani's voice came in the barbed whisper of thousands of termites. "The Phyrexian off-load sites. We'll slay the guards and take back the boughs."

Brow furrowing, the mage said, "It is a thing of black corruption, now. How can it be taken back?"

"Leave that to me," Multani said ominously. He melted down into the tree bough.

It was a brief council—there was no time for words.

Mages mounted their spider steeds and set off through the foliage. Their sleeve-lights slid away in the leaves. The elf archers—young folk with eyes sharp in the night—did not need them. They split up, some trooping up the boughs, others swinging from vines to adjacent trunks. The druids left with the same arcane silence as Multani himself—there one moment and gone the next. The apes outdid them all for silent grace, though. They swung through the boughs, their arms kin to the branches that carried them.

The defenders of Yavimaya rose toward its corrupt canopy.

The tangle of roots below and the tangle of boughs above joined each tree to its neighbors, making Yavimaya one great organism. The forest was a thinking thing, and Multani was its consciousness. Rising through branches, splitting and reassembling himself, he knew the will of Yavimaya: Drive the Phyrexians back onto undead boughs, and destroy them and their ships.

Multani ascended. He felt the tickling feet of giant spiders across his back. Down their barbed legs dribbled armor spells, sent from the hands of elf mages. They gathered massive magics from the green darkness all around. Elf archers seated themselves in nearby crotches, nocking arrows and testing their aim. Great apes clambered into lofts where they could hurl themselves down on Phyrexian heads. Clouds of shimmering sprites darted through the air. They bore spears, swords, and daggers and had adopted the tactics of battleflies. They could strip a Phyrexian in moments.

The forces converged on a huge bough that teemed with Phyrexians. It was a staging ground beneath a landed cruiser. The ship was as huge and black as a thunderhead. It hung in branches that had been corrupted by Phyrexian contagions and resurrected as undead wood. A huge ramp lay open. Monsters in their hundreds coursed down. There would be no attacking them at the ship. The wood had become monstrous itself. This staging ground, though—it was living wood. The Phyrexians had not had time to corrupt it, but already they prepared contagions to pour into crevices and crotches.

Multani seeped into the vast bough. He slipped up just beneath the bark. There, in the quick of the tree, knotholes were plentiful. They were his first weapons—mines beneath monstrous feet.

The rest of his forces were ready. The battle would begin with Multani.

Spreading himself through the vast bough, he triggered the dilation of thousands of knotholes. They yawned wide. Claws and talons dropped into those knotholes. Wood closed to trap the legs.

Suddenly caught, thousands of Phyrexians thrashed.

A heavy rain began. It was not water that fell but arrows. Their stony heads smashed through carapace and rammed into chests and throats and guts. The juices there sank into the arrowheads and the magnigoth down packed within. It swelled massively. In popping succession, Phyrexians exploded. They burst like bugs. Plates gave way. Gray organelles spewed outward. Heads vacated shoulders. Legs separated from torsos. Scales ripped back, and skin sloughed off.

Where monsters slumped, Multani released them. The shattered bodies tumbled away. More beasts staggered into the open holes and were caught. Multani sent sucker stalks up through the bark. They wrapped legs in tenacious tendrils, which widened into inescapable branches. Up torsos they went and then squeezed. Like pinched sausages, Phyrexians burst.

The last of the exploding bolts found their marks. Phyrexians slumped and slid from the killing bough.

Out of the black night, shadows took substance. On giant legs they came. Globular eyes gleamed. Mandibles dripped venom. These were giant spiders. Aback them rode sorcerers—thin, elven, their fingers dancing with power. Spells roared out. Incantations lit rodlike legs before vaulting through the emptiness. Green light painted boughs and broke over Phyrexians. Green spores clung to every tissue.

Plants rooted themselves. Lichens ate away armor. Weeds sank their taproots into blood streams. Saplings split muscle and bone. Blossoms packed air holes. The invaders of the forest were in turn invaded by the forest. In mounds of leaf and vine, more monsters died.

A new rain began—muscle instead of shafts. From their lofted perches, great apes dropped in their hundreds. They hurled living Phyrexians after dead ones. They ripped limbs from Phyrexian troopers and bit chunks from Phyrexian heads.

This was all in the first moments, before there was a foe to fight. These were holes underfoot, arrows and spells out of darkness. With the arrival of the apes and the spider-mounted mages, though, the battle had changed. Phyrexians knew how to fight such creatures. With howls of fury and hunger, monsters attacked.

Yavimaya's horrors were nothing compared to the terrors of Phyrexia—elongated skulls, fang-choked gobs, horn-tipped joints, clawed arms, leg pods, tentacles, talons, stingers. The black tide crashed against the spider mages. It was all bug flesh in those first moments. Then the spiders were shredded, and it was elf flesh and ape flesh flung on dark winds. Spells misfired. Wild magic jagged through treetops. It hurled up the hackled shadows of Phyrexians.

Multani entered vines, lashing them across the monsters. He plucked them up in ones and twos and threes and threw them from the bough. It was not enough. He could not open knotholes—not with elves and apes among the monsters. He could not grow suckers to grab whatever fought above. Behind the slain mages were ragtag armies of elf infantry. They died as quickly and surely as the mages had. There was simply no stopping these beasts.

Even as he fought onward, Multani sent his mind out to Gaea. *Massacre. They cannot be stopped. We must withdraw.*

Gaea did not speak to him. He knew what she would say. *If you withdraw now, they will never be stopped.*

Help us. Help your children. Bring the others. Bring every child beneath your canopy. Else, we are lost.

Why do mortals ever pray? Multani wondered to himself. Why do gods never answer?

The elves were dying like elves. Unflinching, they sacrificed centuries of life.

Phyrexian corpse crews followed in the wake of the advancing lines. They dragged fat chains tipped with long hooks. Wherever the monsters found a body, dead or alive, they would thrust the barb through the soft flesh of the ankle. Four or five elves would fit on a single hook before the corpse crew would swing it away to dangle beneath the cruiser. The chains cranked upward. The specimens were loaded on the ship for study.

Gods might never answer, but Multani would.

He emerged from the tree. He took his form from the quick of the bough. A huge hillside of living wood, Multani flung his fingers out in wooden spikes. They pierced Phyrexians in their scores.

The monsters writhed like spitted roaches. Multani gripped them, splitting them open. This was vengeance pure and simple. While he slew scores in his fists, hundreds flooded past him.

He was losing the Battle of Mori Tumulus. He was losing the Yavimaya war.

Then new allies came. From the volcanic caves beneath Yavimaya, they galloped upward. Never before had Multani's mind laid hold of such creatures. They lurked forever in the twilight world beneath the forest—half green and half red. Their skin was part scale, part rock, their bodies part saurian, part ground sloth. They had tigers' teeth and bulldog faces and feet that were claw and hoof both. The smallest were the size of a man, and the largest the size of two elephants. Most amazing of all were their tongues—longer, more powerful, more dexterous than elephants' trunks. They galloped up the tree boles as if charging across flat ground.

The druids had summoned them. Their enchantments had awakened the slumbering lizards. Kavu. These things were called Kavu—an ancient druid word meaning "ever watchful" and "carved from stone."

Up every bole, Kavu swarmed. In a heartbeat, they fountained out of the darkness and crashed into the Phyrexian lines. Lizard tongues lashed out, snatched up carapaced monsters, and drew them into fangy mouths. They crunched them. No sooner was one Phyrexian swallowed than a second was caught and a third. . . .

Phyrexians withdrew up the bough. The hundreds that had flooded past Multani now fled the other way. He snatched up handfuls of them and crushed them. Kavu got the rest. Soon it was a full-scale retreat.

Forgive my mortal terrors, Gaea, Multani thought. *I should have known you had defenders other than me. You are the world mother, not the forest mother.*

Gaea did not respond. She never spoke to Multani, but he sensed what she would say. You have other defenders as well—allies from old foes.

Yes, Multani said in realization, *allies from old foes.*

Most of the Phyrexians had flooded back onto the black bough where their cruiser waited. It was their beachhead, their haven from which they could launch new attacks—or so they believed.

Multani reached wooden hands into the heavens. A throat opened in him. Out rolled incantations as ancient and dark as those that had summoned the lizards. Words vaulted into the black heavens and called down an even more powerful, even more venerable foe.

Lightning leaped from the black sky. It cracked through a hovering plague ship, transfixing it. Energy poured through its top and out its keel. It leaped onward, through two more ships before its killing hand reached down to the pitching treetops. The bolt scintillated through a cloud of battleflies. They dropped, red-hot, from the air. With clear intentionality, the lightning strike slammed into the beached cruiser. Smoke rose from every seam. Flame burst from rotten wood.

Trapped in flames, Phyrexians oozed glistening-oil from countless cuts. Their blood caught fire. They thrashed.

The lightning gripped the black bough like a hand. It did not let go, did not descend through the tree as natural lightning would. Instead, it held on and shook the bough. Burning Phyrexians fell. Desiccated wood flamed. The cruiser caved and cracked.

Welcome to Yavimaya, my old foes, Multani thought. *Welcome fire and lightning!*

The rot-riddled bough exploded. Hunks of wood and metal and Phyrexian flesh shot into the night.

CHAPTER 12
In Tsabo Tavoc's Web

Phyrexian cruisers filled the night sky above the prison yard. Ships hovered scarcely a hundred feet above the walls. They hung so low that Gerrard could see the flush ports where Phyrexian waste spattered down.

He reached a shackled hand out of the guard tower window, grabbed the lantern that burned there, and cracked it from its casing. He hurled the flaming thing at the belly of a ship. It struck the lip of a sewage port and smashed against the dripping edge. Lamp oil splashed across the black base of the ship. A crimson jet of fire roared up through the waste dump, ignited methane, and set off an explosion that bulged the undercarriage of the ship. Fiery hunks of bug-flesh dribbled from the spot.

The brigands in the yard cheered, united by Gerrard's defiance. Their hope was short-lived.

Hundreds of black cords uncoiled from the rails of the cruisers. They seemed the deadly tentacles of enormous black jellyfish. The cables unrolled to dangle just above the upturned faces of the prison throng. Down those threads slid Phyrexians. Hackled and horned, avatars of death, they plunged toward their prey.

"Free the others!" Gerrard shouted even as the beasts dropped among the prisoners. "Fight for your lives! Fight toward the ship!"

Ship! That single word ignited the yard. There was hope for escape.

Phyrexians claimed their first victims even before setting claw to ground. Talons clamped on heads and crushed them like eggs. Spiked tails gored and lifted gap-mouthed prisoners. Stingers sank into eyes and pumped blackness. Hundreds of prisoners died in that first moment.

Hundreds more fought back. From the guard armory rose crossbow bolts, piercing the black hordes that dropped from the skies. Those prisoners who had swords used them, chopping legs out from under monsters. Others used the shackles or iron bars that had formerly held them captive. Even the bricks of the prison turned deadly. Torches rammed in Phyrexian mouths. Hunks of glass slit throats. Whatever came to hand became a weapon—even the dead claws of the killers, even the sand of the yard.

Some prisoners fought bare-handed. Knuckles cracked chitinous temples. Fingers jabbed segmented eyes. Teeth bit through strangling claws. Feet smashed thoraxes. Phyrexians were flipped and thrown, knee-capped and bludgeoned, throttled and eviscerated. In the horrid spray of oil and blood, prisoners and Phyrexians were almost indistinguishable.

Gerrard and his comrades had their own troubles. The man ascending to release them had been slain on his way up. Monsters landed atop the tower roof. It buckled beneath their weight. Two had crashed through the windows to fight the shackled crew.

Gerrard ducked the scything claws of the first. He somersaulted across the floor of the tower and rose behind the second beast. It was a lumbering monster—a once-human head atop a lupine body fitted out with steel attachments. Luckily, the thing's neck was no canine thing. Gerrard wrapped his shackles around its throat. The chains bit in. The beast thrashed. Gerrard rammed it up against its comrade. The strangling Phyrexian tore the back out of its compatriot. Gerrard tightened his hold. His shackles ground against vertebrae, and the lupine beast fell dead.

Tahngarth quickly finished off the other monster. Hands cuffed behind him, Tahngarth kicked once to spin his foe around, and a second time to bury his hoof in its shredded back.

The Phyrexian convulsed and bucked, falling to the floor.

Tahngarth drew forth his hoof. Acid hissed on his leg and poured out across the planks.

The minotaur spat angrily. "That one burned."

"You must have punctured the spleen," Gerrard said, pointing at the corpse. White smoke rose around the body. "At least spleen is what I would call it."

Sisay knelt beside the fallen Phyrexian, draping her chains in the sizzling stuff. "You don't suppose—" She pulled her hands away, and the links shattered like glass. "I'll be damned."

"Let's hope you won't," Gerrard replied. He used his own shackles to scrape acid from Tahngarth's now-raw leg. His chains also grew brittle. He shattered them. "I've got a gruesome hunch . . ." Scooping up some Phyrexian oil-blood, he laved Tahngarth's legs with it. The sizzling smoke ceased.

Hanna watched intently. "Their blood—it neutralizes the acid?"

Gerrard shrugged. "If I had this stuff in me, I'd want something that could neutralize it."

The minotaur broke his own chains. "Now, as long as the floor doesn't give way—"

Phyrexians suddenly crashed through the rafters. They fell in a frenzied black storm, striking the floor where the corpses lay. The weakened wood held for only a moment. It broke open and hurled the beasts down through the core of the tower.

Clinging to the windowsills, the crew watched as a score of Phyrexians fell to a twisted death on the collapsing stairs below.

"That was miraculous," Gerrard panted.

Sisay stared down grimly. "We'll need a couple dozen more miracles if we're going to get to the ship."

Holding herself up with one hand and clutching her bleeding side with the other, Hanna said, "And a couple more when we're back on board."

Gerrard's eyes were intent. "Orim's got miracles." He edged toward Hanna.

That movement was ill-advised. The stairway within the tower had provided not only access but stability. With the steps gutted, the tower twisted on its four posts. It seemed there was only one way down—one very fast, very horrible way.

"Hold still!" Sisay shouted.

Gerrard lurched to a stop. The platform lurched as well. Nails whined in warning. Joints slowly pulled open.

"We're going to fall, aren't we?"

All around, heads nodded ominously.

Sisay said, "The question is whether we can survive."

"The question is whether we can land on Phyrexians," Tahngarth interrupted.

Glancing toward the ruined roof, Gerrard smiled. "The question is whether we can do both."

He gingerly climbed the inner wall of the listing tower until he could stick his head through the ragged hole in the roof. Lunging, he yanked something down—a tangle of black cords left by the Phyrexians that had landed on the roof. Gerrard hung from the mass of them, his feet swinging free in the center of the wreckage.

Through gritted teeth, he said, "Thought we could . . . take advantage of . . . a few loose ends." He managed to free one of the ropes. Bumping into the far wall, he flung a rope to Tahngarth. "This is your old trick . . . hanging below *Weatherlight* in Rath."

Wrapping the cord around his arm, the minotaur swung free. "Let's hope the Phyrexians are safer pilots."

"Hey!" Gerrard protested. He flung a rope to Sisay. "I saved you, didn't I? Saved us all, and flew out—"

"To crash on Mercadia," Sisay reminded as she let go of the collapsing frame.

"I got us out of there too," Gerrard defended as he bounced against the wall beside Squee.

The goblin clambered onto Gerrard's shoulders. "Squee killed Volrath."

A shrieking moan came as the tower failed. Gerrard hurled himself across the folding space. He snatched up Hanna in his arms and took two running steps up the slanting wall. Squee clung miserably to his shoulders and let out a shriek of his own. Gerrard flung himself and his passengers out the shattered rooftop, now pointing sideways, and into the fiend-charged air. Sisay came just behind him, and Tahngarth brought up the rear.

They swung out beneath one of the great black cruisers that eclipsed the heavens. Below them, thick mobs of Phyrexians swarmed the yard. It was onto their heads that the guard tower fell.

It rushed down like a gigantic club. Monsters looked up and cringed. The tower smashed them to the ground. Wood splintered. The framework cracked. Beams bounded out in a killing storm.

"I was always good at crashing things," Gerrard said as they swooped above the yard. He lifted his gaze from the wreckage below. "Speaking of crashes—"

With a violent crunch, Gerrard, Hanna, and Squee smashed into a descending Phyrexian. The superior mass of the three heroes knocked the monster loose. It fell, legs kicking crablike until it struck ground. Its shell split wide.

Tahngarth executed a similar attack, though on purpose. His four knuckles had never packed such a punch. The minotaur's first roundhouse staved a monster's skull. It died on the vine. Tahngarth set his hooves on the beast and flung himself onward, knocking another beast free. By releasing the first strand and transferring his weight to others, he made a quick circuit of the lines, moving toward the prison walls. Each blow counted for two, fist followed up by shackle. Each kill slew another as the massive creatures crashed to ground atop their comrades.

Sisay attained the same effect with a bit more finesse. She used an acid-dripping shard of her shackles to burn through adjacent cords. Monster after monster plunged beneath her. The next few

Phyrexians down the line slid into sudden emptiness. She swung past Gerrard, Hanna, and Squee.

Gripping a new cord, she shouted "To the ship, then?"

"To the ship. Hang on," Gerrard told his riders.

He too switched his handhold. To drop down into that yard would be certain death. The only hope was to swing line to line until they reached the brig wall and could climb down to where *Weatherlight* was docked below.

* * * * *

First, I fought you in a hole in the ground, Tsabo Tavoc thought gladly, and there you escaped me. I am not a creature for holes in the ground. Then I fought you aboard your own ship, and you drove me off. I should have known not to attack the heir of the Legacy ensconced in his Legacy. But now, she clicked her new legs on the rocky cliff where she stood—stronger legs, fitted with blades in their joints—Now you hang in my web, Gerrard.

Tsabo Tavoc waded through fleeing brigands. They seemed to think there was salvation for them beyond the cliff—or at least there was damnation in the brig. It did not matter to Tsabo Tavoc. On another battlefield, in another time, she would have allowed herself to float in the tide of agony that her troops created. Such was her right. This battle was different though. Benalia had been granted her, but one Benalish warrior thought to stop her. She cared nothing for the shouldering sheep. She cared only for that single strange man built out of all time to serve Urza in his war. Tsabo Tavoc had been similarly built—fearfully and wonderfully made.

She picked her way toward the prison. Some of the prisoners were so blind with panic, they fled into her legs, cracking their brains. Tsabo Tavoc dismembered a few, not intending to but not avoiding it. She must be careful. The blood would make her grip less sure, and in any web—even one's own—grip was life.

Reaching the base of the prison wall, she ambled up the sheer face of cut stones and hurled herself into the air. She caught one of the lines hanging above the bloody yard and climbed toward those pathetic little creatures. She climbed toward Gerrard.

* * * * *

Orim stood at the ship's gangplank. She had been the one who lowered it—after the first fifty prisoners had bloodied their fingers clawing to get aboard. They fought each other. One climber's back was sliced through with a broken bottle. Another had suffered a spontaneous amputation of his left leg beneath the knee. Countless legs had been torn bloody by hands below. Orim had tried to stanch all that blood. When she could not, she let the deck run red, lowering the gangplank lest there be more.

Now there would be more blood. Already *Weatherlight* had taken on six hundred prisoners. They would fill every hold and crouch in the bilge as she raced away. Gerrard had come to gather an army. Instead, he gathered refugees. *Weatherlight* could not safely hold many more. The others would fight. There would be blood.

Worst of all, Gerrard was nowhere to be seen.

"Cast off the plank," came a voice at Orim's shoulder. It was an ancient, wise voice. It brooked no disagreement.

Orim spun, looking at the blind seer. "I cannot sentence them to death."

"You do not sentence them," he said. "You grant reprieve to these others. But if you do not cast off that plank now, even those you have spared will die."

She was pale. "What about Gerrard, Sisay, Hanna, Tahngarth—?"

"That is why you must cast off," the seer said. "If you do not, they will die. Gerrard has saved all those he can. He has his army. Elsewhere, battles scream for that army. Let's save your friends and the world."

Orim drew a deep breath. She closed her eyes, sending her inner self down into that place of peace she had discovered in the forest of the Cho-Arrim. With bliss suffusing her, she reached down and flung away the plank.

Amid the angry shouts and screams, she calmly walked to a speaking tube, flipped it open, and said, "Karn, take us up."

* * * * *

Gerrard hung above the yard. He had nearly reached the wall—it lay fifty feet below and fifty feet ahead.

Suddenly, a huge, agile thing rose up before him. He knew her immediately.

"Tsabo Tavoc," he hissed.

The spider woman was a gigantic bundle of legs and poison. Her beautiful face made a wan smudge on the nighttime.

"I am glad you remember."

Gerrard shifted, pulling Hanna tighter against him. She was growing weak from blood loss and was slipping. "You cannot win."

"I already have. Benalia is mine."

"You cannot defeat all of Dominaria."

"I cannot, but my master can, and he will."

"You cannot defeat me," Gerrard responded, anger in his eyes.

"I already have."

Tsabo Tavoc lunged. Her barbed legs struck Hanna, hurling her away. Without a sound, Hanna fell. Gerrard struggled to grasp her. The spider woman intervened. She gripped the cord with four legs and flung Squee off with three more. With the last, she wrapped Gerrard as she had wrapped Tahngarth. This time, the joints of her legs bristled with blades.

"I don't know which to do, to take you back to my master, or to . . . enjoy you myself."

Gerrard canted his head. "I'll decide for you." He jammed his shackled wrist into her leg joint. The band forced the leg open. Gerrard yanked his arm free and dropped from her.

Tsabo Tavoc's limbs raked out to grab him from the air, but she was too slow. It little mattered. He would die in the fall. . . .

Except that *Weatherlight* hovered below, catching them all. Soundless, the refugee vessel had nosed up under them. Now, with its crew safely aboard, *Weatherlight* streaked away.

Tsabo Tavoc glared after the ship. There would be no catching them.

Still, Gerrard was defeated, fleeing with his tail between his legs. Benalia was hers. Her objective was accomplished. Her master would reward her with the greatest command of the war—Koilos.

If Gerrard dared show himself there, he would be hers.

CHAPTER 13
The Metathran Awake

Urza and Barrin strode up a Tolarian hillside, toward a rocky prominence called the Giant's Pate. While battles raged the world over, this island was a place of calm. Tolaria was a tiny isle, distant from all trade routes. It lay within a tangle of winds that made it almost impossible to find. Swathed in magics and patrolled by helionauts, Tolaria was among the securest sites in Dominaria. It was also Urza and Barrin's home.

For a millennium, they had worked here, training new generations of artificers and preparing for the present invasion. Here, they had taught the precocious Teferi, who now was a planeswalker himself. Jhoira of the Ghitu also learned here. Multani had come to Tolaria to grow the hull of the great ship *Weatherlight*. Even Xantcha had dwelt here—in the heartstone that now rested in the head of Karn. This island had given birth to every great Dominarian artifact and artificer. It had also given birth to legions of bioengineered warriors—the Metathran.

102

That was why they had come today, to awaken the two Metathran commanders who would lead the Dominarian armies at the Battle of Koilos.

The planeswalker and the mage reached the Giant's Pate. Barrin panted. He was in superb shape for a several-thousand-year-old man, seeming only in his mid-fifties. Still, an ascent up the Giant's Pate could make a thirty-year-old pant. Barrin's breathlessness came in part from his memories of the place—of the deep black gorge below, once rife with Phyrexians. He had fought his first Phyrexian invasion from this hilltop, had once flown an ornithopter low over that fast-time rift to save the life of Urza Planeswalker.

Urza did not pant. He did not even breathe. He was too deep in thought. His gemstone eyes gleamed sharply as they swept the horizon. Behind him lay the vast sprawl of the artificers' college of Tolaria—blue-tiled roofs above curving white walls. Before him stretched the time-gutted wilderness.

Tolaria had suffered a cataclysmic explosion that left it a place of temporal scars. Time gashes, they were called—deep temporal chasms where time ran at a snail's pace and tall temporal plateaus where time fled away to eternity. Urza had caused the cataclysm, of course, and he had subsequently found ways to benefit from it. He set up laboratories in fast-time hills, where weeks of research could be done in days, where bioengineered generations could reproduce every year. As to slow-time sloughs, they were most useful for storing food, artifacts, and even creatures.

"There," said Urza pointing toward a series of tightly packed time shells. Some were nearly black, fast-time zones where sunlight was rapidly swallowed. Others were lightning-white slow time where radiation doubled and redoubled. "The Curtains of Time. That's where we stored the Metathran commanders."

"Thaddeus and Agnate," Barrin supplied. "You must remember that though it's been a century for us, for them, it will have been only a few hot minutes. They'll expect us to know their names."

Urza turned his gleaming gaze on the master mage. "And you must remember that these two are perfectly engineered for their roles. They have no expectations other than the ones I have given them."

Barrin shrugged, hiding the motion in a gesture down the far side of the Giant's Pate, toward the Curtains of Time. "Let's go get them."

Marching down the Giant's Pate was always easier than marching up. The path was smooth, worn by a thousand years of foot traffic. It led down to a bower of wild grapes and up toward the Angelwood, a mild slow-time paradise. Urza and Barrin turned off the path, cutting through blackberry thickets. Beyond, they approached a gleaming white wall. It shimmered brilliantly, a barrier of energy. In the brightest fold of that curtain, the Metathran commanders waited. There, time was almost nonexistent.

Urza's gemstone eyes grew dark. He could shape and color his body however he wished. For Barrin, protections were a bit more elaborate. He waved one hand around himself, evoking a shroud of blackness that sank into eyes and skin. He seemed a man of midnight, his clothes hanging on personified emptiness.

The two strode, side by side, to stand before that brightest of spots. Through blackened sight, they could just make out two white capsules within the gleam. Each was ten feet tall and six feet wide—a living sarcophagus that shielded the commander within from a century of sunlight. Explosive charges would blast the capsule doors—and the men strapped to them—back into the main time stream.

Urza stood to one side, and Barrin to the other. It would be death to stand directly before those capsules when the charges blew.

"Are you ready?" Barrin asked.

"Bring out the commanders."

It was a simple spell, one with no gestures, no words, no components that partook in time. Such things would have halted the effect once it entered the time curtain. Instead, the spell was quick as a thought, as immediate as recognition.

Bolts exploded. They outlined the doors in a radiance brighter that the sun. Within the time rift, the blast was instantaneous, but in the normal temporal flow, the blast spread out through the air like bleach wicking through fabric. It formed a brilliant halo about the caskets. The doors left their frames. The gaps widened by inches. Thick plates of steel cleared the case. The figures strapped to the doors showed through. Enormous and mantled in fire, Thaddeus and Agnate rode, faces pressed against the padded inner doors. The Metathran were eight feet tall, blue skinned, and powerfully muscled. They seemed fiery demons as they soared out of the time curtain.

The first of the doors broke through the temporal field. Its metallic face burst the zone and dragged normal time in vortices behind it. The door brought with it the deafening roar of the explosion. Then came the clap of the temporal field closing, water after a diver. With the same fierce bellow, the second door crashed through the temporal wall. Vast energies spent themselves on that re-entry. This was by design, lest the doors fly for miles, killing their riders. Just beyond the time curtain, the doors toppled, side by side. They struck ground in a pair of terrible thuds. Steam and smoke hissed in circles around them, momentarily hiding their occupants.

Barrin cast a second spell. Wind leaped from his fingers, rushed beneath the steaming hunks of metal, and slowly lifted them into the air. The spell bore the doors away from the ravening curtain of time. Slicing through the blackberry thicket, the air-sleds and their occupants came to rest on the path to Angelwood.

Barrin and Urza followed. As they went, they shed the ebony protections they had donned. By the time they stood on the path, they had regained their common aspects. The wreaths of smoke dissipated, revealing the two commanders who would lead the armies of Dominaria.

They were gigantic. Each commander was three hundred pounds of muscle and bone. They were human, yes, but only barely so. Their rib cages were as strong as rhinos', their arms as powerful as gorillas', their legs as long as horses'. They were not body only. These two were great minds, trained in every strategy of war, honed from inception for their task.

Thaddeus rose first. Straps that held against the rocket blast of the door were no match for his flexing arms. They snapped, whipping back to flog the rocky path. Heaving himself up from the padding, the great gladiator rose. Two heads taller than most men, he seemed taller still because of the silver-white hair that stood like flame from his head. Thran emblems tattooed his cheeks and forehead, announcing his name and generation. Blue, armored shoulders towered over Barrin. Bright eyes gazed from beneath a jutting brow.

"The invasion has begun?" Thaddeus asked, his voice as deep as a bear's growl.

"Yes," Urza replied simply.

Thaddeus nodded in understanding. His jaw rippled. "My army stands ready?"

"Yes," Urza repeated.

The commander's eyes shifted down to where Barrin knelt beside the other door. "What of Agnate?"

The Master Mage raised his head, drawing a hand back from the man's neck. "He's not breathing. There is no heartbeat. Perhaps the blast was too much—"

Thaddeus strode to the spot. He was there in two steps. His feet pinned the door down, and his hands ripped the straps loose. In the same swift motion, he hauled his counterpart free and laid him supine on the stone. Thaddeus balled a fist and pounded massively on the man's breast.

Agnate's body lurched under the assault, but he did not stir.

Thaddeus drew a deep breath and forced the air into Agnate's open mouth.

"He must live," the massive man growled as he pounded Agnate's breast again. Aside from the blow, there was no life in him.

"How strange," Urza mused, staring down at the sight. It was strange indeed. Agnate's musculature was perfect, his figure the pinnacle of eight hundred years of genetic research. He seemed a sculpture, flawlessly rendered, but cold. "It has been only minutes since he was placed in that capsule. What could have slain him?"

"The shock of the blast might have done it," Barrin said, kneeling beside the lifeless figure as Thaddeus worked him over. "Or perhaps the capsule failed, and the solar rays—"

"We could assign both armies to one commander," Urza thought aloud.

Thaddeus reared up from the most recent breath. "I cannot fight without him. All our training . . . no, more than that . . . all our lives—" he pounded the still breast once again— "we share the same flesh, the same mind. We are genetically identical. We think each other's thoughts. I cannot fight without him." He breathed another gale into the man's lungs.

"I am seeing a flaw in your design," Barrin said to Urza.

Agnate suddenly spasmed, as though his spirit had leaped back into his body. He gasped and clutched his hand over Thaddeus's fist. Agnate's eyes opened, that same sky-blue. Awareness filled them and realization a moment later.

He sat up. Thaddeus pulled him to his feet.

"The invasion has begun," Agnate guessed.

Staring intently in his counterpart's eyes, Thaddeus nodded and smiled. "Yes."

"Our armies await us?"

"Yes."

Urza shot a knowing glance at Barrin. "What were you saying about a flaw?"

Barrin shrugged. "They do not have to fight alone now but what about a week from now? A month? A year? Perhaps they will."

"Perhaps you will have to fight without me," Urza replied, "or I without you."

Agnate turned, bowing curtly to Urza. "Master Malzra, where does our battle unfold?"

"A desert, perfect for deploying troops. I fought once there myself. Everyone has fought once there. We will engage Phyrexian ground armies to take back the Caves of Koilos."

* * * * *

Tsabo Tavoc arrived at Koilos.

She pivoted within the piloting bulb of her private fighter. The craft was her own design—a one-person vessel fitted with a flying harness that allowed her to access the powerstone controls with all eight of her mechanical legs and both of her human arms. It flew faster than any other Phyrexian vessel, bore more armor, and had a ray cannon for each of her legs. Its main body was the spider woman's piloting bulb. The rest was drive core and metal deadliness. When she led an aerial armada, the fighter straddled the command cruiser, replacing its traditional bridge. Tsabo Tavoc replaced its traditional crew.

Just now, though, she arrived without her armada. They were busy hunting down the last vermin in Benalia. They needed her no longer, so complete was her victory. Her master had been pleased. The other commanders were still mired in combat in Yavimaya and Shiv, in Jamuraa and Keld. They hadn't even found Tolaria yet. Benalia was the first great victory of the early war, and Tsabo Tavoc was made second-in-command for the entire invasion. Her master had been wise to promote her—and wiser still to send her far away from him. Black widows have a way of eating their mates.

Soon Koilos also would belong to Tsabo Tavoc. She would stand before her master and ascend his throne. Then she would conquer even Lord Crovax.

The fighter skipped lightly above a desert rill and plunged into the slanting darkness on the other side. Tsabo Tavoc's legs moved in precise jabs within the piloting bulb. The ship leaped to her touch. It slid down into the belly of the dark terrain, following an ancient hollow.

This was an historic place, she knew. Megheddon Defile, it had once been called, the clearest overland route to the Thran city of Halcyon. Down this hollow, when it had been a narrow valley, had marched the Thran in their war against the Phyrexians. They had been utterly destroyed in that war, through the grand wisdom of the Ineffable. Somehow, though, they had managed to shut him away from his world, from Dominaria.

Tsabo Tavoc's fighter soared from the encroaching cliffs and out onto the wide, flat plains of Koilos. A distant outcrop appeared on the horizon.

It was all that remained of the once-towering extrusion on which Halcyon had stood. The caves beneath that outcrop—what had been called the Caves of the Damned—held a permanent portal to Phyrexia. That was the gate closed to the Ineffable when he was banished from Dominaria six thousand years before. That was the gate opened again by Urza and his brother Mishra at the beginning of the Brothers' War four thousand years ago. It had been closed again by the traitor Xantcha and remained that way— the Ineffable willed it so—until the invasion had begun. Now, the gate was wide open, the only land portal in the early war. It belonged to Tsabo Tavoc.

She was to keep it open, to bring through the vast land armies arrayed across the first sphere of Phyrexia. More importantly, she was to battle Urza Planeswalker, who would inevitably bring his forces to close the portal.

With a final few flicks of her barbed legs, Tsabo Tavoc sent her fighter screaming over the caves of Koilos. A beautiful sight opened before her. Rank upon rank, they awaited her arrival— Phyrexian troopers, witch engines, dragon engines, negators, gargantuas, shock troops, vat priests, sand crabs, raptors. . . . One hundred thousand of them, they filled the desert like thorny crops and spread to the horizons.

As Tsabo Tavoc's fighter soared overhead, they welcomed her with an awful shriek of joy. Their leader had arrived, their great mother. "Tsabo Tavoc!"

CHAPTER 14
Strange Saviors

In Yavimaya's darkest hour, Multani toured a lightless place. The Heart of Yavimaya was the eldest and largest magnigoth in the forest, a five-thousand-foot-tall tree. Its root bulb bulged above the nearby canopy. Foliage spread in four vast rafts up its manifold trunk. The tree's crown was a huge, lofty forest in its own right. Normally this was a place of eternal and holy light but not now. The Heart of Yavimaya was now a ravaged battlefield.

For two days, Phyrexian troop transports had hovered above the canopy. Down webby lines, monsters slid. They dropped from their cords atop the Heart of Yavimaya.

It was a sacred site, as large as a great city. In ancient times, Multani had excised a piece of the tree's core, gifting it to Urza Planeswalker. From that wedge of wood grew the hull of Urza's great skyship *Weatherlight*. No thinking creature dared live on the Heart of Yavimaya—not elf nor sprite nor druid.

That bark, too holy for the feet of fey, was desecrated by the claws of Phyrexians. Every branch became a roadway for the demonic army. Phyrexians swarmed it, bending every fiber of the crown with

110

their black weight. They ripped the leaves off. They peeled back the green tendrils. They drove killing spikes down into the living wood. As they had done throughout the forest, the Phyrexians turned life to unlife.

To lose this tree—this most sacred tree—would be to lose everything.

No thinking defenders dwelt on the Heart of Yavimaya, so the tree defended itself. It transformed the spikes driven into it, infusing them with the ancient power of green. The killing shafts gained life. Black and green mixed and blended. The spikes that had cracked down into the tree's vast boughs shot suddenly upward. Each was as sharp as a spear, as stout as a lance. They drove themselves through the Phyrexians standing above. Ebony wood impaled monsters. First to die were those who sat upon or straddled spikes. Next to die were all the rest. Spikes grew rampantly. They jutted even from the healthy flesh of the tree. Once the secrets of death had been learned by the Heart of Yavimaya, they were whispered through every grain.

The Phyrexian city had become a sudden necropolis.

Victory.

Multani walked the battlefield among the writhing beasts. Not a Phyrexian remained free. Every last one had been skewered. They hung overhead. Their oil-blood rolled quiet and golden down the shafts. Barbed legs shivered in agony. Claws clutched air.

Multani walked onward. He approached a human-looking leg, the pierced foot of a one-time man. Above the creature's hips was the shaggy body of a ram. Instead of fur, though, the thing was covered in spines that oozed poison like sweat. The bestial torso of the monster seemed strange above these strong, human legs.

Multani reached out, setting his fibrous hand on the riven foot. Through feverish flesh, his mind touched its mind.

He saw a vision of another place. The beast gazed in horror across a different killing field. He saw not treetops but a convoluted tumble of red-black ground, like muscle laid open. The sky seemed a reflection of the ground—a crimson mass of coiling energy. Between ground and sky hung impaled tens of thousands. They were not Phyrexians. They were men, and women, and children. The Phyrexians there walked quietly among the dying folk. In their midst sat a madman. He smiled and sipped from a delicate cup and sang songs to himself.

From the Phyrexian's mind, Multani gleaned a name for this horrible world—Rath—and a name for the madman—Crovax.

This was their foe. This was the man—the monster—who had assembled the armies of invasion. Crovax had slain tens of thousands of humans and elves on his own world. For them, the Heart of Yavimaya had exacted revenge.

Multani released the foot of the dying beast. His mind broke contact. The scene of horror in Rath was replaced by the scene of horror in Yavimaya. There was little difference. The Heart of Yavimaya had become as hellish as a hillside in Rath. Life had learned the tricks of death.

"Perhaps this is what must happen," Multani mused grimly to himself. "Perhaps to defeat these foes, we must become like them." What victory was that? Once they had become their foes, the Phyrexians would truly have won.

A great sadness swept through Multani. The Heart of Yavimaya was horribly disfigured. All that was green had been shredded. All that was smooth had turned to spikes. The crown of Yavimaya's most sacred tree had become a cemetery.

Feeling weak, Multani dropped to one knee. His vinelike hand settled onto the tortured bark. His mind fled inward, through the fibers. He sensed the tree's agony. Every spike that had grown rampantly upward had also grown rampantly down. When green life had allied with black death, it had formed a cancer that ate away living flesh. The Heart of Yavimaya was dying, impaled on the same spikes that slew its foes.

Multani reeled.

Defeat.

The Heart of Yavimaya was dying. It was becoming Phyrexian. The forest could not be saved.

Gaea, hear me. In defeating these monsters, we become monsters ourselves. The forest is lost, slain as Argoth of old—turned from living wood into tools of death.

Gaea did not speak to him, but he sensed that she also was dying.

That filled Multani with a new passion: anger. Yavimaya and Gaea would be saved by him if they would be saved at all.

Multani marshaled red fury. He had allied with red before—with lightning and fire, with Kavu lizards and lava. They had not destroyed the forest. They had been conformed to the power of life.

Ah, there—there was the great difference. The Heart of Yavimaya had conformed itself to the power of death. Instead, it should have transformed its foes with the power of life.

Multani smiled. The aerial roots that formed his teeth were a ghastly jumble. He knew what he must do to save the forest.

Closing thistle-blossom eyes, Multani sank down on the bark. His fingers twined themselves deep into the crevasses there. His mind followed into the agonized wood. He melted. His body of vines sloughed on the outside of the huge bough.

Pain suffused Multani. It might have slain him except that he tapped its power. He used agony to reach down past the cancerous crown and into the tree's immemorial bole. Multani cascaded down the trunk. He took anger with him. Five thousand feet down, he reached the root bulbs and spread farther. Through the hundreds of trees that surrounded this forest giant, he went—through the thousands that touched upon them, and the millions beyond. To each, he conveyed his fury at the death of the Heart of Yavimaya.

He summoned them, the vast and endless forest. He summoned them.

Let's teach these black monsters the ways of life, he told them. *Let death be swallowed in victory!*

The forest rose to his call. The spirits within each tree took his fury into themselves. Ancient souls stirred for the first time since Urza Planeswalker had been trapped among them. A huge welling force—the forest itself—roused. Yavimaya had always been sentient, but now it was awakening. Tiny leaves of desire united. Individual surges of power gathered into a single column of green force.

The locus of that mana cyclone was the Heart of Yavimaya itself. Its wood flared phosphorescent. Its bark glowed as energy seeped out the creases. Green power whirled up through the aching tree. Rotten wood woke to new life. Rings lost to time renewed themselves. The surge of power fountained through the tree, blasting into the spike-filled crown.

Green strength rushed through deep-driven spikes. It flooded the stalks and washed away all darkness. Magic pressed into every space, every tissue. No room remained for corruption. The spikes turned healthy and whole.

Multani soared up the Heart of Yavimaya, glad for its salvation. What he sensed in the next moments, though, was beyond his dreams.

The power did not cease in the tips of those spikes. It flowed into the creatures impaled there. Through glistening-oil and acid lymph, it passed. Just as the forest's soul reinvigorated dead wood, it enlivened the monsters pinioned there. They writhed. They growled ghastly growls. The forest was not done with them. It formed cell walls. It thickened glistening-oil to sap. Veins hardened into vines. Bones became heartwood. Muscles became quick. Skin turned to bark. The warriors of Phyrexia slowly transformed to beasts of wood.

The forest was converting its foes.

One by one, the new army of wooden warriors drew themselves up off the spikes that had previously impaled them. They climbed down. Every last one was now made of wood. It was as though Multani had brought into being an army of his own offspring.

The Phyrexian necropolis had become a true city.

The Heart of Yavimaya had been saved.

Out of corruption, a sacred race had been born.

Multani arose. He assembled himself from peeled leaves and stripped boughs. A bundle of ivy filled out his torso. The power he had gathered glowed out of every leaf tip. His aura drew to him great masses of foliage. Multani became gargantuan. He towered above the wooden warriors, who stood there, watchful beside the spikes that had once slain them.

The giant man knelt, laying his hand on one of the warriors. His consciousness leaped into the wooden man. There was Phyrexian fanaticism here still and the will to fight, but that was all that remained. This creature had become a child of the wood, a locus of Yavimaya's spirit and will.

Multani drew back. He surveyed the others—a sacred army. "You were once the damned. You were once Phyrexian. No more. Now you are born of Yavimaya. The forest brought you out of death into life. He who gave you first birth is no longer your father. She who gave you second birth, she is your true mother. For you, Yawgmoth is no more, and Gaea is all."

Thousands of clenched fists—gnarled in tough bark—rose to the sky with the shout. "Gaea!"

"Fight for her now. Fight the evils you once were to save the good you have become. Fight for Gaea!"

"Gaea!"

* * * * *

Phyrexians were thick in the elf kingdom of Civimore. They were thick everywhere. The great Kavu lizards grew fat on fiend flesh. No bloodlust or cunning was necessary for the Kavu. The Phyrexians were so thick a beast couldn't yawn without one falling in.

The king, of course, was dead. Half his elf subjects were dead too. The other half did what they could to hide. Occasionally they charged out to die, shouting oaths to their lovers and mothers— better than dying with craven pleas. That was one thing the forest would not do. It would die, but it would not plead for its life.

There was no end in sight. Either these gray-skulled devils would inherit Yavimaya, or these red-scaled lizards would. As for the forest folk—as for elves and apes, druids and green-men—they were merely shifted to the base of the food chain. Death descended on each one, extinction on them all.

What were these new beasts? They swarmed up the boles and bounded through the crown. More Phyrexians? They seemed it, with their brow ridges and horn-studded shoulders. Why, then, did they fall on their own kind? Why ram those claws beneath carapace and rip it out by its roots?

Phyrexians took exception. They turned on their apparent brethren. Fangs clamped down on heads but couldn't bite through anymore than they could have bitten into the side of a tree. Stingers struck against bellies and spattered their poison impotently on the surface. Claws did little more that scratch the beasts' hardened hides. Heedless, the wooden warriors killed their brethren.

So, what were these strange things? They seemed outward Phyrexians but inward children of the forest. They fought like the minions of death, but they fought for the minions of life. Garlands twined their knobby skulls. Sucker branches poked out between their claws. There were even little berries here and there—sweet-tasting berries that burst within Phyrexian mouths when they thought to taste brains instead. Deadly and sweet, tender and tough—these were strange saviors indeed.

And what was that gigantic mound of sticks shambling in their midst? Had it been smaller, it might have seemed Multani—but this thing was colossal! It stomped Phyrexians in their tens. It batted them aside in their hundreds. It destroyed them in their thousands.

Victory?

Could it be that the forest would not die, that it would kill the killers? Who could be thanked for such a victory?

There was no name for any of these mad beasts. Such things had not been seen in the world since the Phyrexians left it six millennia ago. The only word that came close to describing these strange monsters was the name chanted low on all their vined lips.

"Gaea."

CHAPTER 15
Dark Destinies

Gerrard stood on the deck of *Weatherlight*. The ship soared along Benalish shores through coiling rills of cloud. Lifting his captain's spyglass, he glanced abeam.

Other ships bobbed there, strange small ships—the remnants of whatever arcane air defenses Benalia had had. They were drawn to *Weatherlight* as ducklings to their mother. Gerrard had not known there were other flying ships on Dominaria. He had almost blasted the first one from the sky before he had made out the symbol of the Seven Clans on its side. Then more came. While *Weatherlight* crossed Benalia, flying its refugee army away from the Phyrexian armada, it gathered this ragged fleet. Most of the other ships were small, one-person fighters. A few had crews. A rare few even had enough room to take on some of the prison brigade.

A humorless smile lit Gerrard's face. Who would have thought he'd become the commander of a flying armada, leader of a small army, defender of Benalia, bane of spider women? Without trying, he'd become what everyone wanted him to be. They didn't want a saint. They wanted an honest fighter—someone who saw evil and tried his damnedest to knock it flat.

Even so, his damnedest hadn't been enough for Benalia. Tsabo Tavoc had overwhelmed it. Sometimes, a fighter's damnedest wasn't enough.

"Perhaps it would be better to be an infallible savior," Gerrard mused darkly, "to cast out demons and heal the sick—" A pang of guilt stabbed through him. *Healing the sick . . .*

Turning away from the ragtag armada, Gerrard hung his spyglass from his belt, strode to the hatch, and descended a stair to the companionway below. *Weatherlight's* engines sent a hum through the wood all around. The lanterns in the hall glowed wanly over sleeping warriors. Gerrard stepped past them to a door that spilled light into the corridor. Ducking his head, he strode into the sick bay.

It was overloaded. On bunks and floor mats lay folk injured in the brig battle. These were the worst cases—amputations, skull injuries, sucking wounds, lacerations, multiple contusions. Other, less infirm soldiers slept atop crates in the hold. Orim swooped back and forth among the twenty-some patients, giving what aid she could. Most were unconscious, whether from agony or soporifics. Gerrard headed straight across the sick bay to a single bunk.

"Hanna," he breathed, taking hold of her hand and brushing blonde locks back from her sweaty face. "Has the bleeding stopped?"

She looked up at him through a cloud of pain. "I'm not sure. Yes. Orim packed it tight." She tried to sit up. "I shouldn't be taking up one of these bunks—"

"Lie down," Gerrard soothed, easing her back. "Orim can't tend you unless you are here. You're here for her, not for you."

"I should be navigating."

"No," Gerrard insisted. "Sisay can do it. Besides, we'll not be planeshifting. We'd lose our armada." He gave a little laugh. "For that matter, we're not exactly sure where we're bound. I was counting on the old man's advice, but nobody can find him. He's probably squirreled away somewhere. We can use the time to rest, all of us—a little sailing before the next fight."

Hanna curled in a spasm of pain. She clutched her stomach.

Gerrard held her hand, staring at clenched eyelids. "Orim! Over here. Something's happening."

Orim looked up from the man she tended, a double amputee at the knees. Her eyes were grimly determined beneath the turban she wore. In her bound hair, Cho-Arrim coins gleamed. Drawing a white sheet over the twin tourniquets, Orim made her way across the crowded sick bay.

She gave Gerrard an apologetic smile. "We're doing our best. There's not enough space, not enough supplies—"

"Something's wrong," Gerrard broke in. He gestured to Hanna, curled on the pallet. His eyes were pleading.

Orim nodded and knelt beside the pallet. "She's been doing this for the last hour. I've cleansed the wound and applied opiates. I fear to give her more, lest they poison her. I've tried every spell and meditation. Even Cho-Arrim magic is no match for this plague."

"I'm fine, really," Hanna said through gritted teeth. With an effort of will, she straightened. "I need to get back to the bridge."

"Let me see the wound," Gerrard said.

"It's nothing," Hanna interrupted, "just a little blood, just a little infection."

Orim's jaw muscle leaped. "I'm going to pull back the gauze. It's time to check the wound anyway."

Tears standing in her eyes, Hanna nodded.

With quick and expert motions, Orim drew back the bed-clothes, exposing Hanna's midsection from her hipbone to the first rib. The bandage showed a small smile of blood. Beyond the fabric, Hanna's skin was smooth and pink.

"That doesn't look so bad," Gerrard said hopefully.

Orim pulled loose the gauze. It came away only reluctantly. Its warp and weft clung to the seeping flesh. A great weighty gob came loose. Crimson blood and black rot were mixed on the packing. Orim drew it aside, setting it in a silver tray.

The wound was a canyon in Hanna's stomach. Perhaps three inches deep, the infection had carved ragged walls down through skin and muscle. A glossy gray membrane stretched across the base of the wound. The corruption that ate away at her flesh dribbled down atop that membrane.

"That's the peritoneum," Orim said. "It protects her organs. If the disease spreads beyond that—"

"We have to stop it," Gerrard murmured intensely. "Can't you cut away the infected flesh?"

Orim shook her head. "That's how it got this big—I cut away the rot, but it returned. The roots of the infection are too long. Look." She pulled back more of the dressing gown. Beneath the pink of Hanna's skin, gray tendrils of corruption spread outward, up to her neck, around to her spine, and down to her knee.

"We have to stop it. You have to find a cure."

"Yes," Orim replied quietly, repacking the wound. "Yes, I know."

"All right," Hanna said. "The show is over. I'll be fine. Orim's the best healer in Dominaria. She'll—" She stopped, gripping her side.

Gerrard pulled her hand away and clutched it tightly. "You're right. You'll be fine. Orim will heal you. I've ordered her to. We're destined to stay together—"

Hanna laughed. "You've never known what you were destined for."

Smiling, Gerrard nodded. "You're right. But I always knew what I wanted, and I always wanted you."

As she finished bandaging the wound, Orim said, "Gerrard always gets what he wants."

"Damn straight."

A familiar voice echoed through the speaking tube. "Orim, is Gerrard down there?"

He answered with levity he didn't feel, "Ah, the third goddess summons! What is it, Sisay?"

"You'd better get up here. We're coming up on something."

"On my way," Gerrard answered. He bent, kissing Hanna. "Get some sleep. Orim will give you something. I need you rested. By the time you wake, we'll be halfway to a cure." Turning, he threaded his way through the crowded sick bay and out into the hall.

Beyond the murmur of the wounded, the hum of the ship's engines was omnipresent. It was a comforting sound—straightforward power. In the face of that roar, no obstacle seemed insurmountable. How could a little disease resist such power?

Gerrard gained the deck and climbed to the forecastle. Beyond the prow was a strange sight.

Low above the sparkling waves, a lone Phyrexian cruiser flew. It seemed almost an island instead of a ship, except for its speed. The cruiser's black mass left a churning sea in its wake, waves driven up by the force of enormous turbines.

"What are they doing down so low?" Tahngarth asked. He leaned on the rail.

Gerrard lifted his spyglass, extended it, and peered down. "They seem to be fishing."

Along the lower rail of the Phyrexian cruiser were batteries of harpoons. Scaly crews manned them. They worked diligently, loading and firing. Long white jags burst out from the guns, seeming to wriggle in the air as they descended toward the sea. They sliced the water with a diving motion. Beneath the glassy surface, they surged along. Four white shots converged on a school of fleeing dolphins.

"Just like Phyrexians to kill dolphins," Tahngarth hissed.

Gerrard shook his head grimly. "Just like them to kill merfolk."

Through the spyglass, he saw. The bolts below ripped into the undulating tail-fins of fleeing merfolk. Those shots seemed somehow to be self-guided. Each one burrowed straight up the spine of a creature. All life fled the bodies. Lanced corpses floated to the surface and lolled on the waves. The cruiser drove on, just above them, with no apparent attempt to retrieve the kills.

"What are they doing?" Tahngarth snorted. "They'd not waste a whole cruiser on harpooning, would they?"

"Those aren't normal harpoons."

Gerrard trained the spyglass on the crews at the guns. Whatever they loaded into those launchers wriggled like snakes—not snakes, centipedes. Long thin legs extended from the main body. They hungrily lashed the arms of the crews that loaded them. One gunner dragged his fist down the length of a centipede, flattening its legs against its bony body and straightening the whole beast. The gunner then jabbed the thing into the launcher. A shuddering second later, the centipede flew from the ship into the water and struck a merman, carving its way up his spine.

"Spinal implants," Gerrard said in realization, "just like the one Volrath used to control Greven. They're killing merfolk and then—"

Before he could say it, the spyglass caught movement among the slain merfolk. They lifted lolling heads. Their limbs jerked horribly. The dead things turned and stared in awe at the vast ship. Their backs were long, raw wounds where the former spine had been ejected. The flesh was as torn and corrupted as the gash in Hanna's stomach.

"Oh, that's it," spat Gerrard, folding the spyglass. He whacked Tahngarth's chest. "Let's get to the guns. We'll sink that mermaid-killing, zombie-popping, black-boil-on-the-butt-of-the-world slave ship."

Lifting an eloquent eyebrow, Tahngarth said, "If you say so."

"Battle stations!" Gerrard called out between cupped hands. Flipping open the speaking tube beside the port-side ray cannon, he repeated the command, "Battle stations! Signal the fleet. We go down in a strafing run. Any ship with a gun, follow *Weatherlight*!"

Sisay's voice replied, "Aye, Commander. I thought you'd have something to say about this. How close do you want us to pass?"

"Close enough to clip their horns," Gerrard called back as he strapped himself in behind the cannon.

Tahngarth rubbed one of his own horns. "That's close."

"Drive them into the sea. Let 'em rust beneath the waves. Let 'em feed the sharks."

"Aye," was all Sisay said.

The ship pitched sharply forward. Her prow dipped past ragged white clouds. The black cruiser came into view directly beyond the figurehead. Air spilled up past the gunwales. *Weatherlight* plunged into a dive. Her engines mounted up, trailing coils of vapor. The manifolds roared. The airfoils trimmed backward. Wind screamed off their streamlined tips. All that noise might have alerted the monsters below, but the ship punched through her own sound envelope, outrunning it.

Weatherlight was an axe head rushing down to split the vast ship below. Beside her and behind her swarmed the ragtag fleet. Every last gun buzzed, its charge building.

The blue-green sea welled up below. The black cruiser above it grew as well. It swelled to fill the whole world. Only when every gun turret and conduit showed clear across the horrid thing did Gerrard give the order.

"Fire!"

Red bursts leaped from his cannon. Plasma smacked against a canister engine, cracking through the armor shell and releasing geysers of sulfur. Tahngarth's gun spoke twice. The first charge ripped away a whole section of wall. The second painted the harpoon deck in killing fire. Phyrexians and their damned spinal centipedes writhed in agony as the blast burned them to nothing.

The amidships cannons added their fury to the battle. Red flack spread from all sides of *Weatherlight*. As she snapped out above the rankled mid-ridge of the cruiser, even her rear gun came to life. Squee clung there with savage glee. He unleashed a fiery barrage that stripped the Phyrexian's answering fire from the sky. The rest of the armada blasted away as well.

Explosions rocked the outer shell of the ship. Fires belched out from within.

"Pull up!" Gerrard ordered as *Weatherlight* shot fore of the craft. "Take her high in a rollover reverse. Prepare for a second attack run!"

The ship launched herself skyward. She climbed with the same eager speed with which she had plunged. The rest of the armada struggled into her slipstream.

Gerrard glanced over the rail. The cruiser was striped with destruction. Inky smoke rolled up from its rent hull. All across it, Phyrexians lay dead.

"That'll teach them—attacking defenseless merfolk!" Gerrard hooted.

Sisay stood the ship on end and rolled her over, climbing all the while.

"Not as defenseless as you think," Tahngarth barked.

Gerrard peered down again.

Huge columns of water blasted up out of the deep. They surrounded the crippled ship, overtopping it. The arcs of water broke and fell away from vast hooks and thick cables. A sheet of spray flung up, carrying in it an enormous net. With unimaginable force, every line that had snagged on the cruiser went taut. The ship struggled in vain to stay aloft. The force below was too great. The bow of the craft crashed into the waves. It sank with preternatural speed. Lightnings awoke across the cruiser as power cells contacted the water. Energy surges opened more cracks in the ruined hull. The pressure of the seas lengthened these fissures. Underwater explosions mounded water high.

In deep and boiling oceans, the cruiser sank with all hands aboard.

Gerrard stared in amazement. He gabbled, "Uh, c-call off the next attack."

A heavy hand settled on his shoulder. Tahngarth's voice rumbled. "The seas can take care of themselves."

Nodding numbly, Gerrard said into the speaking tube. "Captain, let's maintain a high altitude. We wouldn't want to get too close to those nets."

"Aye."

CHAPTER 16
A Dreamed Man

Victory.

From the Heart of Yavimaya to the seas all around, there was victory in the forest. Elves filled the crowns, their songs twining in freshening wind. Sprites drifted in swarms so thick they seemed chandeliers lighting the wood. Druids strode ancient paths amid deep root bulbs. Their songs of joy were basso drones that reverberated through watery grottos. Beneath even them, in the volcanic caves of the Mori Tumulus, Kavu lizards lay slumbering. They had gorged on Phyrexians and would be sated for years.

Many Phyrexians had met their ends in the bellies of Kavus or of the leviathans that swam the deep water tubes. Others had been blasted apart by druid spells or torn to ribbons by sprite pike swarms, or blown open by elven arrows. Their remains even now were being scoured from the forest. Elves tended pyres that turned the last of the monsters to ash. Burning brands set fire to the rot that riddled magnigoths. Black coils of smoke bore the stink of Phyrexian oil-blood away from the canopy.

Yavimaya would not lose all its taste of those creatures. Elves and sprites naturally purged what darkness they could, but the forest had knowingly taken some of the evil into itself. Yavimaya had gained a sort of immunity. She bore the memory of Phyrexia and knew its weaknesses.

The final battle for the forest had been waged by woodmen, the folk who had once been Phyrexian. They combined the fanatic power of their heritage with the patient strength of the forest. Eternal defenders. Once the battles were done, woodmen clutched themselves against the vast boles of the forest. They lingered there, immobile for days or weeks. They breathed through leafy stomas and were nourished on sun and rain alone. Herds of arboreal goats passed them unknowing. Wood spiders attached webs to their knobby heads. Should another Phyrexian descend into the forest, though, the woodmen would awaken to slay.

Victory. Multani breathed it in. He had often petitioned Gaea during this war, always receiving a silent but undeniable answer. Now was time for praises, not petitions. Multani spread his mind down into the great tree where he knelt. His consciousness expanded. Individual identity gave way to collective soul, to archetype, to divinity. He took on the body of the forest. Each tree was a single muscle fiber, each vine a neuron in a vast, thankful thought. Before that thought was full-formed, though, an idea intruded.

A perfect creature walked the land. He did not walk Yavimaya but another ancient forest across the sea—Llanowar. A perfect creature, his spirit had been forged in a great red furnace and was tempered in war.

Never had Multani sensed such a creature, not in all the billion creeping things of his forest. Here was a man—an elf—with the relentless perfection of a dream, but he was real.

Gaea, what is this walking vision?

Multani knew he was to be silent and still, to sense this creature in Llanowar across the sea.

Among the watchful blackthorns of Verdura, this perfect one had first appeared. A month ago, he came into being out of midair, trailing the stink of Phyrexian spaces. Out of corruption, he was born incorruptible. Tall, with long silvery hair in numerous braids, steely eyes, and steely armor, the elf was mantled in glistening-oil and blood. Dust clove to him. He fell to his knees. The escape from his former prison had been desperate.

Eladamri was his name, called the Korvecdal in Rath—a uniter among his own people.

Behind him came a woman. She seemed to step around an invisible corner. She was born of the same dark womb as he, but was human. With hair of red flame and muscles corded over a lean frame, she was a child of Phyrexian furnaces. The elf had saved her from the hell where she had dwelt. Her name was Takara, prisoner of Volrath, daughter of Starke.

To Eladamri's other side stood another woman. As weary as her comrades, she did not drop down. A war woman, she kept her weapon—a chain and blade construct called a toten-vec—ready in the pulsing air. Her eyes and hair were dark, her face intense, her frame a taut coalition of muscle and bone. She, too, was an orphan raised in Rath. Wicked parents make monsters of some and heroes of others. This one was a hero, Liin Sivi by name. She would guard her companions to the death.

Gaea, these are not perfect folk. These are heroes, true, but not divinities. This Eladamri is no more pure than a Kavu, parented by leaf and flame in equal measure. This Takara is embittered by long imprisonment. This Liin Sivi—chains and blades are myriad already in Dominaria. What makes these three divine?

He knew he was to keep silent and still and sense them.

Up from Verdura they marched. They sought forest—Llanowar. Travelers' tales told of them. In every village they entered, folk asked them where they had been, how they had come to Verdura. Eladamri told their story, simple and certain. He warned of the hellish kingdom to come, of demons pouring down out of storm clouds, and of cataclysm tearing Dominaria apart. At first, he seemed but a brain-baked fool, wandering in dust with two other lunatics.

Then reports came of demons raining from the clouds over Benalia and Yavimaya, over Zhalfir and Shiv and Keld.

Villagers flocked to Eladamri. If this man had known of the coming monsters, surely he would know how to fight them. Eladamri did know. He told them what to do, how to make arrows that would pierce carapace skulls, how to mix glistening-oil poisons, how to stab all the hearts of a vampire hound. The people listened to every word. When he said he could not linger on the road to Llanowar, they heard that he had a messianic mission there. They followed him. They preceded him. Runners went ahead to the forest kingdoms, telling the glories of the elf who was coming, who had raised an army on the road and who would fight the monsters that came to destroy Llanowar.

Fhedusil, King of Staprion, sent Steel Leaf warriors to intercept this man and his army. Savage-shorn and tattooed, elves crouched at the forest eaves. Past Freyalisean eye-patches, archers watched the man approach.

Eladamri strode sternly. Sweat glinted on his brow. Eyes sparked beneath. Takara lingered at his right hand, allowing petitioners one by one to approach the man. Liin Sivi lingered at his left, keeping back the rest of the crowd.

The Steel Leaf elves emerged from the forest to bar the way. They were immediately surrounded by the believing throng. That is enough to sway most men, but these were elves. In the name of King Fhedusil, they demanded that Eladamri halt his human army and turn them back to Verdura. His followers took great exception.

Eladamri himself did not. He said only this: "May you survive the coming plague." He turned to go.

The Steel Leaf did not allow it. They demanded in the name of the Staprion Elfhame that Eladamri accompany them to see King Fhedusil but that he turn back his human army. Again, Eladamri's followers took exception.

Again, Eladamri did not. He told his followers, "Go to defend your homes. I have an army of my own awaiting here." He gestured into the trees, where Steel Leaf warriors crowded in their multitude, peering through their stylized goggles.

Just now, Multani's senses traveled in the midst of the elf throng. They strode among colonnades of stately trees. They ascended spiral stairways that wound around trunks. Overhead, just beneath proud crowns of green, spread villages and cities of wood, with conic towers and wide-curving plazas, lookout posts and cozy huts. At their center stood the exalted palace of the Staprion Chief.

I must go too, Gaea. I must see this savior of the elves.

Moving across the world was more difficult than moving through Yavimaya. At every edge of the forest, an ocean covered the land.

Multani leaped above the sparkling waves, riding on currents of pollen. The rarefied life of those tiny spores could barely hold him. It was a long leap to the nearest landfall.

Below appeared a great jungle of kelp. Multani swept down out of the pollen, skipping across the plants. Their leaves crowded atop the waves, ten miles of salty respite before he surged again into pollens on the trade winds.

Land appeared ahead, a black line too still to be water. Where there was land, there was green. In a mere thought, Multani reached it. He plunging into cliff-top woodlands as a child into a pile of leaves.

This was not Llanowar. These woods were but scrub on the edge of farmed fields, windbreaks and no more. Still, Llanowar was not far. A patchwork of hickory and sumac led across the undulating fields. Multani leaped through them. He moved with the quick surging motion of water. Beyond were redbud and alder, which led in turn to juniper and fir. Llanowar loomed on the horizon. Multani was there in a moment.

He breathed again. To be among these great trees—this root tangle and colonnade and crown—it was almost like his own Yavimaya. Magnigoth was replaced by quosumic, Gaea by Freyalise, the volcanic Mori Tumulus by the Dreaming Caves, but otherwise, this might have been Yavimaya.

Except that Llanowar had a spirit of its own. Reserved, refined, reticent, the soul of Llanowar stared at Multani through the leaves.

Forgive me this intrusion, honored Molimo—

Why come you here, Multani of Yavimaya? came a thought that was as much accusation as question.

Circling through the bark of one great forest giant, Multani could sense the angry heat in the heartwood. *I come to see this man, this Eladamri.*

As with all outsiders, he is nothing, came the reply.

He is nothing, but Gaea makes something of him, said Multani. *I come at her bidding.* It was only a slight exaggeration.

At the name of Gaea, a troubled rumble came to the great mind of Molimo. *Freyalise rules Llanowar, not Gaea—*

Gaea rules all Dominaria, even if your elves do not know it, Multani replied. *Freyalise is no goddess. She is but a planes—*

Be quick, then, Multani! See what you must. Do what you must, and leave.

Yes, Molimo. As you bid.

Smiling inwardly, Multani continued on his way. Molimo would suffer his presence now because he had no other choice. He would suffer it later when fiends started falling from the sky.

In the time it had taken Multani to skip across the ocean, Eladamri and his entourage had nearly reached the treetops. There was no missing the path he had taken. Every fox shied from the trail of the throng; every coney poked its wondering head out at them. Eladamri marched forward in the company of Steel Leaf warriors and their sleek, shouldering hounds.

Even now, they ascended to the palace of King Fhedusil.

Multani coiled up through vast vines, some as fat as trees elsewhere. He surged to the high court of the Staprion Elfhame.

It was a glorious palace of white wood, grown through complex magics out of the crown of a quosumic tree. The tree's boughs spread wide, an enormous hand holding aloft the palace. Foliage rioted across woodland murals and up tall towers with roofs of living thatch. Green pennants snapped among the leaves. Wide courtyards, hanging gardens, blooming bowers—it was a beautiful court in the treetops. Yavimaya had no such magically constructed halls. An elf from Multani's homeland might have thought it all pretentious, though today it seemed only wonderful.

Multani seeped out into the quosumic's leaves and saw it all.

Eladamri stepped beneath a gate of twining vines and out into the main courtyard. To his right hand walked Takara. Her eyes were hard beneath her shock of red hair. To his left hand strode Liin Sivi, gripping the toten-vec at her waist. All around them marched tattooed warriors. They walked with him as though they were his bodyguards. Their bright-dyed hair made savage gardens around Eladamri. He progressed up the winding way toward the high court.

The doors of the high hall swung wide. More guards, King Fhedusil's elite, stood aside to let the visitors through.

Multani withdrew from the leaves, slid into the living thatch on the roof of the grand palace, and peered down.

The high court within was opulent in shaped wood, inset with gold and silver. At its far end, atop a red rug and backed by a wall of glass, stood a huge black throne. There sat King Fhedusil. Ancient but powerful, the chief had white hair that spiked within his crown. His limbs were thin and long, with the same sinewy strength of tree roots. Across one gnarled knuckle he wore a ring of Staprion nobility.

King Fhedusil gazed, patiently amused, at the man who had been called the Seed of Freyalise.

Eladamri entered the throne room. Takara and Liin Sivi accompanied him, as did a score of Steel Leaf warriors. The rest kept the throng back behind a wall of pikes.

Eladamri approached the king's dais. He motioned for Takara and Liin Sivi to remain behind. They complied, in their own turn holding back their elf escorts. Alone, Eladamri strode to a dense rug of red and blue before the throne. He knelt there in front of Fhedusil.

"I have come to serve you, Majesty."

A querulous look filled the face of the Staprion king. "From all I have heard, I thought you would expect me to bow to you."

Eladamri raised his eyes and stared levelly at the ruler. "I expect nothing of any of you except that you fight when the fiends fall from the sky."

131

Smiling ironically, the ancient elf sighed. "Ah, yes, the prophecies—"

"They are not prophecies. They are only reports. I am not a prophet, only a man who has seen the armies that are coming. In my former world, I united three tribes and led them in revolt against these Phyrexian killers. Here, I do not wish to lead anyone, only to provide what help I may against a common foe."

"Really?" the king responded. "And what sort of help could you be?"

"I can tell you how they will fight. I can tell you that only warriors must remain above. The rest must abandon this palace. It and all other great structures in the canopy will be attacked first."

Multani was impressed. Perhaps Eladamri was not as pure as the elves dreamed him to be, but he was honest and bold.

"Abandon the palace?" echoed the king incredulously. "All go below?"

"Yes. I will stay here with your warriors, but you and the others must go below to survive," Eladamri responded.

King Fhedusil nodded once last. Then he stood. With a simple gesture, he sent his own guard from beside his chair to lay hold of Eladamri. Simultaneously, guards seized Liin Sivi and Takara. The throng beyond the high court fell to a shocked silence.

Into that hush, the king spoke. "It is a black hour for our world, yes, Eladamri. But blacker still when a man who has a sliver of fore-knowledge uses it to rise to the top of a nation. To use a piece of gossip to become a false prophet—"

"I have never claimed to be a prophet," objected Eladamri as he struggled against his captors.

"Perhaps not a prophet, but a war-profiteer," snapped the chief. "You are not the Seed of Freyalise, as has been said of you."

"I dispute none of this," Eladamri pleaded. "I am a warrior, pure and simple. I have been dreamed by these people into something I am not."

Suddenly, Multani understood. The people of Llanowar needed a leader, and King Fhedusil, for all his age and wisdom, would not be sufficient to the task. Gaea had found a man, a sufficient man, and was dreaming him into divinity.

"We are done dreaming," the king insisted. "We are done listening to idle foolery. We will not abandon our palaces in the sky. 'The kingdom of Hell is at hand!' you say. We will not follow you!"

Multani saw it before anyone else. He saw it in the multitudinous vision of the living thatch. Portals opened above Llanowar. Thousands of small portals. Through them dropped tens of thousands of plague bombs.

Sliding down from the thatch into a great branch in one corner of the high court, Multani took form. Leafy brows and bristly lips, twiggy hair and spore-filled eyes—Multani charged into the midst of the assemblage.

"I am Multani of Yavimaya. Listen to this man! Even now, portals open overhead. Fiends are falling from the skies!"

"Guards! Arrest this apparition!" the chief shouted, finger jutting out toward Multani. "Take them to the stockade!"

"We must go below," Eladamri and Multani choroused. Guards dragged at them.

Something tore through the thatch above. Glimpsed in a flurry of straw, it seemed a small meteor, though it was a constructed thing—a spherical machine. The plague bomb smashed down. It cracked the hardwood floor as though it were an eggshell. The bomb struck King Fhedusil, slaying him instantly. It hit the far wall and bashed its way into the king's chambers. A moment of silent terror followed. Then from the hole in the wall, white clouds of plague spores spewed outward.

"Down to the roots! Down from the crown! We must go below!"

CHAPTER 17
The Metathran Pincer

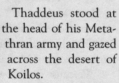

Thaddeus stood at the head of his Metathran army and gazed across the desert of Koilos.

Koilos. This was holy ground. Here the Phyrexians had first been driven out of Dominaria. Here, Urza and his brother allowed them back in. These two events were father and mother to the Metathran—the only parents they would ever have. When Phyrexian bloodlust mixed with Dominarian terror, the Metathran were gestated. Over the last thousand years, they had one by one been born—as strong as rhinos, as tireless as fire ants, as loyal as hunting hounds, as sterile as mules. The Metathran were raised to maturity, trained in weapons natural and otherwise, and stored away like stockpiled arms. In slow-time caverns, temporal loops, and cryo-chambers, they were kept. Chill cradles, these had been, made less so by dreams of this hot desert and the battle over this holy place, Koilos.

Here, the Phyrexians would be driven from Dominaria.

Thaddeus breathed deeply. The dust of Koilos entered his lungs and, from there, his blood. The scent of Phyrexian glistening-oil filled that breath.

In well-ordered companies, the Phyrexian army filled the vast desert below. Scuta, bloodstocks, and troopers stood arrayed on the outskirts, ready for an all-out charge. Behind them lay the main encampments, fortified with miles of trench work. The ditches had been dug by giant Phyrexian worms. Beyond it all was Koilos—a broad, dark plateau of stone above a wide cave. That throat descended into the belly of the world. From it issued a constant tide of monsters. Beautiful monsters.

Thaddeus ached to slay them. He understood and appreciated these foes. Their bodies were as huge and superbly twisted as his own. Thaddeus's own sagittal crest and brow-ridge were designs Urza had modeled after Phyrexian craniums. These modifications made the head a ramming weapon and allowed for powerful jaw muscles that could deliver a severing bite. Thaddeus's face was augmented with stronger bones, leaping muscles, and fangy teeth. His chest and arms bore the powerful benefits of bruin architecture. Equine implants bulged his legs. Thaddeus and his army were as unnatural beasts as the Phyrexians they had been designed to kill. There was but one difference. The Metathran fought for good. The Phyrexians fought for evil. Otherwise, they might have been brothers.

Lifting his hand in a visor over glimmering blue eyes, Thaddeus gazed out beyond even the Caves of Koilos. There, Agnate and his Metathran troops arrayed themselves. Agnate was his true brother. He and Thaddeus were biologically identical, trained together, meant to fight as an opposing pair.

Though a hundred miles of desert and a hundred thousand Phyrexians separated them, Thaddeus could hear his brother's thoughts as if they were his own.

Advance?

Nodding in agreement, Thaddeus lifted his hand in a long arc. "Advance!"

He strode down the desert embankment. His boots pounded the ground. Dusty ghosts rose. In the next moment, forty thousand other boots stepped into the march. The ground trembled under their tread. The tremor rolled down the slope and beneath the feet of the waiting Phyrexians. In their midst, the wave of noise crashed against another wave sent from the army of Agnate. The Phyrexians would be caught in a war on two fronts, in the Metathran Pincer. They would writhe in that claw but never escape. They would die.

Thaddeus marched in the midst of his personal guard—eight warriors, four to either side. Each bore a powerstone pike, which could pierce even thick metal, shred whatever flesh lay beneath, and drag itself clean through. Powerstone swords rode their hips for closer combat. Daggers at their ankles awaited intimate engagements. Similarly arrayed Metathran troops spread all along the front line. They could receive a full-out charge if the Phyrexians made any move.

So far, the monsters remained in their ranks across the center of the desert. They were smart. They did not want to charge up a hill nor to spread the already long front farther. Still, it meant Thaddeus and Agnate ate up easy ground on either side. The noose tightened.

"Halt!" Thaddeus called as they reached the base of the hill, just within stout bow range. "Archers to the fore!"

The shout echoed down the line. The march snapped to sudden stillness. Archers flooded ahead. They formed two lines, front ranks kneeling. From powerful shoulders, they unpacked stout bows that could shoot over a mile. The shafts they nocked were six feet long and tipped with powerstone-chips, devised to seek Phyrexian oil-blood.

"Ready?" Thaddeus called. "Loose!"

Ten thousand bowstrings shuddered. Ten thousand arrows vaulted into the sky. They moaned as they went. Their thick shafts arced hungrily upward. In moments, those huge black arrows were so high they seemed starlings. The shafts reached the heights and descended in a deadly hail. They roared down toward the lifted heads of the tightly arrayed monsters. Soon ten thousand of them would be impaled.

The shafts entered a silvery cloud. In an eye-blink, they dissolved.

"What is it?" Thaddeus wondered aloud.

The silvery cloud rose, following the path the arrows had taken. It arched above the desert and coiled down toward the Metathran army. The swarm shimmered as it came. It descended with the same speed as the arrows.

"Battleflies!" Thaddeus warned. "Lift shields!"

The order shot out among the troops. Thaddeus and his personal guard yanked the shields from their backs and crouched beneath them. The battleflies fell. They cracked against the metal like hail from a tin roof. Where flesh was exposed, the metal wings of the beasts clove. Ears and noses and fingers were severed. Razor wings sliced through brows and imbedded in the skulls beneath. Shoulders were masticated. Metathran who had awakened after five hundred years died in instants. The moments after were filled with jittering and deadly swarms.

Thaddeus reached gauntleted hands out from beneath his shield and crushed battleflies as if they were deerflies. The living Metathran all around did the same. Razor wings fell to the ground. Soon, the swarm had thinned enough that the warriors of Dominaria stood and smashed the killing creatures beneath their boots.

"Forward!" Thaddeus ordered, pointing his sword across the desert.

Leaving their brave fallen where they lay, the Metathran army surged toward their waiting foes. If anything, the lacerations across their tattooed faces only whetted their appetite for Phyrexian blood. Swatting the last few battleflies that followed them, the warriors marched double-time. Pikes and swords ran red. Soon, they would run golden.

"Why haven't they moved?" Thaddeus wondered through gritted teeth.

He suddenly had an answer.

The ground erupted before him. It seemed a volcano had burst from the cracked desert. Dirt hurled out in a pelting spray. In the midst of that fountain of soil emerged something enormous. It had a black hide that jutted hairs as stout and sharp as daggers. A huge mouth, formed of three triangular lips, fronted the gigantic worm.

Chunks of rock turned to sand on those lips and slid inexorably inward. Worse, five more of the giant beasts appeared to either side, extending in a wall before the charging Metathran.

These were the beasts that had dug out the Phyrexian trenches. Now, they would dig out the Metathran themselves.

One of Thaddeus's personal guard, running with sword lifted high, attacked the beast before them. His blade sank into the mucousy upper lip of the thing. The weapon disappeared to the haft. A sucking sound followed. The warrior disappeared with it. That mouth, which could pulverize rock and dust, ground the man inward until he was but a red smear on dark lips.

The worm lurched forward, its daggerlike hairs driving into the ground. A second guard, hewing at the lower lip of the thing, fell beneath the advancing monster. Hairs pierced him in a hundred places. His life gushed out. When the beast landed atop him, he burst open.

Thaddeus roared. He hurled his powerstone pike into the bloody lip of the thing. The weapon bit true. Its head ground muscle to pulp and dragged its way deeper. It dug through lip and oral cartilage. The shaft slipped away after the pike's gnawing head.

"Use your pikes!" Thaddeus commanded.

Three more of the weapons sank in the worm before him. Each pierced and dug and drew itself inward. The beast lunged, bellowing through ruined lips. Hot, bloody breath shot out before it.

Thaddeus stepped back. If this worm were like every other, its brain would straddle its alimentary tube. It was only a matter of time before the pikes reached it.

The worm entered a sudden convulsion. Its head spiked the warriors crowded up beside it. Metathran fell back. The monster sprayed gore as it flopped. All along the line, worms were dying. One by one, they issued last gasps and dropped to stillness.

"Form up!" shouted Thaddeus, dragging a hand across his crimson face. He pointed to avenues between the dead hulks. "Form up! Advance!"

Thaddeus led his troops between dagger-walls. Beyond, the Phyrexian forces still waited. They were cowards, hiding behind battleflies and worms. What would it take to goad them into charging? Perhaps they would simply wait for the Metathran to overrun them. Thaddeus was glad to oblige.

The first flood of Metathran had only just cleared the field of dead worms when movement began along the Phyrexian lines. Their advance line charged.

Oh, but the cowards! They did not send true Phyrexians even now. That line of rushing things—it glinted metallic. Artifact creatures, machines—and what strange machines! They were perhaps four feet long, with a snakelike central body made up of metal nodes in a line. The things scuttled rapidly forward on metallic legs, their tails jutting up like scorpion stingers above them. They seemed mechanical centipedes—simple-looking beasts, with no apparent weaponry except for that barbed stinger. A thousand of them broke from the Phyrexian ranks and undulated forward.

Thaddeus strode to meet them. His powerstone pike was gone, even now chewing its way through the dead hulk of a trench worm. His powerstone sword was out. It gleamed in his hand as he charged. All along the Metathran line, blades flashed.

These creatures did not so much seem centipedes but metallic spinal columns. . . .

The lines converged. With a glad shout, the Metathran met beasts they could at last fight.

Thaddeus did not shout. He was too busy dodging aside. A war centipede launched its stinger at his face. He swung his sword. Steel flashed, striking the giant bug behind the stinger. The blow sparked on hard metal, slid, and caught the soft copper cables that strung them together. With a flash of arcane power, the blade severed the creature's tail from its scaly body. The momentum carried it on. Metal knobs crashed into Thaddeus's chest, knocking him back a pace. Spikes along the centipede's back scourged his shoulder and neck. The artifact creature tumbled in two writhing halves on the ground.

All around Thaddeus, the desert was alive with twitching hunks of centipede. Among them lay many, many slain Metathran. Their mouths had been sliced open, and pulpy blood disgorged from them. The corpses shuddered as if something were crawling through them.

There was no time to see more. Another centipede hurled its stinger at Thaddeus. He was slower this time. Gritting his teeth in determined fury, he dragged his reluctant blade before him. It sliced only air. The beast vaulted over the sword tip and struck Thaddeus's face.

The blow made his vision go white. There was a sharp, strange looseness in his lower lip. Next instant, his sight returned. With it came blood—his own blood—in a crimson cloud.

Wrenching his blade up in desperate defense, Thaddeus hewed the centipede in half. It spun, crippled, in the air and dropped by his feet. Thaddeus chopped at the wriggling thing and managed to slice it into three more pieces.

Dripping, Thaddeus reared upward. His face bled profusely. The centipede had sliced through his lower lip. His gums were cut open, exposing the roots of his teeth. He would heal quickly enough—with hyperclotting, regenerative flesh, and blood storage sacs—but the wound angered him.

Thaddeus lashed out at another centipede but was too late. The thing launched itself at a nearby Metathran. The warrior met the attack with a cry. Darting past his sword, the centipede drove its barbed tail *into* the warrior's mouth. With whiplike legs, it thrust deeper. The warrior goggled in astonishment as the creature wormed quickly down his throat. In moments, the head of the thing clutched the man's severed lips. Eyes going dark, the Metathran dropped to his knees and fell on his face. His body twitched and his mouth gushed pulpy blood.

Why would anyone, even Phyrexians, create such a monstrous machine? There were easier ways to kill a man than to drive a creature down his throat.

A sudden, wet snapping sound came from the fallen man. Grisly spikes popped out of the skin all down his back. The Phyrexian centipede had replaced the warrior's spine. Dead as a slab of meat, the Metathran moved and rose. Horribly, it rose.

"Zombies," Thaddeus managed to splutter through his torn lip.

They were all around him. Thaddeus wheeled. His sword hacked into one of the zombies—a former member of his personal guard. Thaddeus's blade cut a chunk out of the undead warrior's belly, but it was not enough. He stepped back and swung again. The zombie's head bounded free. No blood came, drained already. In the clean cut, Thaddeus could make out the severed esophagus and windpipe and the sliced centipede that had become the warrior's spine!

"Zombies!" Thaddeus shouted in warning to the other Metathran that pressed up behind him. "Slay them!"

The order spread quickly down the line. Living Metathran hewed into unliving ones. These warriors were bred to follow orders, and they did, destroying their former comrades mercilessly. Even so, emotion had not been winnowed out of them, and these warriors, every one, felt the acute dread of the slaughter.

I once believed we were like the Phyrexians, Thaddeus thought, sending the idea across the battlefield to his distant brother. He paused to cleave the corrupted brain of one of his own men. *Now I know how truly different we are.*

There came no direct answer, but Thaddeus sensed that his counterpart agreed. Agnate and his forces even now fought the same horrible, desperate battle.

* * * * *

With a glad heart, Tsabo Tavoc watched the carnage. It was exquisite to feel the plunging rupture of the spine's descent through flesh. It was delicious to wander the dead minds of the spine-grafted Metathran.

There were two of those blue-skinned creatures—two *living* ones—whose thoughts called to each other. It was a simple enough thing for Tsabo Tavoc to reach up and pluck the thoughts from the very air.

Yes, Thaddeus, she purred to herself. You are nothing like us, as you will learn all too soon, all too painfully. In my turn, I will learn it as well. I will parse every tissue of you, Thaddeus of the Metathran.

CHAPTER 18
One Hero Dies, Another is Born

That first moment after the plague machine rocketed into Staprion Palace, the court of Llanowar was paralyzed. Their chief was dead. Their savior was accused of fakery. A strange green man had formed, screaming of fiends from the sky. Then came the plague spores, spilling out on the air.

Only Liin Sivi kept her head. She was used to the solitude of decision. It was a simple thing, really. Rushing the chief's throne, she dragged her toten-vec from her belt. One foot landed on the chair arm and the next on the chair back. She vaulted up the wall. A final toehold on a knothole sent her high enough to hurl out the toten-vec. Chain paid out smoothly, and the blade cut the top corner of an ancient tapestry. The corner plunged beneath her. Liin Sivi rode it like some thief in the Mirage Wars. She kicked the fringe out ahead of her. The carpet spread with beautiful precision over the hole in the wall. It covered the spot, temporarily trapping the plague-spore cloud.

Of course, no plan is utterly perfect. The contagion that had already seeped into the palace was flung outward. It swept across elves. It rolled over Liin Sivi too, though this was an elf plague. While it stung her skin, it melted theirs. Virulence sank into their pores. Flesh reddened and turned gelatinous. Elves melted like wax creatures. They oozed together across the marble floor. Those behind scrambled back and away, trampling others in their haste to escape.

Outside, plague bombs tore through the treetops.

"Flee downward!" Liin Sivi shouted. She saw that her own skin prickled with rash. Striding toward them, she bellowed, "Follow Eladamri downward!"

The green-man shucked quosumic leaves to slip free of the guards that held him. He turned, barging a wooden shoulder against a tall set of double doors. They flung back, barking against the walls of a dark chamber beyond.

"Here, the royal stair! It winds down within the quosumic. It is the safest way."

A guard roared, ramming his spear through the green-man's belly—as useless as stabbing a bush. "Only the king and his guard may descend there."

Eladamri yanked the spear from Multani's gut and bowled the guard over. "The king is dead. We will be as well lest you follow me downward. Come! Swiftly." Spear raised high, he strode through the doorway and down into the lantern-lit gloom beyond.

Still, the folk hesitated.

Liin Sivi snarled, "You heard him!" She whirled her toten-vec. The crowd surged toward the door. They followed Eladamri.

Liin Sivi spotted a shimmering shield hung upon the wall—the enchanted coat of arms of the Staprion royal house. She strode to a chandelier tie-down cord, grabbed the line, and sliced it. A massive chandelier in the center of the chamber plunged. The rope yanked her up along the wall. With one hand Liin Sivi held to the cord as her feet ran up the smooth face. She snatched the shield from its mount. Brandishing the thing overhead, she continued to run up the wall. The rope hurled her to the rafters. Liin Sivi leaped onto a hammer beam and released the cord. A terrible crash came below. The chandelier shattered before the throne. Giving no heed, Liin Sivi climbed the black beams, reaching the thatch. Three chops of her toten-vec opened a hole large enough to crawl through. A fourth allowed the shield to come after her.

Liin Sivi climbed onto the green roof. It was sharply pitched, on all sides merging with the canopy of leaves. Above the shaggy peak, the blue sky was crowded with small portals opening and closing.

As each gate would swell into being, a plague machine would plunge through. No sooner had the bulk cleared the device than it would slam shut again. All across Llanowar, plague machines fell from the skies. They whined in air and crashed through treetops and hammered the boles of the ancient forest. After they struck, plague clouds hissed out on the wind.

Liin Sivi sniffed in annoyance. The gods-damned Phyrexians did not even want to take this forest, only destroy it. Typical. She'd lived her whole life in the shadow of those heartless, mindless, soulless roaches. She knew how they swarmed, and she knew how to stomp them.

One plague machine dropped free of its portal and plunged straight for the rooftop.

With another snort, Liin Sivi rushed up the green slope, shield in hand. If that machine entered the throne room, thousands would die. A direct hit could tear through thick wood, but what of a glancing blow? Staring upward, she vaulted to the peak of the roof. For a moment, she lost the plunging machine in the sun. Lifting her hand to block the light, she still could not make out the death sphere. Its whine grew to a deafening shriek. Only the device's growing shadow told her she stood in the right place. She swung the shield to one side and braced on the king beam of the palace.

A clang like a giant bell sounded. Liin Sivi was crushed flat against the rooftop. The sphere cracked away, whirling to impact a nearby tree.

Rising tremulously, Liin Sivi dragged numb fingers from the shield's handles and shook them out.

Another scream mounted—another sphere plunged. Squinting up into the sky to find her target, Liin Sivi ambled toward the site.

"Damned Phyrexians."

* * * * *

"Damned Phyrexians!" Takara hissed.

She dragged an elf away from the bloody slough where his friends lay—red gelatin and bone. The elf's own legs dribbled away to nothing. Arteries emptied behind him. His eyes rolled one last time—eyes that had seen hundreds of years of peace in Llanowar. They died seeing this.

Releasing him, Takara breathed raggedly. Her fiery hair was pasted to her forehead, and her back ached excruciatingly.

This plague was the worst she had seen, faster, more virulent than other strains. No doubt this contagion had been developed in experimentation on countless Skyshroud elves. Takara herself had been a test subject for the human plague. These tiny motes of elf-virus prickled the large, gray infection across her back.

Yes, Takara was dying of the plague. She had been dying when Eladamri and Liin Sivi had rescued her from Rath. Her companions knew but no one else. They had treated the sore every night, sterilizing it with rye spirits and soothing its ache with aloe. Still, it had spread.

When the bomb hit, Takara's first impulse had been to flee downward with the others. But why? She was doomed one way or another. Up here, she could help a few people before she was eaten away to nothing. Takara wasn't being noble. She wasn't so much saving elves as choosing her own time to go.

Scrambling across the body-strewn floor, she caught up an elf child. The little girl, perhaps no more than two, stood just beyond the shouldering multitude. She screamed. Tears streaked her white cheeks. Takara lifted the girl in her arms and held her tight, whispering comforts into her ears. She did not know this dialect of Elvish but consolation sounded the same in any language.

How like this child she had been. Her father had been a

grotesque little servant of evil. Her home had been red-skied Rath. She had not been alive for even two decades before she was dying of plague—a child screaming in chaos all her life.

"Take her!" Takara demanded, grabbing an elf man who pushed among the throng. "Take her!"

He began to plead, his old eyes filled with mortal fear. This was an elder elf, perhaps a millennial elf, long beyond his century of child-rearing. Still, he reached out for the girl. He cooed, patting her sobbing back. With new purpose, the old elf shoved his way into the crowd.

Through her pain, Takara smiled. If this child was her miniature likeness—screaming in chaos all her life—then saving her was as close as Takara would ever come to saving herself.

She moved back out among the wounded. Any moment another bomb would hit. Then she and everybody left in the chamber would die.

Takara realized with surprise that she would miss Eladamri and Liin Sivi. The three had made a fair team. More surprising, still, she hoped they would miss her too.

* * * * *

Liin Sivi was too slow to deflect the fifth plague bomb. It plunged from the heart of the sun. She knew of it only by the whistle that became a whine and a shriek. The sun was blinding. The shadow of the bomb jittered across the sloped roof. Liin Sivi flung herself beneath that shadow and braced the shield over her head.

The plague bomb struck to one side. It tore through the thatch as if it were air. It smashed the king beam. The roof slumped massively beneath Liin Sivi's feet. A thunderous boom came below, with a brittle, crackling sound. The hiss of the plague spores was unmistakable. So were the shouts of the elves.

The plague hadn't time to kill them, though. One wall of the high court caved and fell inward. A hundred tons of wood toppled in giant killing sheets. Dagger-splinters stabbed down afterward.

The roof buckled and failed. It crashed like a bellying wave.

Liin Sivi rode the green tide. She could do nothing else. Timbers crashed to the floor. Giant knots fell in blood puddings that once had been elves. White, killing spores seeped smoky through every crack. Liin Sivi fell to her knees on the shuddering thatch and braced herself.

The far wall crumpled under the roof's plunging weight. Beams roared as they tumbled over each other. In four sections, the thatch crashed to the floor of the ruined high court.

A sudden quiet filled the air. No more crashing. No more screams. Before Liin Sivi stood the tall doorway where even now the last of the refugees fled. Behind her lay the silent wreck of the high court. Not a single moan came from the tumbled ruin. All the elves had been eaten by plague. There were no humans except—

There she lay, red hair tangled amid thatch. A cracked rafter had run her through, spearing the gray rot that filled her back.

Liin Sivi bowed her head. Takara had been a worthy companion. To die this way, twice killed, in the midst of strangers . . . She'd chosen her time.

"Good-bye, Takara," Liin Sivi said. "You will be missed."

Another whistling shriek mounted above.

Drawing a ragged breath, Liin Sivi strode to the giant doors and entered the resinous darkness within. They made not a sound as they closed over the bright world. Liin Sivi set the bolt and descended after the refugee crews. She descended after Eladamri.

* * * * *

Eladamri led the refugees down the royal passage. No king had been this deep in centuries. No lamps lit the way except those torn from walls higher up. The ragged stairs, carved from dead heartwood, spiraled down around a vast emptiness. A fall would bring death by lance-long slivers on the way down. It was a certainty . . . proven many times over already.

Screaming began above. The refugees knew what that meant. They pressed up miserably against the walls and waited for the body to plunge past. It did, narrowly missing an elf woman and her son. Into the dark pit the man fell. His screams grew hollow. They were interrupted by glancing impacts and ended at last by death.

"Downward," Eladamri commanded softly, leading the way.

In time he reached a region where giant webs had caught a number of the bodies. Eladamri advanced, cutting the gruesome figures free, lest their presence bring hungry spiders.

"What am I doing here?" he wondered under his breath, holding a flickering lantern high to stare at one of the bloodied victims. "Why am I leading these people?"

More screams above interrupted his thoughts. He glared up, clutching the wall. Lanterns showed the spiraling ascent. They lifted to see what came down the shaft. Voices joined themselves to the rolling scream. Something pounded one wall, ricocheted off, descended across the emptiness, and impacted the opposite wall. It struck the folk there, seemed to stick a moment on pulverized bodies, and tumbled downward again.

"A plague bomb!" Eladamri hissed in dread realization.

Once it came to a stop, its panels would open and spew contagion. It would contaminate them all and even the caves below, where they had hoped to shelter. All was lost, unless the contagion could be contained. . . .

Dropping his lantern to the stair, Eladamri swung his sword along the stairway. The blade cut through fat cobwebs. He gathered them in a net in his free hand. Once there were enough strands, he sheathed his sword and experimentally spread the web. His timing would have to be perfect.

If only he were the perfect man he was believed to be.

The plague pod bounded down, followed by a flurry of tumbling bodies.

Eladamri gritted his teeth and flung the net outward. It enveloped the globe. Its sticky bands wrapped around the spore panels in the side of it. The sphere tore past. Eladamri released it, though the clinging strands yanked jealously at his hand. He hunkered down to keep from getting hurled into the void. The racing ball almost ripped his hand off before the strands tore free. Beyond the edge of the stair, Eladamri glimpsed the ball as it plunged away through webs and darkness.

Perhaps the strands would hold. Perhaps the spores would not emerge. Eladamri had done all he could, and it would have to be enough.

Bodies fell past in a wet, conglomerate paste.

Eladamri snatched up his lantern and picked his way farther down the spiraling stair. "What am I doing here?"

* * * * *

Multani moved through Llanowar, awakening great tree spiders. Their webs would save the wood. Their webs and the ingenuity of this Eladamri. There was more to this elf than the man himself realized.

As Multani rushed from tree to tree, mustering the defenders of Llanowar, he felt new power surge into him. It was Molimo. In his reticent and reluctant way, the spirit of Llanowar lent his strength to this foreign spirit. Multani smiled with mushroom teeth. The forest needed champions, mortal and immortal, and it was making them—Eladamri and Multani both.

CHAPTER 19
Bombs for Phyrexia

"There it is, see?" said the blind seer somewhat absurdly. He jabbed a withered old finger beyond the prow rail. Wind tore at his white hair and old robes. "Llanowar."

"Yes," Gerrard responded grimly.

The vast forest spread in all directions beneath *Weatherlight*'s bow. Llanowar's once-green crown was black with Phyrexian corruption. Spidery figures moved en masse through the great canopy. Above, in blue air and white cloud, huge black shapes clustered. From them dropped thousands of bombs. There were no aerial defenders here. With impunity, the monsters rained plague down on the forest.

Gerrard leaned to the prow speaking tube. "Battle stations, everyone. Signal the fleet. Prepare to engage those . . . whatever those ships are."

Turning to the blind seer, Gerrard said, "Thanks for the tip. With Benalia fallen, Llanowar especially will need our help."

"Help them, and help yourself," the old man said cryptically from the shadows of his broad hat.

Gerrard's brow furrowed. "We could have been here hours sooner if we'd been able to find you. Where were you?"

"I live half in truth, half in dream," the man replied evenly. "When I cannot be found in the one, I can be found in the other."

Gerrard sighed, shaking his head as he strode toward the portside ray cannon. "You've wasted time."

The seer took a deep breath and murmured, "I never waste time."

Gerrard strapped himself into his gunner's harness. He powered up the machine and turned it through all three axes. Across the forecastle, Tahngarth did likewise. The two amidships gunners climbed into position. Crew scrambled across the decks and up into the bridge.

Turning in his traces, Gerrard glanced toward the bridge. He saw a familiar figure clamber into the navigator's seat.

"What the . . . !" he hissed, flipping open the speaking tube. "Hanna! What are you doing in there?"

"My job." Her response came curtly through the tube. "You've called battle stations, Commander."

"You can't navigate in your condition."

"Take us up, Sisay!" Hanna called suddenly. "Those aren't ships!"

Gerrard turned about, seeing the black, hovering mass in the clouds. No, they weren't ships. They were nothing at all, holes opening and closing in the sky.

Weatherlight pitched backward and rose. The clustered shapes shrank to a long, thin horizontal line. They seemed the surfaces of lakes, seen on edge for a moment as the ship emerged from below. *Weatherlight* soared higher. Beneath her, the line spread out into a cluster of shifting shapes.

"What are they?" Gerrard asked.

"Portals," Hanna shot back. "Small portals. Thousands of them. They are weak, not like the ones we've seen before. Each creates a mild spacio-temporal distortion. Together, the effect is massive."

Weatherlight vaulted up over the portals. From above, they did not seem so much holes in the fabric of reality as blurred areas, like the wavering of heat energy off gray coals. Beneath those shimmering spots, mechanical spheres hurtled down. They gave out long screams on their descent to the canopy. There, they crashed and spewed disease payloads.

Hanna's voice came again. "They each can transport perhaps a few hundred pounds of material before shutting down. Together, they'll destroy the forest with plague."

That word on her lips made Gerrard angry. He drew a breath and gritted his teeth. "Signal the fleet. Open fire!"

His own gun was the first to bark. Crimson energy burst from the steaming muzzle, as bright as heart-blood and as hot as lava. Gaseous plasma surged out to smash against the field of scintillating spheres. It engulfed a dozen of the small portals and ripped through the spaces between them.

Fire spoke also from Tahngarth's gun, the two cannons amidships, the belly gun, and Squee's artillery at the tail. Lines of power streamed down from *Weatherlight*. The surges were joined by the multifarious attacks of her armada. Hoppers sent orange fire, helionauts blue. Plasma bolts, lightning blasts, disruption fields—energy poured down on the portals.

Gerrard gave a whoop, unloading shot after shot. It felt good to be fighting again, blazing through the invaders.

"It's no good, Commander," shouted Hanna over the speaking tube. "The portals don't exist on this side. We can't destroy them from above. We'd have to fly below and risk plague contamination. Up here, we're just destroying the forest."

Standing in his traces, Gerrard peered down over the rail. The flack of their shot ate through the canopy, vaporizing wood and setting the forest ablaze.

"Cease fire!" Gerrard shouted. "Signal the fleet! Cease fire!"

As his cannon darkened, Gerrard's mood did likewise. How could he fight an enemy he could not shoot? These portals were too small to fly through, too numerous to shut down, too intermittent to predict, too deadly to fly beneath. The Phyrexians had learned how to defeat Gerrard. They had paid in glistening-oil for Benalia, but they had bought it. Now, they would buy Llanowar without shedding a drop.

His voice was heavy as he leaned toward the speaking tube.

"Suggestions?"

"Say again, Commander?" Sisay asked for them all.

"Suggestions. I want suggestions. How can we fight these portals?"

Only silence answered from the speaking tubes. Beneath *Weatherlight*, the glimmering sea of portals slid away. Only the mournful wind and the whine of the fleet's engines spoke in the hush.

"Shall we bring the fleet about for another pass?" Sisay asked quietly. "Or shall we ship for another battle, elsewhere?"

"I don't know," Gerrard replied. "I don't know."

*   *   *   *   *

Orim stood on the poop deck, gazing aft. She had clambered topside in hopes of dragging Hanna from her post. The impossibility of that quest was soon clear. The impossibility of this battle was clear as well.

"Bring us about," Gerrard's voice came sullenly through the tubes. "There must be something we're missing."

Orim shook her head in empathy. She had repeated those same words countless times as she stared at the rot that was killing Hanna. *There must be something I'm missing.* It was Orim's own impossible battle. Without Hanna, how would the ship find her way? How would Orim and Sisay find their way? And Gerrard— he would be utterly lost.

Already, they were lost. The ship roared out above Llanowar, trailing its faithful fleet close behind. They cruised above the field of portals. Not a gun woke fire on those devices. They seemed to form a placid and illimitable sea.

Water. It triggered memories of a far-off place—of Cho-Manno, the Cho-Arrim, and their water magic. When she had left her beloved, she had sworn to take the power of the waters with her. Orim gazed at the shimmering portals. How could she find power in such black waters? If only she could meditate, could draw from the reservoirs within her, perhaps she could find a cure to this plague.

Orim gazed down in desolation on the portals.

Weatherlight stirred a strong, long wake in the portals.

Suddenly, Orim knew. It was a simple thing, the sort of thing Hanna and Sisay would understand implicitly.

Spinning on her heels, Orim rushed to the bridge door. She flung it back and descended.

The cramped room buzzed with activity. Gerrard had arrived on the bridge to consult with Sisay at the helm. Reports poured out the speaking tubes that blossomed here and there: The metallic voice of Karn asked for attack status; the signal officer relayed other ships' queries. Ensigns scrambled up through the lower hatch and back.

Hanna was busiest of all. She worked feverishly at her navigation console. The compass and stylus that walked across a chart of Llanowar dragged telltale lines of red in their wake. Her fingers were knotted in crimson where she clutched her belly wound.

Orim's breath caught at the sight. Blood did not bother her. Its implications did—especially *these* implications. Rushing to Hanna's station, Orim knelt, grabbing her friend's arm.

"Hanna, you have to get below—"

"I can't," she snapped, her voice more exhausted than annoyed.

"You can, once we get rid of those portals."

"Get rid of—"

"We couldn't planeshift to Benalia because of the three portals over it. You said they caused spacio-temporal distortions that shunted us to the side."

"Yes, but what does all this—"

"Our own shift envelope is much stronger than any of these. Even at normal speeds, we leave a wake in the portals below. If we were to—"

"Yes," Hanna said. Despite the horrible pallor of her face, a brief and beautiful flush came to her cheeks. "Sisay! Captain! Take us up!"

Without question, Sisay drew back on the helm. *Weatherlight* responded as though the ship were her own body. Even Karn ceased his questions below, seeming to understand.

Only Gerrard was caught off-guard. He went to one knee and spilled against the bridge stanchions. His face smashed against the bulwark.

Jiggling his head, Gerrard growled out, "What is it? Danger?"

Hanna laughed dryly, "Only for the Phyrexians."

Standing placidly at the helm, Sisay shouted over her shoulder. "What's your plan, Hanna?"

"A nosedive," the navigator returned, "right through the portal sea. We'll see how many we can drag away in our slipstream."

A grin lit Sisay's face. "I like it! Gerrard, you'd better call off the fleet. Tell them to circle and wait for our return."

Clawing his way forward, Gerrard rubbed a lump under his beard. "Wait a minute. What are you three planning?"

"Just the salvation of Llanowar," Sisay said lightly. "More power, Karn." She steered the ship into a near-vertical climb. The air grew thin all around. Clouds dragged away from *Weatherlight*'s raked airfoils. "You asked for suggestions."

With a rueful nod, Gerrard clutched the speaking tubes and barked, "Signal the fleet! Tell them to circle until further orders!"

"That's a dear," Sisay said. "Hanna, how's our position?"

Peering through the sight arrays that jutted above her navigation desk, Hanna replied, "Yaw four degrees port, and let the keel cut for another thousand feet, and we'll be ready for the dive."

"Will we have the velocity for a shift?" Sisay asked.

"Velocity won't be the problem. It's whether we've got time between the portals and the treetops before we crash," Hanna replied easily.

Sisay laughed. "That's the kind of problem I like. Here we go." She shoved the helm hard to fore.

Weatherlight's engines ceased for a moment. She lolled upward in a weightless arc, rolling her stern skyward. Dominaria swept smoothly from aft to fore.

Squee, still strapped to the stern gun, squealed as his feet swept out toward the sun.

Then, greedy and inexorable, Dominaria grasped *Weatherlight* and yanked her down. Creaks ran stem to stern. The prow seemed to stretch away from amidships, and it from bridge and spankers. The airfoils folded tight along the centerline, spilling air instead of grabbing it. *Weatherlight* plunged.

Squee was still squealing. Even so, his view of the skies was not as terrifying as everyone else's view of the land. Llanowar seemed a leopard, crouched to spring.

Weatherlight's engines engaged. Intakes dragged a deep breath. A white-hot column of energy formed within the engine. Fire burst from exhausts. To the ship's terminal velocity came impatient force, ramming it down.

Llanowar sprung. The forest roared up to swallow the ship. Its rot-black treetops groped into the sky. The sea of portals seemed only a slim membrane above that reaching place. In moments, *Weatherlight* would punch through the portals and into the tree-tops.

"Shift to where?" Sisay shouted over the roar of the engines.

"The course is laid in," Hanna called back. "A place in need of Phyrexian bombs."

There was no more time. *Weatherlight* impacted the plane of portals. They swept from prow to poop in a heartbeat. Spacio-temporal stresses clawed across the deck. Bombs, half-emerged, hung in countless portals, too slow to catch up with *Weatherlight*. Squee and the folded wings cleared the portals.

"Shift!" Sisay shouted, staring at the ground as it soared up to meet them.

The ship hurtled all the faster. Wind tore at her rails. The black treetops resolved into individual boughs, and the ruined houses on those boughs, and the running figures among them. A jump-envelope welled out from the forespar. It swept a wide wake, encompassing thousands of portals.

"Shift!" Sisay shouted once last.

An enormous bough rushed up to smash through *Weatherlight's* windscreen—except that no bough remained. Black and green had given way to jittering gray.

Beyond the ship's rail, the envelope rattled. It held back the hissing, glaring emptiness between the worlds. Chaos churned and spun. Nightmare forms reared their heads out of darkness and dissolved again before they were fully created. Lines jagged away in recursive ribbons. There seemed no more horrible place in all the multiverse. . . .

Until chaos transformed at last, solidifying into tortuous Rath.

Overhead, red clouds roiled like boiling blood. Below, red rills coiled like flayed muscle. Arrayed all across those hellish hills were army after army of Phyrexians, waiting to invade.

Weatherlight's planeshifting envelope dissolved around her. Heat and smoke washed over her prow. Airfoils swept out to grab the bitter air. She slowed, leaving in her boiling wake a field of portals.

From those toppling, spinning devices, plague bombs hailed. They fell among the troops arrayed there. Devices meant to slay elves fell instead among the monsters that made them. Many were crushed under the pounding things. Others were mowed down as the spheres bounded across the ground. Bombs rolled to a stop and spewed white spores out across the shrieking hordes.

"Nice work, ladies!" Gerrard shouted, whooping.

Orim was cradling Hanna's bleeding, unconscious figure in her arms. "Get us out of here! Get us back to Llanowar!"

Gerrard staggered across the pitching deck toward the two women. "You heard her!" he rasped out, kneeling before Hanna and wrapping her in his arms. "Planeshift!"

CHAPTER 20
The Fires of Shiv

Tumbling head over heels, Barrin was hurled into the red skies over Shiv. He'd been in the middle of a losing battle in Keld when he was yanked away by alerters—artifacts that sniffed for glistening-oil. They went off massively. A full-scale invasion was beginning over Shiv. The volcanic land was the world's only source of manufactured powerstones. If the Phyrexians captured or destroyed the Shivan mana rig, Urza could not build new machines of war.

Still, it was rude to be literally hauled out of one battle and flung into another.

Barrin righted himself. Brimstone breezes fled into his robes, plucking away the last stink of battle in Keld and replacing it with the stink of Shiv. He gazed at the land.

Here, the flesh of the world was but a fragile crust, suppurating with lava. In every direction lay calderas and smoking crowns, seas of magma, hissing vents, ropy coils of rock, basalt cliffs, gnarls of obsidian, pumice, ash, sulfur. . . .

In the midst of the fiery desolation towered the mana rig. It was a massive, ancient factory, set crownlike on a basalt headstone. A huge dish of metal girded either end of the rig. One wing was anchored into the ground. The other perched on enormous articulated legs over a sea of lava. Atop these dishes, great domes rested. Between them ran a long hall, built up like the porticoed temple of some forgotten god. From the structure, veiny pipes ran down the cliffs and into boiling lava. The tubes conveyed red-hot magma up into the structure, there to turn the heat of the world into powerstones and living metal—weapons to slay Phyrexians.

A massive portal—larger than those at Benalia, Zhalfir, Yavimaya, or Keld—gaped wide in the sky. The first three Phyrexian cruisers advanced from the darkness. Shiv painted their bows red. Each ship was the size of the mana rig. Hundreds more crowded behind.

"Where is Urza?" Barrin hissed, yanking the alerter brooch from his sleeve and hurling the blazing thing away.

As if in answer, the air beside Barrin shimmered. A creature formed itself from spectral winds. Urza's gemstone eyes glared out of his materializing skull. The figure grew an armored war-stole, done up in gleaming sigils. A shaft of radiance formed in his hand. It became a great war-staff. Urza lifted his other hand, grasped the blazing brooch on his own sleeve, and vaporized the thing.

"Glad you could make it," Barrin said with quiet irony.

Urza lifted an eloquent eyebrow. "Exigencies of war and all that."

Barrin gestured outward. "Here's an exigency for you."

Nodding solemnly, Urza said, "The Metathran ships are en route. Until they arrive, it's you and me, friend. We cannot hope for goblins and Viashino to stand against—"

"Look!" Barrin said, pointing toward the emerging ships.

The three cruisers blazed with sudden flame. Giant fire dragons swarmed the ships, breathing destruction across them. Huge though they were, the wyrms seemed small against the black vessels. Still, there were hundreds of serpents. Their wing beats flung back bolts of black mana. Their fangs crunched Phyrexian crews. Their incendiary breath was only augmented by glistening-oil. Flames belched from their mouths and spattered across the hulls of the great ships. Rails melted. Conduits ruptured. Engine cells cracked.

"Rhammidarigaaz," Barrin said wonderingly as he watched the leader of the fire drakes. A millennium ago, the young male had fought beside Urza and Barrin in a war with angels. Indeed, Barrin had ridden him into battle. Today, ancient and huge, Darigaaz would fight beside them in a war with devils. "He has mustered his people."

"A boon, yes," said Urza, "but they will not be enough." He pointed beneath the ships.

Dragons, mantled in black goo, plunged from the skies. Some struggled all the way down before crashing on lakes of fire. Others were dead even before they fell, ripped in half by ray-cannon blasts or eaten away by corruption-machines. Alone, these dragons could not destroy the ships. They would be slain, every last one.

Rhammidarigaaz saw the futility. He trumpeted a call and led his folk in a peeling dive away from the ships. Scores of dragons followed in a coiling ribbon. Leathery wings bore them away from killing fire.

Burning and trailing smoke, the cruisers slid unimpeded through the portal.

"Now it is up to us, my friend," Urza said grimly.

Side by side, the master mage and the planeswalker soared toward the emerging ships. They readied sorceries and summonations, energy flickering across their war robes. Barrin lifted his sleeves, evoking blue sparks in swarms around his hands. Urza's war staff beamed with crackling lightning.

One thing bothered Barrin, though. Darigaaz would not have committed his folk to so deadly an attack only to break off moments later . . . unless he were buying time or creating a diversion to mask some greater effect. . . .

Movement below caught Barrin's eyes. Panels atop one of the mana rig's domes shifted aside and slid down into pockets. Barrin knew the facility intimately. There had never been such roof sections when he'd worked it.

. . . creating a diversion to mask some greater effect . . .

Barrin swept his arm out against Urza's chest, intending to halt him. The mage's hand swam with blue sparks, which rattled out across Urza's figure, delivering myriad shocks. The mistake would have killed a mere man. Urza was not even close.

Eyebrows smoldering, the planeswalker said, "What is it?"

"Something's happening below," Barrin said, indicating four huge tubes that jutted slowly up from gaps in the mana rig dome. "An attack of some sort. It might prove deadly to fly into the path of such—"

Barrin's explanation was made moot. Lava erupted in four boiling columns from the tubes. This was no flare of simple vulcanism but focused geysers of the stuff. As straight and hot as new-forged steel, the liquid rock stabbed skyward.

One fountain of spray rose just before Barrin. He and Urza fled reflexively back but not before the column had evaporated their beards. Barrin's robes actually burned. Urza's war-stole only smoldered.

As if in repayment for the shocking touch, Urza grasped his burning friend. Water suddenly drenched Barrin's clothes and hair. He flipped soggy locks backward and scowled his thanks.

The lava jet that had briefly ignited them rose to its peak. It arced over and rained molten rock down atop the lead cruiser. Fires flared on the ship, and subsequent explosions threw away some of the lava. More lava piled on. Sections of hull melted and caved. Phyrexian crewmembers rushed to shovel the stuff. They burst into spontaneous flames and exploded. Their carapace and bone became shrapnel, killing those who came after. Phyrexians popped like corn.

The sheer weight of molten rock overloaded the ship's engines. It listed, its port side slumping in a succession of jolts. The ship fell into a banking spiral. Turning and slipping, spewing smoke and dripping lava, the cruiser corkscrewed down. A roar mounted up. Steam hissed from ruined engines. Countless seams failed. The cruiser augered into a rubble field.

The other two ships had suffered similarly under the lava bombardment. One shuddered as its power core went critical. It exploded in a fireball, flinging scrap and bone, magma and muscle in a star burst. The concussion made the world leap. Visible waves of force rolled in spheres out from the blaze.

The third craft had already been cruising downward when the blast cracked the sky. Waves of force flung it faster to ground. It came down across a volcanic ridge and cracked like an egg. The prow fell down one side of the ridge and the stern down the other. Both sides flared in cross-section. Scabrous figures leaped out of them.

Other creatures, hidden in the rocky crevices, emerged. They seemed crocodiles attacking prey. They lifted war clubs and axes, bringing them down on Phyrexian backs. Savagely, they slew the invaders. Savagely, they hurled the dead into hissing cauldrons. Their bodies flared a moment and were gone. What few monsters escaped the slaying lizard men were swarmed and mauled by other defenders—scrubby and small.

Barrin nodded, impressed. "It looks as though the Viashino and goblin tribes are well prepared for this battle." He rubbed a non-existent mutton chop. Curls of scorched hair came off on his fingers. "As long as the rig can shoot columns of magma, cruisers and plague engines haven't a chance. Perhaps our meddling is not needed."

"The Phyrexians have more tricks up their sleeves," Urza said, seeming almost affronted by the rig's successes. He blinked in concentration and regrew his burned goatee.

He was right. Next moment, the gaping black portal poured out squadrons of smaller, faster ships—rams and dagger-boats and dragon engines. They seemed a waterfall, cascading with hungry speed from the hole in the sky. In mere moments, they would crash down on the rig below.

"Intercept!" Urza shouted. He winked out of existence.

"You could have taken me," Barrin groused to the empty air. From the dark corners of his mind, he dragged out his last teleport spell. It was a blue sorcery, but there wasn't a thimbleful of water in a hundred square miles. Drawing on his memories of distant Tolaria, Barrin charged the spell. Space folded around him and opened again.

Barrin was suddenly beside Urza. They both floated just above the mana rig's aerial dome. Phyrexian ships plunged toward them.

Urza was already unloading his arsenal. Rockets leaped from his gauntlets. They shrieked upward and smashed head-on into the plunging craft. Each rocket drilled deep into its target before detonating. Dragon engines and dagger-boats turned to fire and shrapnel. Ship after ship exploded. Through smoke and fire, more vessels fell.

The ram engines were harder kills, almost solid metal. Urza's rockets could only dig small divots in them.

Barrin turned their strength into weakness. He produced a Serran tuning fork from the folds of his robes, summoned the mana of far-flung fields, and struck the fork on his battle staff. It rang, its tone absolutely pure. The sound doubled and trebled, rising incorruptible to the ram ships above. It spread through solid metal and shook every fiber. The ships rang like giant bells. Cracks raced through them. Shuddering, they disintegrated into iron filings.

Still, more ships plunged from the sky.

Flinging fireballs and firestorm phoenixes, shatter spells and immolations, Barrin and Urza dissolved the engines before they could reach the rig. The sky was full of flame and smoke. Molten metal rained down all around. The fight was intoxicating—all too intoxicating.

While Barrin and Urza fought a falling sky, a new threat arrived. As silent and smooth as a black shark, a Phyrexian cruiser nosed up beside the mana rig. Its plasma cannons lit.

Fire stabbed into the rig. Walls split, walkways peeled away, stanchions collapsed.

The cruiser's black-mana bombards hurled corruption.

Thran metal sloughed and buttresses failed.

"There!" Barrin shouted through the firestorm.

Spells lashed down from the planeswalker and the Tolarian mage. Lightning scrambled across the cruiser, cracking armor. Fiery stones hailed over the hull. It wasn't enough.

Phyrexian cannons and bombards kept up their killing fire.

A whistle overhead announced that a pair of flaming dagger-boats had slipped past the spell work. Side by side, they plunged to impact the dome of the rig.

Twin explosions ripped the roof. The dome shuddered and sank. Half of the facility slumped toward the cliff's edge.

"It's no good!" Urza shouted as he pulverized a dragon engine. "They're breaking through!"

The dome and the central colonnade cracked away from the rest of the rig.

"They're destroying it!" Barrin roared. Spells stormed up from his fingers.

The loose sections of the rig did not fall from the cliff, though. Instead, they rose on vast, articulated legs. The dome wasn't failing. It was separating to fight on its own. It seemed a huge praying mantis. Massive legs lashed out from beneath it. They caught hold of the cruiser's prow and yanked it brutally downward.

The Phyrexian ship plunged. Its bow cracked against the basalt cliff. Metal buckled and shrieked. Boulders calved from the outcrop and poured down atop the cruiser. One massive stone fell like a fist on its bridge, collapsing it. Sparks and smoke spewed from tortured metal. The ship slid downward. Its hull ground against the cliff as it fell. With each impact, chunks of armor broke away. They tumbled separately into the lava and caught fire. Then the whole wreck splashed in crimson oblivion.

"Impressive!" Barrin shouted.

"Yes," Urza replied through the spell storm. "But until the portal is closed—"

Boiling rock suddenly mounted up from the lava tubes behind them. Barrin flung Urza and himself away from the eruption. Air turned to steam in anticipation. The sweat in Barrin's pores hissed out. His clothes reignited. Pillars of fire hurled past.

Lava rolled heavenward, crashing through the remaining ships and splashing higher still. It gushed into the throat of the portal. It filled the gigantic device like water in a shallow hole. Puffing smoke, the portal slammed shut.

Ruined ships plunged, tearing away from each other and driving themselves like spikes in the volcanic hillsides. Where they struck, they punched holes to the hot core of the mountains. Out oozed lava.

Suddenly, there was stillness. The portal was gone. The Phyrexians were gone. Only hellish Shiv remained.

His goatee having burned away for the second time in one hour, Urza snorted. "I seem to have underestimated the rig's preparedness."

Barrin beamed as he patted out the flames on his robes. "Congratulations are in order."

"Congratulations," Urza said flatly.

"Not for me," Barrin replied with a laugh. "For the head of the rig, your former student—Jhoira."

Urza nodded, drifting down toward what was left of the mana rig. The section that had broken loose now ambled over the rocky ridges of Shiv. It seemed almost a guard dog, spoiling for a fight.

"I thought I knew everything about this rig."

"Me too," Barrin said with a wry shrug. "Jhoira seems to have taught it a few new tricks. By the way, you might like to fix your goatee before you see her again."

An irritable whoosh rushed over Urza, restoring beard, brows, hair, and robes to their impeccable best. He looked scornfully at the burned-out mage.

"What about you? Have you any laundering spells? Any darning sorceries?"

Spreading charred robes, Barrin replied, "Not on me. What you see is what you get."

Urza nodded silently, grinding his teeth. The two drifted down, watching the lava tubes retreat into the dome of the rig. Plates slid from their pockets and slowly crept back over the openings. With a rattle and clank, they settled in place.

Barrin and Urza dropped down among the towers of the facility. The flying sorceries released them. Boots came to rest on an arched balcony of smooth metal. Stately robes and tattered rags settled.

Barrin sighed as he felt the warm solidity of the metal beneath his feet. "Where do you suppose we will find Jhoira?" he wondered aloud.

"Right here." The voice came from a tall archway of interlaced metal. Within it stood Jhoira herself. Forever young, the dark-haired, dark-eyed Ghitu woman wore work coveralls and an over-loaded tool belt. She also wore a sardonic expression. "I thought you'd show up for the fireworks."

"Very impressive, my dear," Barrin said genuinely, approaching her. He held his arms out. "Do you mind a little dirt?"

Jhoira embraced him. "Never have," she said into his ear. "It is good to see you, Master Barrin."

"And you, Jhoira," he replied. "It is also good to see what provisions you have made for the defense of the rig."

"I had some help," Jhoira said, gesturing behind her.

Through the metal archway came a huge, robust figure. The dragon walked upright on powerful talons, balanced by a lashing tail. A talismanic belt and neckpiece were the only clothes he wore on his scaly belly, though his wings hung behind him like royal robes. Horns rose in a manifold crown from his ancient face.

"Darigaaz!" Barrin said happily.

Jhoira coughed into her hand. "Lord Rhammidarigaaz of the Shivan Fire Dragons."

"Of course," Barrin replied, bowing low. "Thank you, Lord Dragon for the valiant aid of you and your folk."

In a voice like rumbling rocks, Darigaaz replied simply, "This is my home."

Urza bowed to the dragon as well. "Shiv is your home, and Dominaria is home to all of us. We hope we can count on your aid in defense of the world at large."

The dragon seemed almost to smile. "I have already begun such efforts. I am gathering the dragon nations. We will fight for Dominaria."

"Excellent," Urza said. He turned to Jhoira. "You have done well, my dear. Remarkably well. But this isn't the last Phyrexian attempt on Shiv. I trust you have made arrangements should the Phyrexians appear beyond the reach of your lava tubes."

"She has indeed," came a new voice. Teferi stepped from the shadows of the arch. The lithe, spark-eyed man walked easily to

Jhoira's side. He bowed to each of his former masters. "Shiv will not fall into Phyrexian claws. I will save it, as I saved Zhalfir."

Urza strode suddenly forward. He breathed—a sign of concentration—and his visage reddened. "You cannot take away this rig. It is mine."

"It belonged to the Viashino before you, and to the Thran before them," Jhoira said. "Besides, we are not taking your rig. We are taking Shiv. We are saving my home."

"You would deprive us of powerstones? Thran metal?"

"No," Jhoira responded, stepping between the two planeswalkers. "We will leave you the mobile portion of the rig. Even now, it crawls away to a safe distance. It will remain for you to use. This portion, here, and all of our homes, though—these will go with us."

"You are dooming Dominaria," raged Urza.

Teferi shook his head placidly. "No. You are the one doing that, my friend."

Urza's eyes blazed. The Might and Weakstones showed clearly. "I will *save* our world."

"You do not promise that," Teferi said. "You have promised only to destroy the Phyrexians, whatever the cost. Our homes will not be part of the cost."

"You will not take this land! I forbid it!" Urza roared.

Teferi shrugged. "Forbid if you wish. Even now, we are phasing out. A planeswalker cannot step through time, Urza. Unless you leave now, and take Barrin and Darigaaz with you, you'll be stuck here with us for dozens or hundreds of years. It is your choice."

Urza quivered, speechless.

"Now, masters," Jhoira said. "Leave now or be trapped for centuries. Good-bye."

"Good-bye, Jhoira, Teferi," Barrin said. "Fare you well."

Without a word, Urza angrily clutched Barrin's hand and Rhammidarigaaz's claw. The three stepped away from the rig. They plunged into the Blind Eternities.

CHAPTER 21
Big Game Fishing on Rath

"Prepare to planeshift!" Gerrard called, kneeling with his arms around Hanna.

The navigator lay unconscious just beside her console. Her stomach wound wept blood.

Orim worked diligently over her, laying hands on the site. Silvery sorcery enveloped her fingers.

"My magic hasn't worked before on this plague, but . . ."

Sisay stood nearby at the helm. She steered the ship through Rath, up and away from the Phyrexian troops they had just bombed.

"We need a navigator to planeshift."

"Damn," Gerrard growled. He flipped open the speaking tube above Hanna's desk. "Karn, lay in a planeshift back to Llanowar."

"It'll take him time," Sisay warned.

"Stay high, then, and let's hope these bastards haven't got any airships close by."

"Ships spotted!" Tahngarth shouted from the starboard bow gun. "A squadron of fighters—perhaps two score!"

With back-swept wings and blazing ray cannons, the Phyrexians came on. Deadly shafts of energy ripped out from the converging fighters and flashed all around *Weatherlight*. One beam tore through the starboard rail just beside Tahngarth. It gouged a groove across the forecastle, vaulted through the air amidships, and clipped the helm.

"Evasive!" Gerrard called.

"Yes, yes! Of course, evasive!" Sisay snapped. She rolled the wheel hard to starboard.

Weatherlight listed. Rath's sultry winds crashed against the turned keel and spilled up both gunwales. Her manifolds sucked hot air. Engines struggled to grip the wind. Another volley of ray fire flashed past. A bolt caught the hull just beneath the main engine, burned through the bilges, and boiled a barrel of wine in the hold. Had it not been for that merlot, the beam would have cracked the power core. As if sensing its near demise, the engines surged, hurling *Weatherlight* back the way she had come.

The ship vaulted angrily up from the turn, finding herself in sudden and lethal company. Phyrexian fighters swarmed her. They jagged, their wings as sharp as claws. Squee at the aft gun flung ray fire at them. Most of the glowing flack slid past, tumbling in air. One fighter was too slow. Squee blasted it. The ship skipped and flared. It plunged to cut a long furrow in the flowstone below.

The Phyrexians returned fire. Their guns blazed. Rays leaped after *Weatherlight*, eating through the skin of her airfoils.

"Tuck those things, Karn," Sisay shouted, "while we've still got them to tuck!"

The wings folded with an angry snap like ladies' fans. The engine roared to keep the ship aloft. It rocketed above Rath's rolling rills. For a moment it left behind the swarm of ships.

The sudden jolt of speed made Tahngarth growl in his traces and cling to his gun. Wind ripped at his eyes. The bull-man gave a whuff of breath. He gazed blearily beyond the rail. The plague portals flashed past. They still rained bombs down on the Phyrexian troops. Tahngarth's lip curled into a sneer, which disappeared a moment later.

"They're not dying!" Tahngarth shouted in the speaking tube. "They're not even being eaten away. The plague has no effect on Phyrexians!"

Sisay's voice rang irritably through the tube. "No more bad news, Tahngarth!"

The minotaur's eyes grew wide. "Bad news, Sisay! More ships. A whole armada. Dead ahead."

Sisay stared beyond *Weatherlight*'s thundering bow. There, ships spread in a thick blanket above the ground. They rose gradually into a great black shaft. The flying machines seemed a horrid tree joining the red ground to the coiling heavens. There were tens of thousands of ships.

"Gerrard! I need you at your gun!" Sisay shouted.

Still crouching beside the navigation console, Gerrard replied, "Hanna needs me here. Turn the ship!"

"Yes, yes, evasive!" Sisay retorted through gritted teeth. She muttered, "*You* try evasive action with folded airfoils and no navigator." A dark smile spread across her teeth. "Here's your evasive action!" She shoved the helm forward.

Weatherlight dived above the ragged hills. Her pursuers closed in at her flanks. Red shots ripped her hull. Heedless, the ship clove into a narrow trench in the hillside.

The fighters swarmed down after. The lowest ship miscalculated. A gnarl of stone rose fistlike to smash against its belly. The craft bounced. It spun, spitting sparks, and cut through a neighboring fighter. The other ricocheted off rock, impacted the far side of the ravine, and rattled back and forth for a mile more. The remaining ships, thirty-some, crowded into the turbid slipstream of *Weatherlight*. Bolts of cannon fire charged the air. They tore struts and wing panels and glass from *Weatherlight*.

"Dat no good. Squee show you turds!" Squee shouted.

He fired. The beam sank directly into a fighter's forward intake and was sucked into the engine. It produced a sudden burst of speed, ramming the craft into the fighter before it. Both fighters blew up from the inside out.

At the helm, Sisay smiled. She lofted *Weatherlight* over the sudden terminus of the rift. Phyrexian fighters impacted the rock wall—one, two, three, four. Admiring her handiwork, Sisay steered the ship across the plateau beyond.

Weatherlight soared beneath the Phyrexian fleet. There was little room between the cruisers and the rumpled ground. Had *Weatherlight*'s airfoils been extended, they would have scraped ships and soil both.

Some score of Phyrexian fighters pursued her into the gap. The tight confines forced them to fan out in *Weatherlight*'s trail, bringing them into range of the amidships guns. Bolts jabbed back. Twice, plasma stole Phyrexian ray fire from the air. A third time, the energy smashed into a fighter, limning every console of the ship and igniting the bones of its pilot. They glowed through muscle and shell until the cooked monster slumped in its seat. The ship plunged. The fighter's wing man, distracted by the fireball blossoming below, steered too near a cruiser's landing spine. The massive metal rammed through the cockpit and scooped its pilot out in mush. The fighter spun around that pivot thrice before falling and exploding.

Most of the small ships clung tight to *Weatherlight*'s stern. Their fire stabbed viciously outward. It punched holes in the stern castle, vaporized sections of hull, and tore away lengths of rail. A particularly well-placed shot destroyed the starboard gun amidships.

Sisay hauled hard on the helm. The prow angled toward the ceiling of Phyrexian cruisers. They were stacked to the skies. It was precisely the sort of obstacle course Sisay needed. She stood the ship on end. *Weatherlight* spiraled in her ascent. She roared past the starboard hull of the first cruiser. *Weatherlight*'s port gun amidships flared, cutting a line up the superstructure.

Engines shrieking, the fighters followed the rocketing craft. Half of them did not survive that first swerve, impacting the black belly of the cruiser. Eight explosions in a line gutted the hull there. Even as the cruiser dipped, spewing soot, the other fighters vaulted past, higher into the stack of war vessels.

Among massive hulls, Sisay steered. The ship climbed with furious speed. Fire and black mana awoke from Phyrexian cruisers. The shots were late, missing *Weatherlight* but blanketing the fighters in her wake.

Screaming, *Weatherlight* shot to the top of the column. En route, she scraped away another five fighters. As Sisay rolled the ship into a level orientation, she smiled.

"Not bad flying, if I do say so myself." She sent *Weatherlight* in a stooping dive, falcon-swift, pulling clean away from her pursuers.

"Dem big ones comin' behind us!" shouted Squee through the tubes.

Cruisers drew away from their aerial stack, edging into *Weatherlight*'s trail.

"How's that planeshift coming, Karn?" Sisay called.

The silver man's voice rumbled like distant thunder. "Planeshift whenever you are ready."

"Wait!" Orim shouted suddenly where she tended Hanna. "First take us low. Strafe those Phyrexian troops!"

Gerrard stared incredulously at her. "What?"

"I've got an idea for a cure. I've got an idea to save Hanna."

"Take us low!" Gerrard commanded.

* * * * *

Her healing magic could not combat this damned plague. Spellwork had only fizzled hopelessly from her fingers, unable to sink into the wound and purge its blackness. Still, she had tried, clinging to stanchions and seats as the ship rolled through her courses. How like the Phyrexians to devise a contagion that destroyed all flesh but their own.

"All flesh but their own," Orim had whispered in realization as she hunched above Hanna and Gerrard. "All flesh but their own!"

If she could only harvest some of that Phyrexian flesh, immune to the effects of the plague, she could extract from the monsters' blood the immunity factor. She could distill it, make of it a serum that would grant immunity to anyone.

"Planeshift whenever you are ready."

"Wait!" Orim shouted suddenly where she tended Hanna. "First take us low. Strafe those Phyrexian troops!"

It had taken little convincing to win Gerrard over, only two words—"cure" and "Hanna."

"Stay with her here," Orim said, giving Gerrard's hand a squeeze. Her fingers left a bloody print on his knuckles. "She needs you. I can't help her here, but up there," she nodded toward the prow, "I can."

Weatherlight dipped into a steeper dive, bringing Orim easily to her feet. It felt as though some divine hand lifted her, urging her to the fore. Clutching the bridge rail, Orim found her way out onto the deck. Beyond the glassy confines of the bridge, *Weatherlight*'s plunge was a dizzy thing. The crimson sky sucked its muscular belly up away from the roaring craft. The scarlet ground swelled up to engulf it. All across the heaving world, Phyrexian troops waited, rank on rank, prepared to march.

Behind *Weatherlight*, massive war cruisers broke into pursuit.

Leaning into the terrific motion of the craft, Orim strode from amidships to the forecastle. With each step, *Weatherlight* dropped away beneath her. She felt she was lunging forward across a cloud. She reached the starboard bow gun and the irate minotaur strapped to it.

"I need you, Tahngarth. Hanna needs you."

He tossed his hands up in submission. "Yes. I can't draw a bead on ships behind us." Yanking at the buckles and straps, he disentangled himself from the harness. "We ought to be shifting any moment now."

Orim shook her head, wind jingling the coins braided in her hair. "Not until we perform one task." She motioned him to follow. They came to the capstan. "We've got to release the anchor."

"Release the anchor?"

"Just a big fish hook, and we're trolling for big fish," Orim said. "I need to get some Phyrexians. They've got a cure for this plague in their blood."

Without another word, Tahngarth shoved the locking lever.

The capstan whirled. Chain paid out. *Weatherlight*'s weighty anchor plunged from her prow.

Orim watched as it dropped. Fifty feet, a hundred feet, a hundred fifty. "Good!"

Tahngarth threw the lever. Cams squeezed the capstan wheel. Ratchets clicked, slowing and stopping the chain. The anchor jolted to a halt, swinging above the ranks of Phyrexian troops.

"Excellent," Orim amended as Tahngarth came up beside her. She turned, signaling Sisay to ease the ship lower. *Weatherlight* dipped gently, bringing the anchor down into the enemy army. Orim signaled to hold altitude.

The anchor skimmed just above the heads of armored scuta. Beyond them stood Phyrexian troopers. The anchor struck one of their heads and spattered it. Bell tones followed as the rest of the contingent were struck. The arms of the anchor dragged parallel lines of destruction through the ranks, but no beasts caught on its flukes. The impacts drove it back on its chain.

"We've got to go lower," Orim said.

"If we grip land, the ship will rip in half," Tahngarth noted.

Orim scanned the fields ahead and then signaled Sisay lower. *Weatherlight* swooped down. The anchor trailed under her keel. It twirled about its shank. The flukes spun like drill bits. Into the troops they descended. It ripped into them, stabbing, cutting, grinding, macerating. Hundreds of Phyrexians were torn to tatters by the spinning thing.

"Quite a weapon," Tahngarth approved.

"I need whole bodies," Orim said flatly.

The stock cracked against a boulder, flinging the anchor up to clang against the belly of *Weatherlight*.

"This isn't working," Orim growled.

"Wait," Tahngarth said, "look."

Striking the ship had stilled the anchor. With slow, easy motion, it swung down into the Phyrexian troops. Its bills impaled a pair of Phyrexians, driving the flukes through them and out the other side. The two beasts squirmed on the throats of the anchor while a third and a fourth were impaled.

"Pull up!" Orim shouted, motioning to Sisay. "Pull up!"

Weatherlight soared up from the tumbled plains. The anchor followed it skyward, bringing four impaled Phyrexians. Tahngarth shoved a pin into the capstan and leaned against it. Orim set her own pin and lent her back as well. Two other crewmembers saw the need and helped.

A massive bolt of black mana soared overhead, narrowly missing the ship and crashing into a hillside below. The charge ripped a deep chasm in the land.

Five cruisers pursued *Weatherlight*. The foremost ship sent another mana blast.

A barely perceptible wave spread from *Weatherlight*'s bowsprit through the air. The jump envelope enwrapped her and the four Phyrexian captives jolting up her side. It spread from stem to stern and closed just before the black mana blast arrived. Rath folded up and slid away, leaving only the hissing space between worlds.

CHAPTER 22
The Web of Tsabo Tavoc

Agnate was stalled out. He and his forces battered an immovable wall of Phyrexians. The front was a slaughterhouse.

Metathran blood—vermilion from the air that suffused it—crazed across the ground in ankle-deep puddles. Higher than ankles it rose, up armored calves, past massive thighs and powerful stomachs. The Metathran were baptized in their own blood.

They gave as good as they got. Power-stone battle-axes flocked in the sky, darted like eagles, and cleft Phyrexian heads.

With Metathran blood mixed the humors of Phyrexia. Glistening-oil, gray matter, orange acid, black venom, pink lymph, yellow bile—the Metathran had cloven every tissue and organ in the vile monsters. They had cut their way straight through but could gain no ground for all of it.

"Forward!" Agnate growled as he hauled his battle-axe down from overhead.

The blade chunked through a scuta's cranial shield. It found paste within—only a shallow layer of vestigial nerve. The axe bit deeper, sliding between bony plates. It macerated white-matter but did not stop the scuttling beast. There were no pain receptors in the organ, and the motor cortexes lay deep beneath the knobby crest. The scuta drove on, a gigantic horseshoe crab, and rammed Agnate.

He fell atop the scuta's skull shield. Blood-slick, he would have slid down to be picked apart but for his axe. Yanking on the haft, Agnate climbed the beast. He kicked a foothold in the vestigial face. Agnate rose and chucked his axe free.

The scuta bucked, struggling to throw him off. Agnate crouched and caught a handhold in the bony wound. He swung his power-stone axe again. It clove into the thing's head. Metal stuck in bone. It was just what he wanted. Gripping the axe haft with both hands, Agnate hurled himself off the beast's back. He hauled hard on the weapon. The axe quivered in the bony cleft but did not pull free. Agnate's weight flipped the creature. Its thin legs lashed the air, struggling to roll over.

This was how you killed a pill bug.

Since his axe was mired beneath the beast, Agnate drew his sword. He hacked between the rows of legs. Viscera within fountained black. Legs spasmed in agony. Agnate struck again, slicing through flesh and straight back to grind along the skull shield. A final attack divided the wriggling beast in half. Agnate strode through the severed middle. He reached through streaming muck and yanked his axe out.

It was a victory, hard-won, but Agnate had not gained an inch of ground for it. Scuta lay all around. In their midst lay dead Metathran. What good was such slaughter?

Hewing a Phyrexian trooper, Agnate sensed sudden jubilation. He lifted his head above the horrible tumult and saw a glorious sight.

Thaddeus and his command core had broken through. They ran in a thick pack through the inner ranks of the Phyrexian soldiery, killing as they went.

Agnate's growls turned to cheers. He could kill forever in this awful battle if only Thaddeus could advance.

The charge was glorious. Thaddeus ran at the head of a hundred of his best fighters.

Most of the warriors were members of his personal guard. They had survived the trench worms, spinal centipedes, and Metathran zombies to charge beside their commander. Others were fleet-footed grenadiers who pulled hand-bombs from their shoulder sashes and hurled them in their line of charge. They paved the way with shattered hunks of Phyrexians. The rest were heavy infantry—massive Metathran bred with extended shins, knee caps, pelvises, and ribs, so that their own bones formed subcutaneous armor.

In addition to the Metathran fighters were Urza's war machines. Tolarian runners loped like metal emus and shot exploding quarrels from ports along their sides. Dog-headed su-chi warriors pounded in their midst, with hands powerful enough to tear the mechanical forelegs from a Phyrexian bloodstock. Falcon engines shrieked down in waves overhead, impacting monsters, grinding in their guts, blasting through the far side, and rising to swoop down on other beasts.

It was a glorious charge. These hundred warriors and two score machines were cut off from the main army, yes, but they tore the belly out of the Phyrexian lines. They each killed hundreds. Every slain Phyrexian brought them ten running paces nearer to the Caves of Koilos.

There, the Phyrexian command center lay. In those tight confines, a hundred Metathran would be equal to ten thousand Phyrexians. Thaddeus and his troops would plunge through to the command core, slay the land-army's leaders, and press on to shut down the portal. This bloody business could be concluded in the next few days.

"To the caves!" Thaddeus shouted, lifting high one of the swords he held. "Break through to the caves!" His forces took up the call.

A wave of Phyrexians swept toward them, perhaps five hundred strong. Falcon engines screamed into their midst, impaling one in five. They flopped to ground as their innards were ground away. Four hundred more rushed onward. Grenadiers hurled their bombs in great overhead arcs. The crude devices fell in the midst of the running wave. Gray smoke belched out, shrapnel tearing through the Phyrexian lines. Many fell in pieces. Others struggled on with stumps of leg or arm streaming golden. Two hundred more came, unaffected.

So, it would be two to one. Thaddeus smiled. His teeth were limned in vermilion. It was for fights like this that he bore two swords.

The first blade struck a charging bloodstock. Thaddeus sidestepped the attack. His sword lanced with the precision of a marksman's arrow. It clove between flattened ribs and speared through the bloodstock's heart. The beast opened its mouth to scream. Only blood emerged. It pitched forward, dead as it ran. Its mechanical forelegs did not need a heart to live, and they struggled on. The bloodstock's head dragged on the ground, battered bloody by its own thudding hooves.

The other sword tangled with that of a Phyrexian trooper. Slower, more humanlike, this vat-grown fighter was cunning, trained in the arts of sword work. Blades clanged. Horned shoulders crashed. Both warriors halted in their charge, unable to win past. Steel raked steel. With depthless snake eyes, the infantryman studied its foe. Through a segmented mouth, it hissed. Something that smelled like creosote oozed from chitinous lips.

Thaddeus flung the thing back with one sword and brought the other to bear. The Phyrexian blocked the attack with a quick backhand parry. Thaddeus followed the block with a stab that should have eviscerated the beast. It spun easily aside. Thaddeus plunged forward, catching himself. The Phyrexian turned, sword high, and brought it down to cleave Thaddeus. Twin swords caught the blade in air and hurled it away. The two blades fell in a scissoring motion, catching either side of the creature's neck and slicing through. The monster's head bounded free.

Thaddeus drove onward. He had fallen back in his column.

They carved through the wave of death, near to breaking through. Thaddeus ached to be in the vanguard.

Vaulting the dead, he shouted again, "To the caves! To the caves!"

* * * * *

Atop the Caves of Koilos, Tsabo Tavoc had arranged a kind of tea party. There was no such thing as tea among Phyrexians, of course, and no notion of a party—which was why the spider woman had to borrow a human term for this experience. To sit on this high spot—breathing the fetor of battle, seeing compound deaths in compound eyes, witnessing the killings by her children and the murders of them—it was a banquet of sensations that could only have been akin to fine tea and pleasant banter.

That one, there—Tsabo Tavoc had thought, gazing down on the speckled blades as they rose and fell in the opening attack—*that man-monster Thaddeus, he gives me greater diversion than any of you, my children. I would like him to come to me. I would like him to win his way to the caves.*

A simple wish, it was. For Tsabo Tavoc, wishes became realities. Her will went out to her children, her killers. They held Commander Agnate and his contingent to a single plot of land, hurling themselves suicidally into that meat grinder just to keep the meat grinder in place. Before Thaddeus, though, Phyrexians melted, their will bowing to the will of Tsabo Tavoc. They fought as they fought because they wanted what she wanted.

He came. Mustering five score of his warriors, he broke through and charged, just as she wished.

Tsabo Tavoc felt every blow of his swords. Her consciousness lurked within each of those bashed-out brains. She fled away in the dying moments, only to surge up again in another warrior. He killed her countless times, each death freshly excruciating. Normally, Tsabo Tavoc enjoyed the anguish of others, the killing, but with this one she enjoyed the dying. Her mind swept out through her folk like a wave, crashing whitely against Thaddeus and his warriors and then retreating before him. She channeled him inward. Each loud assault was followed by an inexorable undertow that dragged him deeper.

There was such pleasure in the battle. Tsabo Tavoc was awash in regret as she pulled her mind away from the carnage.

Why draw the fly in unless the web is ready?

My children. I call to you.

Their response came in a quickening of pulses, in deep breaths in deep caverns. Her minions at the portal lifted their heads. Tsabo Tavoc saw what they saw—the wide, dark portal chamber. It centered on a pediment stone that shone like a mirror. The gleaming pediment radiated wires to the ceiling. Mechanisms it had powered six thousand years ago still huddled in the dark reaches.

This site was devised by the Ineffable himself in ancient days, when he was not yet a god but only a Thran. On one side of the shiny pediment, the darkness was filled with Phyrexian troops in rank and file. They marched toward the ascents and the battle. On the other side yawned a wide portal. Phyrexia lay there, beautiful and verdant beneath a blazing sky. Fields of metallic grass held great armies.

Tsabo Tavoc sought no warriors just now. She wanted more powerful denizens. Her will crowded through the streaming portal and sank down through the ground. She wanted creatures that lived deep in the Fourth Sphere of Phyrexia, amid mile-high furnaces and belching fire. She spotted them.

They were unnaturally tall, unnaturally thin, their flesh clinging like old paper to their bones. In red robes, the creatures walked metal causeways. They dipped long poles into pits and poured jerkied flesh into vats, feeding overlarge fish. These were vat priests. They compleated every newt, making it a perfect war machine.

Spheres and worlds away, Tsabo Tavoc smiled.

Her vat priests lifted their heads.

It was simply enough done. She needed only place the image of Thaddeus in their minds. She felt the saliva run along their withered jaws. They would obey her summons. The vat priests would send their most sanguine minds to Koilos to have a look at Thaddeus.

Satisfied, Tsabo Tavoc's consciousness sifted back upward. Her mind withdrew into the Caves of Koilos. When the Ineffable had walked the world as a Thran, these had been called the Caves of the Damned. As she returned to the delicious battle, Tsabo Tavoc thought how right that name had been.

Certainly for Thaddeus, they would once again be the Caves of the Damned.

* * * * *

My sword unmakes another. I see the tip chop through the thing's belly. It splits wide like a shirt ripping. Out spill strange, dark, wet shapes. The monster comes to pieces. It seems not even to have the will to live.

They cannot kill me. It is almost brutal to slay this way. They are no match for me and mine. It is like cutting grain to kill these Phyrexians. It is like chopping wildflowers, except that these flowers shriek and gush.

Another goes down. It seems to be almost bowing to me. I split its back. My sword cuts through, separating meat from bone as if filleting a fish. I charge through the muck of it. My foot crushes a panting lung.

I am too well made. Urza has done too much to make me. He has winnowed away humanity, knowing his foes will destroy all that is human. Urza perfected my inhumanity so that I could fight Phyrexians and not be destroyed. I am a greater monster than these things I slay. I am a vat-grown monster whose leash is held by Urza instead of Yawgmoth.

The sword hacks through a scuta's shield and the knob of bone beneath. It splashes brain on my feet and chops through to the monster's spine. The creature slumps atop scuttling legs. Dust rolls up around the settling beast. I vault over it and cut through a Phyrexian trooper. It is so surprised by my assault that it stands, gaping, though its shoulder is cut through down to the sternum.

I am too well made.

* * * * *

Thaddeus and his hundred had broken through. They drove like demons through the Phyrexian hordes.

Agnate was still mired in the slaughterhouse of the western front. He fought amid encroaching corpses. Dead Metathran lay in lurid intimacy with dead Phyrexians. Legs and arthropods jutted in heaps, part redoubt, part hazard. Killing another beast, Agnate peered beyond the thing's bulk.

Thaddeus fought in the sere distance. Oh, to battle at a run, so fast and free! It must have been glorious.

Agnate reached out his mind to his counterpart. Above the mad din, he sought. In all that killing lunacy, Thaddeus was lost. Agnate could not touch his comrade. A greater presence filled the battlefield—a greater mind in jealous possession.

It mattered little. Thaddeus would prevail. They knew each other's minds even when they could not touch. Thaddeus was too busy in the running battle.

It must have been glorious.

CHAPTER 23
The Dreaming Caves

This place was not fit for the elves of Llanowar. They were accustomed to colonnades of quosumic trees, to hanging vines in vast highways, to leaves among the clouds and days beneath the sun. This place had no trees but columns of tortured stone. It had no vines but giant blind serpents that crawled the cave floors. In place of heavens, there were groins of rock. Instead of sunlight, there was blackness.

It was worse than that. Crowded here in these haunted caves, the elves knew that even now trees and vines and skies were decimated. This place might not be fit for elves, but neither was their home, anymore.

Eladamri walked among the refugee rabble. They sat shoulder to shoulder in a large, dark cavern. Liin Sivi strode in silent

184

watchfulness behind Eladamri. She kept at bay the refugees, who teemed about him in their terror. They had feared to come here. It was a place that lived in their common mind—the Dreaming Caves, the underworld home of the dead.

True enough, since they had arrived, strange, moaning spirits seemed to flit all around them.

Eladamri was no prophet. He was a warrior. For him this was not an underworld but a bunker, not a place of the dead but of the living.

Were these the only survivors in Llanowar? Could they even be considered survivors? Perhaps a hundred had died in the palace. Perhaps a hundred more had died in the flight downward. How would these thousand die? Starvation? No, they would not last so long. They would die in a trampling stampede.

One old elf, clutching a squalling child, had summed up all their fears—"The Dreaming Caves . . . bring nightmares . . . to life!"

The refugees had brought a wealth of nightmares with them. Visions of hurtling plague bombs shone in their wide eyes. Shrieks of dying countrymen echoed through their ears. Shame at leaving their dead nobles . . . royal rings unclaimed on stilled fingers . . .

Perhaps the Dreaming Caves did have that power. Here, beneath miles of root, the air was charged with green mana. Merely breathing it induced a waking sleep. The very rock hummed in sympathy with the hearts of the people. Perhaps these caves did pluck thoughts from their mind and send them spinning through air.

One man's private terrors paraded before whole families. The very real deaths of hundreds above were recombined into the surreal deaths of hundreds of thousands below.

Refugees staggered about the caverns, wringing their hands and wailing. Others fought their comrades, thinking them ghosts. Still more fled shrieking into deeper places. They fell into nests of white serpents, which awoke to find warm meat. They dropped into wells that plunged to the boiling core of the world. They fled into the manifold stomachs of Dominaria, where she devoured her own children.

Terrors came true.

Eladamri had to stop all this. He had not saved these people yet. He had brought them out of one death and into another.

Not for long. If they could dream of horrors, they could dream of beauties.

Lifting high the lantern he had brought from above, Eladamri strode with sure and measured step among his folk. He headed for a prominence of rock on the far side of the cavern. To reach it, he would pass through the main mass of refugees. The staging was perfect, as if he had dreamed it into being. As Eladamri went, he sang an ancient ballad of the Skyshroud elves, his people on Rath:

> I walk the groves of Damherung.
> Below a dappled sun go I
> And sing of Volrath's coming doom
> Beneath a brilliant sky.
>
> O forest, hold thy wand'ring son
> Though fears assail the door.
> O foliage, cloak thy ravaged one
> In vestments cut for war.

The refugees did not know this hymn, but they would think they knew it. The caves carried his voice among them like a breeze that promised rain. Music swallowed remembered shrieks. Echoes became memories. They knew this hymn, and as he walked among them, they put aside jangling terrors to sing.

> For what are leaves but countless blades
> To fight a countless foe on high,
> And what are twigs but spears arrayed
> To slay the monstrous sky?
>
> O forest, hold thy wand'ring son
> Though fears assail the door.
> O foliage, cloak thy ravaged one
> In vestments cut for war.

The murmur of the song rose, drowning the last of the moans and shrieks. Even Liin Sivi, walking behind him, sang. Voices joined, strengthened, grew, until it seemed the throat of the world sang with them.

> *Though death has guile and killing power,*
> *Though bloodlust rules the steaming tides,*
> *It's life that wrestles hour by hour*
> *And finally abides.*

> *O forest, hold thy wand'ring son*
> *Though fears assail the door.*
> *O foliage, cloak thy ravaged one*
> *In vestments cut for war.*

By the time he had reached the gnarl of stone, the whole of the cavern sang—some stridently, some quietly, some merely in gentle hums. The refugees watched this elf whom they had seen first in the treetops, whom they remembered from ages upon ages.

Eladamri lifted his face. Lantern light shone across it. He was not old for an elf, in the midst of his second century, but his profound eyes and prominent nose and jutting chin gave him the look of a sage. In the lantern glow, he seemed the only solid thing in a world of shadows. Eladamri spoke.

"Llanowar will rise again," he said simply, without preamble. The words struck the air and made swimming visions of the forest. "Green leaves grow out of black ground. Green shoots rise from charred wood. Moments of defeat are swallowed in millennia of triumph."

These words were not enough. He needed to speak not words but visions.

"I see bright birds darting among the overspreading boughs of a quosumic. Children swing on the vines that hang there. Red camro fruits burst from flowery folds. Morning breezes pluck dew from the leaves and carry it in cool bands of mist through the crown. From every hollow comes the sound of singing, of laughter."

A gentle murmur of merriment moved among the folk. They were gladdened by this dream tree.

"Yes," Eladamri continued, "we are there. All of us. We dwell among the clouds, friends of the sun. This day is but a sad memory. It is swallowed in lifetimes of joy. We are there, resting in the heights. Lie down, my friends. Lean your heads on the warm bark of the tree. Breathe her sweet pollen and sleep awhile."

With the rustle of ragged clothes and the murmur of weary souls, the refugees settled to ground. One by one, they sighed into sleep and dreamed of a perfect tree.

Eladamri smiled to see it. At least they could rest. At least they would cease trampling each other and rushing off into doom.

"That was well done," said Liin Sivi behind him.

"Someone had to do something," Eladamri breathed.

"Yes," came a new voice, tremulous and panting, "someone has to do something."

Eladamri turned to see a bloodied elf emerge from a nearby tunnel. The man was a peasant, his shift charred and his shoulder blistered from burns. He had not descended with the refugees from the High Court.

Raking a breath, he said, "You must come to us. You must do the same for us! We came from the forest floor. Our village was struck. There are five hundred. You must come to help us as you helped these here."

Eladamri's eyes glinted darkly in the cavern light. This desperate man would interpret the look as mystery and power. In fact, Eladamri felt a doubt that bordered on panic. He had done what he could for these desperate folk—the work not of a savior but of a compassionate warrior. He had done no more than anyone else would have done.

Why, then, had no one else done it?

"I will go see what I can do."

A light pierced the terror of the elf's face. He seemed to breathe for the first time since he had spoken. He bowed deeply. Eladamri could hear the burned skin on his shoulder crackle with the motion. The man's grateful breath quickened.

In utter darkness, even the faintest ember seems a beaming sun.

Eladamri was that faint ember. His glow had drawn nations, and as they bowed, their hopeful breath stoked the fire in him. They needed a savior. They were making a savior. He could only receive their adoration and use it to save as many as he could.

Perhaps that was all a savior ever was.

"Lead me to them," Eladamri said, catching the elf's hand and lifting him from his bow. "I will go where you lead. Take my lantern. Let it guide you."

The elf shook his head. "Keep your lantern. I want them to see you. I want them to see who I have brought." He squeezed his thanks and turned to lead Eladamri away.

Lifting his lantern, the Seed of Freyalise strode along a ledge of stone at one side of the cavern. Most of his folk slept in contented clusters. A few remained awake. They watched in quiet admiration, their eyes reflecting his light.

"They will not suffer your absence long, Eladamri," Liin Sivi said behind him. "They will come looking for you."

As he followed his guide down into a narrow shaft of slanting stone, Eladamri answered, "Let us hope we are not gone long."

"I cannot keep them back, you know," Liin Sivi said. "My totenvec can keep back foes but not friends. That was Takara's job."

Eladamri's breath caught. The bombing of the palace had been chaos—the flight downward, the terror of collective nightmare. . . . He had forgotten about his companion. "She didn't—"

"No," Liin Sivi replied simply.

Eladamri steadied himself, setting a feverish hand on cold stone. The rock drank his heat. Before him, the passage descended to deep darkness. Chill air crowded past from spaces below. It seemed Dominaria was breathing. It seemed her breath was cold.

"Just a little farther," the elf assured. He was small and sure-footed, like a cave cricket.

Eladamri and Liin Sivi picked their way across a rubble field where hunks of stone had calved from the encroaching ceiling. Beyond, the passage squared up, seeming almost a mine hewn from rock. Eladamri's footsteps echoed in whispers all around him. At the end of the corridor, the elf stood before a vast cavern. Eladamri's lantern barely shone in the blackness.

He stared at the lantern. Its wick was little more than a nub. Reaching to the neck of his robe, Eladamri grabbed the collar and hauled hard. The fabric ripped easily free. He opened the lantern, lit the strip of material, and fed it down into the wick slot. The collar filled with oil. Fire flared. Eladamri closed the panel and lifted a blazing lantern.

Its light shone out over a cavern filled with crouching figures. Their eyes gleamed. They looked not to the light but to the light-bringer.

"Let's go down to them," Eladamri said.

"Yes," the elf said, scrambling down the slope.

As Eladamri descended, Liin Sivi spoke, "We should go back."

"I cannot go back," Eladamri said. "They have glimpsed hope. It would kill them for me to leave."

"You cannot just sing to these people and make pretty speeches. Look at them, Eladamri. Look at them."

He did. His heart went cold in his chest. It was not merely darkness that swathed them. It was death. They were rotting. Their flesh boiled off their bones. Teeth showed through rags of lip. Eyes wept in lidless sockets. Breath raked into and out of riddled windpipes. Shoulder bones showed white through sloughing flesh.

"They are still alive," Eladamri said.

"But for how long?" Liin Sivi replied, clasping his shoulder. "You cannot save them."

Eyes hardening, Eladamri pulled away from her. "These are the Dreaming Caves. I cannot save these folk, but their dreams can."

He descended the final pitch of the hillside and was among them.

Eladamri lifted his lantern, peering in gladness across the hordes.

"Behold, children of Staprion—dread has fallen from the skies, but hope rises from the world. Gaea has not forgotten you. Freyalise has sent me to you. She wants you to rise, whole, into the

light. Come to me, brothers and sisters. Come. Believe. Be healed.
We will rise. We will save our homeland. Come!"

Liin Sivi stood on the slope, her hands sweating on the hilt of
her toten-vec. She would not cut down allies, certainly not plague
victims. She could only watch as they surrounded Eladamri, pressing on him, swallowing him in their rot. In moments, he was gone.
Even the light of his lantern was eclipsed in that clamor of heads
and hands.

There was only darkness now, darkness and death and the wails
of the dying.

Suddenly, the lantern beamed forth again. It rose, clutched in a
healthy hand. Its rays spilled out over more healthy flesh. Where
there had been scaly heads and skeletal arms now there were flow-
ing locks and young muscle. Where there had been rot there was
now vitality. It was as though light itself healed them—rebuilding
bodies, renewing spirits.

At the center of that glow was Eladamri. His robes seemed lit
from within.

Hands reached for him, touched him, and came away whole.

Liin Sivi released her weapon. She rubbed fists in her eyes. Was
this another delusion of the Dreaming Caves?

Waves of power, of belief, swept in visible rings from Eladamri.
This was no dream. This was truth.

Mouth agape, Liin Sivi dropped to her knees.

Eladamri sang gladly to his people:

> *Though death has guile and killing power,*
> *Though bloodlust rules the steaming tides,*
> *It's life that wrestles hour by hour*
> *And finally abides.*
>
> *O forest, hold thy wand'ring son*
> *Though fears assail the door.*
> *O foliage, cloak thy ravaged one*
> *In vestments cut for war.*

CHAPTER 24
Heroes' Meeting

Orim's sick bay seemed a menagerie. Rats and flying squirrels paced in makeshift cages. Mounds of what seemed fish eggs occupied airtight vials across her desk. Four dead Phyrexians lay nearby. They seemed giant, overturned cockroaches. Only one true patient remained—Hanna. She languished in feverish sleep on the far side of the room. It was for her that the menagerie existed. It was to save that one human that Orim had worked so tirelessly over Phyrexian corpses.

From those corpses, Orim had tapped every fluid she could find—glistening-oil, green bile, saliva, gastric juice, venom, lymph, cerebral-spinal fluid, even cardiac liquids. Gladly these vat-grown creatures had no reproductive fluids. Using a centrifuge and Cho-Arrim water magic, Orim separated each fluid into its component parts. The lymph and blood contained many of the disease-fighting compounds, and comparing the materials common to them allowed Orim to narrow the immunity substances. Then, it was a matter of applying distillations of each part on plague-infected flora and fauna from Llanowar.

The Benalish aerial armada had proven itself quite intrepid in gathering test subjects.

The immunity substance, as it turned out, was a black platelet suspended in glistening-oil. It could not reverse the disease, but it prevented its spread. Uninfected leaves treated with the substance were made immune to the plague. Infected leaves did not worsen but neither did they improve. No cure, this, it would at least prevent the disease from spreading, flesh to flesh and person to person.

Squee had gathered rats from the bilges—healthy beasts that had feasted on hardtack and ale. The black material was gobbled greedily by the beasts. In mere moments, they proved immune. Infected flying squirrels from the forest also liked the taste of Phyrexian immunity, and their disease ceased its advance.

Now, it was up to Orim. She would not test this substance on any person until she had tested it on herself. After dissecting Phyrexian corpses, Orim had little stomach for the curative caviar, but she would do anything for Hanna. Drawing a deep breath, she lifted the jiggling black mass to her mouth. The spoon slid reluctantly over her teeth.

Tiny, cold spheres settled on her tongue. They felt like minute beads of glass, sliding down behind her teeth. They tasted of oil. She dared not chew but only swallowed. The platelets crowded down her throat. They slid into her belly. It felt chill and dark. The sensation spread from her stomach into her blood. Was it only her mind, or did this feel like a tiny invasion? A shudder moved through her, the coolness spreading under her clothes and out to her fingertips.

"That should be enough time," Orim sighed.

She lifted a knife from her worktable, set its tip on her biceps, and drew the blade down in a brief, deep cut. It was almost painless, the knife was so sharp. The blade came away. A drop of crimson welled up from the slit. Putting down the knife, Orim lifted a plague infected leaf, opened the cut, and crumbled the black corruption into the wound. Every instinct she had—not only as a healer but as a living being—shivered at the sight of those black flakes adhering to the cut flesh.

Clamping a cloth over the spot, Orim closed her eyes and hissed. This strain of the plague was virulent enough that it would turn the skin necrotic in moments. She needed wait only those moments to see if she had devised a serum or if she were joining Hanna on the road to death.

Pulling the cloth away, Orim drew the sides of the wound apart. She peered down into perfect, red flesh. A deep, thankful breath filled her. She said a silent thanks to the powers of healing and water.

"Oh, Hanna," Orim said, though she knew her patient still slept. "The first hope. It cannot save you, but it can save others. I'll keep working until I have a cure." Dashing tears from her eyes, Orim snatched up a vial of the platelets and approached Hanna.

She lay on her side, knees drawn up over the belly wound that was killing her.

Sitting on her bunk, Orim reached out gently to stroke her friend's hair. Hanna was so thin. Her face seemed skin stretched over a skull. Her eyes were visible beneath translucent lids. Her neck was a bundle of straining cords. Only her hair was as it had been—streaming gold. Fondly, Orim drew her fingers through the strands.

"Hanna, wake up. I have something for you."

A shuddering breath went through Hanna. She rolled to her back. She eased her legs downward. They seemed as thin as sticks beneath the blankets. Blue lids pulled back from bloodshot eyes. Orim bit her lip to see the chronic pain there.

Hanna muttered weakly, "Something . . . for me?"

"It's not a cure—but it will stop the disease from advancing." Orim held up the vial. "It'll keep a healthy person from catching it."

"Thank you," Hanna said, reaching up. She did not clutch the vial but Orim's arm. "Use it on someone it can save."

Orim's eyes clouded. "There is enough. I want you to take this. It will buy time."

Not releasing her friend's arm, Hanna drew aside the gown. The bandages that looped her midsection seemed loose, as though she had shrunk. Even beyond the edge of those bandages, her skin was gray from shoulder to thigh. Tendrils of corruption reached farther, to elbow and knee.

"Time for what?" She covered herself again. "Please, give it to someone it will save."

Orim sadly patted her friend's cheek. "Gerrard has ordered it. Now, open up."

Her eyes hard and angry, Hanna took the spoonful.

"I won't give up, Hanna. I'm going to find a cure."

"Thank you, Orim," Hanna said quietly. "Thank you. . . . I need to sleep."

"Yes," responded the healer. She drew Hanna's blankets up to her shoulders. A chill went down her spine. One day, and sooner than later, she would be drawing these blankets up over Hanna's face. "Sleep, dear girl. Sleep."

Turning, Orim retreated to her worktable. Hanna breathed in quiet rest as Orim gathered the rack of vials. She pushed back the sick bay door and climbed the stairs. The tiny bottles rattled as she rose.

Here, beyond the Phyrexian corpses and the caged test-creatures, *Weatherlight* ceased to be a laboratory and became a warship. An ensign hurried down the companionway above, reading from a page in his hand the names of the refugees who were to eat next. Orim continued on until she reached the amidships hatch. She climbed through to stand on the deck.

Gerrard crouched on the deck, working with a crew who were easing the repaired port-side ray cannon back into its moorings. He was bare to the waist and sweating, though a steady breeze came over the prow to him.

Orim approached, lifting the rack of vials. "I have it, enough serum for the ship's whole complement and some left over."

From the grease-track where he knelt, Gerrard looked up. "You have it? A cure?"

"Not a cure. I have an immunity serum."

He was on his feet. "Will it help Hanna?"

Orim shook her head slowly.

An angry line knitted Gerrard's brow, but he managed to say, "Good work. You've saved us."

"Most of us."

"Administer the serum. Once everyone is treated, I want you to set aside the rest—as much as you can spare—for a gift."

"A gift?" she asked.

"We're landing in the treetops. Not the whole armada, just *Weatherlight* and her immune crew. The ship herself should somehow ingest some of the serum, to make her hull impervious. I'll ask Hanna how—"

"Ask Karn," Orim suggested.

Nodding stiffly, Gerrard said, "I want to take the rest of the serum to whomever might survive there, as a sign of our alliance. We'll land in the center of the devastation—there's a ruined palace down there—and we'll search until we find the native people."

Orim's eyes shone. "Good. Perhaps we'll also find more Phyrexians. Give me more Phyrexians, and I'll give you more serum."

Gerrard nodded, his eyes like poniards. "I'll give you more Phyrexians."

* * * * *

It was no easy task for Multani to find the refugees, down so deep. The Dreaming Caves lay below Llanowar's water table. Most roots sank no lower than this subterranean sea. Its bed was a shelf of granite a hundred yards thick. The Dreaming Caves hid beneath. The Phyrexians could not have found them there, and even Multani would not have except for the guidance of Molimo. He showed the way. Though most roots did not plumb the water table and crack the granite shelf, quosumic tap roots did.

A tree that stands thousands of feet tall plunges equally deep.

Still, the way was not easy. Multani spiraled down a quosumic tree that pulsed with agony. The tree's crown had been eaten by plague. Not a single leaf remained. Half the branches were destroyed. Rot-plague girdled the bole in five separate rings. To move through dying wood was terrifying. Every impulse cried out that Multani should escape. Instead, he coursed lower, beneath the fecund humus, through the frigid underworld sea, through even granite, to the caves.

Multani emerged from the taproot precisely where the refugees had. He assembled a body for himself out of albino tendrils and glowing lichens. Cave crickets became his eyes and blond roaches his fingers and toes. It was a spectral form, venous and shimmering, but it was the only life he could gather in these deeps. Surely, he would be no more ghastly than the refugees themselves. He followed their footprints.

Something strange—a fresh warm breeze rolled up the passage toward him. It felt like the soft tides of air that bring spring rain. It smelled of lightning. Here, three thousand feet below the overworld, blew breezes redolent with life. It was impossible or at least miraculous.

Surely that breeze would circle the Seed of Freyalise.

Multani followed it. Through winding ways, it went. No longer did he track a trail of blood and tears but now a breath of hope.

He reached a wide cavern. The folk there not only *breathed* hope. They sang it. In fire circles they gathered, singing and speaking, eating and healing. The fires were impossible. There was no fuel, no ventilation. They burned even so. The food, also, was ludicrous—groppa wine, dried apples, braid bread, honey butter, arbor grapes, onion chives, and game hens. Some circles ate lesser fare, mere trail rations, and others feasted on eel and cheese and the board of kings. It was dream food. Still, it nourished them as surely as the fires gave them warmth and light. Those who believed health were healed. Those who made themselves glad were glad.

One man had taught them to dream beauties, and they had dreamed him into glory. He was just ahead, walking among the multitude. Eladamri's hands gently lingering in theirs and awoke health.

Multani approached. Even in the enthralled throng, a man made of roots and tendrils was a strange sight. The people parted before him.

Eladamri lifted his face to behold a man with cave-cricket eyes.

Multani bowed, a wry smile on lips of white moss. "Greetings, Seed of Freyalise. I bring news from the forest."

The man's eyes were changed. He was no simple elf now. He was something more. Divine forces had conspired to make him a tool, and he had at last allowed himself to become one.

"Do not tell me here, amid the throng. I would not let your news resound needlessly through these Dream Caves."

He was wise. Word of atrocities above could awake atrocities below.

Multani said simply, "You will not escape this throng, and so—" he took Eladamri's hand. Through touch, he sent his thoughts.

The palace tree is destroyed, with all who remained above. This is despite the ceaseless labors of giant spiders to contain the contagion. So too, plague ravages the trade house of Kelfae and the port of Wellspree of the Jubilar. Throughout the forest, death is rampant.

Eladamri gazed bleakly at the tendril man. *This is not news. We knew all above was destroyed by the bombs.*

It is worse. The first ship has landed in the ruins of Staprion Palace. The smell of oil-blood pervades the ship and its crew. They descend within the palace tree, following the route that led you here. You must take a war party up to battle them.

Yes, answered Eladamri simply.

You are their savior now. You must save them.

And I was a warrior before. I will gladly fight these monsters.

* * * * *

Gerrard led Tahngarth, Sisay, and a party of warriors down the winding heart of the tree. In one hand, he clutched a lantern and the jar that held the last of Orim's serum. In the other, he clutched a sword. Death in one hand and life in the other.

Gerrard snorted, slashing a cobweb that draped the treacherous path. He paused, peering into the gloom below.

"Someone's down there." He lifted the lantern. Its light beamed against the splintery hollow of the tree, tracing out the spiral stairs.

It showed more webs, and dead elves hanging in them. "Someone's alive down there. I can sense it."

Tahngarth stared over his shoulder and lifted an eloquent eyebrow. "You can . . . sense it?"

"There's a presence. A power I can't quite describe."

The minotaur rumbled quietly. "Since when have you been a mystic?"

"I sense it too," Sisay said behind him. "A fey power."

Sheathing his sword, Gerrard cupped a hand to his mouth. "We come in peace. We come with serum to stop the plague."

A voice came from below, resonant like the voice of the wood itself. "Since when do Phyrexians come in peace?"

"We are not Phyrexians."

"You smell like Phyrexians."

"It is the plague treatment," Gerrard replied. "Its immunity is derived from Phyrexian blood. We have been treated. We have brought more for you."

The voice was dubious. "We have found our own cure, one that does not make us reek of Phyrexia."

"Your forest is cured? It does not seem so to me. Do you prefer the reek of rot and death to the reek of oil-blood?"

The voice was angry. "Who are you?"

"I am Commander Gerrard Capashen of *Weatherlight*, here with Captain Sisay and First-Mate Tahngarth."

A laugh answered. "Oh, yes, Gerrard—the Korvecdal."

"The Korvecdal?" Gerrard laughed as well. "No, I'm no Uniter, just an honest fighting man." He took a long breath. "How did you know?"

"I know because I am the true Korvecdal, the true Uniter."

Even as the stately figure ascended into the lantern's glow, Gerrard realized. "Eladamri of the Skyshroud! What are you doing here?"

"It's too long a tale," said the elf. A retinue of elf warriors came behind him. "Let it simply be put that you and I have traded places. Once you were thought the Uniter and I the common hero. Now, it is as it is. Let us trust that higher powers understand this chess match."

"I don't trust any powers but my sword arm and these friends."

"Which, again, is as it should be."

"And one of those friends devised this serum," he said, holding up the jar. "It has saved the crew of my ship. It can halt the plague among your people."

Eladamri's eyes seemed brighter than the lantern. "My people, just now, are safe from the plague. It is the forest that languishes."

"Then, give this serum to whatever druid or nature spirit might make use of it to heal the forest."

Suddenly, a figure took form between the two men. He was a green-man, made of splinters and vines. His eyes were a pair of seed pods, his teeth a row of mushrooms.

Other men might have shied back from the strange creature, but Gerrard himself had learned maro-sorcery from such a man.

"Master!" Gerrard said in sudden recognition. His knees buckled. His fingers went nerveless around the jar of serum. It slipped free, plunging toward the hollow of the tree.

Multani's viny arm shot out, snatching the jar from the air. "Thank you, Gerrard."

"I-I feared you . . . I feared you were dead," stammered Gerrard.

"I feared the same for you, many times over," Multani replied, lifting Gerrard to his feet. "It is good to know fears do not always prevail." He spread fibrous arms through the darkness. "Welcome, Gerrard and *Weatherlight*. . . . Welcome to Llanowar."

CHAPTER 25
The Battle of Urborg

"Come away from Keld," Urza said, appearing suddenly out of nowhere.

Barrin did not even startle. He didn't care enough anymore to startle. He'd been crouching here beside the fjord, watching frigid water mound up with the rising tide. Foam stole tentatively across the sand bars and kissed the keels of Keldon longships. In less than an hour, the warships would stand in twenty feet of water. Then Barrin and his erstwhile foes, the Keldons—gray and massive and impatient on the docks—would ship together for more wars in Western Keld.

"Come away from Keld," Urza repeated.

Barrin squinted up at him. "How dare you? You told me this battle was everything. You told me I'd just have to forget what these . . . what these beasts did to Rayne. So I did. I did just like you said. And now you so blithely call me away?"

Urza stared back, his eyes like twin candles. He stood on a black fist of basalt beside the fjord and seemed just another stony extrusion. Beneath woolen skies, his war-robes were dark except where snowflakes pasted themselves.

"This battle is no longer everything."

"Damn you, Urza," Barrin said bitterly.

Sea spray vaulted up behind the planeswalker. "It's the army, not the battle. That's why you had to forget about your wife. I needed this army. I need them for a better fight."

"What better fight?" Barrin asked wearily.

"Urborg."

Barrin barked a laugh. He couldn't have imagined a more ludicrous response. "Urborg? A cesspool of liches and ghosts and zombies, brimstone and malaria? Yes, oh, yes, that's a better fight."

"Urborg is key to the next phase of the Phyrexians' plan. They cannot be allowed to gain it."

Shaking his head dispiritedly, Barrin said, "Why not? Urborg deserves them. They'd probably be at home there."

"That's the reason, exactly. They would be at home," Urza replied evenly. "Koilos and Urborg. If Yawgmoth gains footholds there, he can straddle the world."

"All the better to punch him in the groin," Barrin growled. He flung a shard of basalt out to skip across the foaming flood.

"You sound angry, my friend," Urza said. He stepped down from the rock and approached. "These northern climes are wearing on you."

Barrin stood. He gazed at a gray wave that struck the pebble bank and sent rocks tumbling toward the shore.

"Benalia is lost. Zhalfir and Shiv are gone. Now Keld is falling too. I thought I could forget Rayne in war but not when war screams—'Loss! Loss! Loss!' "

The planeswalker shook his head. Icy wind tore at his ash-blond hair. "It is not all loss. Yavimaya has won. Llanowar has won—"

"Llanowar!"

"Yes. I understand that your daughter was instrumental in the victory."

"Hanna," Barrin breathed. He closed his eyes, imagining her bright smile. The face he saw, though, was that of Rayne. "I should go congratulate her."

A strange shadow passed across Urza's gemstone eyes. "Soon, my friend, but not yet. Urborg awaits us. I want you to convince the Keldons to sail to Urborg at best time and rendezvous with you there. Meanwhile, you'll be mustering the Serrans who survived the fall of Benalia. We will need their angel armies."

"Serrans and Keldons?" Barrin looked sick. "Strange alliances."

"Stranger and stranger," Urza agreed. "Dominaria will not be saved unless all Dominarians fight. I am arranging a great coalition among the many nations of the globe. Those who stand alone will fall. Those who unite will conquer."

Barrin stared appreciatively at his friend. "I never thought I'd hear Urza Planeswalker admit needing help from anyone."

Urza shrugged away the comment. "Of course, Lord Windgrace and his panther warriors will join us. I'll be bringing elf warriors from Yavimaya and helionauts from Tolaria—"

"Helionauts," Barrin interrupted. "Tolaria will be vulnerable without them."

"We all must make sacrifices," Urza said.

Barrin shrugged, staring across the rising tide. Already, two of the Keldon longships bobbed levelly on the flood. Up stout gangplanks marched Keldon warriors, crates loaded on their backs.

"All right. I'll do what you ask. The Keldons and Serrans will be there at best time. We'll fight your battle for you. We'll drive out the Phyrexians and leave the place to the liches."

"Good," Urza said simply as he began to disappear. "I'll look for you there."

*   *   *   *   *

Barrin flew in the midst of an angelic host. Their wings gleamed white above a pitching sea. Wind whistled from perfect pinions and set songs in the air.

This was how Serrans flew—enmeshed in music. It was why

their attack squadrons were called choirs. Each creature knew her part. Each flew in precise pitch with the others. Like fish in a school, who sense the movement of the whole in pressure points along their sides, angels knew by harmonies and dissonances where they flew, how they fought, and whom they slew.

Barrin was at home among these inhuman glories. He rode ahead of them, aback a winged horse conjured from thin air. The creature seemed a thing of cloud—white and gleaming, halfway between solidity and mist. Still, it was powerful. Wings spread wide on the wind. With each surging stroke, the beast's neck bent. Its hooves churned the air as though it leaped steeples.

Of course, Barrin did not need a winged steed. He could fly with a mere thought, but he had been inspired by Teferi's phoenix flocks. There was something appealing about riding into battle on a creature of pure imagination. This horse would not tire. It would not bleed. It would not foam or spit or die—all the filthy things that true flesh had done over and over the last long weeks.

As glorious as the angel choir behind him, as magnificent as the ideal creature beneath him, Barrin could not keep his spirits from slumping. He was sick of war, sick to death of it. He didn't mind killing Phyrexians. He minded watching Phyrexians kill angels and Keldons, elves and Metathran and humans. He minded knowing that lives were mere chess pieces in a match between Urza and Yawgmoth.

Barrin was tired of being a pawn.

"There," he murmured, looking dead ahead. Though he was still a hundred miles out, a gazing enchantment brought every detail in crystalline clarity to his eyes.

Beyond the alabaster wings of his mount, Urborg loomed up out of the sea. It was a black and awful chain of islands. Dormant volcanoes hissed sulfuric steam into the air. Pestilential swamps stretched beneath forests of dead trees. The air waved with nauseous heat and rattled with a billion billion bugs. The only solid ground was muck. The only water was poisoned. The only living inhabitants were allies of, or slaves to, or prey for the unliving. Ghouls, liches, zombies, wraiths—necromantic horrors all.

That was the normal aspect of Urborg. Since Phyrexians had moved into the neighborhood, things had gone significantly downhill. Now, the skies teemed with dragon engines and undead serpents. Like devil rays, they drifted in lazy circles around the isles—guardians and watchdogs for the forces below. There were plenty of forces below. Three Phyrexian cruisers had landed. They sat atop long pylons sunk in the marshes. These were the command centers. Troop transports in their hundreds had also landed, off loading Phyrexians especially bred for swamp combat. The officers of these units rode small airship through the swamps, wedge-shaped chariots with batwing airfoils.

Despite Urza's best intentions, the Phyrexians already ruled Urborg. Now Barrin and his angels would fight demons for possession of hell.

More than Barrin and his angels. . . .

He glimpsed eight huge rags of sail stretched on the wind. Keldon longships. They tore parallel lines through an angry sea. Reaching full out, they seemed to plan a ramming attack on the main isle itself. Knowing Keldons, it was a surety. They would drive their ships up as far as they would go, perhaps a thousand yards into the salt marshes, ram whatever Phyrexian landing craft they could find, clamber up on the decks, and kill, kill, kill.

Oh, yes, the Keldons would have a grand time today.

Above them, seeming almost their reflection in the sky, soared a squadron of airships—Tolarian helionauts. Each looked like a galleon, its fore and mid decks encased in a dome of glass and steel. From the center of the aft deck rose a mechanical arm topped in whirling blades. Defensive spines bristled at prow, gunwales, and stern. Three pulser guns pivoted fore and aft, but the true weapon of the ship was the whirling blades.

Those blades proved themselves now. Darting down with the speed of eagles, Tolarian helionauts swarmed the island.

Dragon engines rose to do battle. Skulls craned backward to belch flame. Mechanical claws raked out. Tails scourged the air. On leather wings, Phyrexian dragon engines leaped into the sky and bathed their foes in a river of fire.

The helionauts plunged into the blazing flood. Flames licked across polished metal. Fire left a blush of steam in windscreens. Tolarian pilots rubbed away the condensation and shot through the flame. Pulsers spat streams of disruption fire. The charges jagged across the sky to impact dragon engines. Blue energy sparked and danced across their metal frames. It held them in a paralyzing grip, just long enough for the blades to come to bear.

With spinning scythes, helionauts sliced through dragon engines. Wings were sheered from the beasts. Heads chopped free. Even ribs ground to shards and dust. Hunks of dragon engine fell from the air.

It was not as easy as that, though. From a volcanic vent below, more dragon engines arrived like shooting steam. These were larger beasts. The others had been only keen-eyed sentries. These dragon engines were decked for war. They jetted into the sky straight beneath the helionauts. Wings surged once last and folded beneath wicked shoulders. Dragons rammed helionaut hulls.

Planished metal buckled. Joints failed. Great holes gouged in the sides of the ships. Out spilled crews and ruined mechanisms. One craft was struck so hard it bounced upward and chewed the belly out of another. They both plunged from the sky. A third helionaut began spinning drunkenly beneath its whirling scythes. It veered like a gyro and dropped, destroying a dragon engine on its way to ground.

The remaining helionauts filled the air with pulser blasts. Charges chased dragon engines through the sky. Power lay hold of them, paralyzed for a moment. Before the ships could tear them apart, though, other dragon engines attacked. Helionauts hailed down.

Barrin suddenly regretted the gazing enchantment. What was the good of seeing a battle that was still miles away?

Then everything changed. Dragon engines tore each other apart.

Barrin blinked, wondering what he saw. Suddenly, he knew.

Down upon the Phyrexian dragon engines soared real dragons—Rhammidarigaaz and his dragon nations. The ancient Shivan wyrm led four other dragon lords, one for each of the colors of magic. They flew wing and wing, onetime foes turned stolid allies. In the wake of these five great dragons flew whole serpentine nations. They poured from the sky as the Phyrexians had geysered from the ground.

Darigaaz flew in the vanguard. Fireballs rolled from his claws and baked dragon engines. Lava spouted from his throat and melted them in midair. To his one side flew the green dragon lord, trailing spores. They clumped onto Phyrexian engines and grew rampantly, cracking their joints. The white lord of dragons followed. It only flew, its pure wings cleaving through Phyrexians like light through nightmares. The blue dragon lord meanwhile sent spells out to rip the air from under scabrous wings. The black dragon and his folk, though, were fiercest of all. They smashed atop their evil brethren and ripped them apart with bare claws. Hunks of dragon engine fell to crash spectacularly in the swamps.

More things crashed in the swamps. Keldon longships—dagger-like with their mainsails reefed and outriggers cut loose—glided with surreal speed through the salt marshes. Rams split dead trees in their path. Keldon great swords clove Phyrexian troopers clawing to board. Arrows poured out from the decks, from this distance seeming ripples spreading from the prow.

"Arrows?" Barrin wondered to himself.

The first longships at last ran aground, a thousand yards inland. From the rails leaped massive Keldons in their hundreds, but also others—lithe, quick, slender. Elves. Urza must somehow have arranged their passage with Barrin's Keldon warriors. Strange coalitions. Brawny and scrawny, arrogant and elegant, Keldons and elves rushed side by side into battle.

Beyond their lines, Phyrexian shock troops rose from rock grottos to slay. They were as thick as maggots on a corpse and outnumbered the Keldons and elves a hundred to one. At their head, gliding aboard wedge-shaped air-chariots, rode black-armored commanders.

"They'll need help down there," Barrin decided. Helionauts and dragons ruled the skies, but Phyrexians ruled the ground. Barrin lifted his hand in an attack signal and sent his winged steed into a steep dive.

Angels swept down behind him. Their song rose an octave into a shrill whistle. The music lost none of its glory, only becoming more inhuman.

In moments, they had dropped from the blue heavens to the black swamps. Dead trees flashed past in gray stripes. Angels darted like silver blades in their midst. Depthless water churned below the hurtling hooves of Barrin's steed.

Ahead, a Phyrexian commander roared forward atop his air-chariot.

Barrin gathered the power of islands and seas and sent a blue enchantment ripping out from his fingers. It twined in air and grasped the chariot. The vessel flipped over and drove downward, ramming its driver headfirst into a mud embankment. The chariot bounded up to crack against a tree and rattle to ground. Only the driver's legs jutted from the mound, and they were broken and still.

The shock troops beyond continued their charge.

Angels jagged out before Barrin. Their magna swords sliced Phyrexians. Blades bit into spiky shoulders and cut clean through to hunched legs. They cleft heads and gutted chests. Magna swords ran black and golden with guts and oil. The angel song had become a bloody thing, part battle hymn, part requiem.

Barrin lashed out with a rainbow of sorceries. His first spell turned Phyrexians on each other. His next sorcery infected hundreds more with carbuncles of rust. Catching his breath, Barrin unleashed a simple but effective fireball, melting metal and bone and flesh. As he gathered another enchantment, Barrin's steed smashed hooves atop Phyrexian heads.

Still, there were so many shock troops—too many. Phyrexians rose from every hollow and every deadfall. Plague-infected claws sank into angel throats. Pincers ripped wings from their sockets. Stingers pumped venom into pure hearts. Serrans dropped like moths.

The Keldons fared even worse. They held a nearby ridge but were surrounded by Phyrexian slashers. Elven arrows did nothing against the metal beasts, all legs and blades. Keldon swords only clanged helplessly against them. Shoulder to shoulder, the strange allies were being ground to pieces.

"Break through!" Barrin called to the Serrans. "Break through to the Keldons!"

The battle shifted. Angels gathered up behind the winged steed. Barrin and his beleaguered troops rose from the swamp. Black-mana spells followed them up, claiming two more Serrans. The rest escaped. It was a tattered group, angry and wounded, that broke from one overwhelming battle only to enter another. They had lost many comrades already and would lose more in moments.

Barrin's winged horse punched through curtains of moss. Angel wings tore the rest to ribbons. Sloughs beyond teemed with mosquitoes. Leather-backed shapes moved darkly through the water. Perhaps they would keep the Phyrexians from pursuing.

The dead forest gave way to a stinking lake, beyond which rose the ridge where the Keldons and elves stood surrounded.

Barrin led his aerial units out across the inky waters. They would be too late. Shock troops and slashers closed in. Even now, the shores boiled with black figures rising to join the Phyrexian ranks. They surged up eagerly behind the pressing armies and lent their putrid claws to the killing.

Except they were killing Phyrexians.

Ghouls climbed in their thousands from the rank water. The remains of their former clothes and skin and muscle draped in tatters from their skeletons. They shambled with a hungry will up among the Phyrexian troops and piled atop them. Horns pierced their rotting flesh. It didn't matter. Blades chopped limbs from their bodies. It made no difference. Ghoul flesh clambered onto Phyrexians, gumming up every joint, choking every throat, burying every beast.

Mouth hanging open in amazed horror, Barrin diverted his troops up and away from the carnage. Angels jagged skyward behind the winged steed. As Barrin gazed down at the strange tableaux, he glimpsed, in the crest of a rotten stump, the black-garbed necromancer that had raised the ghouls. Its face was a patchwork of desiccated flesh over white bone. It was a lich, an undead creature itself—but it was Dominarian. It mustered its minions to fight Phyrexians.

Just before the winged steed carried Barrin beyond a stand of trees, he glimpsed a small, acknowledging nod from the lich, the sort given by comrades in the thick of battle.

Strange coalitions.

Barrin leaned down against the glimmering neck of his mount and clutched it, panting sickly.

CHAPTER 26
A Plaything for Tsabo Tavoc

They did not expect us to penetrate this far, Thaddeus told himself.

He climbed a dust embankment and crashed against a new wave of Phyrexians. His sword rammed deep into the jowls of one beast. The blade sliced upward alongside a four-foot fang and to the root. With a violent, wet lurch, the tooth was pulled from its socket and fell into Thaddeus's grasp. Flipping the thing over, he clutched the root like the hilt of a sword.

The Phyrexian bowled into Thaddeus. Rolling onto his back, Thaddeus set sword and tooth side by side on the creature's thorax. It impaled itself on the twin spikes. Amid a gush of glistening-oil, Thaddeus kicked out and flipped the monster over. The corpse tumbled down the hillside. Thaddeus rose, sword in one hand and tooth in the other.

They had not expected us to penetrate this far. No trench works, no palisades, no defensive batteries. All they have are these

211

suicide squads, hurling their bones on top of us. It will not be enough.

"Forward!" Thaddeus commanded, tooth lifted high. His sword lanced into the olfactory cavity of another monster, hewing into brain. The stuff sluiced like gray pudding down the nasal shaft and poured over Thaddeus. The beast slumped. Beyond hackled shoulders, the cave appeared. "Into the caves!"

Striding up the fallen hulk, Thaddeus hacked the head from a snakelike Phyrexian and ran down its twitching body. His corps followed, perhaps fifty fighters. He had lost half his troops in the mad, mile-long charge to the caves. The Phyrexians had lost hundreds. The Metathran that remained were the best fighters Thaddeus had. They would carve their way to the command core and down to the portal and set off enough bombs to seal it. Victory at Koilos was almost in hand.

* * * * *

Thaddeus and his strike force were but glinting helms in the distant fighting. They couldn't have penetrated so far. Something was amiss.

Agnate peered at the scene from atop a mound of dead. More died each moment, adding to the cairn of flesh. Phyrexians and Metathran fought ferociously, spilled each others' blood, and lay down side by side like brothers—huge and twisted brothers. The adversaries this day seemed descendants of the first feuding brothers who had battled over this same dirt clod six thousand years before.

A Phyrexian foot soldier scrambled up the mound of dead. It was humanlike, its torso shot through with metal struts that reinforced its biological spine. Gray muscles torqued among gears. It smiled as it came, teeth like a line of bones.

With a yell, Agnate brought his axe down on the soldier's head. It had expected the attack. It turned an armored shoulder to the blade. Steel met steel instead of flesh. Agnate's blade clung to the magnetized shoulder-piece. The soldier lunged back, ripping the axe from Agnate's grasp.

It clutched the hilt and brandished the blade with a yell.

The Metathran commander drew a dagger and hurled it. The knife clanged against magnetic struts and clung there, shuddering.

"More weapons?" the beast taunted, clutching the dagger.

Agnate stepped backward down the hill of death and stared incredulously. "It speaks."

"It thinks too. It plans. It uses your weapons against you." The four-armed thing hurled itself at him, swinging axe and dagger in a dual attack.

Agnate ducked under the axe—the worse of the two blades— but took the dagger in the shoulder. Clasping his hand atop the weapon's hilt and the beast's claw, Agnate ran beneath the Phyrexian's arm and rushed up the hill. The dagger anchored the monster's arm, forcing its joints into unnatural alignments. The wrist popped first, then the twin bones of the forearm broke, the elbow yanked out of joint, and the shoulder separated from the metal framework. One final surge, and the arm came off altogether.

Agnate wheeled, pulling the dagger from his shoulder and flinging the severed arm away.

The Phyrexian crouched atop the dead pile, its life streaming from the amputation. Still, bonelike teeth gleamed with a smile.

"Commander Thaddeus is doomed. Tsabo Tavoc wants him. Tsabo Tavoc gets him."

Agnate coldly approached the creature and drove his dagger into the thing's skull. Fingers eased from Agnate's axe, and he retrieved it.

It thinks . . . it plans . . . it uses your weapons against you. . . .

Agnate hissed, standing. The whole thing was a trap. Thaddeus was being drawn in, his strike force decimated and he . . .

Tsabo Tavoc wants him. . . . Tsabo Tavoc gets him. . . .

Taking a moment to chop his axe into the flank of another Phyrexian, Agnate flung his mind out across the battlefield. He reached for Thaddeus, an instinct since the moment of their creation. Twins, identical in body and mind, they had forever fought in tandem. Always, they had known each other's mind—

Not in this battle. A greater mind interposed itself between them. Agnate could only batter his thoughts against that solid and seamless presence.

Tsabo Tavoc wants him. . . . Tsabo Tavoc gets him. . . .

* * * * *

He fights beautifully, magnificently. He fights like a lion.

Tsabo Tavoc took a deep, satisfied breath. Lids closed over compound eyes. She had no desire to see the cave that ensconced her. It was the battle beyond that she watched with inner eyes. Distally, she experienced the slaughter of thousands of Metathran and felt the murder of thousands of her own children. Proximally, she sensed armies of warriors arriving even then through the portal, red-robed vat priests among them. In the middle distance, she felt Thaddeus.

He kills with such grim pleasure.

Tsabo Tavoc shifted her legs. A tremor of ecstasy moved through the mechanisms as Thaddeus clove the head of a gargantua. She had not intended to sacrifice that one. Gargantuas were hunched things of gray muscle, their feet as wide and rooted as trees. Flesh like rhino hide plated their torsos. Scythe claws could divide a man into five sections. Grotesque swells of bone covered their bulbous heads. Within lurked brains built for bloodlust and obedience. It took a century to grow a gargantua—a century and implants from ten separate species. Thaddeus had killed it in a moment. That was a costly loss—and yet all the more piquant because of it.

Thaddeus and his forty stormed the cave mouth. The gate guard lined up before them, claws and teeth at the ready. She would not thin their blood. If Thaddeus were to gain his way within, he would need to gain it honestly.

Tsabo Tavoc propelled another gargantua up before Thaddeus.

It raked its claws outward and caught Thaddeus as though he were a grasshopper. One simple squeeze and—

Tsabo Tavoc took a shuddering breath as she felt Thaddeus's sword slice the tendons of the beast's wrist. Flexors balled up beneath the elbow and extensors, splaying the claws uselessly back. It was a glorious strike. The pain was exquisite.

Thaddeus dropped to the ground.

The gargantua had another arm. It grabbed Thaddeus. It clenched its fist. There would be a brief spray and the gurgle of meat between claws—

Except that two of those claws were lopped off by the Metathran. He vaulted through the bloody space and ran up the gargantua's scaly arm.

Tsabo Tavoc smiled. He was good. What would it be next? Heart? Spine? Throat? Brain?

The gargantua's dead claws flailed at Thaddeus. They cut shallowly into him.

He reached the beast's shoulder. There was something in his hand—long, white, and curved. It shone point-on for a moment before the tooth plunged into the gargantua's eye. It sank through cornea and humors, up the optic nerve. The tooth bit into brain, cracking out the top of the skull.

Tsabo Tavoc did not withdraw from the gargantua as it slumped down in death. She wanted to feel that tooth through her mind, that black welling tide of death in every tissue. She wanted to suffer Thaddeus's victory. It would make her own triumph all the more sweet.

Thaddeus was inside the cave. He and twenty of his warriors had fought their way in. They would strike for the command core. They would all die but one. Thaddeus would be hers.

Ah, war is a glorious enterprise.

Tsabo Tavoc opened her compound eyes. She stood on eager legs and ambled out into the cavern beyond.

* * * * *

The gargantuas were fearsome beasts, but they died as had the sand worms, spinal centipedes, Metathran zombies, scuta, bloodstocks, and shock troops. Thaddeus's hundred had been winnowed to a simple score, but they had carved their way into the Phyrexian fortress. Now it was only a matter of discovering the fortress's heart, and tearing it out, and feasting on it.

"Gather up!" he shouted. The Caves of Koilos picked up his voice and hollered it back at him. Thaddeus smiled. The sound was good.

As they advanced, the twenty warriors converged on Thaddeus.

"We drive for the portal. Once it is closed, we'll clear out the command center. How many pikes remain?"

Four of the warriors lifted high their pikes.

"Good. Take the vanguard. Axes take the rear. Swords take the flanks. Slay only those beasts who give battle. This is their beach-head. They will defend it furiously. Don't be drawn away from the main group and the main objective—the portal. How many grenades?"

Eighteen of the twenty had bandoleers.

"Excellent. That will bury the mirror podium in a half-mile of rock. Downward."

The final word was not spoken before pikes bristled across the vanguard and axes gleamed at the rear. Thaddeus himself took to the right flank, knowing the first turn would cast him in a blind corner. Muscular and vicious, the strike force rushed to the gap. Pikes rounded the corner, intent on whatever lay beyond.

Flesh lay beyond—flesh and horns and fangs. Pikes sank into the shrieking wall of monsters. Impaled, they came on.

Jaws as large as a bear trap clamped the head of one pikeman. Triangular teeth converged, closing in an inescapable bite. With a crunch, they severed the man's spine. His body dropped away, hands yet holding the haft.

A man in the vanguard released his pike, drew his sword, and stabbed. The blade buried itself in a beast's belly. It sliced through scales and muscles and plunged into some black organ beneath. The Phyrexian shrieked. Acids sprayed from its stomach. They ate away the man's hand and arm to the elbow. He died beneath his falling foe.

The tumbling monster dropped sideways, crushing the third pikeman.

The fourth vaulted up the beast and drove his sword into the head of another. Steel cracked bone and brain. The monster— what seemed a giant ground sloth but could have been almost anything in that murk—was unimpressed. Its fist pounded its own head, crushing the pikeman and driving the sword deeper.

The vanguard was gone, and only ten feet gained into the cave.

"Forward!" Thaddeus commanded, taking the van.

His sword cut between two huge eyes. They peeled back on opposite sides of a split visage. Thaddeus kicked a foothold in the bisected sinus cavities and vaulted atop the hissing beast. He climbed the thing.

"Forward!"

Thaddeus's sword hewed a path through beasts. Slick with glistening-oil, his boots reached ground. He advanced into the dark.

Battle sounds suddenly hushed. Thaddeus whirled. Even the light of the entrance was lost. It was as though a door had slid silently closed behind him.

Thaddeus kept his sword at the ready. He reached to his belt, grabbed a flare, and broke the thing in half. A red flame shot from each edge. The light gleamed dimly off walls of smooth stone.

How did I get separated?

He spun, glimpsing movement out of the corner of his eye. Turning fully around, he watched for shadows against the dark wall. No one was there.

He should have looked up.

A metallic spider leg knocked his sword away. Crushing weight flung him to his back. His flare skipped angrily across the floor. Thaddeus struggled to grab a grenade. It was no good. His hands were pinned. He was trapped.

In the sulfuric half-light, a voice spoke. It was as omnipresent and alien as a cicada chorus: "Tsabo Tavoc wants you. Tsabo Tavoc will have you."

CHAPTER 27
She is So Light

Where once rot and death had filled the treetops, now music and life reigned.

Of course, the ravages of war remained—whole crowns had been eaten away, whole villages destroyed, whole families wiped from the face of Dominaria. The heights of Llanowar were gashed open to the skies. It would never be the same. Even after suckers grew to twigs and branches to boughs, the forest would forever bear the taste of glistening-oil. It was the curse of the cure.

The celebrants were not blind to all they had lost. That knowledge only deepened their joy. The disease had been stopped. One cure had come from below with the Seed of Freyalise, the other from above with the Scion of Benalia. Gerrard had granted immunity to those who were healthy, and Eladamri health to those who were sick. Between the two, they had saved Llanowar.

The feast spread through the eight treetops where once the

Staprion Elfhame had extended. Every last bit of corruption had been scoured away. Many boughs were bared to their quick. Tender new bark struggled to close exposed sections. With the aid of Multani, branches budded; leaves fanned into air. Vine networks sent tendrils to the ruined reaches. Sunlight streamed into the ancient heart of the wood.

What remained of the former palace was pulled down and fashioned into an altar and shrine for those who had fallen. Elves whose hollows were destroyed wove hanging nests of aerial roots. Giant spiders lent their spinnerets to string gossamer highways through the canopy.

Perhaps Llanowar would never be the same. Perhaps it would be better. All of it was because of three foreigners—one from a different forest, another from a different nation, and a third from a different world.

Multani, Gerrard, and Eladamri stood side-by-side on a lofted curve of high bough. The noontime sun warmed their shoulders. Below, in the broad lap of the tree, thronged the survivors of Staprion. On thread-ways to either side lingered the faithful of Jubilar. Other elves, farther out on the adjacent trees, had arrived from as far away as Kelfae and Hedressel. All had come to glimpse the elf rumored to be the Seed of Freyalise and to observe his strange and powerful comrades from afar. All had come to cheer and revel.

The adulation had given the men little chance to trade words. Since reaching this overlook, they had been busy with hand-waving, smiling, and nodding.

Gerrard was unwilling to delay longer. He reached out to Multani, a hand of flesh grasping a hand of vine. The crowd loved the gesture, their roars vaulting gladly up.

Over the uproar, Gerrard said, "I am glad, after all these years, to know that you live, Master Multani."

The green-man smiled, snail-shell teeth showing between rose-petal lips. "It is no easy thing to kill a maro-sorcerer. We don and doff our bodies as you do your clothes. I will not die, not truly, while Yavimaya yet lives."

Nodding in realization, Gerrard said, "Very truly, then, the last months brought you near to death."

"Yes," Multani replied. His eyes—twin fish swimming in socket-pools—flickered in remembered pain. "The Battle of Yavimaya is won, as is the Battle of Llanowar, thanks to you and Eladamri."

Eladamri turned to his comrades, clasping their hands. Again, the revelers cried out gladly.

"I am only a tool of higher powers," said Eladamri humbly.

"As are we all," Gerrard said with a laugh.

"As are we all," Multani agreed. "Still, Llanowar owes you both a great debt."

Drawing a deep breath, Gerrard said, "I would like to collect on that debt." His two companions looked surprised, but Gerrard waved away their concern. "It is the smallest of prices for you and the forest but the dearest treasure I could beg."

Eladamri stared seriously at his friend. "Whatever you ask."

"Whatever is in our power."

"It is in your power," Gerrard said. "Take us to *Weatherlight*. I will explain there."

Without a moment's pause, Multani's viny arms reached out around his companions, encircling them. More stalks and stems insinuated themselves through the framework of the nature spirit. His body grew. Long arms branched from his shoulders. Tendrils reached up to encircle boughs overhead. Multani pulled free of the overlook where they stood. Brachiating beneath the overhanging branches, Multani carried the two saviors of Llanowar over the head of the crowd.

Below, the people cried out in thrilled amazement.

Multani seemed a spider dangling from his thousand legs and picking his patient way across the canopy.

Ahead, *Weatherlight* rested in the broad crook of a quosumic tree. Even at midday, the ship gleamed like a jewel box. In addition to running-lanterns, she had been decked with festive lights for the celebration. The prison brigade thronged the deck, quaffing elven wine and cheering. A contingent of once-xenophobic Steal Leaf warriors had joined them, trading war stories. Above it all, in the noontime skies, the Benalian aerial armada swarmed. They seemed almost living fireworks, circling joyously.

With strange solemnity, Multani bore Gerrard and Eladamri toward the festive folk.

As they approached, the cheers and oaths quieted. Wine jacks ceased rising to lips, which in turn grew respectfully still. Everyone aboard *Weatherlight* knew the weight on Gerrard's heart. They knew the boon he would ask of Multani and Eladamri. The crowd separated as the green-man arrived.

Multani lowered himself into the midst of the people and released his passengers.

Gerrard set his boots to the familiar planks. "Below," he said simply. He gestured toward the hatch and led the way downward.

Grim jawed, Eladamri followed. On legs of twining wood, Multani shuffled after. They descended into the ship's deserted companionways, down to a single room that glowed with lantern light. Though it held numerous bunks, all were empty save one. In a chair beside the bunk, Orim the healer lingered. Her eyes were tired beneath black, coin-coifed hair. Tawny hands moved fretfully along the sheets.

Another woman lay beneath those sheets—this one a seeming skeleton. Her face was drawn and bone white. Her closed eyelids were gray. Even her thin lips were taut with pain, making a death's-head grimace.

Gerrard went to his knees as if his legs had been cut from beneath him. He clutched her hand—as light and curled as a dead twig.

"Hanna. Can you hear me? I've brought some friends, a savior and . . . and a god."

Eladamri's eyes were dark beneath his lifted eyebrows. Multani lingered in silence just behind him.

"They are going to take you to a place where you can be healed. Caves beneath the forest. Thousands were healed there, healed with a touch. They're going to take us down where you'll be made whole again."

Swallowing grimly, Eladamri said, "You must understand, Gerrard, it is a matter of belief. The caves make belief real."

Gerrard's gaze was bright with anger. "I'll believe you. I'll believe anything. Just make her well."

"Yes," Eladamri replied heavily. "If there are greater powers at work in us, she will be healed."

There were no more words to say after that. Multani stooped. Every fibrous stalk grew a sudden silky down across it. His fingers opened in milkweed pods. His arms became a cottonwood blanket. Tenderly, he reached beneath Hanna's still form and lifted her in her draping sheets.

"She is so light," Multani murmured before he could stop himself.

Gerrard's eyes clouded. "Take her ahead of us. Eladamri will lead us—Orim and I—down to the caves. Take her and let the caves work on her. Let them begin their work." A tragic hope lit his face. "If there is justice in the multiverse, she'll greet me herself when I get there."

Wordlessly, Multani bore Hanna from *Weatherlight*'s sick bay. He climbed to the deck, followed by Gerrard, Eladamri, and Orim.

Silence surrounded them. If the three men were the saviors of Llanowar, the woman they bore in their midst—skeletal within her pure white sheets—was the martyr. The ravages of plague were painted plain across her, and yet her former beauty shone through. That she was Gerrard's love was whispered among the prison brigade and the Steel Leaf elves. One by one, the revelers went to their knees—one by one and then ten by ten. They saw on Hanna's face the daughters and sisters and mothers they themselves had lost.

Tendrils sprouted from Multani, catching hold of a nearby network of vines. Without pause, he drew himself and Hanna smoothly over the rail and began his descent.

Gerrard watched, his gaze dipping lower and lower until she disappeared from sight. A shuddering breath moved through him.

A hand settled on his shoulder, startling him. He turned, seeing Eladamri's solemn face—prominent nose and chin, eyes profound and piercing. It was no wonder the elves saw a leader in this man.

"Choose the ten who believe most in you. I will take Liin Sivi and the nine who believe most in me. Their faith will help."

Nodding numbly, Gerrard leaned on the rail, staring.

"I would be . . . honored to be included in the company," came a solemn rumble at his side. Gerrard looked up to see Tahngarth, no more than a looming shadow in that bright company.

Once, the minotaur had considered Gerrard a spoiled, selfish, and angry young man. Somewhere along the line, the bull-man's opinion had changed—perhaps because Gerrard had changed.

He clutched the minotaur's four-fingered hand. "I would be honored."

"You'd have to drive me off with a stick," Sisay volunteered, coming up behind the minotaur.

"Squee too," the goblin said on his other side. He crouched back from Gerrard's desolated stare, lifting his hand as though he expected a stick to fall any moment.

"Sisay, Squee, Orim, Tahngarth—yes, thank you all," Gerrard said gratefully.

Something massive moved among the kneeling soldiers. They scurried up and back. A gasp went through the group. In their midst rose a steaming specter. Hissing heat peeled away from muscles of silver.

"Would anyone like a shoulder ride?" Karn asked.

* * * * *

Gerrard, Eladamri, and their comrades descended within the Palace Tree. They gradually left behind the sounds of festival. First came the creak of growing wood, then the slosh of subterranean seas beyond the root walls. At last, only stone silence remained.

All the while, the party's lanterns bathed the tortuous descent in flickering light. Ragged splinters jutted from every wall. Giant cobwebs laced the spiraling way. The corpses had been removed, but still it was a haunted place.

Eladamri abjured the company to banish doubt and embrace hope. He sang a cycle of elven songs. His folk joined him, all but the ever-watchful Liin Sivi.

Gerrard and *Weatherlight*'s command crew meanwhile traded

stories of their travels—of Hanna steering the ship past the Rathi slivers, of her heroism inside the Stronghold, of her encyclopedic understanding of *Weatherlight*, of her pinpoint navigation, her shy wit, her laughter. They spoke of courage, strength, and wisdom, not illness or death.

At last, the way opened. Eladamri's songs grew only louder as he progressed beneath a series of ribbed archways and down into the Dreaming Caves. Beautiful visions flowed from the singers' mouths and coiled in air around them.

Eladamri lifted his lantern. The light reached out across the cavern and splashed tepidly over a figure below.

Multani had formed himself into a great, woody altar, cradling the sick woman. Hanna seemed a figure laid on a pyre. It was clear she had not healed a whit.

Gerrard stopped in his tracks, panting. He closed his eyes and stooped, setting hands on his knees as if he had been struck in the belly.

Eladamri approached. "You must bring her back, Gerrard. Bring her into our minds—whole and healthy and happy."

Breath hitching in him, Gerrard stood. A manic light came to his face. He smiled a cheerless smile. He raised the wick of his lantern so that his face glared brilliantly.

"Have I told you, Eladamri, of the woman I love?"

An approving look came into the elf's eyes. "No. Not nearly enough. Tell me about her."

"She has the most beautiful hair," Gerrard said, blinking. "The color of wheat—spun gold. She doesn't ever do anything with it. She just pins it back out of her way. She doesn't have to do anything with it—"

"She puts grease in it," Squee blurted.

Gerrard laughed, a little too harshly. "Yes, bearing grease and engine oil and soot from a coal box—this is her makeup kit. She always looks great." Images of Hanna formed in the air—her smile, her glad eyes, her lithe figure kneeling beside some hunk of hardware.

"Yes," Eladamri said. "I see her. Tell me more."

Gerrard grasped Eladamri's shoulders and said fervently. "Did I tell you she saved my life on Mercadia? She pretended to be an elevator mechanic. Dressed up in Mercadian laborer's clothes. She tried to make herself look fat and grubby, but she's too tall, too statuesque, and even with grease and soot she's about the cleanest looking creature in the multiverse."

Before Tahngarth's eyes swam visions of that bright day, Hanna and Squee and the boy Atalla plotting to free the captives.

"More. Tell us more," Eladamri insisted.

"She sabotaged that cage pretty well. She shut it down for a week. Fact was, next time we left the city, we flew out on wings of cloth, like angels . . ." Gerrard gagged on his words. He reached out to his comrades. "She's the smartest one on board, don't you think?—trained on Tolaria. Hanna's dad is the Mage Master Barrin, but she outstrips him in artifact knowledge. Remember her rebuilding the engine in Mercadia? Remember her threading the needle over Benalia? Remember?"

Visions swam brightly before the eyes of the comrades.

"Come!" Gerrard said. "See for yourselves. Look on her perfect skin, her blushing cheeks—the sweetest smile you ever saw. Come over here, let me show you. So thin and strong, perfect health! Let me introduce you."

Dragging at Eladamri, Gerrard led the group rapidly, excitedly to the place where Hanna lay. The swarming visions followed them. Airy spirits encircled the woman, caressing her. They seemed at first to be holy raiments and then to be healthy flesh. The mists wrapped her atrophied muscles and filled them out. Belief cloaked her gaunt frame in strength. The grim set of her teeth became a smile, the sunken sockets became bright blue eyes. It was the old Hanna—strong and glad and whole.

"Do you see?" Gerrard shouted. "Do you see?"

"Yes!" Eladamri replied. "I see!"

Gerrard slid his hands under Hanna and lifted her. "Do you see!"

The glamour did not come with her. The delusion of health peeled away from her skin. Misty muscle dissipated to gaunt infirmity. The eyes that had seemed open were closed now, had never opened. Her loveliness was a skull.

"Oh!" Gerrard said in sudden shock. "Oh!"

Eladamri clasped his arm. "It's all right. It's all right."

"No, it's not all right! Nothing is all right!"

"You did all you could," Eladamri soothed. "Our belief can't heal her—I realize that now. It is only her belief that could heal her. If she could awaken from this coma, she could save herself. Otherwise . . . You did all you could."

"Oh!" Gerrard repeated, falling to his knees. He looked up piteously at his comrades. "She is so light!"

CHAPTER 28
Why Heroes Fight

Thaddeus awoke, pinioned beneath the spider woman Tsabo Tavoc. Her compound eyes gleamed like twin gemstones in her pallid face. Her mouth segments twitched in concentration as she stared down at him. The massive weight of her body pressed on him in eight spike-tipped feet. Above her head, a smooth rock ceiling gleamed with myriad lanterns. They sent tendrils of smoke up across the wall to gather and coil in the vault. The swirling soot made a black halo above the spider woman's head.

"He awakens," she said in Phyrexian.

From birth, Thaddeus had learned languages both human and inhuman. He was fluent in Thrannish and so could parse out Phyrexian.

A seeming smile formed across the segments of Tsabo Tavoc's mouth. She withdrew slightly from him. Her fingertips were gory. A scalpel in her hand ran with blood. The red stuff steamed in the cold, wet air of the cave.

Again came her buggy voice. "How admirable."

The Phyrexian commander gathered her legs beneath her and shifted away. Her horrible weight remained on him. Only then did he realize it was not she who held him down. Spikes did. Driven through wrists and ankles, shoulders and hips, they pinned him to an examination table.

Thaddeus bucked on the steely block. Joints pried hopelessly against the heads of the spikes. None budged.

Thaddeus hissed. He should have been able to rip the spikes out. His arms were somehow unresponsive. An aching weakness filled his chest. Lifting his head, Thaddeus glimpsed the reason.

His blue flesh lay open to red innards. From the notch in his throat to the ring processes of his pelvis, he had been sliced open. Each layer of living flesh—skin and muscle and tendon—had been meticulously flayed back one by one. Pins identified important structures. Similar tags rested on his organs. Numbered slips of paper clung to his liver, his spleen, pancreas, stomach, viscera. Tsabo Tavoc had even sawn away one after another of his ribs, revealing gray lungs and flailing heart.

"Do you see how quickly he discerns his condition?" Tsabo Tavoc asked, her voice buzzing. She approached. The gory scalpel twirled deftly in her grasp. "Awake but moments, and he understands what we are doing here, understands he will never again be whole. He will die, and he knows it. See how quickly he calms? Truly, he is the pinnacle of humanity."

Thaddeus tried to respond. All that emerged was a red spray across his throat. He could produce no sound, could feel no breath between his lips.

Tsabo Tavoc loomed up above him. "Are you missing something?" she asked, holding up a larynx. "Quite a costly contrivance, this. A descended voice-box allows you to speak, but at risk of choking. It is too bad your master felt so tied to human physiology, retaining such weaknesses as this. Of course, you needn't worry about choking anymore."

Approving hisses rose from figures packed around the edges of the cavern.

Turning his head, Thaddeus peered past dissection carts and

experimental apparatuses to glimpse the watchers. Red-robed vat priests stood five rows thick around the cavern. They leaned avidly toward Thaddeus. Their eyes gleamed beneath the folds of their hoods. Desiccated flesh clung to skull-like heads. Scabrous hands hung loose beneath priestly sleeves.

Tsabo Tavoc made a long slice in Thaddeus's thigh.

He twitched as each successive neuron was severed. His eyes rolled in his head. He would not have cried out even if he had had the vocal cords to do so, but a raking sigh emerged from the stoma in his throat.

"Here, though, is significant improvement," Tsabo Tavoc said, neatly drawing back folds of skin to reveal muscles and their neural networks. "Do you see the myelin sheaths on these nerve bundles? They speed impulse. This nerve cluster travels to the base of the spine, where lies the cortex that processes sensory and motor information for the legs. At the base of the spine rests the innovation—a second cerebellum encased in the coccyx. It speeds response time, allowing Metathran extraordinary agility. It also prevents paraplegia. A Metathran can fight on, despite a broken back. A similar though smaller node controls the arms."

There seemed genuine appreciation among the vat priests. They produced an inhuman sound, halfway between the purr of a cat and the hiss of a roach.

"Compare to the original design," Tsabo Tavoc said, withdrawing from the table where Thaddeus lay. Her legs clicked across the stony floor.

Thaddeus turned his head to watch her. She reached another table where lay another form—a human woman. She had been tied in place instead of spiked, but she was similarly cut open. The woman shivered in dread at the Phyrexian's approach.

Tsabo Tavoc picked up one of the scalpels and sliced a long, deep line down the woman's leg. "Here, we have larger deposits of adipose tissue. These are not intended to power the skeletal muscles but rather to provision the whole body with food should famine occur. It is another concession to breeding ability. If this woman is bearing young, she will need extra fat deposits. The adipose tissue makes her a slower fighter. Her pelvis is inefficiently wide, as we have seen, and this bundle of leg neurons reaches not to the base of her spine but to her brain. The uterus—prone to numerous diseases and chronic breakdown—takes up an inordinate portion of the abdomen. All in all, this is a crude design, intended for child-bearing instead of war.

"The males are no better. They bear external genitalia that are extremely vulnerable to injury. Both genders are subject to intermittent madness caused by these systems. Humans and all the indigenous creatures of Dominaria still rely upon sexual reproduction. Such is the way for creatures that live beyond the salvation of Yawgmoth.

"Only these Metathran have ascended. They are nearer to Phyrexians than any other creature. They are in some senses lost cousins of ours. Urza has made them so." Tsabo Tavoc lifted her gaze from the gory thigh muscle. She raised the scalpel thoughtfully and set the red tip on her own cheek. "One wonders, had we not launched this invasion, how long it would have taken Urza to make all Dominarians into Phyrexians."

Absently setting the knife on the table, Tsabo Tavoc strolled to the middle of the floor. Her eyes gleamed philosophically in the lantern light. "Here is the great irony." She flung one bloody hand out toward Thaddeus. "This pinnacle of glory was created not for its own sake. The Metathran were created to defend humanity—squalid, imperfect, imperfectible larva." She gestured toward the woman lying beside her. "Urza has engineered a warrior that can be spiked at wrists and shoulders, ankles and hips, can be cut open without anesthesia, can withstand a multiply broken back and still fight. The whole reason this creature exists, though, is to defend beings too weak to escape simple rope bonds, creatures that must be heavily drugged to bear the rigors of vivisection. The cream of humanity came into being to defend its dregs."

Tsabo Tavoc could not have anticipated what happened next. Even in her compound eyes, she did not see it.

The flayed woman had found the scalpel Tsabo Tavoc had left. She had used it to cut the bonds on her arms. She lurched up from the examination table. With a swift motion, she cut those around her legs. Roaring, she lunged off the table, scalpel raised to stab.

It was a futile gesture. She could not have wounded let alone slain Tsabo Tavoc. She could hardly have stood with one leg sliced open. It didn't matter. The woman held a fury that could not be denied.

A vat priest caught her before she could reach Tsabo Tavoc.

Shrieking, she rammed her scalpel into the vat-priest's skull. It was her final act. Her abdomen disgorged itself on the priest's clawed feet. He collapsed. Together, the compleated Phyrexian and the incompleated woman fell, dead, to the floor.

Silence settled. Tsabo Tavoc stared down with mild interest at the bodies. The spiracles along her sides breathed slowly as she drew in the aroma of death. "As primitive and inefficient as these humans are, they fight all out of reason. It matters little. They die either way."

Thaddeus thrashed against his spikes, unable to escape.

Tsabo Tavoc once again turned her attentions on him.

* * * * *

Gerrard gently lay Hanna in her sick bay berth. She was no better for her sojourn in the darkness. Gerrard was much worse. Hope had fled from him. If Orim could not save Hanna, if Eladamri and Multani could not, she would not be saved.

"How will I fight unless you are with me?" he whispered, kissing her lightly. Her lips were as dry as paper. "What will I fight for?"

Hanna was more than his beloved. She was his heart, his courage. He fought for her. Before she entered his life, Gerrard had been a bitter young man. If he lost her now, what was he? There would be nothing left but fury. There would be no difference between Gerrard and the Phyrexians.

"Oh how I will slay them," Gerrard said bitterly as he clutched Hanna's skeletal hand. "I will be my own plague. I will rot them away. I've had enough of portal wars and serums. I want a fight, a real fight. I want teeth against knuckles and broken noses and knives in the eyes."

"I have a fight for you," came an elderly voice at the sick bay door. The blind seer hobbled slowly into the chamber. "Not I, but Dominaria. You have lost Benalia, and saved Llanowar. Now there is Koilos."

"Koilos? A hole in the desert," Gerrard hissed.

The old man shrugged. "More than that. At Koilos the Phyrexians were first driven from the world. At Koilos they first returned in the time of Urza. Now, it is their only land portal. If that hole in the desert is lost, all is lost."

Gerrard shook his head bleakly, gazing at Hanna. "All *is* lost."

"Grief can wait," the old man replied. "Koilos cannot. The Metathran have been beaten back. One of their commanders is captured and near death. They need you and your ship. They need the Benalish air fleet, the prison brigade, elf shock troops, and their leader Eladamri."

"Eladamri?" Gerrard blurted. "He has a nation to rebuild. He won't go."

The blind seer sighed. He eased himself to sit on a bunk. "He will go. Saviors are not builders. The heir to Staprion wishes that he go. No, Eladamri's work is done here but not so at Koilos. He and his elite warriors will go. Multani, too, will go.

"Multani!"

"He was present for the birth of this living ship. He provided her hull from the Heart of Yavimaya. He goes with us, in the very wood of *Weatherlight*. He will heal her every wound. In some senses, this is his ship." The old sage lifted an eyebrow. "In some senses, you are his as well. Multani trained you. He wants to see how his old student does. You cannot blame your masters for taking an interest in your doings."

"My doings?" Gerrard echoed.

"Yes. Your doings. Koilos is your fight, Gerrard."

Gerrard stared down at the dying form of his beloved. "Of course. It's a fight Hanna would approve." His mouth flattened into a bitter line. "And, besides, at Koilos there are plenty of Phyrexians to kill."

CHAPTER 29
Battles Won and Lost

Weatherlight topped a ridge of sand above the plains of Koilos and soared down the far slope. Gerrard's gunnery harness held him in place as the deck dropped out beneath him.

"There are the buggers," he growled.

Ahead and for miles to the horizon camped Phyrexian troops.

"Attack formation!" Gerrard shouted into the speaking tube. "Signal the fleet. Strafe the troops. Ray cannons, plasma jets, goblin bombs. Kill 'em with whatever you've got. Let's let them know Benalia's revenge has arrived."

A cheer rose from the prison brigade. They crowded the decks, elven bows clutched in their eager hands. Among them were Steal Leaf troops. Their leader, Eladamri, stood at the prow. He lifted high his longbow, nocked a flaming arrow, and sent the shaft streaking away. It raced ahead of *Weatherlight* and sank among the Phyrexian troops. The shaft cracked through black scale. It punched into oil-blood. The creature ignited, blazing blue. Elves and prisoners whooped excitedly.

"Fire!" Gerrard shouted. "Fire!"

All along the decks, elves and men drew arrows from pots of

233

burning pitch. They set notch to string and loosed. From *Weatherlight*, rings of fire spread. Where those flaming waves touched ground, Phyrexians blazed and flared and exploded.

Gerrard unleashed his own fire. Red-hot bursts of energy leaped from the barrel of his ray cannon. They stabbed faster than arrows. The bolts ripped through monsters and their sleeping sties, tore apart trench worms, blasted through pens of live food. From Tahngarth's gun, another bolt roared. It cut a parallel trough to Gerrard's attack. Each line of energy felled hundreds of Phyrexians, but there were hundreds of thousands.

Benalish assault ships dropped down to *Weatherlight*'s beam. They loosed their own arsenals, not as flashy, but in their own way deadly enough. From the stern hatches of round-bellied bombers, gray goblin bombs rolled. They dropped in twisted lines. Smoke barked up where they struck. Chunks of scale and bone tumbled through the mounded smoke. Hoppers jagged like serpents' teeth above the armies. Their quarrels pelted down in a deadly hail.

Gerrard loosed another volley of ray cannon fire. He gazed appreciatively at the broad line of destruction that his armada cut through the Phyrexian hordes.

"They've got no airships. It's like shooting fish in a barrel!"

He spoke too soon. The beasts might not have airships, but they had brought cannons. Fire spat from entrenched batteries. Crimson and black, rays roared skyward.

One bolt struck a falling stream of goblin bombs. It ignited them. In midair, they detonated. Each new explosion triggered a second and third. Like a fuse, the line of bombs carried their explosions up toward the stern of the bomber. Shrapnel tore into the fuselage. The detonations went to completion. A white blaze erupted around the ship. A thousand explosions roared out. Hunks of ship cascaded down.

Another beam rippled through a line of fighters. One after another, they flew into the radiance and were cloven in two. Halves spiraled down in fiery wreckage.

A third bolt—this placed best of all—smashed into *Weatherlight*'s port airfoil. The spars lit with fire. The canvas flashed away to nothing. *Weatherlight* listed hard to port and began to roll over.

"Take her up!" Gerrard cried even as his latest shot raked the enemy lines.

"I know! I know!" Sisay shouted back through the speaking tube.

The starboard airfoil slapped closed, and the ship's engines roared. *Weatherlight* lolled upright and rocketed heavenward.

"Signal the fleet! Break off the assault!" Gerrard ordered. He braced himself against the hot casing of the gun. *Weatherlight* jigged up through a rack of clouds. "Rendezvous at the Metathran camp. Land and repair!"

He had breath for little more. The ship ascended like a comet. Gerrard and his crew and their fugitive armies held tight to the meteoric craft. It vaulted just ahead of the cannon fire, outpacing killing heads of flame. The Benalish armada straggled upward in the great ship's wake.

In canyons of concealing cloud, *Weatherlight* leveled out. Gerrard gave a gusty sigh.

"Let's hope for a better reception from the Metathran."

* * * * *

Within his tent, Commander Agnate stared bleakly at the tactical maps of Koilos. They lay in a sloppy stack across his field table. Once, they had been neatly stored, each in its own tube. Once, Thaddeus and Agnate had strolled their compasses easily across lines of topography. Now, the maps bore the fretful, fruitless scribbles of a commander in a hopeless engagement.

Agnate was trapped. His forces had been winnowed horribly by the last, disastrous assault. Fifty thousand Metathran had marched into battle behind him, and twenty thousand had fled. They had made camp here, twenty miles beyond the caves—out of reach of the monsters. Members of Thaddeus's army slowly joined them. The field was lost. The Metathran were in full rout. Thaddeus's force was equally reduced. Thirty thousand of them remained, but they had lost their commander.

Thaddeus was easily worth ten thousand troops.

He is worth more than that, Agnate mused bitterly. Thaddeus was the other half of his mind. Even distance could not block their shared thoughts—until Tsabo Tavoc. She knew of their bond and targeted it. She tore the point from the compass, leaving only a lead nib to turn, hopelessly alone.

Agnate could not think without Thaddeus. Together, they had planned an assault of a hundred thousand Metathran on a hundred thousand Phyrexians. The Metathran ranks had been halved, and the Phyrexian ranks had doubled. Agnate had positioned paper troops in various arrangements throughout the broad plain. Even with a four-to-one kill ratio, no Metathran would remain to possess the field. It would be suicide to attack now and swifter and surer suicide with every passing hour.

A sound intruded on Agnate's bleak reverie. He had blocked out camp sounds—crackling fires, conversation, strummed lyres— and so the slow-mounting roar startled him alert. Lurching up from his camp stool, Agnate caught his head in the peak of the man-sized tent. With a growl, he ducked and emerged. The flaps slapped angrily together behind him.

Mounting thunder filled the dusty sky. It was unmistakable— the approach of airships. The Phyrexians were bringing sky machines to destroy them.

Agnate shook his head grimly. I couldn't make a damned decision myself, and now they have decided for me.

All around, Agnate's troops stood stunned, staring upward. His indecision had infected even them.

"To arms! To arms!" Agnate bellowed. "Train the guns! Wake! It's time to die."

Soldiers snatched up their swords and pikes. They cranked crossbows. They scrambled to rip covers from cannons and wheel them about. Blocks of powder slid down the barrels of bombards. Powerstone charges mounted within ray cannons. Shouts filled the air. It was a sound that heartened Agnate after days of silent fear and indecision.

"You might not want to fire on these," came a voice abruptly at his side. "These are your reinforcements."

Agnate whirled, sword raking out, and found himself staring at the grim visage of Urza Planeswalker. The man's face was battle weary. His ash-blond hair was disheveled and singed—though only a moment's attention would make it perfect. Urza had not had a moment to spare.

"Master," Agnate said breathlessly, dropping to one knee.

"Call off your gunners!" Urza replied with quiet urgency.

"Gunners, stand down!" Agnate commanded without standing. His call went down the lines. To Urza, he said, "Reinforcements?"

"Coalition forces. Airships, a Benalish army, an elf strike force, and a replacement for Thaddeus," Urza said simply.

"There will never be a replacement for Thaddeus."

"We will see."

Suddenly, the sky was split by a hurtling ship. The vessel clove the air into canyons of white exhaust. The ship was sleek and large, unmistakable to any Metathran's eye. This was *Weatherlight*—Urza's angel. Her lines were etched into the dream minds of all Urza's children. Her lines meant salvation.

It was a ragged salvation. One airfoil had burned away, and the other was folded like a praying hand. Burns scored her hull. Frightened faces crowded her rail. In the ship's rocketing wake came an even less impressive swarm of vessels. All were small. Some gave out puffs of smoke. Others whined gnatlike.

Weatherlight cut her starboard thrust and spread her remaining airfoil. She slowed and banked, beginning a long circle around the Metathran camp. If she could land without crashing, it would be a miracle. Metathran were raised to believe in miracles from *Weatherlight*.

Rising to his feet, Agnate watched the wounded war bird and her fledglings circle. "Who is this replacement for Thaddeus?"

"His name is Eladamri. He is a Skyshroud elf from Rath. He is the Seed of Freyalise."

"What is a Freyalise?"

"He is my choice to replace Thaddeus."

"He is not my choice, nor the choice of Thaddeus's troops," Agnate replied quietly. "He is no good until we have chosen him."

"I know."

"And if he fails the test?"

"Then Koilos is lost."

* * * * *

Weatherlight's landing would have been better described as a controlled crash. It was controlled in the sense that Sisay was at the helm, and she was among the best fliers in the multiverse. Also, its engines took orders from a silver golem—undoubtedly the best engineer anywhere. The rest of the crew did all they could—which meant tying themselves to something that would not move and informing their gods they might soon need afterlife accommodations. Aside from these efforts, the landing was simply a crash.

Weatherlight's landing spines sliced into a sand dune. They flung up grit as if it were water. The hull smashed to ground. It groaned under its own weight and bounced briefly aloft again. Sand streamed from a mangled spine. The ship smacked the top of the next dune and knocked the peak off. The keel sawed through packed dust before hanging up on a layer of gravel. *Weatherlight* pitched forward. She slid down the far side of the dune. Sand shoved her sideways. Flinging a blanket of the stuff, *Weatherlight* came to rest on the side of a natural bowl in the desert.

Panting in his gunner's rig, Gerrard spat grit from his teeth and said, "That wasn't so bad."

Suddenly, the bare dunes all around teemed with Metathran soldiers. Pikes, swords, and axes gleamed in their hands as they topped the hills. They kept coming—hundreds, thousands, tens of thousands. Their blue faces were grim, and their boots sent ominous dust clouds up to shadow the great airship.

"All right," Gerrard allowed as he pulled himself out of the tangled traces. "Maybe the bad part is still to come."

In all the surrounding ring of soldiers, there was a single clear avenue. The commander of the Metathran marched there, accompanied by his personal retinue. Garbed in silver battle armor and bearing a naked sword, the commander had a solemnity that bordered on belligerence.

Donning his most winning smile—though just now it was full of sand—Gerrard came to the rail and called out to the commander, "Hail, Friends of Dominaria. I am Gerrard Capashen. I have come to ally my forces with yours."

"I know who you are," shouted the commander curtly. "And I know why you have come. Where is Eladamri?"

"Eladamri?" echoed Gerrard blankly.

"Yes. Eladamri. The Seed of Freyalise. He is to take command of half my army."

Gerrard shook his head in astonishment but managed not to echo the words. "How do you know all this?"

"A god told me."

"I get a lot of that," interrupted the Skyshroud elf from amidships. "I am Eladamri."

"Come," beckoned the Metathran commander. "You must prove yourself to me and to my troops."

"I get a lot of that too," replied Eladamri. "What must I do?"

The commander replied with even steel. "Draw my blood before I draw yours."

* * * * *

It was a duel, like so many others. This had been an age of duels—Urza and Mishra, Xantcha and Gix, Gerrard and Volrath, and now Eladamri and Agnate. It seemed the whole world had come into being between pairs of adversaries squaring off on either side of some table, bringing every weapon, every spell, every ally they had gathered over the years and fighting a duel to the death. Agnate and Eladamri did not fight to the death, of course—but to first blood. There was little difference when both men were weapon masters and both fought with broadswords.

As the gladiators fought, Gerrard watched from a crowded port rail. Beside him stood Liin Sivi, Eladamri's closest companion. Her nostrils flared with every sword blow. In white-knuckled hands, she gripped the hilt of her toten-vec. It was clear she wished she could be down in that battle. She wasn't the only one. Steel Leaf elves watched avidly, shoulder to shoulder with Benalish warriors and *Weatherlight*'s own crew.

Beyond the ship, Metathran filled the sand dunes. It was a natural arena, and Metathran were a naturally bloodthirsty crowd.

Eladamri rushed in. He was the quicker of the two. He knew the cuts and feints taught by wild men and scrappers. His blade lanced toward Agnate's gut. It would be a killing blow if it landed. It was well placed. If Agnate dodged or knocked the sword up, down, or to either side, the tip would catch his flesh and score first blood.

A cheer rose from the deck of *Weatherlight*.

Agnate did not try to knock the blade away or attempt to dodge. He merely caught the sword in a gauntleted hand. He was the stronger. His classical training made him keen eyed and efficient. With a powerful yank, he hauled the blade forward, just above his own sword. Eladamri must either let go or overbalance and sprawl onto his foe's sword.

The Metathran shouted their praise from the sand-dune coliseum.

Except that Eladamri vaulted over his trapped blade. He used Agnate's own strength to carry him in an easy arc above both swords. Eladamri flipped, landing on his feet behind the Metathran warrior and yanking his sword free.

On ship and sand dune both, the watchers cheered.

Eladamri swung his sword in a gutting stroke.

The Metathran commander was no longer there. One step carried him beyond the elf's blade. A second step brought him back during the follow-through, when Eladamri would be defenseless. Agnate's sword stabbed for his side.

Eladamri slid sideways. The stroke nicked armor but missed flesh. Eladamri kicked the weapon away. His foot trailing a swath of sand that temporarily blinded the towering warrior. Agnate staggered back. This would be Eladamri's winning stroke.

Cheers from *Weatherlight*'s deck mixed with growls from the Metathran troops.

Both fell suddenly silent.

Eladamri stepped back, waiting for his opponent to clear his eyes.

In the hush, Agnate's words were heard by all. "You would be a fool to let a Phyrexian clear his eyes."

Eladamri's responded wryly. "You, friend, are no Phyrexian."

The roar of the crowd united ship and sand dunes.

Gerrard was glad. Eladamri was doing it again. He was bringing disparate people together.

A voice broke through the ovation, the voice of a very old, very tired man. "She is asking for you, Gerrard."

Applauding Agnate's escape from a back stab, Gerrard said distractedly, "Who is?"

"Hanna."

Wheeling, Gerrard stared incredulously at the blind seer. "Sh-she's awake?"

The old man nodded, his face shadowed in the wide brim of his hat. "But not for long."

Gerrard shoved his way across the deck. He reached the amidships hatch and descended. It took only moments to clamber down the stairs to the sick bay. It seemed hours. Gerrard fairly vaulted across the room, falling to his knees at Hanna's side.

"You're awake! Hanna! You're awake!"

She smiled a wan smile through rictus lips. "The old man. He did something."

"He's healing you!" Gerrard gasped, though even he knew this hope was false.

"No. He is letting us say good-bye."

"Don't say that!"

Despite the plague's ravages, she was somehow beautiful in that moment. "I have to, and so do you."

Gerrard grasped her shoulders, felt only cold bones in his hands, and let go. "How can I live without you?"

"You lived without me for twenty-six years," Hanna said sadly.

Gerrard's smile was rueful. "We all remember how worthless I was then."

A loud cheer shook the sands beyond the ship.

"What's happening?"

"A duel," Gerrard said. "It's nothing. Someone lost his partner—"

"It's a new world being born, Gerrard," Hanna replied wistfully. "It's a new world, and the partners of the old must say good-bye."

"No." His eyes glimmered intently. "No. I won't say it."

"Then I will die without hearing it—"

"You won't die. You can't—"

"I can, and I will," Hanna said. Her lids slid slowly down her blue eyes. "The old sage's magic cannot last much longer. Good-bye, Gerrard."

"I'll say I love you. I'll say you're everything to me. But I won't say—"

She trembled once last. Her final breath left in a long, sweet sigh.

An ovation roared through the heavens, shaking the ship's vast beams.

"No, Hanna," Gerrard groaned. He leaned over, sliding his arms beneath her. A tear fell on the white sheets. He lifted her. There was nothing in his arms, nothing at all. She was gone. "No, Hanna. No. I won't say it. I can't say it."

A voice came at the door—loud and excited, with a clear Benalish accent. "He's done it! Eladamri has bested the Metathran!"

Clutching that lifeless shell to his breast, Gerrard whispered simply, "Good-bye, Hanna. Good-bye."

CHAPTER 30
The Nine Titans

Urza stood on a sand dune overlooking the duel grounds. His cloak billowed with the breezes of night. One hand clutched his war staff. The other fidgeted at the edge of his cloak. It was a momentous hour.

Below, warriors thronged the sandy arena and the deck of the mired ship. They shouted their excitement to the heavens. In their midst stood Eladamri, victorious above a fallen Agnate. The elf's broadsword dripped Metathran blood. He had cut a shallow slice along the warrior's biceps—the sort a human could heal in a week and a Metathran in a day. It meant nothing and yet everything. Eladamri would command half the Metathran army, leading warriors who believed in him. Perhaps more importantly, he would complete Agnate. Eladamri could never replace Thaddeus, of course, but he could bring fight back to these beaten soldiers. That would be enough.

Victory in the arena and defeat in the ship. Even from where he stood, Urza could sense Hanna's death. Planeswalkers could heal most diseases with a thought but not Phyrexian plague. A futile regret fled through Urza, a wish that he had studied disease processes instead of artifice. It was foolishness. His machines would save millions of lives—they could not be reasonably exchanged for this one life. Even so, this was a loss. Hanna had anchored Gerrard. Without her, he would be a different man, a lesser man. Urza hoped only that Gerrard would still be sufficient to his role.

"I shall have to tell Barrin of his daughter's death," Urza reasoned, "once he has won the battle of Urborg."

Victory in the arena and defeat in the ship. It was a momentous hour. Urza's own labors in the coming minutes were critical. Taking one last breath of the dust of Koilos—a smell that took him back to the days with his brother—Urza planeswalked away from the dune.

He did not step into the chaos between worlds. That was a place for mortals. Urza did not have to travel that way, though sometimes he visited the Blind Eternities when he needed time to think.

Not now.

Urza appeared in the gloaming of a forested hillside. He stood in the minotaur homelands. An-Havva lay below, but he had no interest in minotaur cities. A single cabin stood on the hill. It was picturesque—what seemed a mere hunting cabin. A fieldstone pathway led among wildflowers. Chink logs held aloft a pile of thatch. A queer little chimney contentedly puffed smoke into the air. Quaint and tiny, it was meant to seem so. Its owner had built a cabin that was larger inside than out.

Urza walked up the fieldstone path. Through the soles of his boots he felt the cool stones. They were reporting his approach to the man within. Some intruders dropped dead on the path. Those who stole through the wildflowers fell into a sleep that proved eternal. Urza was not susceptible to such protections. Neither did he wish to circumvent propriety and incur the resentment of another planeswalker.

The door was round topped and rugged. Urza knocked on it with the shimmering head of his war staff.

"Good evening, Taysir. The time has come."

Without a sound, the door swung suddenly inward. A short, thin man stood there, his bushy brows peaked dubiously. Though bald on top, the man had a regular mane of white hair, and his beard was cinched at his sternum. He blinked deep, querulous eyes, and his voice whuffed with bookish intensity.

"Time? Time?"

"Yes," Urza replied. "The hour has come. Dominaria hangs in the balance."

"Doesn't it always?" Taysir replied dryly.

"Who is it, Father?" asked a young woman who appeared at Taysir's side. She seemed a great-great-granddaughter to him. Her shoulder-length hair was black beside his linty locks, her face smooth and bright next to his pruny visage. She saw Urza and scowled. "Oh, it's you."

Apologizing with a smile, Urza made a shallow bow to the woman. "Hello, Daria. It is time for your father to come to the defense of the world."

"If you are taking him, I'm coming with you."

Urza's face turned dark. "This was never part of the agreement."

"It is now," Taysir said quietly. He rubbed his throat, loose folds of skin beneath his beard. Louder, he went on. "We've agreed. We go together or not at all."

"You didn't discuss it with me," Urza quietly protested.

"You need planeswalkers," Taysir said. "She is of our ilk and powerful even in her youth."

Urza considered. "I do need someone to replace Teferi."

Taysir smiled. "Teferi's pulled a Teferi?"

Huffing irritably, Urza said, "Lock your doors. Snuff your candles. Douse your fires. You're both coming."

Daria gave a begrudging grin and hugged her father. "I'll get our stuff," she said, ducking back within the door.

The glow in the cabin windows went dark. The sudden rush of steam up the chimney smelled of cool ash. A moment later, Daria emerged. A pair of packs rode on her shoulders. They seemed small, but as with Taysir in all things, they were larger within than without. Daria shooed her father from the doorway and emerged into the blue gloaming of the hillside.

Panting slightly, she said, "We're ready, Urza Planeswalker."

"Are you ready, Daria Planeswalker?" mocked Urza, his eyebrow hitched ironically. "Take us, then, to the realm of Freyalise."

Canting her head sideways, Daria reached out her hands. "Take hold."

The two ancient planeswalkers rested their hands in hers. The twilight mountainside melted away like watercolors running from a page. Reality puddled and rose again.

It spread itself in a new design, what seemed a vast star burst. It was in fact a huge thistle bloom. Green and gold down extended from a gleaming core. Breezes whispered among the feathery seed pods. Occasionally a stalk tricked free to glide away. No sooner had one tuft floated off than another grew outward.

Beside that enormous bloom, the three planeswalkers floated, as tiny as gnats.

"The Inner Sanctum," Urza said, blinking at the great thistle. "I am not welcome here."

"We are," replied Daria with a quirked smile. Cupping a hand to her mouth, the young woman called: "Freyalise, it is time."

There came no change to the mammoth thistle. No door opened, though a presence emerged from the core of the blossom. Not a single downy tuft shifted. Still, out of a clump of them formed a statuesque woman with delicate, almost fey features. Her blonde hair was shorn short and dyed in the fashion emulated by the Steel Leaf elves. Across her face coiled intricate tattoos in woodland motifs—leaves and flowers whose stems extended down her throat and beneath the white shift she wore. A ring glinted in one nostril, and light mantled her.

Freyalise smiled. Her lips held much the same caprice as Daria's. It was clear these two had become allies in what Urza would call mischief. Still, Freyalise was ancient. She was protector of Fyndhorn and goddess of the Juniper Order, savior of the Llanowar Elves and Patron Lady of the Order of the Steel Leaf. She also was no particular friend of Urza's.

"Time, is it?" asked Freyalise, blinking as if awakening from a dream.

"That's what Daria said," Taysir put in.

"Yes, it is time," Urza answered. "A critical battle is at hand, a dry run for our final target—"

Ignoring Urza, Freyalise extended her hands toward her friends and took them in her arms.

"How are your studies getting on, girl? Your father's a tough master—the minotaurs made him so. No, that's not true. He was tough before the minotaurs. If anything, they rounded his rough edges." Turning to Taysir, she said, "And speaking of rough edges, guess who is visiting me?"

The old man's eyes rolled. He said with infinite resignation, "Kristina."

"Yes!" Freyalise said happily. "Oh, don't tell me you still moon over her."

"No. The Anoba Ancestors took care of that, as well. They said I couldn't have my body back until I 'got shut of the rut.' I did. Get shut. Of the rut."

Freyalise laughed.

"Ahem," Urza interrupted, coughing into his hand.

Freyalise turned. Her eyebrow lifted. "Oh, it's you."

"That's what *I* said *too!*" Daria replied happily.

"Planning another Ice Age, Urza?" Freyalise jabbed.

Urza winced. "I might remind you that your spell to end the Ice Age was as devastating as mine—and cast with the same disregard."

"You two . . ." Taysir said.

Urza continued, "I understand you have no love for me. I expect none. But you have love for the world and its creatures, and that's why we've come. We are sworn—even that bastard Szat—to fight for Dominaria. That's why we come together."

Freyalise strolled easily across the air until she stood before him. "I don't remember your swearing to fight for Dominaria, only against Phyrexia."

"There is no difference," Urza said.

Again came the laugh. "If you had any inkling why that was

247

funny, you might understand why we have so little love for you."
She shrugged. "Oh, well. It is time." Her eyes closed for a moment.
The air around her shimmered with a silent conversation.
"Kristina will be right out."

"Kristina?"

"You need eight planeswalkers to power these contraptions of
yours, right?" Freyalise asked. "Kristina is a planeswalker. Get rid
of Szat."

Urza shook his head. "No, I need Szat. I'll get rid of Parcher.
He's a bit of a lunatic."

"A bit?" said Freyalise and Daria in unison. They traded glances,
and Freyalise said, "This is going to be more fun than I thought."

Another presence shimmered into being. Kristina had deeply
tanned skin and long brown hair done up with beads. She had the
angular intensity of a mage and the presence of an oracle. Taking
shape beside Taysir, she took his hand in hers. Her voice was mel-
lifluous and low.

"So good to see you again, Taysir. We'll be seeing much of each
other in the next months."

He bowed in midair. "Nothing would make me more glad."

Feeling vaguely sick, Urza swept his arm in a broad gesture over
the floating assemblage of planeswalkers. The thistledown Inner
Sanctum of Freyalise melted away.

A stiff salt breeze burst over them, flung up from fifteen-foot bil-
lows. Beyond the rails, the sea was black beneath the Glimmer
Moon. Clouds dragged rags across the sky. A deck of rugged wood
solidified beneath the feet of the company. The ship ran lightless
through midnight seas. The pirate ship was immediately familiar
to them all.

"Bo Levar?" Freyalise asked dubiously. "The cigar smuggler?"

Urza blinked, his gemstone eyes glimmering in the dark. "He
prefers 'interplanar merchant.' After all, the laws of continental
embargo should not extend between worlds."

"Whatever his title, he's a patriot," Taysir said, licking his lips.
"I hope he has a crate of Urborgan maduros."

"You bet," said Bo Levar, leaping down from the dark stern

castle to light among the planeswalkers. He wore the aspect of a young man, with sandy hair and a trim mustache and goatee. "You can have two. The rest are bound for Mercadia. The Ramosians have gotten really fond of them."

"It's time," Urza said.

"You're telling me," Bo replied, shaking his head. "It was easy enough to run a Benalish blockade, but these Phyrexian plague ships aren't as friendly." He sighed. "Still, business can't wait. I'll take these to the Outer Sea of Mercadia, give instructions to my crew, and meet you all—where?"

"At Tolaria, in the Phyrexian rift."

Bo made a gagging face. "You're still working in that stink hole?"

"It's fast time," Urza replied defensively. "I get ten days inside for each one outside."

"Yeah, but it stinks," Bo said. "I'll bring a crate of candellas to cut the air."

Urza clapped his shoulder genuinely. "It is good to have you with us." Spreading his arm toward the others, he said, "We'll see you there momentarily."

Even as Bo Levar replied, midnight sky and ocean swell and the ship between them faded from being.

In their place, a great library formed. Shelves ran away into infinity. Their edges curved in the blue distance. It was said one who walked a straight line through the Library of Commodore Guff would end up walking in his own footsteps. More frightening still, every volume in that infinite place was the history of some place in the multiverse, and the old commodore had read them all.

As the planeswalkers materialized among the books, Commodore Guff himself appeared. He had a raft of reddish-blond hair, an aggressive beard and eyebrows, and an intent eye behind his monocle. The glass fell from his eye and dropped into the book he held. In the same motion Commodore Guff's mouth fell open.

"Are you here to borrow or to return?"

"It's time," Urza said simply.

Commodore Guff scowled. "No . . ." From the red vest he wore, the man fished out a pocket watch—a device the young Urza had fashioned as an apprentice in Yotia. "Well, bother. It *is* time."

Daria gave him a dubious look. "You don't even know what we're talking about."

"There, you are wrong, young lady," the commodore huffed. "We are talking about time, and I know all about time. I know what is supposed to happen in it and what actually does happen in it. I know the difference between history and reality. I have dedicated my life to making reality conform more closely to history."

Daria's expression grew only more unimpressed. "How can there be histories for things that haven't even happened yet?"

Waggling a finger beside his shaggy ear, Commodore Guff said, "And I would ask you how things can happen unless there is history?"

"Damn it," Urza said, growing irate. "We're wasting time."

"Yes! Damn it," Commodore Guff said, tapping his pocket watch. "Damn it! Damn it!" He slipped the device into a vest pocket, seemed to lose it, and patted furiously. Nettled, he looked up. "Do you know what Teferi did? Phased out Zhalfir and Shiv! That'll take about a century to sort out—the little sneak."

"One thing at a time," Urza said, trying to calm the man.

"Yes." Commodore Guff nodded, quietly adding, "Damn it . . ."

"All right, one final stop," Urza said, sweeping his companions away with him in a sudden planeswalk. The infinite library of Commodore Guff ceased to be, though the waistcoated gentleman still clutched a book from it. He slammed the volume closed, noticed his monocle was missing, and patted his vest again.

The crew arrived in utter blackness. Brimstone scented the air. Normally, planeswalkers could see into the darkest corners. Where sight was denied them, it was denied by one of their ilk.

That one circled them even now. His presence was titanic. His flesh was gelid and rubbery. A hint of a long tentacle slipped away into inky darkness. A scaly shoulder showed itself and was gone. A baleful eye watched them all. There came the distinct impression of teeth set in a razor smile.

"Bother!" Commodore Guff said, gaping into the darkness.

"Tevash Szat? Since when does he want to make Dominaria anything but an ice cube?"

The voice that answered seethed gladly. "You know me. Yes. I once tried to freeze the world—no thanks to you, Freyalise—only wishing to preserve it in perfect memory. I fight for Dominaria. How could it be preserved if it is overrun by . . . roaches?"

The commodore sniffed. "You yourself have had dealings with those roaches."

"Yes," the voice allowed quietly. "When the dealings suited me. Losing the world to Yawgmoth does not suit me."

"We are all agreed on that," Urza said. "Szat will be our inside agent. He knows Phyrexia better than even I."

"You spoke of eight guardians of Dominaria, aside from yourself, Urza," Taysir pointed out. "Who is the last?"

"Lord Windgrace. Just now, he aids Barrin in the battle of Urborg. I will send for him when the isles are secure. As for the rest of us—" the gesture was unseen, though it encompassed even dark-swathed Tevash Szat.

Suddenly they stood within a deep, dark canyon. Its floor and walls were black basalt. A dome of scintillating energy shimmered above. A volcanic plateau dominated the center of the cleft. On that prominence rested a weird city fashioned of obsidian. Once, this valley had been filled with Phyrexians, trapped within a fast time rift. They had built—and been purged from—the City of K'rrick. Since then, the gorge had become Urza's private laboratory. In it, nine new wonders had taken shape.

"Titans, I call them," Urza said, breathing happily.

Against the walls of the canyon sat nine monumental figures. They seemed huge warriors, slumped in rest. Each colossus was a suit of power armor. Massive armaments bristled from the hands and shoulders and feet of the machines—ray cannons, plasma blasters, powerstone ballistae, energy bombards, sonic shock generators, falcon engines, and countless other innovations.

"Bother," Commodore Guff said, paging through the book he held. "There's not a single word written on these yet."

"In these suits, we will launch our attack on Phyrexia. First, though, we will assist the coalition armies of Metathran, elves, and Benalians in the Battle of Koilos."

Daria sneered, "It would take months to learn to use these suits."

"Luckily, we have months—two to be exact. The coalition forces plan an attack on the Caves of Koilos in two weeks of normal time. We will be ready by then."

"It *is* time," Commodore Guff said decisively. "Damn it, it's time!"

CHAPTER 31

Sarcophagus in the Sky

Barrin fought a futile, one-man fight over Urborg.

At first, Urza's coalition had held strong, but the Phyrexians were too many, too vicious. They slew the Keldons and Metathran to a man. They drove Serrans and elves and panther warriors from the isles. When the costs of battle mounted, Urza himself had summoned Darigaaz and the dragon nations away to Koilos, and enlisted Lord Windgrace for his titan corps. In the battle of Urborg, he left a single warrior—"My one-man army."

Mage Master Barrin floated high above the rankling central volcano. He surveyed the wreckage of the past month. Helionauts burned on the ground. Longships sank in the brine. Angels lay dead in rainwater swamps and elves in saltwater marshes. Metathran were crucified to cypress trees. Keldons rotted in kelp beds. Muck made them all seem slain pigs. Bugs the size of fish fed on them— worse things too. Phyrexians clambered like roaches over the dead.

There were victories, of course. Two of the Phyrexian cruisers lay in broken heaps. The minions of the lich lord crawled into the fallen hulks like maggots into corpses. Ghouls and scavenger folk tricked away whatever they could and matched claws and teeth with the Phyrexians there. Barrin let them annihilate each other.

A worse battle loomed. This morning, a storm front had formed above the western sea. The clouds approached with slow confidence. All the while, they gathered steam and wrath above the churning ocean. The storm had rolled within a score of miles before Barrin saw what it hid. Along its advancing edge appeared the black prows of seven, eight . . . twelve Phyrexian cruisers.

"If I fight this fight alone, I will lose the island and myself," Barrin reasoned. "If Urza wants this stink-swamp saved—for whatever unfathomable reason—he will have to grant me more aid."

Closing his eyes, Barrin drew a long, deep breath of the brimstone air. He tapped memories of another island, of blue and beautiful Tolaria. Power surged through him, the azure energies of magical manipulation. Space folded. Barrin leaped from one wrinkle to another. Urborg vanished away beneath him, taking its envelope of steamy heat. Koilos formed, equally hot, but as dry as a furnace.

Barrin hovered above sand dunes and rills of rock. In the sheer distance, Phyrexians filled the world. They drilled and rested, fought for the best food and gobbled it down live, rode trench worms and burned their murdered own. In the near distance, coalition armies camped—Metathran, Benalish, and elf, with dragons sleeping in their midst.

Urza would be just beyond them, under that long line of canvas. The fabric hid a deep trench hewn from bedrock by artifact engines. It was Urza's secret bunker, a thousand feet deep, two thousand feet long, and a hundred feet wide. Within the bunker, he kept his secret weapons—the titan engines.

Drifting slowly down to the canvas, Barrin swept his hand over himself. He turned momentarily insubstantial and slid through the fabric.

Cool darkness filled the bunker. Titan engines stood against one wall, seeming watchers in an ancient tomb. In a few of the cannon-toting machines, planeswalkers fiddled, finalizing the settings of their command pods.

At the base of the trench, Urza worked. He had set up his folding travel table, a massive workspace that compacted into a slim panel of wood. Maps of Koilos lay neatly arrayed before the master artificer. He scribed confident lines across them, projecting angles of attack.

Barrin descended beside his old friend. Charred war cloaks settled about the mage's ankles. As Dominaria resumed its hold on him, Barrin let out an involuntary sigh.

"Hello, Urza."

The planeswalker glanced up, his eyes bright in the gloom. "Is the battle of Urborg concluded?"

Barrin bristled at this greeting. He replied just as curtly. "No. I need reinforcements."

Looking back down at the maps of Koilos, Urza said, "There are none."

Shrugging, Barrin pursed his lips. "Then Urborg is lost."

Urza snorted, "Then it is lost."

"So that's it?" Barrin asked heatedly. "A month ago, Urborg had to be saved at all cost, and now you lose it with a shrug?"

Raising his gaze, Urza said, "It is a strategically important site, second only to Koilos. But it *is* second to Koilos. If Urborg cannot be held without reinforcements—and we have no reinforcements to spare—then Urborg is lost."

Flinging his hands out in surrender, Barrin said, "Yes, lost." He leaned against the wall of the trench and folded his arms. "I see you have your final chess match worked out here—your armies, your war engines, your airships and dragons and titans. Was that *Weatherlight* I saw?"

"Yes," Urza replied simply.

"Good," Barrin snapped. "I'm going to go see my daughter—"

"No," Urza interrupted. Something like sadness—or guilt—entered his eyes.

"What do you mean, no?"

"Hanna died two weeks ago."

"What?" Barrin barked, laughing incredulously. "What did you say?"

"The plague overwhelmed her. There was nothing anyone could do."

Shaking his head in disbelief, Barrin said, "Hanna? My Hanna?"

"There was nothing anyone could do."

The mage master's face became a sickly white. He steadied himself on Urza's table, crumpling the maps there. He gazed blankly at those ruined plans. Color suddenly flooded back into his features—blood.

He spoke in a quiet, trembling voice. "There *was* something I could have done, Urza. I could have held her hand. I could have stroked her hair. . . ." His voice failed, but his welling eyes stared imploringly at Urza. "Why didn't you summon me?"

"Urborg had to be saved."

"Don't say that! Don't for one moment say that!" Barrin replied, dashing the tears from his eyes. He lashed out, flinging the maps from Urza's table. They rattled in an angry flock of paper and landed in the dust. "Of course you didn't call me. Your work was always the most important thing. Of course I wasn't there when my daughter died. I wasn't there when she lived. You stole her from me, and that's not the worst of it—I let you steal her from me! Yawgmoth of the Nine Hells!"

"Don't say that name—" Urza said urgently, lifting his hands toward the titans—"not here."

"Where is she?" Barrin demanded. "Where is she?"

"Gerrard buried her. She lies in the sands of Koilos."

"She wouldn't have wanted that. This desert was nothing to her. Tolaria was always her home. I'm taking her to Tolaria, to be buried beside her mother."

"No," Urza said, plucking the maps from the dust. "Tolaria, too, is lost. The gathering of planeswalkers drew Phyrexians. They attacked ferociously. We escaped with the titan engines and every useful device, and detonated the others. Even now, the Phyrexians solidify their hold on the island."

"Solidify their hold?" Barrin asked in angry amazement. "So some of the students and scholars remain?"

"Every battle has casualties—"

"And I have become one, Urza," Barrin said. All the anger had gone from his voice. Only dread clarity remained. "I have spent my life fighting battles I did not believe in because I believed in you. No more. The cost is too high. Belief is too rare. I've been a fool. I fought for things I did not love and let what I loved slip away— first my wife, and then my daughter, and now myself. I'm done. I'm taking Hanna back to Tolaria. I'm fighting for my home and her home and my wife's grave. I'm finally going to fight a battle I believe in—I'm going to fight a final battle I believe in."

Brow furrowing, Urza said simply, "You cannot."

"Good-bye, my friend," Barrin replied, and he was gone.

He had never teleported himself into solid matter before. It was ill-advised, of course. Barrin was through with advice—he was through with nearly everything. The Mage Master of Tolaria materialized beneath the sand of a nearby hill. He took form, his arms wrapped around the buried body of his daughter. When she was first born, Barrin had held her thus, had placed on her a beacon enchantment. It let him find her wherever she was. It had led him to her here, in her grave.

Why didn't I use the enchantment a month ago? Why not a year ago? Why not all those days of childhood when she was building box kites and damming the creeks of Tolaria?

"Hanna," Barrin whispered with his last breath, brought cold within him from Urza's bunker.

The single, quiet word emerged with the force of a blue gale. It blasted away sand, shooting it up through the press of soil. Grains spat from the grave. The wind redoubled. A vortex stripped away particle after particle. Sunlight stabbed down through the thick ground. The spinning shaft widened, carving out the grave. It scoured Barrin's face and mutton chops. It filled his bloodied cloak and cleansed the white cerements that wrapped his daughter. Barrin gasped in sadness. Hurloon myrrh had been used on the cloths, and it exuded the scent of sorrow.

"Hanna," the old mage cried.

The whirlwind tore away the last of the entombing sand. Without its weight pressing on him, Barrin marveled at how light she was. This had been no sudden death but the long agony that comes from chronic neglect.

How could I have been worlds away while she slowly died?

"Hanna!"

Through the angry storm, Barrin rose. He bore his child in his arms. Beyond the circling curtain of dust, he saw the crew of *Weatherlight*. They had rushed to the grave site when they saw the sandstorm begin. Tahngarth stood nearest, his axe lifted to slay any beast that might emerge. Sisay and Orim stared in disbelief at the violated grave of their friend. Dust pasted tears to their faces. Only Gerrard, beyond them all, understood. He saw not the storm but the man in the storm. He saw Barrin's eyes and the guilt there. Gerrard understood. He shared that guilt. Hanna had died while the two men she most loved were busy fighting Phyrexians.

It was more than Barrin could bear. With a nod to Gerrard, he took Hanna away from that sandy place.

The roar of the cyclone was replaced by the roar of the oceans. The sands of Koilos reshaped into the stony cliffs of Tolaria. It was the simplest teleport Barrin had ever cast. He knew the spot intimately—the unmarked grave of his wife, near the sea. Here, a young Jhoira once escaped the rigors of the academy. The teleport was as simple as returning home.

Barrin stood above the slab of rock where his wife lay. He ached to lay his daughter to rest beside her. He ached to die with them.

Tears streaming down his face, Barrin dropped his head back.

The sky above was dark, not with storm clouds but with Phyrexian ships. There were a score of cruisers and as many more plague ships. Smaller vessels peeled away from the main fleet to pursue Tolarian refugees in tiny boats. Beneath the crowded fleet, columns of black smoke rose from the ruined academy. Perhaps the Phyrexians had bombed the buildings to oblivion. Perhaps it had been Urza. Their works were often indistinguishable.

"I have been a fool," Barrin told himself.

Without laying his daughter down, Barrin cast a simple water spell.

Beside his wife's grave lay another natural crypt in the stone. Barrin had always believed he would lie there when his time had come. He had never imagined his daughter's death. Beneath the stone lid of the crypt, the spell took shape. Tiny jets of water bubbled up, lifting the lid and sliding it slowly aside. Water wept down the stony walls of the tomb. By the time the lid had glided to one side, a small clear pool lay beside the stones.

Drawing a deep breath, Barrin hugged his daughter's body. "The last time I saw you, you were heading into Rath. We fought, I remember. I'm sorry. We also said good-bye. I didn't think that that good-bye would be our last. I was wrong about everything. Everything." Gently lowering her into the grave, he sighed deeply. "Good-bye, my angel."

He stood, watching solemnly as the lid slid back over the crypt. Darkness slowly swallowed up his daughter. The last of the water dripped from the edges of the lid. It grated quietly into place.

"Sarcophagus." Barrin whispered the old Thran word as he stared at the spot. "Flesh eater."

He would find his own sarcophagus in the sky.

Barrin rose into the air for the last time in his life.

In ancient days, Urza lost his brother to Phyrexia. In his rage, he had unleashed a blast from an artifact called the sylex. That blast had sunk continents and reshaped Dominaria. It had also made Urza a veritable god.

Barrin was no god. He did not have a sylex. He did not wish to sink continents, but he knew the spell Urza had cast. It would be enough.

Above him, massive ships floated like leviathans. Barrin made no move to hide. A single man rising through a smoky sky was hard enough to see, and those mountainous machines were oblivious to so small a threat. Barrin ascended in their midst. Black killing things. They would not know what hit them.

Closing his eyes, Barrin drew upon the power of his fury. Lava. Brimstone. Fire. He thought of Shiv and Rhammidarigaaz. He thought of the mana rig pumping red-hot stone like a giant heart. Rage welled in him. He was its vessel. Hatred shaped the spell, but he needed more power.

Barrin drew mana from Tolaria beneath him. He remembered Karn's birth in the first Tolaria. He remembered the war with K'rrik in the second Tolaria. He remembered Jhoira and Teferi, *Weatherlight* and the Metathran, Rayne and Hanna. As blue mana coursed into him, Barrin tapped other lands as well—verdant Yavimaya, militant Benalia, undead Urborg. He drew all the power into himself and became a living sylex.

His insides boiled. Beams shot from his eyes and his fingertips. Power sought escape in every extremity. It crept its way up legs and arms, across face and chest. Hair stood on end and hurled energy from its tips. Pores opened and beamed. Every wound ever struck on his body burst open and shone. His flesh could not contain the radiance. Soon, Barrin glared like a second sun.

Those were not light rays, though, but power rays. They roared out red from him. The air sizzled with them. Beams struck the ships. They cut metal as though it were water. They turned Phyrexian armor to pudding and Phyrexian flesh to ash. They pierced to engine cores and cracked powerstones.

Cruisers and plague ships spewed smoke through a thousand sudden holes. Engines went critical. One machine blazed apart. Its own shrapnel melted in the energy it unleashed. Four adjacent cruisers lurched and exploded. They tilted on end. Daylight sieved through their riddled hulls. Ship to ship, destruction spread.

Not a cannon was fired, not a plasma burst unleashed, but there was holocaustal fire in the heavens. Below, it was the same. Oceans boiled. Trees flash-burned. Rocks melted.

Whatever creatures had stood on Tolaria were blinded by the flash, and deafened by the concussion, and dismantled by the raw power. Phyrexians, scholars, students, hinds, fleas—all died in that moment. Their struggles were done. Their bodies were gone. Even the ground on which they stood turned to wax and ran.

Only Rayne and Hanna were safe, sealed into their sarcophagi. How like Urza had Barrin become.

At last the blast spent itself. It left a hole in the sky. No ships remained. No clouds either. The beaming sun seemed dim and gray.

Cold waves crashed into boiling seas. Whirlpools laid the ocean depths bare. Water churned silt as red as blood.

Where once had been a verdant island was now a molten slab of rock, hissing into the sea. Tolaria was gone forevermore.

So too was her onetime lord, Mage Master Barrin.

CHAPTER 32
The Battle is Joined

Eladamri strode at the head of his army, Liin Sivi at his side. He wore the elven armor and livery of his Steel Leaf warriors. He carried a powerstone pike, just like the tens of thousands of Metathran that marched behind him. Their belief armed and armored him. Belief made Eladamri the savior of elves and the commander of Metathran.

Lifting high his powerstone pike, Eladamri shouted, "Charge!"

His folk took up the shout. It became a fierce war cry, mortals storming the gates of hell.

Those gates were well guarded. The desert before Eladamri swarmed with Phyrexians. For a mile in every direction, monsters ranked. In deep trenches lurked Phyrexian throats—living stomachs that would swallow anyone who happened across them. In cannonades and bombard embrasures, Phyrexian gunners tested aim and range. In spell towers, sorcerers prepared black-mana magics. In sanctums, priests tended flesh eaters. They waited eagerly.

Not all waited. Other beasts marched forward. In side-by-side phalanxes, they advanced. Their claws and hooves flung up shimmering clouds of salt-dust in their wake. The vanguard bristled with scuta. Their cranial shields gleamed black under a merciless sun. Next came bloodstocks. Their metallic fore-hooves churned the ground. Phyrexian shock troops filled up the main body of the army, the most vicious fighters of all. They all advanced—not marching but charging.

Eladamri leveled his powerstone pike. His jaw clenched. His eyes gleamed like twin poniards.

Liin Sivi prepared her toten-vec.

The two lines approached—one blue and silver and the other black and iron.

A whine rose behind Eladamri's division. The noise intensified to a shriek. The air directly overhead suddenly thronged with gleaming birds—falcon engines. They cut the sky to ribbons. Bending razor beaks toward the Phyrexian lines, the birds dived. A manifold crackle followed as falcons smashed through scuta shields. From the holes they punched came a whirring sound and geysers of macerated meat.

The Phyrexian front lines crashed down. Over their scaly backs, bloodstocks galloped eagerly. They bore no shields except the bone armor beneath their skin. They bore no weapons except the scimitar claws that sprouted from their fingers. Their fangy throats were filled with roars as they smashed against Eladamri and his army.

Powerstone pikes rammed into bloodstock bellies. The weapons tore through bony plates and ate deeper. Bloodstocks clawed their way up the shafts that impaled them. Pikes chewed through Phyrexian spines. Their hind legs went limp. Mechanical forelegs bore the creatures forward. They sank scimitar claws into elf faces and Metathran necks.

Eladamri himself was almost torn to pieces. He released his pike—mired in a bloodstock's midsection—and ducked under a pair of swiping claws. With a roundhouse kick, he flung the claws back to stab their owner. The bloodstock impaled its own eye and tore its neck wide. Glistening-oil sprayed in a golden cloud.

Blanketed in the monster's gore, Eladamri raked his sword from its sheath. With one chop to the neck, the bloodstock fell before him. His powerstone pike clawed its way out the monster's back. Eladamri clambered past the beast and retrieved his pike.

A terrible creature reared up before him. It seemed a giant crab. A huge pincher clamped onto Eladamri, lifting him from the ground. Carapace cut into his sides. Biting back the agony, he hurled his powerstone pike at the thing's back. The weapon cracked off of chitin and rattled uselessly down among clicking legs.

The claw tightened. Eladamri felt his hip pop. He hacked at the claw's joint. The sword's tip imbedded between scissoring plates. Yanking sideways on it, Eladamri levered the pinchers slightly open. He could not escape, but neither could the monster cut him in half.

A Phyrexian foot soldier climbed the crab's back to hew Eladamri's head from his shoulders.

Sudden fire blazed from the sky. The foot soldier was gone, dismantled by a ray cannon beam. The carapace of the creature was eaten away also. Its guts showed in white cross-section beneath the shattered shell. The beam sliced onward. It carved a smoldering line deep through the Phyrexian troops.

Behind that beam came a welcome sight, the roaring hull of *Weatherlight*. Another ray cannon blast ripped down from the other side of the vessel. *Weatherlight* blazed past overhead. Her guns plowed furrows through the monsters. Directly abeam of the great warship flew a ragged fleet of smaller fighters. Some shot cannons of their own. Most hailed quarrel bolts down atop monstrous heads.

Dropping from the dead claw of his captor, Eladamri lifted his sword high and let out a Skyshroud battle cry.

In elf and Metathran throats, the shout echoed across the bloody field.

* * * * *

Gerrard heard the battle cry go up, and it hardened his angry heart.

The gun before him was already blisteringly hot. He loosed another round. A ray roared from the smoking muzzle. It soared, a great fist, and slammed into a Phyrexian cannonade. The guns below liquefied atop their gunners.

Gerrard watched them writhe. He spat through gritted teeth. His spittle sizzled off the cannon. Spotting another gun bunker, he squeezed off a line of fire. The shot hurled down into the long, low embrasure. It brilliantly lit the space within. Figures shone for a moment, silhouetted in fire. The roof blew wide. A great gray gout of smoke belched up from the scar.

The scar. A huge black crater, with gray tendrils radiating out across once-healthy flesh. . . .

He poured fire down on the roaches. He ripped their black shells and watched the white meat ooze from beneath. He tore out their nests and stomped on the vile maggots. They were vermin. Worse, they were living rot, they were hunks of walking plague.

Gerrard's cannon spoke again. Four pulses leaped out. The first came to ground with such force that it rolled across Phyrexians, mowing them down in a line a thousand feet long. The second struck the rising shot from an ensconce bombard. Energy ripped the bombs from the sky, turning them to whistling fireworks. The third spattered flame across a whole regiment of monsters. The final bolt sailed low above the ground and impacted the entrance to the Caves of Koilos.

Weatherlight pulled up sharply. It had been their plan—Gerrard's plan—to cut Eladamri an avenue of destruction through the Phyrexian forces. Eladamri would drive across the smoldering ground and straight for the caves, cutting one edge off the Phyrexian defense. Then the ship would fly to Agnate's contingent and cut a similar swath for them.

Weatherlight rose at the end of her run. She thundered into the heavens.

Gerrard distractedly clutched the gunners' straps. He should have ordered the maneuver. He did not. Sisay knew what she was doing. The ship vaulted high above Phyrexian cannonades. Fire followed them up. Its tepid tongues licked the screaming machine. One shot spacked against the new spar, grown by Multani. It hissed sap but did not burst into flame. The engine surged. *Weatherlight* leaped skyward, shucking the fire with an airless boom.

"Prepare for second strafing run!" Sisay shouted through the tube.

Weatherlight topped out her ascent, slipping sideways to bring herself about. Ahead lay Koilos. Air spilled past the hull. The world soared suddenly up beneath her. The line of battle was there, just ahead. Agnate and his troops fought.

Weatherlight nosed down toward the bloody front.

Gerrard swung his gun down. The machine shuddered as a charge built within. He spotted a line of trench worms. The cannon belched energy. The shot looped as it descended and corkscrewed into one of the huge worms, frying it.

. . . When he had been a child, Gerrard and Vuel had skewered caterpillars with twigs and watched them struggle to walk. . . .

Another flare spilled from his gun, rolling over the Phyrexian hordes and baking them in their shells.

. . . He and Vuel used to pour lamp oil down an anthill and light it on fire. . . .

The third shot struck ground just in front of a cannon embrasure. It pulverized the ground. The cannon drooped forward, unleashing its venom into the backs of its own creatures.

. . . Wasps emitted an acrid wisp of smoke just before the magnifying glass made their abdomens crack. . . .

Agnate would be able to drive forward over this swath. *Weatherlight* and the rest of the armada had paved a road in bodies. Sure, plenty of Phyrexian cannons and bombards remained, but Sisay and her other gunners could take them out on subsequent passes. Gerrard unstrapped himself. He had another task ahead.

. . . It had taken all day and two gallons of lamp oil to dig up the anthill, but when they found the queen, all the bites were worth it. They cut open her abdomen and pulled out the white eggs and crushed them and watched all the workers try to carry them away. They laughed with that last fire, the queen dragging herself through it all, picking at the dead eggs while her torn-open abdomen curled up and crisped. . . .

Tsabo Tavoc. She had done this. She had brought these bugs, these maggots here. She had brought rot and plague. Gerrard would find her and cut her open as she had cut open Hanna. He would drag out her eggs and crush them and kill her slowly, just the way Vuel had shown him.

A hulking presence loomed up behind him. Tahngarth. The sky raced past. The minotaur's eyes were grave. Gerrard saw his reflection, small and hunched, in those eyes.

Tahngarth said, "The strike team is ready."

Gerrard nodded, pulling himself from the gunner traces. Another gunner, waiting nervously beside the minotaur, slid himself into the spot and resumed fire. Gerrard stared blankly at him.

"We're coming up on the drop site," Tahngarth urged. "You need to pull on your hauberk and arm yourself." Tahngarth pounded the hilt of his sword against the Hurloon battle armor he wore.

Nodding numbly, Gerrard lifted a breast-and-backplate and slid them on.

"Are you sure you're up to this? Hanna's death—"

Gerrard's eyes flared. "Yes. That's it, isn't it? Hanna's death. Yes. That's it."

Turning, he stalked to the prow. He shoved his way through the Benalish strike team. Gerrard peered over the ship's rail, seeing that Sisay edged *Weatherlight* up just above the caves. Phyrexian cannons struggled to turn about and fire on the hovering ship. Just as rapidly, *Weatherlight*'s own guns took out their entrenchments.

From the prow speaking tube, Sisay's voice shrilled, "Can't hold her here for long."

Without answering, Gerrard flipped the capstan lock. As chain rattled out, Gerrard vaulted over the rail. He landed with his feet on the arms of the anchor and rode its plunging weight downward. The prison brigade gave a cheer to see their leader's bold advance. They too flung themselves overboard, gripping the chain. It dropped before the yawning mouth of the Caves of Koilos.

Out of that debouchment lumbered a huge figure—a Phyrexian digger.

The anchor crashed down atop it. The vast head of the monster staved beneath the anchor's crown. The beast collapsed, and Gerrard rode it to ground. He leaped free of anchor and digger both, cleaving the head of the beast's handler. Turning, he hacked through a Phyrexian foot soldier that rushed him. Tahngarth landed beside him, bringing his sword to bear. The two friends pushed back the monsters, widening the circle.

One by one, Gerrard's small army landed. Two hundred Benalish fighters dropped down atop the dead hulk. Gerrard led them. He and his comrades moved out, killing as they went. They were like a plague, spreading from a single point out to infect an entire organism.

Gerrard liked the image. He liked killing these monsters. Vuel would have liked this too. Poor Vuel. Poor Hanna. Gerrard had lost too much. He'd lost everything.

Somehow Tahngarth did not seem to be enjoying himself. He fought sure, and slew, but there seemed no gladness in it.

Gerrard shrugged off the thought. He caught a monster's claws on his sword, chopped them off, and pierced the beast's skull. He advanced into the caves.

Tahngarth will have fun when we find Tsabo Tavoc and slice her open and crush her babies.

* * * * *

He was exquisite. Such an angry killer.

Deaths cascaded like pure water through Tsabo Tavoc's mind. They refreshed her, invigorated her. They made her teeth itch.

This one will be easy to capture, Tsabo Tavoc told herself. Reckless, angry, blind. He will be easy to catch and fun to dissect. He is, after all, Urza's bioengineered savior. If Thaddeus is a work of art, this Gerrard is a masterpiece.

Tsabo Tavoc scuttled from her deep cave, up to capture her prey.

CHAPTER 33
The Fight Inward

Weatherlight soared past overhead. She bled fire down onto the Phyrexians. Her cannons glowed. Prow, amidships, stern, and keel, destruction bloomed from her.

Fire raked over a Phyrexian contingent. The flesh beneath chitin flashed away in gray smoke. Scales and bones stood upright a moment longer as bodies fled in sooty ghosts on the wind. Hundreds of monsters fell. Their superheated shells crumbled to white powder.

Weatherlight unleashed another firestorm, cratering the battlefield. Glass splashed out to wrap Phyrexians in searing blankets. Half-melted stones pelted the menagerie. Flesh was scoured from bodies. Other cannon blasts laved acres of sand in flame. Phyrexians marched as far through the holocaust as they could. At last, their cores reached the combustion threshold. They exploded. One blaze ignited a second and third. Where once had marched a whole regiment now lay a highway inward, paved with soot.

Agnate charged onto that highway. He clutched a battle axe in both hands. The vast blade fell with angry vengeance. It clove into the segmented mouth of a Phyrexian footman. The blade bit to the throat, splitting jaw and pallet.

The beast fought on. Its claws rammed beneath Agnate's breast-plate, punching holes in his side. Fingers clenched. Organs severed and bled.

Letting go his battle axe, Agnate gripped the impaling claws with one hand and the beast's elbow with the other. Twisting quickly, he rammed the elbow, breaking the joint. It popped loudly, and bone and gristle separated. One more yank, and the arm came off, streaming oil-blood.

Undeterred, the Phyrexian lunged with its good arm.

Agnate drew the dead arm from his side and thrust its gory claws up before him. The Phyrexian grabbed its severed arm, giving Agnate the chance to yank his battle axe free. He swung it in a broad circle and lopped the thing's head off.

The body jigged a moment more, uncertain it was dead, before flopping to ground.

Agnate trod over it. His axe haft felt strange in his hand. It was not just glistening-oil and Phyrexian white matter. Something else was wrong. His fingers felt numb, jangled. His arms were sluggish.

He had been only fighting—not fighting toward something. This Eladamri was his match, was worthy to lead the Metathran, but he was not Thaddeus. Agnate could fight beside this savior of elves but not toward him.

O Thaddeus, in dying, you killed me, thought Agnate bleakly as his axe split the breast of a bloodstock. *If you only lived, I could fight.*

I do live . . . Agnate. . . . I live. . . .

The thought was weak on the wind, but it was there. It entered Agnate like a freshening breeze, breathing life into him.

He lives. I can yet fight. He lives.

Agnate lifted high his axe. It streamed the life of Phyrexians, anointing Agnate and his troops with oil.

"To the caves!" he shouted, as Thaddeus had in the first assault on Koilos. "To the caves!"

That axe fell, harvesting more glistening-oil.

Agnate fought with fury. There was nothing to lose now. Either he would fight to Thaddeus's side, or he would die trying.

Either way, the fight would end in joy.

* * * * *

Tsabo Tavoc paced patiently around the table where Thaddeus was pinioned. The man lay wide open. Any human would have died long ago. Not a Metathran. Their organs visibly regenerated. They had an infinite capacity for pain and no capacity for despair. They had no instinct but to fight Phyrexians. Even in a coma, Thaddeus was fighting Tsabo Tavoc. He was sending his dreams to his comrade.

Cruelly idle, Tsabo Tavoc reached one of her slender hands into the man's open abdomen. She clutched his spleen. She squeezed, cutting the organ into four wedges.

"That will take some time to heal," the spider woman whispered in her cicada voice. She smiled. Plates shifted back from filed teeth. "In the meantime, keep fighting me, Thaddeus. Keep calling your friend. Bring him here. Fill him with mad hope. I will lay him beside you. You will die together. Isn't that what you hope for? There is no better hope for the folk of Dominaria, but that they die with those they love."

Tsabo Tavoc straightened. She breathed, well satisfied with her work. Flicking a look at the vat priests on duty, she thought, *Do not let him heal.* Then she set out for the portal. That was the spot Gerrard hoped to reach. That was the place her surprise would be waiting.

The spider woman's feet made glad clicking sounds as she left the chamber.

* * * * *

Urza hung within his titan suit. This should have been his heaven. Ensconced in the heart of his greatest invention, surrounded by ten thousand tons of machine and armor and weaponry—Urza should have been thrilled.

His full-body harness was keyed to every fiber of the war suit. His feet moved the feet of the engine; his fingers made the machine grasp and crush. With a thought, he could launch falcon engines from aeries on the suit's back. On a whim, he could fire the ray cannons that ringed the titan's wrists or ignite the plasma bolts imbedded in the titan's eyes. His every running step would slay hundreds. His every fiery breath would ignite thousands. In this suit, he could stomp with impunity up to the Caves of Koilos and tear it apart like a boy ripping up an anthill.

Urza should have been thrilled, but his hands felt numb. He couldn't stop swallowing. It was absurd. His physical body was merely a convenient projection of his mind. He need suffer no physical ailment in the world—unless, of course, it had its root in his mind.

What is wrong with me? Urza wondered as he fitted the last conduits to his brow. Perhaps it is the whole Barrin business.

Could that be? Surely not.

Barrin had been a good man—a good friend. Planeswalkers habitually avoided friendships with mortals due to the inevitability of loss. Through the use of slow-time water, Barrin had become functionally immortal. He had been a fine choice of friend, if a planeswalker allowed himself such things. Barrin's death was a great loss, true, but Urza had expected great losses. War had its casualties. He was willing to lose even himself if it meant defeating Phyrexia.

So, why this melancholia? It could have no physiological basis. Urza had no true physiology. It could only be that he was sad because some rogue part of his mind wished to be sad—a strange and not wholly satisfactory mechanism, the mind.

The battle is raging, Urza, spoke a snide mind into his. It was Tevash Szat. The cockpit of his own titan suit had been specially designed to fit the god-demon form he preferred. When do we get to go a-slaying?

Heaving a needless sigh, Urza returned the thought. *Is everyone ready?*

From the others—Taysir, Daria, Freyalise, Kristina, Lord Windgrace, Bo Levar, and Commodore Guff, each in his or her own specially designed titan suit—came affirmative replies.

Szat thought irritably, *It's about time. Your Metathran are already wading waist-deep in their own blood.*

Then we should best wade in ourselves. Urza's heart caught in his throat. He had spoken those very words to Barrin at the opening of the war. *Let us go.*

The canyon that held the nine titans was suddenly loud with the groan of hydraulics and the thrum of engines. Szat's titan suit reached overhead. Its enormous fingers, each tipped in swords as large as plows, clasped the canvas that hung there. He ripped it down, the thick cloth tearing like tissue. Bright sunlight stabbed down into the trench. It splashed across shoulders of Thran metal and bristling armament. The colossi clasped the edge of the trench, digging their fingers deep. They kicked footholds out of solid rock. Massive but agile, they climbed from the crypt that had held them.

Three miles distant, Phyrexians glimpsed this awesome arrival. Where once there had been but silken folds of desert, now appeared gargantuan figures—veritable gods. They cast shadows as large as villages. They were spangled with the light of the sun. Time stood still as they rose. Every mortal breath hushed. Every heart skipped a beat.

Szat vaulted first from the trench. His titan suit was as black as his soul, so dark that it seemed a living shadow. He landed, shaking the ground, and stared at his glorious figure.

With a deep, demonic laugh, Szat reared his head back and bellowed fire to the skies. From the suit's mouth, flames shot high enough to burn a hole in the clouds. Szat stomped his feet—towers pounding the desert. Wide rings of dust rolled up around him. Szat drummed vast knuckles against his Thran-metal breast. From him came a deep tolling like a dirge bell.

It was enough exultation. Since he had first begun training in the Phyrexian gorge, Szat had wanted to battle in the suit. He wanted blood. Szat charged across the empty desert. His every footfall sent tremors through the ground.

Phyrexians and Metathran, who had paused in their battle, fell now to their knees. The concussions yanked the ground from under them. Phyrexian ray cannons wheeled madly about to bring this new menace into the crosshairs. Red rays leaped out at the thundering titan. Most cut wide and leaped onward to slash through clouds a hundred miles away. A few beams cracked against the giant's armor and were deflected away. They slid off as if he were made of mirrors.

Szat returned fire. His wrist guns blazed to life. Beams blossomed into the air before him. They tore into trenches, pulverizing those within. Rays ripped through readouts and carved out cannonades. Dead husks of Phyrexians bounded through the air.

Szat ran up behind the Metathran lines. It seemed he would crush his allies. At the last, he leaped. His enormous figure hurtled overhead with all the silent weight of a meteor. Clearing the front, he crashed to ground in the midst of Phyrexian troops. His boots struck first, slaying hundreds. His knees struck next, crushing hundreds more. Szat's hands rammed into a cannon embrasure. Claws plowed through dirt. They sank deep, cracking rock foundations, and flexed around the hot guns. Yanking, he hauled the guns loose. He flung them away to crash, burning and blasting, among enemy troops.

Laughing, Szat spat another gout of flame heavenward.

This is not as I had planned, Urza sent to the other seven titans. He rushed toward the other side of the battlefield. They, too, were running but not directly into the fray. Each planeswalker had been assigned a wedge of the battlefield in forty degrees of arc. Each was to reach his or her position before the whole titan squadron advanced. The point was to create an inescapable noose, and to unnerve the beasts before attacking. *This is not as I had planned.*

Freyalise, whose suit was green tinged from the living components implanted in the metal, answered for all the rest—*You should have planned for Szat to be Szat.*

From his own snow-white titan suit, Urza responded, *This*

changes nothing. The rest of you, attack as planned. Eladamri and his troops can cut through whatever creatures Szat allows to flood past.

Taysir reached his designated spot. Mechanical feet pounded to a halt. Dust rolled up around the enormous, hunched figure. Powerstones of every color winked through the clouds. *I am ready.*

As am I, answered Kristina.

Looks like all of us, Bo Levar replied.

I've lost a cannon! Commodore Guff broke in. *Blast!* As if in answer, a bolt leaped suddenly across his frame, cutting fifty feet into the rock where he stood. *Nope, there it is.*

Charge! Urza shouted.

As one, the eight titans leaned into their strides and broke into a tectonic run.

Koilos rumbled like a drum struck by countless mallets.

Urza unleashed a volley of ray cannon fire and vaulted the Metathran troops. As he flew, he shot, and as he shot, he shouted—*Charge!*

* * * * *

These titans are a pleasant surprise, Tsabo Tavoc thought. The massacre of her folk moved through her. Deaths mounted up in great crashing waves that battered her heart. It was a thrilling sensation, the sort that, if indulged too long, would leave her without an army. The Ineffable had millions more, of course, but Crovax frowned on excessive massacre of his troops—unless, of course, he was the one doing it. No, as delicious as these titans were, they had to be stopped.

Awake, my children. The time has come to feed.

Urza was not the only one to have a few tricks hidden in reserve.

Tsabo Tavoc felt the vast, ancient creatures rise from the dusty barrows where they had slept.

Witch engines. They were engines, yes, but as alive, as fleshly, as any biologic beings. Headless, featureless, the enormous creatures consisted merely of a gigantic central body that bristled with quills. From their hunched and shaggy backs fell storms of sand.

They rose on impossibly thin limbs, white and thousands like the tentacles of a jellyfish. They did not use those legs to stand on—the hoary monsters could float or fly—but instead to tear ships from the skies and lift whole platoons to their fangy mouths. Best of all, the beasts could regenerate as quickly as a wound was struck.

Yes, my children. Welcome to the feast.

Through the compound eyes of her collective mind, she saw the arcane guardians loom high and soar toward Urza's titans.

CHAPTER 34
The Death of a Warrior

"What the hell is that thing?" Sisay shouted to no one. Hanna was gone, Orim tended injuries on deck, and Gerrard and Tahngarth fought in the caves. There was no one to shout to, but some things must be shouted. "What the hell is it?"

Weatherlight banked, soaring swiftly to one side of a rising hummock of bristly spines. It was a creature, a Phyrexian monster as massive as a cloud. Beneath its shaggy white body dangled thousands of long legs. With its legs, the beast plucked the battlefield. Writhing forms—Metathran, elf, and human—struggled in the grips of barbed claws. The limbs hauled them up into mouths beneath the creature.

Sisay cringed away. "Whatever it is, it's about to be dead."

She wheeled *Weatherlight* hard about. The ship's keel skidded on buffeting air, caught hold, and cut a tight, clean semicircle.

The bristly creature swept up before the bow.

Mounting on her new course, *Weatherlight* blazed to life. Her engines roared.

Squee had moved to the starboard prow ray cannon. It barked. Energy roared in superheated shafts out from the gun. Rays plunged from the bow, struggling to escape the hurtling ship. They crashed into the spiny mass.

White puffs of smoke went up. Quills curled acridly. Pink skin split open to a muscle mass that seemed writhing maggots. Awash in yellow blood, the maggot-muscles ebbed down ragged hunks of bone.

"Die, monster!" Sisay growled through clenched teeth.

It was no good. The yellow tide of blood welled up over bone. White hunks of muscle fused.

"Those maggots are machines," rumbled Karn through the speaking tube. "I see them through the running lights. They fragment to absorb damage and then join together to regenerate flesh."

Weatherlight had not even passed the beast when its pink skin had closed. New spines jutted obscenely from the scar. Tentacles slapped at the stern of the ship.

"Damn it!" Sisay roared. "How're we supposed to kill that thing?"

From the speaking tube came a shout—Orim, on deck with a wounded ensign. "The anchor. We harvested Phyrexians with it before. Hook that beast, and we can drag it."

"Or it can drag us," Sisay replied.

"Do it," Karn said. "The engines will hold. The chain will hold."

Sisay shook her head. "It'll rip the hull in half."

Another presence spoke to Sisay out of a wooden boss in the bridge ceiling. "Do it," Multani echoed. "The hull will hold. It will heal."

There *was* someone to speak to. Sisay grinned eagerly. "Yeah. Let's do this. Orim, if you've got that gunner stabilized and strapped down, I could use you at the capstan."

"On my way." Beyond the wind screen, Orim picked her way to the prow.

Weatherlight cut a long smooth arc out over the battlefield. In her wake, Phyrexian cannons bled fire into the sky. A few bolts struck, ripping holes in the hull.

Multani worked quickly to regrow the sections. Where energy lashed the engines, Karn healed the spots with Thran metal. All the while, Orim hunkered by the rail.

The ship roared into her new flight path. Ahead, the witch engine rose. Its legs reached out toward *Weatherlight*.

"We'll have one shot at this," Sisay warned. "We've made it mad enough. This'll make it furious."

"This'll make it dead," Orim called back through the capstan tube. "I learned a little about fly fishing among the Cho-Arrim."

Sisay snorted. "Cast your line."

Orim pulled the pin from the capstan. It spun. Chain paid out loudly. The ship's massive anchor plunged downward through the boiling air. Ten fathoms, fifteen fathoms, twenty fathoms.

"Ratchet that off, Orim!" Sisay called. The healer hauled hard on the capstan's lever, and the rattling chain grumbled to silence. "Karn, I'm going to need your eyes on this one. I want to sink the flukes in that monster's maggot heart. And help me keep the ship trim. That thing could flip us end over end."

Instead of words, Karn answered in a surge of the engines. *Weatherlight* vaulted higher into the reeling skies.

A cannon blast clipped the starboard gunwale, cutting a trough through it. Another ripped through the port-side airfoil. The ship dipped, heeling to starboard.

"Fold them!" Sisay ordered Karn. She pointed the prow at the midsection of the beast and held her course. "Fold the airfoils. We're going in full speed."

With a loud clap, the wings folded. The ship's engines thundered. *Weatherlight* leaped out ahead of a volley of plasma bursts. She clove the air like an axe head, outrunning even ray fire. The anchor swung up beneath the keel.

"Bring us in low!" Sisay ordered. The ship plunged.

Below, the witch engine swelled out grotesquely. It had reared up. Its countless mouths gnashed the bodies of its latest victims. White arms groped toward *Weatherlight*.

Squee fired a series of bursts. They cut a swath through the forest of lashing legs. The ship soared down that avenue. More fire blazed from Squee's gun. Hunks of severed white leg pelted across the deck. Toothy mouths hissed fetid fumes at the fleeing craft. The anchor swung down, cracking across the hard jaws.

"Got a nibble!" Orim shouted.

Sisay hauled back on the helm. *Weatherlight* jagged upward. The anchor swung down, digging itself deep in one of the monster's mouths. It sank away.

"Make that a bite!"

Links slashed through the thing's wet white flesh. In the maggot storm of the beast's innards, the anchor at last lodged on something solid.

The prow deck bulged upward beneath the straining bolthead. Green mana flowed through the wood, strengthening it to steel hardness.

"Let's flip it!" Sisay growled.

Weatherlight vaulted just above the hairy, horrible beast. Chains whipped tight against the monster's bulk. Metal burst flesh and sawed deeper. The witch engine roared from its myriad mouths. *Weatherlight* nosed toward ground. Her anchor chain cut brutally deep, spreading the walls of the laceration widely apart. The ship's keel shot forward, just above the maggoty canyon it carved. She roared down.

Legs flapping into the heavens, the witch engine slowly toppled. Its spiny back flipped down to the battlefield. Cannon fire meant for *Weatherlight* smashed instead into the riven monster.

Spotting Phyrexian armies beyond, Sisay shoved the helm all the way forward. The ship dived sharply, dragging its captive down behind it.

"Let's see how you regenerate this," Sisay growled.

Weatherlight avalanched down the skies. She seemed about to impact the battlefield when she drew sharply level. Her keel smashed the heads of Phyrexians. Landing spines jutted, slicing more of the beasts. Those hewn in half by the rushing skyship were lucky. The rest stood in the path of a great bristly ball.

In its first revolution, the witch engine's legs were shredded. Sections of muscle smashed down atop Phyrexians, crushing them. In its second revolution, the engine pounded its folk into paste. In its third, the anchor chain sawed through it.

Equal halves of the monster split from each other and rolled away across the battlefield, spewing destruction. Maggot-machines flung free. They pelted the monsters into the ground. The torn halves of its skin emptied themselves. The last of the witch engine's essence pattered away uselessly.

Sisay hauled back on the helm. *Weatherlight* climbed into the heavens. "That's the way to cut 'em! Good work, Orim!"

The healer smiled grimly. "I could use a hand reeling in the anchor."

"Leave it be," Sisay said. "I'm not done fishing."

* * * * *

Did you see that? Bo Levar sent to the other planeswalkers. He was busily ripping legs from another witch engine. The giant monster grew replacements faster than he could pull them loose. It climbed his multicolored titan suit. *Did you see what* Weatherlight *did?*

Indeed! Commodore Guff replied. A witch engine straddled the shoulders of his titan suit. Hundreds of mouths gnawed at the power conduits. *Bother these buggers!*

We cannot expect Weatherlight *to save us*, Urza replied. Three of the vast beasts swarmed him. Cannon blasts from his wrist rockets tore into them. The wounds closed as quickly.

Impatient, Bo Levar growled, *Rip 'em open. They can regenerate as long as the maggot machines are together. Rip 'em open and dig away the machines. These beasts are like cigars—without their wrappers, they come to pieces.*

He rammed his clawed fingers deep into the witch engine before him. With an almighty roar, he tore back the thing's skin, splitting it open and spilling billions of writhing machines. The tear deepened. Wriggling white maggots showered across the titan suit. Ignoring them, Bo kept ripping until the two hairy halves peeled away from each other. He flung the empty halves down onto the Phyrexian hordes.

Well done. Urza said, ripping one of his own tormentors into chunks. *It seems we can learn from* Weatherlight *and her crew.*

Where once scores of witch engines had menaced the titans from the sky, now hailstorms of maggots fell to ground.

Szat burned the beasts as they fell. He draped the dead husks over his shoulders like trophies. *Nothing can stop us, now! See? Even the puny mortals are driving for the cave mouth. Victory is in reach.* He crowed, pouring maggots into his mouth and spewing them forth in flames. *Nothing can stop us!*

* * * * *

Maggot-engines plunged in a thick cascade ahead.

Rhammidarigaaz banked sharply into clear air. The dragon nations—red and black, blue and white and green—followed.

Plasma cannonades hurled blanketing fire toward them. It seemed crimson silk unfolding on the wind. In moments, it would slay them all.

Darigaaz led his folk in a steep dive toward a Phyrexian division below. The cannonades ceased their fire. Even Phyrexians would not vaporize their own troops.

Rhammidarigaaz did it for them. He spat flames on the Phyrexian vanguard. It ate them away.

The dragon nations shot out over the main body of the Phyrexian army. Breath baked bugs in their shells. Talons cracked Phyrexian skulls. Wings hurled monsters like leaves.

There were spells too. Darigaaz drew volcanic might into the crystal of his scepter. Lava churned within the pure glass. It gathered into a whirling vortex. Light blazed forth and brimstone hailed out. The fiery hunks of stone whistled as they fell. They stuck to gray flesh and burned their way through.

Scuta shuddered, struggling to throw off the burning things. Shock troops thrashed as magma sank between ribs. Bloodstocks slumped dead and smoldering on still-charging legs. Wherever lava and air and oil met, beasts exploded.

This was no Urborg. The coalition was winning this time. Darigaaz could feel it. *Weatherlight* and the Circle of Dragons ruled the heavens. Metathran and the Steel Leaf elves ruled the world. Gerrard and his prison brigade ruled the underworld. All the while, Urza and his titans closed the circle around Tsabo Tavoc.

With a hiss of volcanic steam, Darigaaz vaulted skyward. His dragons coiled like a deadly veil behind him. As plasma mounted up from cannons, Darigaaz and his folk plunged in another strafing run.

Fire belched down. Phyrexians rose in ash.

This was no Urborg.

* * * * *

Agnate and his forces fought forward down a path of soot. *Weatherlight* had paved the way. Burning beasts and fields of glass led to the caves. Agnate's army marched with grim fury. They owned this highway. They cleared Phyrexians like weeds. Agnate's battle axe grew dull—it had split so many skulls, so much chitin. Still, it was a deadly club, and Agnate's rage made it a lightning bolt.

The axe smashed a Phyrexian skull. Horns atop that pate bent inward. The monster staggered. Agnate kicked its belly. He strode over the fallen thing.

Another hailstorm of maggots began. The wriggling mechanisms cracked against helms and shoulder pieces. They fell in treacherous fields before the Metathran, who kicked them aside. Anyone who fell was swarmed and suffocated by the maggots.

"Forward!" Agnate shouted above the hail of creatures.

They had almost reached the cave mouth. The place was already a charnel house. Gerrard and his prison strike force had been brutal. They had slaughtered hundreds. Phyrexian oil-blood formed a shallow marsh. Bodies lay like flagstones in a vast floor. Even now, a platoon of the prison brigade guarded the gates. They cheered Agnate and his troops as they broke through.

Eladamri, Liin Sivi, the Steel Leaf warriors, and the other division of Metathran approached from the opposite highway of death. The pincers drew inexorably together. The Phyrexians caught between those two claws would be sliced to pieces. Those outside were even now being stomped to death under the feet of titans.

After so much killing, after such impossible legions of fiends, it seemed strange so suddenly to rush up beside his own allies. Arms that had spent hours wielding swords and axes now opened in glad greeting. The long parted halves of the Metathran army were reunited before the gates of hell.

Agnate did not allow himself the luxury of joy. Neither, he noted, did Eladamri. The two commanders converged at a stride, approaching the head of the prison contingent. The defenders of Dominaria were ragged and bloody, but grim smiles filled their faces.

"Welcome to Koilos, commanders," the shaggy Benalish leader said. "Gerrard and the rest of our brigade are locking down the caves within. We have prevented Phyrexian incursion from above. I gratefully relinquish command to you."

"Thank you," Agnate said with a level nod. Turning to Eladamri, he said, "And I relinquish my command to you. Lead this army in after Gerrard. He will need every sword arm he can muster."

The elf commander stared amazedly at Agnate. "I was about to offer you my command."

Agnate shook his head. "I have more pressing business. Lead these troops."

With no further word, Agnate marched past the soldiers, into the yawning cave. He tossed aside the battered battle axe. It clanged against a wall of stone. It would be useless in the tight spaces in the caves. Agnate drew his sword and dagger.

Gerrard had done well. Phyrexian bodies littered the floor, with only occasional human corpses among them. The bunkers were burned out, the guard stations smashed, the nooks scoured. He had been thorough—furiously so. Agnate approved.

. . . *Agnate . . . stay away . . .* a weak voice said in his mind. . . . *They are luring you. . . . It is a trap. . . .*

I will always seek you, Agnate responded. He strode down burned out corridors toward that voice. *The trap is sprung. Gerrard is killing the killers. There are none left to trap me.*

. . . *I know. He has been here. He has . . . slain them . . .* The press of Thaddeus's mind told that he was near, quite near.

Then he has freed you!

. . . *Gerrard could not . . . free me. No one could. Do not seek me. . . .*

Agnate shook his head angrily. *I am almost there. Wait for me.*

. . . *No, Agnate. Do not . . . It is a trap. . . .*

He was just behind that corner. Agnate bolted around the dark turn. Beyond stood a shattered doorway and the chamber where Thaddeus lay.

What was left of him . . . He was spiked to a slanted table. His limbs were gone, flayed away tissue by tissue. All of it was stored in solution jars on shelves behind him. They had cut away his pelvis too, and his spine, bone by bone, up the lumbar curve. Abdominal organs occupied various silver trays. Pins jutted from them. Vat priests lay in bloody ruin beneath the samples.

Only Thaddeus's ribcage and head remained. The aorta had been expertly sutured, allowing his heart to maintain pressure through the man's upper body. A large, round rock had even been leaned against the diaphragm to press the muscle up toward the lungs. He breathed through a scabby stoma in his throat. His eyes, in utter despair, watched Agnate approach.

"What have they done?" Agnate gasped, staggering toward the ruined man.

. . . *I told you . . . seeing me this way . . . is a trap you will never escape. . . .*

Agnate shook his head. "No. Urza will build you a body. You won't die this way. New legs, new arms, new organs."

. . . *I am done fighting for Urza Planeswalker. . . . I am done fighting. . . .*

"I am not," Agnate declared, staring into Thaddeus's tearing eyes. "I will slay a hundred thousand Phyrexians to avenge you."

. . . Don't you understand? We are Phyrexians. . . . Fight all you wish, Agnate . . . you are fighting only yourself. . . .

The Metathran's eyes were hard in his blue skull. "Why did Gerrard leave you in agony?"

. . . He told me . . . you were coming. He said you would . . . want to see me. . . .

"He was right."

. . . They've trapped you . . . forever. . . .

Agnate stared down at his trembling, bloody hands and the weapons he held in them. "Yes. You are right. You were right about everything—except one thing. I *can* free you."

. . . Yes. . . . Free me. . . .

Agnate dropped his knife. It clattered beside the corpse of a vat priest. With both hands, he lifted high his sword.

"Good-bye, my friend."

. . . Good-bye. . . .

The sword fell. Thaddeus was free.

Agnate turned away and folded to his knees. His sword dropped to the stone floor. He buried his face in sanguine hands.

Agnate was twice trapped. He would never forget Thaddeus's pleading eyes, suffering in their ruined flesh. Nor would he ever forget the stroke that closed those eyes forever.

CHAPTER 35
The Seven-Legged Mother

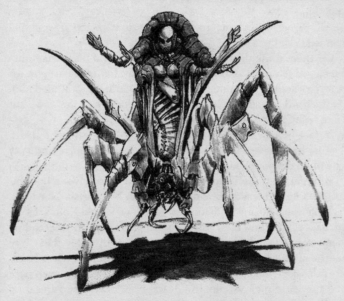

Tsabo Tavoc drew a long breath through swollen spiracles.

Thaddeus's death was intoxicating. He had died slowly, consciously. It was the best death, a perfect bouquet—intense, quiet, virtuous, patient, doomed. Agnate's sword had given a final piquant burst of emotion—regret, love, terror, release. The only scent that lacked in that death had been hatred—pure, hard-edged hatred.

Agnate exuded it now. His sword had drawn all the welling despair up through its hilt and into a new man. There, it became hate. Thaddeus's death had been intoxicating, but Agnate's hatred was thrilling.

Tsabo Tavoc breathed the glad reek of it.

Agnate was not the greatest hater in the caves, though. Gerrard was. His fury had been strong at the mouth of the cave. It had grown only more powerful with each head he had lopped, each gallon of glistening-oil he had spilled. Gerrard fought as though he battled Death itself. He was a fool. No one could beat Death except Yawgmoth. Gerrard's hatred would lead him to the Ineffable.

All things had come to fruition just as Tsabo Tavoc had planned.

Let them think they are winning. Let Urza and his titans stomp the ragged remnants of the Koilos land army. Let Eladamri post his guards in the blood-painted caves he has won with tooth and nail. Let Gerrard advance toward the portal, believing he can shut death away from himself and all Dominarians.

In fact he will be drawn through, Tsabo Tavoc thought gladly, the first in a harvest of souls. He will be drawn through, and they all will be drawn through.

At great cost, the Dominarians had won themselves a bottomless pit. Gerrard could not close the portal. Nor Taysir. Nor Urza. As long as it remained, Phyrexia would always hold Koilos. Dominarians would fling their sons and daughters into the pit, calling them warriors and freedom fighters though in truth they were human sacrifices to implacable Death. They would battle a ceaseless tide of Phyrexians, not realizing the womb cannot keep pace with the vat. Koilos was not lost. It was transformed into an eating machine that would swallow millions.

Tsabo Tavoc smiled. Plates slid in her segmented mouth, drawing back from filed teeth.

She had won Benalia. Now, she was winning Koilos. Her crowning glory, though, would be the moment she presented the savior of Dominaria, the champion of Urza, to Yawgmoth. He would reward her. He would unseat Master Crovax and give Tsabo Tavoc command of the Rathi overlay.

Shackled and brimming with hate, Gerrard will be yours by day's end, Great Lord Yawgmoth.

* * * * *

This felt good—killing them like this. Leaving them in pieces behind. Somehow, when the monsters were chopped up and sloppy on the cave floor, they seemed cleaner than when they breathed and scuttled and walked. That's how he thought of it—cleansing the caves.

Torches held high, Gerrard and his contingent rounded a corner. Two monsters launched themselves from the darkness beyond. No longer did they fight in phalanxes. Now they fought like trapped dogs.

Gerrard's torch fell away. His sword rammed into the rushing chest of one. Steel lanced between obscene ribs. It sank deep, rupturing the heart. Oil sprayed around the edges of the blade.

Even dying, the thing fought on. Its knobby arms clamped down on him. Its claws pierced his sides.

Gerrard roared, prying his sword sideways. The blade snapped ribs and tore clear.

The beast slumped, leaning drunkenly on him before it tumbled sideways. Gerrard batted its arms away.

The fight was finished. Three Benalians had slain the other beast—at the cost of their own lives. Their corpses sprawled on one side of the cave.

Gerrard stared at the two Phyrexians. Their flesh was rotten, gray and shabby. Gritting his teeth, he hacked down with his sword. It clove the face of one dead monster. The blade rose. It fell again. He cut the thing's skull in half. The sword slashed down again. It opened the beast's face along the jaw. Gerrard lifted his sword for another strike.

A hand clamped on his shoulder—Tahngarth's hand. "Save your hate. We've plenty more ahead."

Gerrard severed the beast's neck and kicked the head across the chamber. "I have enough hate for all of them." He began working over the other body.

Tahngarth released his shoulder. As Gerrard chopped, he was vaguely aware of the soldiers around him, working to lay out their comrades as was fitting. Only when they had finished did Gerrard kick his way through the Phyrexian remains and lift his gaze.

"Let's go. The portal cannot be far now."

* * * * *

Multani managed to regrow enough of the damaged spar to allow *Weatherlight* a more graceful landing than her last. Still, the ship came to ground like a box of rocks.

It was little more than that just now. Two ray cannons had overheated and melted down. A third had been blasted away. The hull was riddled with ruptures that even Multani could not close completely. The engines ran red hot and barked gray smoke when Karn shut them down. He pulled his hands from the control sockets where they had been embedded and plunged the glowing things into a bucket of water. She would not fly again, not for hours, and would perhaps not fight for days.

Thankfully, she didn't need to. The ship had landed just beside the cave mouth—now in Dominarian hands. The Phyrexians above ground were routed, pursued in their thousands by tromping titans. The caves were filled with Dominarian defenders. All reports indicated decisive victories. Eladamri and his army descended to the portal.

Mantled in steam, Karn ascended from the engine room. He emerged, massive and brooding, onto the deck. Sisay arrived on deck at the same time, descending from the bridge.

The old friends spoke in accidental unison. "I'm going to help Gerrard."

Sisay smiled, fondly running her hand along Karn's massive jaw. "I'm glad to have you at my side."

Another figure rose from below. In the heat of the sick bay,

Orim had doffed her turban. Her coin-spangled hair dripped with perspiration. She mopped her brow with a rag and tucked it into her healer's cloak. A ready supply of powders, salves, and bandages waited in the pockets of that cloak. Her intent was clear.

Seeing her comrades, Orim strode to them. "Everyone's stable below. There'll be lots more injuries in the caves."

In emulation of Sisay's gesture, Karn ran a yet-warm finger beneath the healer's chin. "We'll all go get him."

The healer's eyes clouded in regret. "Not all of us. Not the one Gerrard wants to see most."

Sisay put one arm around her friend's shoulder. "You did all you could. We all miss her."

The silence that followed was broken by a scampering sound and a shrill squeal.

"Squee go to see him, too!" The green little man vaulted down from the bow gun and clasped hands with his friends.

Karn reached out, wrapping the group in an almighty embrace that lifted them from their feet. He strode purposefully across the deck and leaped over the rail. He fell weightlessly but landed like a hammer on an anvil. The folk in his grip smiled with chattering teeth as he walked into the cave.

Sisay managed to speak for them all. "Thanks, Karn, but I need the exercise."

Considering, Karn tromped to a halt, set his friends down, and gestured ahead of him.

"At least let me lead. I may not be a fighter, but I'm a fair shield."

"A shield?" Sisay said, eloquently staring him up and down. "You're more of a wall."

Squee leaped onto the silver golem's back. "G'won, Karn. You lead, long as Squee rides here."

Satisfied, the massive man tromped down into the Caves of Koilos.

* * * * *

This had been a particularly harsh cul-de-sac. Gerrard had lost ten soldiers to only four Phyrexians. As before, he took out his anger on the bugs' corpses.

Tahngarth and the others meanwhile laid out the bodies of the brave fallen. A torch lighted their heads. There were no longer cloths enough to cover faces. The ten lay staring at the ceiling. Stalactites dripped on them.

Gerrard's sword chopped again into scale and meat. Tahngarth no longer tried to halt the mutilations. Perhaps he understood. Gerrard was only doing to these bodies what their plague had done to Hanna.

Wordless and grim, Tahngarth led the rest of the contingent out of that slaughterhouse. They crowded through the narrow exit and into the passage beyond. Their voices made watery echoes as they headed deeper into the cave. With them went the angry light of the torches.

Gerrard was left with his own torch and the one that tended the fallen.

Cold darkness closed around him. It felt deadly. Gerrard was at home among deadly things. The smell of glistening-oil wreathed him. Positioning a torch at the heads of the four Phyrexians, Gerrard raised his sword. It hung there like a scorpion's tail. The blade fell. A monster's head rolled free with a sound like stone grating on stone. . . .

Gerrard whirled.

A huge, round stone rolled down a track beside the door. With a boom, it sealed off the chamber's only exit.

Gerrard rushed to the stone. He grasped its cold edges and heaved. It did not budge in its track. The corridor beyond was silent and empty.

A rushing sound came behind Gerrard. He spun. Something vast dropped from among the stalactites. Numerous legs riled, outlined in the light of his torch. It was a giant spider—Tsabo Tavoc.

She landed on the torch, extinguishing it with her abdomen. In the sudden murk, legs clicked.

Gerrard lunged, sliding across the bloody cave floor to his fallen comrades. He snatched up the second torch and rose into a crouch. He waved the torch before him. Its fingers of flame were too tepid to reach the chamber's farther spaces.

Gerrard hurled the torch, end over end. It fell atop the Phyrexian dead. Fire leaped to puddles of glistening-oil. With a sudden whoosh, the tiny flame became a great blaze.

Shielding his eyes from the intense illumination, Gerrard scanned the darkness. Lurking beyond the glare, enshrouded in blackness, stood Tsabo Tavoc. She watched the burning corpses with glad fascination. Her compound eyes threw back the raving light.

Gerrard strode steadily toward that horrible apparition, calling out to her. "I see you, destroyer. I see you, Tsabo Tavoc. You took my country. You killed my love. Now, I will kill you."

Her voice buzzed like insect wings. "Such delicious hatred. You will make a fine Phyrexian." She withdrew deeper into the shadows. Only the thinnest sheen traced her legs. She seemed a mere phantasm.

Gerrard stalked dauntlessly forward. He himself had become a creature of shadows. "You killed her."

His sword lashed out. It caught one of the spider woman's legs in the conduits behind the knee. Wrenching his arm, Gerrard severed the leg. It rattled against the stone floor.

Tsabo Tavoc backed deeper into the shadows. The light from the burning corpses was faltering. The rear reaches of the cave were utterly dark. "You are powerful. Fearless."

"You killed her!" Gerrard bolted into the blackness.

He glimpsed a fish-white belly before him and rammed his sword up into Tsabo Tavoc's gut. Blood, black in that murk, sagged beneath the impaling blade. He lunged, intent on plunging the sword deeper.

Tsabo Tavoc's legs hurled him away.

Gerrard clutched his sword tightly. It ripped free of the spider woman's body. He tumbled head over heels. Stones bashed him as he rolled. The spider woman's gore looped him. Sprawling against the wall of the chamber, Gerrard panted.

He laughed. His thumb wiped some of the hot stain from his sword, and he tasted it. Salty, acidic—it tasted good.

Gerrard dragged himself to his feet and heaved a glad sigh. "Do you know, that wound I gave you—it's exactly where your plague bomb struck Hanna. That's where the rot began—the rot that ate her away." He strode into the darkness, sword lifted before him. "I'm going to tear you apart the way you tore her apart."

Tsabo Tavoc dropped on him with such speed and force, he was flung supine to the floor. His sword clanged and slid away. Three of the spider woman's legs wrapped about him, constricting tightly. She pressed his chest to her thorax. Blades in her joints cut into him.

Gerrard struggled. It was an inescapable grip. The gore from her belly wound ran down onto his face.

Tsabo Tavoc stared coldly at him. Her compound eyes gleamed in the last light of the burning bodies.

"You have the soul of a Phyrexian, Gerrard, a soul of hate. It makes you powerful, but infinitely malleable."

He felt a sudden, sharp pain in his back. Something gored him. It punched into his spine and poured out a hot, hissing substance. The stuff flooded Gerrard. His limbs shook. His skin blazed with fire. His vision grew acute—angry black lines slashed down around everything.

It was glistening-oil, liquid hatred infused into his spine. He had never known so powerful a passion. He wanted to rip Tsabo Tavoc apart, to kill everyone, to kill himself, but his body was not his own. Hatred burned away his nerves until he hung in hopeless, seething paralysis.

Good, my child, Tsabo Tavoc purred directly into his mind. *Now you understand what it is to be one of us. Had you been my trophy, I would have fitted you with a mimetic spine, here and now. You belong not to me, though, but to Yawgmoth. This infusion makes you mine until we stand together before him.*

Gerrard hung there beneath her, incapable of moving. He belonged here, clutched in his mother's legs.

She stalked forward a few paces. Her steps slowed, as if she were thinking. *Think of your beloved, Gerrard. Think of Hanna, of how I killed her.*

The pangs of hate cut deep, slaying Gerrard.

Mother was pleased. She purposefully crossed the cavern, scuttling past the burning Phyrexians and the Benalish dead. Reaching the door, she rolled back the stone as though it were a pebble and carried Gerrard away into the bowels of Koilos.

* * * * *

Karn, Sisay, Orim, and Squee followed the path of destruction carved out by the Benalish brigade. It led them ever downward, at last to a vast, deep chamber.

There, Eladamri and his Metathran troops had joined Tahngarth and the Benalish brigade. Together, they battled a horde of Phyrexians. Every moment, more beasts arrived. They filed through a huge, shimmering portal on the far side of the cave. The Dominarians were outnumbered two to one, and soon three to one. As long as the portal remained open to Phyrexia, there would be no hope of holding Koilos.

Beside the portal, surrounded by hundreds of Phyrexians, was a mirror pedestal. On it rested a giant book of glass and metal. Lines of power radiated from the spot, coursing into the portal.

"Where's Gerrard?" Sisay wondered as she hefted her sword.

"Lost, or dead," guessed Orim, drawing her wooden blade.

"We must destroy the pedestal," Karn said. "We must close the portal." He charged into battle along with Orim and Sisay.

On his back, Squee shouted, "What you doing, Karn? You don't fight."

With a voice like a distant waterfall, Karn growled, "They don't know that."

CHAPTER 36
At the Gates of Hell

Tsabo Tavoc scuttled down the dark reaches of Koilos.

It was simple from here. Gerrard was hers. He couldn't move, clutched in three of her legs and gripped in the implacable arms of hate. He was as helpless now as a newborn babe. He would cause no trouble.

Think of your beloved, my child. Think of Hanna.

Tsabo Tavoc's other children were far from helpless. They filled the cavern below, driving the Dominarians back from the portal. Her children would be glad to sense her approach. They would open an avenue through the Dominarian host. Her children would press both ways, and Tsabo Tavoc would walk, untouched, through the center of the battle. Anyone else would have called it a gauntlet, with foes and death on either side. For Tsabo Tavoc, it was a parade of coronation. At its end lay Phyrexia and her great reward.

Think of Hanna. You lost her to me, and she lost you to Yawgmoth.

It was a hopeless fight. Phyrexians poured out of their world and into the cavern. Through the portal they came, distorted like visions through rising heat. Beyond that shimmering gate, thousands more filed forward. Rank on rank, they filed into a meat grinder.

Eladamri was one blade of that grinder. He and Liin Sivi led the Steel Leaf elves in a furious drive for the mirror pedestal. Eladamri's sword rang like a bell as he hewed his way. Liin Sivi's totenvec whirled in deadly circles. The elves did their vicious best, fighting for the Seed of Freyalise as if Eladamri were Freyalise herself. For all their fury, though, Eladamri and his troops could do little more than slay. Phyrexian bodies made walls before them.

Across the chamber was another blade in the meat grinder. Tahngarth's sword opened the belly of a monster. Entrails cascaded out. The beast trod on them and slipped. Tahngarth turned and chopped down into the head of another brute. The horned brow was no match for Hurloon steel. The minotaur wrenched his sword free, simultaneously driving his elbow into the eye of a third beast. It fell to the floor and skidded before Sisay.

She fought beside him with equal valor, though less battle lust. An efficient sword swinger, Sisay had time to defend herself and assist Orim. Though at heart a healer, Orim could kill Phyrexians, even with her wooden Cho-Arrim sword. She had only to think of Hanna. All around Orim fought Benalish irregulars, many armed only with their fists and sheer will.

The defenders of Dominaria brought death to hundreds of Phyrexians, but there were thousands. For half an hour, they had fought in this breathless, hopeless battle, and gained not an inch toward the mirror pedestal.

Karn had done the most in that regard. Without bashing in a head or crushing a spine—both of which he was physically able to do—Karn had simply waded into the Phyrexian troops. It had taken them mere moments to discover they could not kill him. It took considerably longer to discover he would not kill them. They mobbed him. He was halfway across the cavern floor before the weight of bodies mired Karn in place. Beneath a living pile of fiends, Karn and his goblin passenger were buried.

Hopeless.

In the next moments, the battle grew worse. The Phyrexians fought with a sudden, unanimous purpose. They pushed back the Benalish brigade and their Metathran and elf allies. A clear path opened in their midst. On one end of that avenue, the scintillating portal stood, disgorging its armies. On the other end, at the lofted entrance to the cave, appeared Tsabo Tavoc.

The spider woman surveyed the scene. Gladness gleamed in her weird eyes. Her mouth plates formed a serene smile. A wound wept blackly on her belly. She clutched something to her thorax, something that dangled like boneless meat.

"Gerrard!" Sisay gasped in realization. She fought toward him.

Orim followed in her wake. Her sword darted with equal thirst. Tahngarth brought up the rear. Perhaps they could not battle their way to the mirror pedestal that powered the portal, but they could fight their way to Gerrard.

Tsabo Tavoc seemed to see the three comrades. Her spiracles deeply inhaled the scent of battle. On four legs, she darted swiftly down the channel of her warriors.

Roaring, Sisay clove the head of a Phyrexian foot soldier. She climbed his falling body, a ramp up the wall of fiends. Claws lashed her legs. Orim slashed the limbs away. A scuta reared up to block her path. She merely vaulted onto its face shield, sinking her wooden sword in the thing's eye. It slumped. Orim scrambled up the bleeding face. Tahngarth climbed afterward.

Tsabo Tavoc scurried past.

Sisay leaped from the wall of Phyrexians into the spider woman's wake. The floor was slick with blood and oil, but Sisay had seafarer's legs. She pelted after the fleeing spider. Tsabo Tavoc was too fast. Sisay dived, extending her sword arm. The blade swept down, slicing into the obscene abdomen. Even as she fell to her face, Sisay twisted the sword. It lodged behind the spider's stinger and ripped the thing out by its roots.

Tsabo Tavoc emitted no scream of pain, but her followers did. Countless claws grasped Sisay and flung her away as if she were poison. She sailed through air and crashed against one wall of the cave.

Orim, cut off by the sudden tide of beasts, leaped away, racing to Sisay's aid.

Tahngarth was not so easily deterred. The mob of monsters crushed up in Tsabo Tavoc's wake, guarding their wounded mother. They were tightly packed like sheep in a slaughter channel. Tahngarth ran across their heads. His hooves pounded skulls, stunning some, crushing others. If they died, they died. His true focus was the spider woman. He might not have caught up to her except that he ran across a throng that also ran.

Hurling himself from their shoulders, Tahngarth vaulted onto Tsabo Tavoc's back.

She crouched, shoved down by the sudden weight.

Tahngarth swung his sword in a decapitating blow.

Before metal could strike flesh, one of the spider woman's legs rose. She blocked the blade and ripped it away.

Tahngarth did not release his sword—no true minotaur would—but he was no match for Tsabo Tavoc's mechanical might. He was flung away as though he were a mere calf. Tahngarth crashed into the opposite wall of the cave. Groaning, the minotaur slid down to lie still.

There was no one to stop her now, hemmed in by her children. Not even Eladamri could fight past that mass of monsters.

Tsabo Tavoc jerked to a sudden stop. One leg seemed caught.

Karn rose, magnificent, from beneath a mound of clawing Phyrexians. They seemed only voracious cockroaches sloughing from his shoulders. In one massive hand, the silver golem clutched Tsabo Tavoc's leg. His other hand won free of the monsters that swarmed him, and he grabbed another of the spider woman's legs. With an almighty heave, he yanked one of the mechanisms from her body.

Sparks popped from the rent socket. Glistening-oil ran. The severed leg convulsed in Karn's grip. He dropped it amid the shrieking horde. They clutched the limb in mournful agony.

Karn grasped another leg and, roaring, yanked it free. The flesh where it had been embedded made a sucking, rending sound as it came loose.

On only two legs, Tsabo Tavoc tottered. She drew one leg away from Gerrard, setting it down before her and struggling to break from the golem's grasp.

Karn was implacable. Above the shrieks of the Phyrexians, his thunderous voice rang out.

"No more. If I must kill the guilty to save the innocent, I will kill!"

He ripped away another of the spider woman's legs. Before he could get another handhold, Tsabo Tavoc leaped away.

She dropped one more leg from Gerrard and ambled away from the silver golem. Her captive hung limp in the grip of a single limb.

Karn struggled to pursue, but the mass of creatures bore him down. He fell like a steel door, impacting the floor with a resounding boom.

Tsabo Tavoc skittered up to the shimmering portal. Her forces sluiced through around her—faithful children everywhere. Spiracles panting, the spider woman turned to gaze out at the battlefield. She smiled. Segments bristled on her face. Her eyes shone with the glossy glow of exquisite pain.

Climbing onto the mirror pedestal and the glass book, Tsabo Tavoc shouted, "You are finished, Dominaria. You have fought me bravely and lost. No mortal can ever defeat Death. I am Death. Embrace me, and I will lead you down to death and up again into deathless life.

"You think we are destroyers. You are wrong. We are saviors. You are but larvae, but pupae—white and unformed maggots. Until you die, you cannot become more. We bring you your death. We bring you to greater life.

"Now, fight if you must, Dominaria. Flee if you can. Either way, it will be the same. We will drag you down to death and save you. . . ."

* * * * *

Glorious words. Glorious, my mother, Gerrard thought, hanging in her grip. *At last, I have lost all to you. Parents, foster parents, family, mentors, friends, and now myself. Only now do I understand. I love you, Mother. I love you with every fiber in me. Thank you for this. Thank you for killing me to make me greater.*

He had never known such love. It made him weak. It made him mad. It made him want to stab her, to tear out her eyes, to rake her brains. If only his body would respond, he would cut his way into her.

Never had he known such love!

Once, he thought he had. Hanna had been her name. He remembered so much of her—golden hair, bright eyes, quiet smile—but nothing of wanting to kill her. He must not have loved her—not like he loved Mother.

She had killed Hanna, Mother had. Mother had killed so many, some with claws, some with minions, some with disease. That's how Hanna had died. Mother had loved her enough to send tiny machines crawling through her. Hanna had been furious. She had not wanted to transcend. She had not wanted . . .

Gerrard's mind struggled to assemble the thought.

Hanna had not wanted . . . She had not wanted . . . to die.

That forbidden thought spread through his mind.

Hanna had not wanted to die.

That single truth killed the manifold lies that swarmed in his head. Love is what he had felt for Hanna. Hate was what he felt for Moth—, for Tsabo Tavoc. The rest had all been lies, had been glistening-oil.

Truth spread through his once-poisoned spine and out along a million neural branches and into the tissues they touched. It gave him back his mind and his body.

He hung there still, his strength returning. He could feel Tsabo Tavoc's leg around him, could hear the cicada drone of her oration. No longer was she in his head. How to escape? It would take monumental strength to break the hold of even one of her legs.

"Pssst," came a sound near Gerrard's ear.

He slowly turned his head and saw a beautiful face—green and wart nosed, with feverish little eyes and barbed bits of bug leg between yellow teeth. Squee. It was no wonder he had passed unnoticed among the monsters in the chamber—hideously beautiful as he was.

"Here," the goblin said, shoving forward the hilt of a sword.

Gerrard's mind was his own—his arm, his fingers. They clutched the pommel. There was no hesitation. He hurled the blade upward, past legs, past gripping thorax, past even the first cut he had made in Tsabo Tavoc's white belly. His blade bit through skin and muscle. It jabbed into gut, slicing it open.

Tsabo Tavoc's words ceased in the air. Her children watched in shocked horror. She jolted and stared down, stupefied.

"For Hanna!" Gerrard shouted. He heaved the sword again into Tsabo Tavoc's belly, ripping it wide.

The spider woman convulsed. Blood gushed hot from her. She gasped, clutching the filthy laceration.

Her minions winced back in shared agony.

The leg that held Gerrard shuddered, loosening.

"Let death improve you," Gerrard growled. He lanced the tip of the blade into the leg socket that held him.

Wires severed. Sparks flew. The leg went limp, dropping Gerrard.

It felt glorious to fall that way, away from the feverish metal, away from the horrid mother of monsters.

He landed atop the book of glass and metal, atop the mirror pedestal.

Tsabo Tavoc hissed. Her three good legs gathered themselves to lunge.

Suddenly, the portal flickered and disappeared. A rock wall stood where once there had been a door to Phyrexia. The monsters that had been marching through that door were cut in half. Hunks of scale and flesh pattered down in a ghastly hail.

Tsabo Tavoc whirled. Her route to Yawgmoth was gone—her legions of demons, her escape. She didn't even have enough limbs left to hold Gerrard and walk.

Gerrard scrambled off the giant book, swinging his sword before him to clear a path.

The portal reappeared. Without even looking back at her quarry, at her armies, Tsabo Tavoc launched herself for the spot.

"Get back on de book!" Squee squealed. "Shut de door!"

Gerrard dived.

Tsabo Tavoc ambled over the corpses of her own troops. She flung herself through the portal.

Gerrard landed on the book.

The gate slammed shut. Only the blank cave wall remained—and the severed right cheek and arm of Tsabo Tavoc. The two hunks of meat flopped to the floor beside a bulbous cross section of her abdomen. The rest of her was on the other side, in Phyrexia.

"She escaped," Gerrard hissed angrily.

The Phyrexians, so long enspelled by their mother's words, now seemed to wake from a standing sleep. She was gone—they knew that first—and wounded and beyond their reach. . . .

But only as long as the portal remained closed. . . .

A wall of hackles, fangs, and claws rose up to tear Gerrard from the book. En masse, the Phyrexians lunged on him.

CHAPTER 37
The Heroes of Dominaria

Gerrard swung his sword. Four of the beasts flew back from the blow, hurled to the ceiling. Two were impaled on stalactites. Two more were broken by the impact. Before Gerrard could even swing again, another beast slumped forward across the pedestal, its torso shattered as though by some incredible force.

Gabbling, Gerrard raised his eyes to see the incredible force. "Karn!"

Gerrard's oldest friend and long-time guardian answered with a nod.

The silver golem swept out his massive arms and clutched five more Phyrexians. He wrapped them in an embrace that broke them like shells in a nutcracker.

As he let their bodies slump sloppily to the floor, he rumbled, "For you, Gerrard, I will kill."

The man on the book nodded back, hacking his blade through beasts. Side by side, Gerrard and Karn fought the minions of Phyrexia.

The prison brigade lifted their swords in a cheer and brought them down in a killing hail. Phyrexians fell in scraps. An elven war cry ululated through the cavern. The Steel Leaf warriors fought with a new vengeance. Metathran blades carved monstrous flesh.

Cut off from their mother and their homeland, Phyrexians died. There were no more reserves. There was no escape. Dominarians marched down from chambers above, and they gave no quarter.

Blood-mantled horns splashed into glistening-oil. Segmented arms twitched in the gore. Stingers pumped venom from severed ducts. Natural spines were hacked in two. Unnatural spines squirmed from dying bodies.

Sisay repaid her hard knocks by lopping the head off a Phyrexian foot soldier. Orim sliced into monsters as though she were hacking cane. Tahngarth whipped his horns in a killing arc. Gerrard spitted a beast through the crown. Karn was a silver tornado, crushing and hurling Phyrexians. In the battle frenzy, Squee wisely clambered onto the golem's shoulders, lest he be mistaken for a monster.

In brutal moments, every scaly back and hackled head fell. One by one, the last Phyrexians died. One by one, swords ceased in the air. There was no flesh left to cleave.

Could it be the battle of Koilos was done? Could it be the battle was won? Dominarian troops flooded down, seeking a foe to slay.

"We did it," Gerrard whispered breathlessly. "Karn, we did it!"

Karn studied bloody hands. "Yes," he said heavily. "It is done."

Sitting astride the golem's shoulders, Squee let out a celebratory cry.

Sisay embraced Orim. "Sometimes the good guys do win."

Tahngarth only stood, gazing grimly at the wreckage all around.

The Steel Leaf elves lifted Eladamri on their shoulders and marched him across the battlefield.

A cavern that, moments before, had echoed with battle suddenly rang with celebration.

It was short-lived. Someone arrived from the caves above, someone whose aura had the same strange power as Tsabo Tavoc's.

Songs and shouts quieted. Everyone in the cavern looked up to see who had come.

It was the blind seer—but somehow, he was changed. His back was straight. The bandage was gone from his eyes, which beamed like twin jewels. His white linty hair had been replaced by spun gold. All the aged decrepitude was gone. In its place, there was a mantle of ancient power. He descended into the cavern along the same route Tsabo Tavoc had passed.

Corpses lay prostrate before him. Living warriors watched in wonder. Reverently, they went to their knees. As the blind seer made his way toward the mirror pedestal, every last creature dropped in obeisance.

Only Gerrard and Karn remained standing. Golden-haired and white-robed, the great man approached the mirror pedestal.

Even Karn dropped to his knees.

Gerrard, his blood dripping down the glass and metal book, glanced incredulously at the silver golem.

Sword still out, he whispered, "You know him?"

"I know *of* him. I know—somehow—I know that he created me."

Gerrard stared open mouthed between Karn and the blind seer. "He created you?"

"Yes, I did," the man said. "I created Karn and the rest of your Legacy. I created even you."

Gerrard's eyes narrowed. "Who are you?"

"I am Urza Planeswalker."

"You're what?"

"I am Urza Planeswalker."

"You're Urza Planeswalker?" Gerrard echoed incredulously. He glanced down at Karn, whose head remained bowed.

"Yes. I am the one who started all this. I am the beginning. You are the end. I have made you and your Legacy for this very hour."

Gerrard shook his head. "What are you talking about?"

A strange smile lit the man's face. "I have watched you fight, Gerrard. I have seen you command your ship, your crew. You have been everything I imagined and more. The result is this—victory at Koilos."

"You are the beginning, and I am the end. . . ?"

The shimmering man gestured to the bloody book. "I first opened this portal by removing the powerstone that closed it. Even now, the two halves of that stone reside here, in my skull. They have made me what I am—Urza Planeswalker.

"I have made you what you are—my opposite, my complement, my counterpart. Just as the stones that once opened this portal are part of my being, so, your very being has the power to close it."

"You *are* the planeswalker," Gerrard said in an amazed hush. He sighed wearily. "So, am I to stay here, on this book, for all eternity?"

"No," Urza Planeswalker replied. "I have the power to open this portal, and you to close it. Together, we have the power to destroy it."

Urza reached to the belt of his white robes and drew forth a mighty sword. It shone like lightning in his grasp. He lifted it above his head.

"Shall we?"

Gerrard raised his notched and bloody blade. The two swords hovered in midair. Then both fell in a singing rush. Together, the blades smashed into the book.

It shattered, flinging glass all about Gerrard. He stood, whole and healthy, in the midst of the lacerating storm. Smoke rolled up from the lines of metal that jagged across the book. Then, they too were destroyed. Metal ran like mercury, sliding to the edges of the pedestal and bleeding down the sides. Even the mirror pedestal lost its gleam. The life went out of that ancient and powerful construct. With a final rolling puff of smoke, the book and pedestal grew still.

Urza sheathed his sword. His voice resonated through the room. "Now and forevermore, the portal of Koilos is closed." He reached up for Gerrard's hand. "Come down."

A little unsteadily, Gerrard took the proffered hand and leaped down beside the planeswalker. The cave wall remained dark. The portal to Phyrexia was destroyed.

Gerrard stared amazedly into the gemstone eyes of the planeswalker. "You made me for this? You created my Legacy, plotted my destiny?"

"I did, Gerrard Capashen," Urza replied quietly.

"I hate you," Gerrard blurted.

"Forgive him, Master Urza," Karn rumbled, still bowing. "He was poisoned by the spider woman—"

"No," Gerrard interrupted. "I mean it. I really do hate you. It wasn't the Phyrexians who took everything from me. It was you. From the beginning of my life, you have destined me to lose everything."

"If you fulfill your destiny, in losing all, you will gain all."

"No. You are wrong," Gerrard said. "I will be your champion, your hero, yes. I will fight the fight I am destined to. But all the while, I will hate you."

Urza's eyes seemed to dim a little with that. "I know. I will count it as one of my own great losses." In that moment, he did not seem the great, ancient, mad planeswalker, but rather an old and lonely man.

Drawing a shuddering breath, Urza went on to say, "Thank you for victory over Llanowar, and victory here." Urza lifted Gerrard's arm high into the air.

"Rise, faithful of Dominaria," Urza shouted. "Arise in victory!"

The cheer that answered shook Koilos like the tread of a titan's boot.

* * * * *

A week later, the Caves of Koilos had been truly cleansed. Every last drop of glistening-oil had been scrubbed away, every last Phyrexian corpse burned. Gargantuas and witch engines, trench worms and scuta had formed a pyre that burned to the heavens for six days. Meanwhile, with due and solemn ceremony, the Dominarian dead had been buried in the desert. Steel Leaf warriors had been laid beside Metathran beside Benalish fighters. The Dominarian coalition had gathered to mourn.

Now fighting and mourning were both done. The time of festival had come.

Armor was polished until its gleamed beneath the Glimmer Moon. Swords were sharpened. Blood and oil were bleached from livery.

Even the titan engines were scoured. No Phyrexian scales remained in mammoth feet that had crushed them. No scorch marks dimmed armor plates. Ray cannons shone as though they had never been fired. Empty of their planeswalker pilots, the titans now stood in a broad circle that stretched from the caves to encompass a large patch of desert. These colossi marked the edges of the festival grounds. Within their circle thronged coalition forces in their tens of thousands. Elf, Metathran, Benalish, dragon—those who had won at Koilos ate and drank, cheered and danced before the caves.

In the midst of the titan circle and above the happy throng hovered a ship that was hope to them all.

Weatherlight was resplendent in the night sky. Her every lantern beamed, casting a glad glow on the revelers. Festival lights traced out her healed hull and her back-swept airfoils. Her deck held a glorious feast—pheasant and boar, eel and salmon, oat-bread trenchers and onion stew, cakes and puddings and pasties. All of it had been brought by Urza Planeswalker to feast the commanders of his victory.

In their ceremonial best, the dignitaries mingled about the board.

Tevash Szat animatedly narrated his exploits to Commodore Guff, who struggled to write down every word for his official history. Nearby, Daria, Taysir, and Liin Sivi sipped merlot from round-bellied glasses. Bo Levar had brought boxes of assorted cigars, one purportedly dating from before the Ice Age and another rolled from tobacco grown by Teferi on Tolaria. Freyalise and Kristina discussed matters in Llanowar with the head of the Steel Leaf warriors. The panther-warrior Lord Windgrace traded stories with Tahngarth about "human folly."

The rest of *Weatherlight*'s command crew enjoyed the repast as well. Sisay split her time between the helm and the banquet table,

Karn between engines and conversations, and Multani between the ship's hull and her guests. Orim, in a Cho-Arrim robe and coin-coifed hair, listened politely as Squee described how he had saved "everybody's butts from de beginning till now." Laughter only encouraged the goblin—laughter and food and wine. They flowed in plenty on the amidships deck of *Weatherlight*.

A quieter group stood at her stern. Over cigars and rye spirits gathered the four men who had fought hardest and lost most in this war. Eladamri, Agnate, Gerrard, and Urza lingered in each other's company. They said very little. They laughed not at all. The merriment below was like music to them. They listened and appreciated but did not join in. A grim gladness gripped them, the sort that needed few words.

Urza spoke those few words. Lifting his glass, he said, "Here's to all we've lost, and here's to us."

Four glasses rose. They clinked quietly together. The four heroes of Dominaria drank.

* * * * *

The three-day festival was over. The revelers slept in their tents. Only a handful of guards remained awake that morning— they and the green-man from Yavimaya.

Multani heard a sound, a strange rumble. There was movement in the desert—vast movement.

Multani rose through the timbers of the great ship *Weatherlight*. He assembled a body for himself out of the living splinters and shards of wood he found along the way. On deck, the pieces piled themselves into legs, a torso, arms, and a head. Two knotholes made themselves into eyes. With them, Multani looked out.

Beyond the tents, on the morning desert of Koilos, strange, twisted shapes were imposing themselves. Hills like flayed muscle. Fields of tortured red. Across those lands were arrayed enormous armies—Phyrexians.

It seemed a vision—this coruscating red world—a premonition of evil. Yet, the tangled land seemed so solid, so real.

Multani had seen such a world once before. He had glimpsed it in the mind of a dead Phyrexian in Yavimaya. That monster had had a name for the world that even now slowly overlaid itself on Dominaria.

Rath.

MAGIC: The Gathering®

Ice Age Cycle

The Gathering Dark
Book I

From Jeff Grubb, best-selling author of *The Brothers' War*, comes the story of Dominaria in the age of darkness, when wizards and priests struggled for supremacy

The Eternal Ice
Book II

Available May 2000

Ice has covered the world of Dominaria. Now Lim Dûl, a necromancer with a taste for power, seeks to awaken a deeper evil.

Read the book that started it all.

The Brothers' War
Artifacts Cycle • Book I
Jeff Grubb

Dominarian legends speak of a mighty conflict, obscured by the mists of time. Of a conflict between the brothers Urza and Mishra for supremacy. Of titanic engines that scarred and twisted the very planet. The saga of the Brothers' War.

The Shattered Alliance
Book III

The Ice Age has come to an abrupt end, but the world's troubles have not left with the receding glaciers.

Available December 2000

Tales of Magic

The Myths of Magic
Edited by Jess Lebow

Stories and legends, folktales and tall tales. These are the myths of Dominaria, stories captured on the cards of the original trading card game. Stories from J. Robert King, Francis Lebaron, and others.

Available August 2000

The Colors of Magic
Edited by Jess Lebow

Argoth is decimated. Tidal waves have turned canyons into rivers. Earthquakes have leveled the cities. Dominaria is in ruins. Now the struggle is to survive. Tales from such authors as Jeff Grubb, J. Robert King, Paul Thompson, and Francis Lebaron.

Rath and Storm
Edited by Peter Archer

The flying ship *Weatherlight* enters the dark, sinister plane of Rath to rescue its kidnapped captain. But, as the stories in this anthology show, more is at stake than Sisay's freedom.

It's all true.
It's really happening.
It's not paranoia.

Reality and nightmare collide when dark forces converge on a world that seems so normal.

DARK•MATTER™

(oNe)
In Hollow Houses
Gary A. Braunbeck
August 2000

The Hoffman Institute may be our only defense against the Dark Tide, but is it part of the solution, or part of the problem? For a team of investigators with their own connections to the unseen world, the answer to that question may be a matter of life or death, sanity or insanity.

Contemporary dark fantasy from the publisher of MAGIC: THE GATHERING® and FORGOTTEN REALMS®

About the Author

Rob King writes books while taking care of his three boys and hoping his wife gets home soon with the pizza. He comes up with his best ideas while walking a seventy-pound collie through the Wisconsin lake country. This idyllic setting has spawned countless bloody battles and befanged Phyrexians.

After one particularly lovely stroll, Rob started this whole mess with Yawgmoth. His novel *The Thran* is a twisted thing. His editor is forcing him to clean up after himself with the current trilogy. A new pair of shoes has moved things along nicely.

There are more interesting tidbits about Rob, but they'll wait for later. The pizza has just arrived.

INVASION ™

INVASION CYCLE • BOOK I

The Phyrexian nightmare begins.

Dominaria faces its biggest threat—an invasion by its greatest enemy, an attack planned for eons by merciless foes. No one is exempt from their terror. No land is safe from their onslaught. In the shadow of the Phyrexian horde, Dominaria has but one hope—the *Weatherlight* and her crew. The time has come to defend hearth and home from invasion.

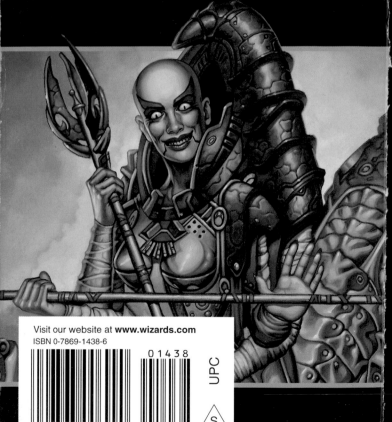